Collector's Library

VINTAGE DETECTIVE STORIES

VINTAGE DETECTIVE STORIES

Selected and with an Introduction by
DAVID STUART DAVIES

Collector's Library

This edition published in 2012 by
Collector's Library
an imprint of CRW Publishing Limited
69 Gloucester Crescent, London NW1 7EG

ISBN   978 1 907360 68 8

Typeset in Great Britain by Antony Gray
Printed and bound in China by Imago

2 4 6 8 10 9 7 5 3

Contents

Introduction

This collection is going to take you back to the time when crime fiction was more glamorous, romantic and intriguing and had more of an element of the dark fairy tale about it than it does today. The detectives were not, as the current crop seem to be, damaged individuals with demons of their own, investigating sadistic and brutal crimes. These vintage sleuth-hounds were eccentric, attractive and remarkable individuals who, without the aid of modern technology, by pure brainwork alone, were able to solve the most puzzling of mysteries. This is escapist entertainment of the finest quality.

Edgar Allan Poe is generally regarded as the 'father of the detective story' due to his creation of the brilliant C. Auguste Dupin, a fellow who could not only deduce what people were thinking but could also interpret the most abstruse cryptogram and read a murder scene as though it were a book. He became the template for all the fictional detective characters that followed. The two main ingredients of a Poe–Dupin tale – a baffling crime and an enigmatic detective who was as fascinating as the mystery he was solving – have become the staple fare of mystery novels and stories. Other writers, taking a lead from Poe, experimented with such a character in their work. Notably, Wilkie Collins introduced a dour, canny policeman, Sergeant Cuff, who was fascinated by roses, into his mystery novel *The Moonstone*; and Charles Dickens gave us the comic yet perceptive and determined Inspector Bucket in *Bleak House*.

However, it was not until Arthur Conan Doyle came up with his detective genius Sherlock Holmes that the floodgates opened. This character appeared in two novels, *A Study in Scarlet* (1887) and *The Sign the of the Four* (1891), with only moderate success, but when Doyle tried his hand at placing his creation in a series of tightly written short stories, Holmes and his narrator friend, Dr Watson, became household names. The tales appeared in the *Strand Magazine* and as a result the sales of this monthly periodical rocketed. Reading these stories it is clear that Doyle borrowed a great deal from Poe in creating his detective – the way that Holmes has the ability to read the thoughts of his companion, for example – but Doyle also added many layers to the original concept. He humanised his detective and injected excitement, suspense, drama and glamour into the tales.

Doyle was soon a well-known and wealthy man as a result of the Holmes stories. It became obvious to other writers that there was money, fame and success in writing detective mysteries and so a trend was set. In no time there were crime-solvers of all shapes, sizes and predilections appearing within the pages of the numerous magazines that filled the newsagents' shelves towards the end of the nineteenth century.

In many ways, it was the proliferation of stories featuring a colourful variety of mystery-solvers that created a passion in the reading public for crime fiction – a passion that has remained and indeed grown over the years. The period between the two world wars saw the emergence of such great detectives as Dorothy L. Sayers' Lord Peter Wimsey, Agatha Christie's Hercule Poirot and Jane Marple, Margery Allingham's Campion and John Dickson Carr's Dr Fell. Their adventures were captured in novels rather than short stories and this period is regarded as the golden age of crime fiction.

During World War II, with its personal traumas and deprivation, the popularity of the detective novel declined. Real life was far more dramatic and grisly than any mystery story. Readers required a different kind of escapism. After the war, the private detective had less appeal and was gradually replaced by the dedicated professional, the common-sense copper on the beat, the dogged inspector from Scotland Yard and the tenacious plain-clothes man. As a result, the colourful, rather eccentric and often amusing independent detective faded into the shadows. The element of fantasy, implicit in the stories prior to the war, was lost. Grim realism and social concerns were the order of the day. Those stories, which readers and writers alike referred to as 'cosies', no longer featured in mainstream crime fiction. Now it was the time for real blood and brutal killings described in gruesome detail. Reality had raised its uncompromising head.

Today crime fiction is a very broad church and its many sub-genres range from the suspense novel, the police procedural and the thriller to the historical crime story, which can be set in any period from ancient Rome to the mid-twentieth century. These narratives are rich and varied but there is a dearth of short stories featuring colourful crime-solvers who are clever enough to engage and entertain the reader for an hour or so. This collection of tales takes us back to those heady days around the end of the nineteenth century when a batch of brilliant maverick investigators tackled a whole range of ingenious and mystifying crimes with their dazzling skill. The writers then were concerned with baffling the reader right up to the final moments when all would be revealed through the idiosyncratic problem-solving methods of the master sleuth.

In this anthology I have included a story by each of the two main progenitors of this fascinating genre. Edgar Allan Poe's 'The Murders in the Rue Morgue' presents Dupin with a classic locked-room mystery which will puzzle the reader up to the last page. It has become the paradigm for all such literary conundrums. 'The Dancing Men' is the Arthur Conan Doyle story I have chosen. Since Holmes solved his first case in 1887, a decade has not passed without the appearance of a new Holmes collection or radio play or film or stage production or television presentation. There has even been a Sherlock Holmes ballet and a musical. 'The Dancing Men' presents the detective with one of his most challenging cases. Interestingly, the story revolves around his breaking of a secret code, a skill in which Poe's Dupin also excelled.

Other luminaries from this dark and mysterious detective world include G. K. Chesterton's Father Brown, the mild-mannered cleric with a brain as sharp as a scalpel, and Arthur B. Reeve's Craig Kennedy who, as a professor of chemistry, uses strictly scientific methods. It was often the case that these detectives were accompanied on their investigations by a Dr Watson figure. Bramah's detective Max

Carrados had an assistant in Parker, his manservant, who was of particular use as Carrados was blind. Jacques Futrelle's sleuth was another scientific fellow, Professor S. F. X. van Dusen, known as the 'Thinking Machine', and he enjoyed great popularity in America in the early years of the twentieth century. The king of scientific detectives, however, was Dr Thorndyke, the clever creation of R. Austin Freeman who referred to him as 'The Great Fathomer'. Thorndyke makes a welcome appearance in this collection in one of his most brilliant cases. Among these relatively famous characters, we also have a smattering of lesser known and neglected sleuths (all with rather odd names), such as Sir Basil Thomson's Mr Pepper, Edgar Wallace's Inspector O. Rater and J. S. Fletcher's Archer Dawe.

These stories represent the early richness of a genre as popular today as it has ever been. All will bring delight to the reader who enjoys the charm of a past era, spiced with a taxing little mystery. The crimes are all there waiting to be solved. You will have great fun joining in the deductive process.

THE AUTHORS & THEIR DETECTIVES

Edgar Allan Poe (1809–49)

A tormented soul whose dark disappointments in life found their way into his fiction, Poe is now generally regarded as one of America's greatest writers. He was a poet, editor, short-story writer and acknowledged inventor of the detective story. His redoubtable sleuth C. Auguste Dupin, whose investigations were related by an unnamed narrator, featured in just three stories: 'The Murders in the Rue Morgue' (1841), which appears in this volume, 'The Mystery of Marie Rogêt' (1842), a fine example of the 'armchair detective story', and 'The Purloined Letter' (1845), which combines the elements of the detective tale with those of a spy story. When Poe created Dupin to perform feats of ratiocination (a word he invented), he did not call him a detective because neither the word nor the profession existed then. Little did he or his readers at the time imagine what a legacy he was to bequeath.

Arthur B. Reeve (1880–1936)

Reeve's mysteries featuring the scientific methods of sleuth Craig Kennedy were the first by an American author to gain wide readership in Great Britain. Reeve created his detective after having been assigned as a journalist to write a series of newspaper articles on scientific detection. His fame was enhanced by silent-movie adaptations of his works. So identified was the author with his character Kennedy that he was asked to set up a science and espionage laboratory in Washington DC during World War I, which he did with some success.

J. S. Fletcher (1863–1935)

Joseph Smith Fletcher, a Yorkshireman born in Halifax, was a prolific writer in the mode of Edgar Wallace, turning out over 120 books in the crime field alone. Despite this remarkable output, he is hardly remembered today, probably because much of his work is mediocre, but there are flashes of brilliance – as in the story in this anthology featuring one of his many detective characters, Archer Dawe, and taken from a short-story collection published in 1909, *The Adventures of Archer Dawe, Sleuth-Hound*. While it is fair to say that as a character Dawe is not particularly memorable, the mystery is cunningly wrought.

Maurice Leblanc (1864–1941)

Leblanc was a French playwright, short-story writer and novelist and most famous for creating the popular rogue Arsène Lupin, the 'Prince of Thieves'. Lupin swaggered through a thirty-five-year career that made him internationally famous. Leblanc often had his tongue in his cheek, his plots being parodies of crime fiction, and on occasion he even had his hero lock horns with Britain's brightest detective Holmlock Shears (also sometimes referred to as Herlock Sholmes). Lupin also had a film career both in silent and talking pictures. John Barrymore portrayed the likeable scoundrel in MGM's *Arsène Lupin* (1932). His colourful character brought Leblanc wealth and fame and eventually the Legion of Honour.

Edgar Wallace (1875–1932)

Wallace was one of the most prolific British writers of adventure stories and crime fiction of all time. In his short life he wrote 173 books and numerous short stories, thus earning the title 'king of thrillers'. He first found success with his novel *The Four Just Men*. As a publicity gimmick he offered a reward to any reader who could describe how the book's central murder was committed. Unfortunately he neglected to restrict the prize to the first person who worked it out. Although he lost a lot of money on the deal, the book became a bestseller and firmly established him as a popular author. He died in the United States *en route* to Hollywood to work on the screenplay of *King Kong*. Although he received a screen credit, he did no actual work on the film.

G. K. Chesterton (1874–1936)

Gilbert Keith Chesterton is now chiefly remembered for his detective stories featuring the deceptively unassumimg cleric, Father Brown. Ironically, rather like Conan Doyle, he viewed his crime-fiction tales as an easy means to supplement his income from his political and religious writings, which he regarded as being much more important. Father Brown was created in tribute to his friend Father John O'Connor, who inspired him and late in life baptised Chesterton into the Catholic faith. The pleasure of the Father Brown stories lies not solely in the unravelling of a conundrum, but also in the touches of sly humour and the author's wonderful manipulation of the English language.

Sapper (Herman Cyril McNeile) (1888–1937)

McNeile's great creation was Bulldog Drummond, the burly thick-eared detective–adventurer, a precursor of James Bond and The Saint. He used the pseudonym Sapper – army slang for engineer – on leaving the forces in 1919 with the rank of lieutenant colonel. With the success of the first Drummond adventure, he was stuck with Sapper for the rest of his writing career. 'The Horror at Stavely Grange' features a Drummond clone, Ronald Standish, who possesses the same kind of cheery bluff courage and swagger as old Bulldog. Standish, a private detective whose motto is 'be sure of your facts', first appeared in this story, which Sapper regarded as his best, in 1927. Six years later he brought out a collection of tales featuring the same character, *Ronald Standish*, 1933, which he followed in 1936 with *Ask for Ronald Standish*. All these tales are a skilful mixture of *Boy's Own* thrills and clever detective work.

Ernest Bramah (1868–1942)

Born in Manchester as Ernest Bramah Smith, he found his way into journalism after an unsuccessful attempt to become a farmer, and from there into writing fiction. He was extremely reticent about his personal life and a rumour circulated that he was a well-known literary figure writing under a pseudonym. Bramah did little to dispel this notion. He created Max Carrados, the first blind detective. Blinded in his youth, Carrados was sanguine about it: 'A new world to explore, new experiences, new powers awakening; strange new perceptions; life in the fourth dimension.' The stories are clever, and while at times the plots strain credibility concerning Carrados's abilities, they are told with verve and humour. Bramah's other great creation was Kai Lung, the teller of fantastic tales in the manner of the narrator of the *Arabian Nights*.

Arthur Conan Doyle (1859–1930)

To any reader of crime fiction, Conan Doyle needs no introduction. He is well known as the creator of Sherlock Holmes, a character partly based on Dr Joseph Bell, Doyle's tutor at Edinburgh University, along with several literary influences mixed with the author's own rich imagination. Holmes was both an armchair detective and a man of action – 'Come, Watson, the game is afoot.' Doyle grew tired of his detective creation fairly early on in his career and killed him off, but later reluctantly resurrected him, mainly because of the lucrative sum he was offered to perform such a feat. Doyle was a Renaissance man with many interests and talents. A writer of great scope ranging from historical novels and science-fiction to ghost stories, he would be chagrined to know that he is now chiefly remembered for giving life to the immortal Sherlock.

Victor Whitechurch (1868–1933)

A canon in the Anglican Church, Victor Lorenzo Whitechurch initially wrote clerical romances and it was only later in life, when he had been appointed honorary canon of Christ Church, Oxford, that he became passionately interested in the detective story. His first effort in the mystery field, *Thrilling Stories of the Railway* (1912), contains fifteen stories, nine of which are from the casebook of Thorpe Hazell, a strong believer in vegetarianism and physical exercise. Hazell was a specialist in railway detection and 'Sir Gilbert Murrell's Picture' is one of his most satisfying cases. Whitechurch continued to write in the genre, often using railways or a clerical setting as a backdrop.

Mrs Henry Wood (1814–1887)

In 1836, Ellen Price married Henry Wood. He worked in the shipping and banking trade in the South of France, where they lived until the business failed. The couple along with their four children returned to London where Mrs Wood turned to writing in order to support the family. She was remarkably successful, turning out over thirty melodramatic mystery novels, her most famous being *East Lynn* (1860). After the death of her husband in 1866, she purchased the magazine *Argosy* and contributed most of the content herself, including many of her short mystery stories, one of which is collected in this volume. When she died of bronchitis in 1887, her estate was valued at over £36,000, evidence of her great success as a writer and editor.

E. W. Hornung (1866–1921)

Ernest William Hornung is almost exclusively remembered as the creator of the master cracksman A. J. Raffles, although he did write other crime fiction. Born in Yorkshire, he lived for a time in Australia in the hope of improving his health, which was never robust. On his return to England in 1886, he married Constance Doyle, sister of Arthur Conan Doyle, and the two men became friends, sharing their great passion for cricket. No doubt Doyle's success in writing detective stories influenced Hornung and he flourished with his brother-in-law's encouragement. Indeed, the dedication to the first volume of Raffles tales, *The Amateur Cracksman* (1889), reads: 'To A.C.D. this sincere form of flattery'. Although Raffles can be regarded as a kind of distaff Holmes, having a less than bright Watson companion in Bunny Manders and a notable address at Albany in Piccadilly, the stories have a different charm and dynamic from the Holmes tales and became successful in their own right. Though in his late fifties, Hornung served in France during World War I, working for the YMCA.

Arnold Bennett (1867–1931)

Bennett was a great English novelist, dramatist and journalist whose major works describe life in the Potteries – the 'Five Towns' of north Staffordshire, where he lived as a boy. However, he did also have a liking for mystery fiction. His novel *The Grand Babylon Hotel* (1902), for example, contains much pure detection. In 1931 he published *The Night Visitor and Other Stories*, the material for which he had drawn from people's dramatic experiences in a large hotel; the adventure of the poet Lomax Harder in the story 'Murder!' features here in our collection.

Sir Basil Thomson (1861–1939)

Thomson was one of those authors who wrote for pleasure in what spare time he had during the course of a busy life. He had a varied career, starting out in the colonial service and serving in several posts in the South Seas. On returning home in 1890, he began writing while employed in the prison service, successively as Governor of Dartmoor and of Wormwood Scrubs. In 1913 he was appointed Assistant Commissioner of London's Metropolitan Police. He was knighted in 1919, and while remaining Assistant Commissioner, he was also appointed Director of Intelligence at the Home Office, in overall charge of every intelligence agency in the country, but in 1921 he fell out with Lloyd George and was asked to resign. The reasons for this remain mysterious. Obviously his work with the prison service and the police influenced his fiction and he wrote a small number of mystery yarns, 'The Hanover Court Murder' (1925) being one of his best.

Jacques Futrelle (1875–1912)

Futrelle, an American journalist, created a most unusual investigator with a most unusual name: Professor Augustus S. F. X. Van Dusen – the Thinking Machine. He is one of the greatest scientific detectives, a master logician who solves cases brought to him by a reporter, Hutchinson Hatch, who also acts as his assistant. In addition to being strong on plot construction, Futrelle's work is notable in that the language, especially the dialogue, seems almost modern to readers today, as does his sense of humour. Futrelle sailed on the fatal voyage of the *Titanic* and went down with the ship, along with several unpublished stories.

Robert Barr (1849–1912)

An editor and journalist as well as an author, Robert Barr created the French detective Eugene Valmont, who acts as his own storyteller. Although born in Scotland, Barr was taken to Canada at the age of four, where he stayed until he had completed his education, hence the French influence in these stories. There are some remarkable similarities between the pompous and vain Valmont and Agatha Christie's Belgian sleuth, Hercule Poirot, although Barr's creation predates Christie's by about twenty years.

Barr was responsible for a series of outrageous parodies of Conan Doyle featuring 'Sherlaw Kombs', which he wrote under the pseudonym Luke Sharp.

Stacy Aumonier (1877–1928)

After a successful career as a landscape painter – he exhibited at the Royal Academy – and an entertainer, Aumonier turned to writing. He did not write exclusively about crime, but was regarded as a great short-story writer. Both John Galsworthy and James Hilton were admirers of his work, likening him to Guy de Maupassant. Perhaps his best and most satisfying crime story is 'Miss Bracegirdle Does Her Duty' (1923), which is both clever and amusing.

Herbert Jenkins (1876–1923)

Jenkins was a prolific writer who created a Sherlock Holmes clone, or perhaps more accurately, a Dr Thorndyke clone, Malcolm Sage, who runs his own detective bureau with his secretary Gladys Norman, his assistant James Thompson, and William Johnson, the office junior who has ambitions to become a Great Detective (shades of Sexton Blake's Tinker). Like Thorndyke, Sage follows clues in a very cold, precise and methodical fashion. In 'The Surrey Cattle-Maiming Tragedy', for instance, he makes deductions simply by reading a map. The tales were written around 1919–20 and were published in book form as *Malcolm Sage, Detective* in 1921. Sage is a lightweight sleuth but the puzzles remain intriguing.

Dick Donovan (1843–1924)

As a short-story writer, Donovan (one of the pseudonyms of James Edward Preston Muddock) was prolific in the extreme. He was a journalist who travelled widely as special correspondent for the *London Daily News* and as a contributor to other publications. In his autobiography *Pages from an Adventurous Life* (1907), he regrets the popularity of his more than fifty detective volumes, preferring his more serious work. These tales tended to feature Donovan himself as the detective hero recounting various adventures with sinister secret societies, super villains and incredible crimes. What the stories lack in finesse they make up for in pace and panache.

R. Austin Freeman (1862–1943)

In creating Dr John Evelyn Thorndyke, Richard Austin Freeman was able to use his own knowledge and experience as a physician and trained scientist to contrive problems with fascinating solutions for his detective. There was a great deal of the author in the character. Freeman, like Thorndyke, was a stickler for accuracy and thoroughness: he would test out the various murderous devices he created for his tales before he allowed himself to publish the stories depicting their use. Freeman invented what has come to be called the inverted detective story, wherein the reader sees the crime committed and knows who the killer is; the suspense comes from wondering how the culprit will be caught. Sometimes Freeman employed this format and sometimes in the more traditional mode he wrote what he called the 'Direct Stories'. 'The Seal of Nebuchadnezzar' (1924) falls into this latter category. Like Holmes, Thorndyke shares his lodgings – a combined home and laboratory at 5A King's Bench Walk in London's Inner Temple – with another doctor, his chronicler, Christopher Jervis. Thorndyke first appeared in the novel *The Red Thumb Mark* (1907) and featured regularly in short stories and novels until *The Jacob Street Mystery* in 1942, a year before his author's death.

VINTAGE DETECTIVE STORIES

EDGAR ALLAN POE

The Murders in the Rue Morgue

What song the Syrens sang, or what name Achilles
assumed when he hid himself among women,
although puzzling questions, are not beyond *all*
conjecture.

SIR THOMAS BROWNE

The mental features discoursed of as the analytical
are, in themselves, but little susceptible of analysis.
We appreciate them only in their effects. We know of
them, among other things, that they are always to
their possessor, when inordinately possessed, a source
of the liveliest enjoyment. As the strong man exults in
his physical ability, delighting in such exercises as call
his muscles into action, so glories the analyst in that
moral activity which *disentangles*. He derives pleasure
from even the most trivial occupations bringing his
talent into play. He is fond of enigmas, of conundrums, of hieroglyphics; exhibiting in his solutions of
each a degree of acumen which appears to the ordinary
apprehension preternatural. His results, brought about
by the very soul and essence of method, have, in truth,
the whole air of intuition.

The faculty of resolution is possibly much invigor-
ated by mathematical study, and especially by that
highest branch of it which, unjustly, and merely on
account of its retrograde operations, has been called,
as if *par excellence*, analysis. Yet to calculate is not in
itself to analyse. A chess-player, for example, does

the one, without effort at the other. It follows that the game of chess, in its effects upon mental character, is greatly misunderstood. I am not now writing a treatise, but simply prefacing a somewhat peculiar narrative by observations very much at random; I will, therefore, take occasion to assert that the higher powers of the reflective intellect are more decidedly and more usefully tasked by the unostentatious game of draughts than by all the elaborate frivolity of chess. In this latter, where the pieces have different and bizarre motions, with various and variable values, what is only complex, is mistaken (a not unusual error) for what is profound. The *attention* is here called powerfully into play. If it flag for an instant, an oversight is committed, resulting in injury or defeat. The possible moves being not only manifold, but involute, the chances of such oversights are multiplied; and in nine cases out of ten, it is the more concentrative rather than the more acute player who conquers. In draughts, on the contrary, where the moves are *unique* and have but little variation, the probabilities of inadvertence are diminished, and the mere attention being left comparatively unemployed, what advantages are obtained by either party are obtained by superior acumen. To be less abstract – Let us suppose a game of draughts where the pieces are reduced to four kings, and where, of course, no oversight is to be expected. It is obvious that here the victory can be decided (the players being at all equal) only by some *recherché* movement, the result of some strong exertion of the intellect. Deprived of ordinary resources, the analyst throws himself into the spirit of his opponent, identifies himself therewith, and not unfrequently sees thus, at a glance, the sole methods (sometimes indeed absurdly simple ones) by which he may seduce into error or hurry into miscalculation.

Whist has long been noted for its influence upon what is termed the calculating power; and men of the highest order of intellect have been known to take an apparently unaccountable delight in it, while eschewing chess as frivolous. Beyond doubt there is nothing of a similar nature so greatly tasking the faculty of analysis. The best chess-player in Christendom *may* be little more than the best player of chess; but proficiency in whist implies capacity for success in all these more important undertakings where mind struggles with mind. When I say proficiency, I mean that perfection in the game which includes a comprehension of *all* the sources whence legitimate advantage may be derived. These are not only manifold, but multiform, and lie frequently among recesses of thought altogether inaccessible to the ordinary understanding. To observe attentively is to remember distinctly; and, so far, the concentrative chess-player will do very well at whist; while the rules of Hoyle (themselves based upon the mere mechanism of the game) are sufficiently and generally comprehensible. Thus to have a retentive memory, and to proceed by 'the book', are points commonly regarded as the sum total of good playing. But it is in matters beyond the limits of mere rule that the skill of the analyst is evinced. He makes, in silence, a host of observations and inferences. So, perhaps, do his companions; and the difference in the extent of the information obtained, lies not so much in the validity of the inference as in the quality of the observation. The necessary knowledge is that of *what* to observe. Our player confines himself not at all; nor, because the game is the object, does he reject deductions from things external to the game. He examines the countenance of his partner, comparing it carefully with that of each of his opponents. He considers the mode of assorting the cards in each hand; often counting trump by trump, and honour by honour, through the glances bestowed by their holders upon each. He notes every variation of face as the play progresses, gathering a fund of thought from the differences in the expression of certainty, of surprise, of triumph or chagrin. From the manner of gathering up a trick he judges whether the person taking it can make another in the suit. He recognises what is played through feint, by the air with which it is thrown upon the table. A casual or inadvertent word; the accidental dropping or turning of a card, with the accompanying anxiety or carelessness in regard to its concealment; the counting of the tricks, with the order of their arrangement; embarrassment, hesitation, eagerness or trepidation – all afford, to his apparently intuitive perception, indications of the true state of affairs. The first two or three rounds having been played, he is in full possession of the contents of each hand, and thenceforward puts down his cards with as absolute a precision of purpose as if the rest of the party had turned outward the faces of their own.

The analytical power should not be confounded with simple ingenuity; for while the analyst is necessarily ingenious, the ingenious man is often remarkably incapable of analysis. The constructive or combining power, by which ingenuity is usually manifested, and to which the phrenologists (I believe erroneously) have assigned a separate organ, supposing it a primitive faculty, has been so frequently seen in those whose intellect bordered otherwise upon idiocy, as to have attracted general observation among writers on morals. Between ingenuity and the analytic ability there exists a difference far greater, indeed, than that between the fancy and the imagination, but of a character very strictly analogous. It will be found, in fact, that the ingenious are always fanciful, and the *truly* imaginative never otherwise than analytic.

The narrative which follows will appear to the reader somewhat in the light of a commentary upon the propositions just advanced.

Residing in Paris during the spring and part of the summer of 18—, I there became acquainted with a Monsieur C. Auguste Dupin. This young gentleman was of an excellent – indeed of an illustrious family, but, by a variety of untoward events, had been reduced to such poverty that the energy of his character succumbed beneath it, and he ceased to bestir himself in the world, or to care for the retrieval of his fortunes. By courtesy of his creditors there still remained in his possession a small remnant of his patrimony; and, upon the income arising from this, he managed, by means of a rigorous economy, to procure the necessaries of life, without troubling himself about its superfluities. Books, indeed, were his sole luxuries, and in Paris these are easily obtained.

Our first meeting was at an obscure library in the Rue Montmartre, where the accident of our both being in search of the same very rare and very remarkable volume brought us into closer communion. We saw each other again and again. I was deeply interested in the little family history which he detailed to me with all that candour which a Frenchman indulges whenever mere self is the theme. I was astonished, too, at the vast extent of his reading; and, above all, I felt my soul enkindled within me by the wild fervour, and the vivid freshness of his imagination. Seeking in Paris the objects I then sought, I felt that the society of such a man would be to me a treasure beyond price; and this feeling I frankly confided to him. It was at length arranged that we should live together during my stay in the city; and as my worldly circumstances were somewhat less embarrassed than his own, I was permitted to be at the expense of renting, and furnishing in a style which suited the rather fantastic gloom of our common temper, a time-eaten and grotesque mansion, long deserted through superstitions into which we did not enquire, and tottering to its fall in a retired and desolate portion of the Faubourg St Germain.

Had the routine of our life at this place been known to the world, we should have been regarded as madmen – although, perhaps, as madmen of a harmless nature. Our seclusion was perfect. We admitted no visitors. Indeed the locality of our retirement had been carefully kept a secret from my own former associates; and it had been many years since Dupin had ceased to know or be known in Paris. We existed within ourselves alone.

It was a freak of fancy in my friend (for what else shall I call it?) to be enamoured of the night for her own sake; and into this *bizarrerie*, as into all his others, I quietly fell, giving myself up to his wild whims with a perfect abandon. The sable divinity would not herself dwell with us always; but we could counterfeit her presence. At the first dawn of the morning we closed all the massy shutters of our old building;

lighted a couple of tapers which, strongly perfumed, threw out only the ghastliest and feeblest of rays. By the aid of these we then busied our souls in dreams – reading, writing or conversing, until warned by the clock of the advent of the true Darkness. Then we sallied forth into the streets, arm in arm, continuing the topics of the day, or roaming far and wide until a late hour, seeking, amid the wild lights and shadows of the populous city, that infinity of mental excitement which quiet observation can afford.

At such times I could not help remarking and admiring (although from his rich ideality I had been prepared to expect it) a peculiar analytic ability in Dupin. He seemed, too, to take an eager delight in its exercise – if not exactly in its display – and did not hesitate to confess the pleasure thus derived. He boasted to me, with a low chuckling laugh, that most men, in respect to himself, wore windows in their bosoms, and was wont to follow up such assertions by direct and very startling proofs of his intimate knowledge of my own. His manner at these moments was frigid and abstract; his eyes were vacant in expression; while his voice, usually a rich tenor, rose into a treble which would have sounded petulantly but for the deliberateness and entire distinctness of the enunciation. Observing him in these moods, I often dwelt meditatively upon the old philosophy of the bi-part soul, and amused myself with the fancy of a double Dupin – the creative and the resolvent.

Let it not be supposed, from what I have just said, that I am detailing any mystery, or penning any romance. What I have described in the Frenchman was merely the result of an excited or perhaps of a diseased intelligence. But of the character of his remarks at the periods in question an example will best convey the idea.

We were strolling one night down a long dirty street, in the vicinity of the Palais Royal. Being both, apparently, occupied with thought, neither of us had spoken a syllable for fifteen minutes at least. All at once Dupin broke forth with these words –

'He is a very little fellow, that's true, and would do better for the Théâtre des Variétés.'

'There can be no doubt of that,' I replied unwittingly, and not at first observing (so much had I been absorbed in reflection) the extraordinary manner in which the speaker had chimed in with my meditations. In an instant afterward I recollected myself, and my astonishment was profound.

'Dupin,' said I, gravely, 'this is beyond my comprehension. I do not hesitate to say that I am amazed, and can scarcely credit my senses. How was it possible you should know I was thinking of – ?' Here I paused, to ascertain beyond a doubt whether he really knew of whom I thought.

'Of Chantilly,' said he; 'why do you pause? You were remarking to yourself that his diminutive figure unfitted him for tragedy.'

This was precisely what had formed the subject of my reflections. Chantilly was a quondam cobbler of the Rue St Denis, who, becoming stage-mad, had attempted the role of Xerxes, in Crébillon's tragedy so called, and been notoriously pasquinaded for his pains.

'Tell me, for heaven's sake,' I exclaimed, 'the method – if method there is – by which you have been enabled to fathom my soul in this matter.' In fact I was even more startled than I would have been willing to express.

'It was the fruiterer,' replied my friend, 'who brought you to the conclusion that the mender of soles was not of sufficient height for Xerxes *et id genus omne*.'

'The fruiterer! – you astonish me – I know no fruiterer whomsoever.'

'The man who ran up against you as we entered the street – it may have been fifteen minutes ago.'

I now remembered that, in fact, a fruiterer, carrying upon his head a large basket of apples, had nearly thrown me down, by accident, as we passed from the Rue C— into the thoroughfare where we stood; but what this had to do with Chantilly I could not possibly understand.

There was not a particle of *charlatanerie* about Dupin.

'I will explain,' he said, 'and that you may comprehend all clearly, we will first retrace the course of your meditations, from the moment in which I spoke to you until that of the *rencontre* with the fruiterer in question. The larger links of the chain run thus – Chantilly, Orion, Dr Nichols, Epicurus, Stereotomy, the street stones, the fruiterer.'

There are few persons who have not, at some period of their lives, amused themselves in retracing the steps by which particular conclusions of their own minds have been attained. The occupation is often full of interest; and he who attempts it for the first time is astonished by the apparently illimitable distance and incoherence between the starting-point and the goal. What, then, must have been my amazement when I heard the Frenchman speak what he had just spoken, and when I could not help acknowledging that he had spoken the truth! He continued –

'We had been talking of horses, if I remember

35

aright, just before leaving the Rue C——. This was the last subject we discussed. As we crossed into the street, a fruiterer, with a large basket upon his head, brushing quickly past us, thrust you upon a pile of paving-stones collected at a spot where the causeway is undergoing repair. You stepped upon one of the loose fragments, slipped, slightly strained your ankle, appeared vexed or sulky, muttered a few words, turned to look at the pile, and then proceeded in silence. I was not particularly attentive to what you did; but observation has become with me, of late, a species of necessity.

'You kept your eyes upon the ground – glancing, with a petulant expression, at the holes and ruts in the pavement (so that I saw you were still thinking of the stones), until we reached the little alley called Lamartine, which has been paved, by way of experiment, with the overlapping and riveted blocks. Here your countenance brightened up, and, perceiving your lips move, I could not doubt that you murmured the word "stereotomy", a term very affectedly applied to this species of pavement. I knew that you could not say to yourself "stereotomy" without being brought to think of atomics, and thus of the theories of Epicurus; and since, when we discussed this subject not very long ago, I mentioned to you how singularly, yet with how little notice, the vague guesses of that noble Greek had met with confirmation in the late nebular cosmogony, I felt that you could not avoid casting your eyes upward to the great nebula in Orion, and I certainly expected that you would do so. You did look up; and I was now assured that I had correctly followed your steps. But in that bitter tirade upon Chantilly, which appeared in yesterday's *Musée*, the satirist, making some disgraceful allusions to the cobbler's change of name upon assuming the buskin, quoted a Latin line about which we have often conversed. I mean the line

> Perdidit antiquum litera prima sonum.
> [The first letter has lost its original sound.]

I had told you that this was in reference to Orion, formerly written Urion; and, from certain pungencies connected with this explanation, I was aware that you could not have forgotten it. It was clear, therefore, that you would not fail to combine the two ideas of Orion and Chantilly. That you did combine them I saw by the character of the smile which passed over your lips. You thought of the poor cobbler's immolation. So far, you had been stooping in your gait; but now I saw you draw yourself up to your full height. I was then sure that you reflected upon the diminutive figure of Chantilly. At this point I interrupted your meditations to remark that as, in fact, he *was* a very little fellow, that Chantilly, he would do better at the Théâtre des Variétés.'

Not long after this, we were looking over an evening edition of the *Gazette des Tribunaux* when the following paragraphs arrested our attention:

EXTRAORDINARY MURDERS

This morning, about three o'clock, the inhabitants of the Quartier St Roch were aroused from sleep by a succession of terrific shrieks, issuing, apparently, from the fourth storey of a house in the Rue Morgue, known to be in the sole occupancy of one Mme L'Espanaye, and her daughter, Mlle Camille L'Espanaye. After some

delay, occasioned by a fruitless attempt to procure admission in the usual manner, the gateway
was broken in with a crowbar, and eight or ten of
the neighbours entered, accompanied by two
gendarmes. By this time the cries had ceased;
but, as the party rushed up the first flight of
stairs, two or more rough voices, in angry contention, were distinguished, and seemed to
proceed from the upper part of the house. As the
second landing was reached, these sounds, also,
had ceased, and everything remained perfectly
quiet. The party spread themselves, and hurried
from room to room. Upon arriving at a large
back chamber in the fourth storey (the door of
which, being found locked, with the key inside,
was forced open), a spectacle presented itself
which struck everyone present not less with horror
than with astonishment.

The apartment was in the wildest disorder –
the furniture broken and thrown about in all
directions. There was only one bedstead; and
from this the bed had been removed, and
thrown into the middle of the floor. On a chair
lay a razor, besmeared with blood. On the
hearth were two or three long and thick tresses
of grey human hair, also dabbled in blood, and
seeming to have been pulled out by the roots.
Upon the floor were found four napoleons, an
earring of topaz, three large silver spoons, three
smaller of métal d'Alger, and two bags, containing nearly four thousand francs in gold. The
drawers of a bureau, which stood in one corner,
were open, and had been, apparently, rifled,
although many articles still remained in them. A

small iron safe was discovered under the *bed* (not under the bedstead). It was open, with a key still in the door. It had no contents beyond a few old letters, and other papers of little consequence.

Of Mme L'Espanaye no traces were here seen; but an unusual quantity of soot being observed in the fireplace, a search was made in the chimney, and (horrible to relate!) the corpse of the daughter, head downward, was dragged therefrom; it having been thus forced up the narrow aperture for a considerable distance. The body was quite warm. Upon examining it, many excoriations were perceived, no doubt occasioned by the violence with which it had been thrust up and disengaged. Upon the face were many severe scratches, and, upon the throat, dark bruises, and deep indentations of fingernails, as if the deceased had been throttled to death.

After a thorough investigation of every portion of the house, without further discovery, the party made its way into a small paved yard in the rear of the building, where lay the corpse of the old lady, with her throat so entirely cut that, upon an attempt to raise her, the head fell off. The body, as well as the head, was fearfully mutilated – the former so much so as scarcely to retain any semblance of humanity.

To this horrible mystery there is not as yet, we believe, the slightest clue.

The next day's paper had these additional particulars:

Many individuals have been examined in relation to this most extraordinary and frightful affair [the word '*affaire*' has not yet in France that levity of import which it conveys with us], but nothing whatever has transpired to throw light upon it. We give below all the material testimony elicited.

Pauline Dubourg, laundress, deposes that she has known both the deceased for three years, having washed for them during that period. The old lady and her daughter seemed on good terms – very affectionate towards each other. They gave her excellent pay. Could not speak in regard to their mode or means of living. Believed that Mme L. told fortunes for a living. Was reputed to have money put by. Never met any persons in the house when she called for the clothes or took them home. Was sure that they had no servant in employ. There appeared to be no furniture in any part of the building, except in the fourth storey.

Pierre Moreau, tobacconist, deposes that he has been in the habit of selling small quantities of tobacco and snuff to Mme L'Espanaye for nearly four years. Was born in the neighbourhood, and has always resided there. The deceased and her daughter had occupied the house in which the corpses were found for more than six years. It was formerly occupied by a jeweller, who under-let the upper rooms to various persons. The house was the property of Mme L. She became dissatisfied with the abuse of the premises by her tenant, and moved into them herself, refusing to let any portion. The old lady was childish.

Witness had seen the daughter some five or six times during the six years. The two lived an exceedingly retired life – were reputed to have money. Had heard it said among the neighbours that Mme L. told fortunes – did not believe it. Had never seen any person enter the door except the old lady and her daughter, a porter once or twice, and a physician some eight or ten times.

Many other persons, neighbours, gave evidence to the same effect. No one was spoken of as frequenting the house. It was not known whether there were any living connections of Mme L. and her daughter. The shutters of the front windows were seldom opened. Those in the rear were always closed, with the exception of the large back room, fourth storey. The house was a good house – not very old.

Isidore Mustè, gendarme, deposes that he was called to the house about three o'clock in the morning, and found some twenty or thirty persons at the gateway, endeavouring to gain admittance. Forced it open, at length, with a bayonet – not with a crowbar. Had but little difficulty in getting it open, on account of its being a double or folding gate, and bolted neither at bottom nor top. The shrieks were continued until the gate was forced – and then suddenly ceased. They seemed to be screams of some person (or persons) in great agony – were loud and drawn out, not short and quick. Witness led the way upstairs. Upon reaching the first landing, heard two voices in loud and angry contention – the one a gruff voice, the other much shriller – a very strange voice. Could distinguish some words of the former, which was that of a Frenchman. Was positive that it was not a woman's voice. Could distinguish the words 'sacré' and 'diable'. The shrill voice was that of a foreigner. Could not be sure whether it was the voice of a man or of a woman. Could not make out what was said, but believed the language to be Spanish. The state of the room and of the bodies was described by this witness as we described them yesterday.

Henri Duval, a neighbour, and by trade a silver-smith, deposes that he was one of the party who first entered the house. Corroborates the testimony of Mustè in general. As soon as they forced an entrance, they reclosed the door, to keep out the crowd, which collected very fast, notwith-standing the lateness of the hour. The shrill voice, this witness thinks, was that of an Italian. Was certain it was not French. Could not be sure that it was a man's voice. It might have been a woman's. Was not acquainted with the Italian language. Could not distinguish the words, but was convinced by the intonation that the speaker was an Italian. Knew Mme L. and her daughter. Had conversed with both frequently. Was sure that the shrill voice was not that of either of the deceased.

Herr Odenheimer, restaurateur. This witness volunteered his testimony. Not speaking French, was examined through an interpreter. Is a native of Amsterdam. Was passing the house at the time of the shrieks. They lasted for several minutes – probably ten. They were long and loud – very awful and distressing. Was one of those who entered the building. Corroborated the previous evidence in every respect but one. Was sure that the shrill voice was that of a man – of a Frenchman. Could not distinguish the words uttered. They were loud and quick – unequal – spoken apparently in fear as well as in anger. The voice was harsh – not so much shrill as harsh. Could not call it a shrill voice. The gruff voice said repeatedly 'sacré', 'diable', and once 'mon Dieu'.

Jules Mignaud, banker, of the firm of Mignaud et Fils, Rue Deloraine. Is the elder Mignaud. Mme L'Espanaye had some property. Had opened an account with his banking house in the spring of the year, eight years previously. Made frequent deposits in small sums. Had withdrawn nothing until the third day before her death, when she took out in person the sum of four thousand francs. This sum was paid in gold, and a clerk sent home with the money.

Adolphe Le Bon, clerk to Mignaud et Fils, deposes that on the day in question, about noon, he accompanied Mme L'Espanaye to her residence with the 4000 francs put up in two bags. Upon the door being opened, Mlle L. appeared and took from his hands one of the bags, while the old lady relieved him of the other. He then bowed and departed. Did not see any person in the street at the time. It is a by-street – very lonely.

William Bird, tailor, deposes that he was one of the party who entered the house. Is an Englishman. Has lived in Paris two years. Was one of the first to ascend the stairs. Heard the voices in contention. The gruff voice was that of a Frenchman. Could make out several words, but cannot now remember all. Heard distinctly 'sacré' and 'mon Dieu'. There was a sound at the moment as if of several persons struggling – a scraping and scuffling sound. The shrill voice was very loud – louder than the gruff one. Is sure that it was not the voice of an Englishman. Appeared to be that of a German. Might have been a woman's voice. Does not understand German.

Four of the above-named witnesses, being recalled, deposed that the door of the chamber in which was found the body of Mlle L. was locked on the inside when the party reached it. Everything was perfectly silent – no groans or noises of any kind. Upon forcing the door no person was seen. The windows, both of the back and front room, were down and firmly fastened from within. A door between the two rooms was closed, but not locked. The door leading from the front room into the passage was locked, with the key on the inside. A small room in the front of the house, on the fourth storey, at the head of the passage, was open, the door being ajar. This room was crowded with old beds, boxes, and so forth. These were carefully removed and searched. There was not an inch of any portion of the house which was not carefully searched. Sweeps were sent up and down the chimneys. The house was a four-storey one, with garrets (*mansardes*). A trap-door on the roof was nailed down very securely – did not appear to have been opened for years. The time elapsing between the hearing of the voices in contention and the breaking open of the room door was variously stated by the witnesses. Some made it as short as three minutes – some as long as five. The door was opened with difficulty.

Alfonzo Garcio, undertaker, deposes that he resides in the Rue Morgue. Is a native of Spain. Was one of the party who entered the house. Did not proceed upstairs. Is nervous, and was apprehensive of the consequences of agitation. Heard the voices in contention. The gruff voice was that of a Frenchman. Could not distinguish what was said. The shrill voice was that of an Englishman – is sure of this. Does not understand the English language, but judges by the intonation.

Alberto Montani, confectioner, deposes that he was among the first to ascend the stairs. Heard the voices in question. The gruff voice was that of a Frenchman. Distinguished several words. The speaker appeared to be expostulating. Could not make out the words of the shrill voice. Spoke quick and unevenly. Thinks it the voice of a Russian. Corroborates the general testimony. Is an Italian. Never conversed with a native of Russia.

Several witnesses, recalled, here testified that the chimneys of all the rooms on the fourth storey were too narrow to admit the passage of a human being. By 'sweeps' were meant cylindrical sweeping-brushes, such as are employed by those who clean chimneys. These brushes were passed up and down every flue in the house. There is no back passage by which anyone could have descended while the party proceeded upstairs. The body of Mlle L'Espanaye was so firmly wedged in the chimney that it could not be got down until four or five of the party united their strength.

Paul Dumas, physician, deposes that he was called to view the bodies about daybreak. They were both then lying on the sacking of the bedstead in the chamber where Mlle L. was found. The corpse of the young lady was much bruised and excoriated. The fact that it had been thrust up the chimney would sufficiently account for these appearances. The throat was greatly chafed. There were several deep scratches just below the chin, together with a series of livid spots which were evidently the impression of fingers. The face was fearfully discoloured, and the eyeballs protruded. The tongue had been partially bitten through. A large bruise was discovered upon the pit of the stomach, produced apparently, by the pressure of a knee. In the opinion of M. Dumas, Mlle L'Espanaye had been throttled to death by some person or persons unknown. The corpse of the mother was horribly mutilated. All the bones of the right leg and arm were more or less shattered. The left tibia much splintered, as well as all the ribs of the left side. Whole body dreadfully bruised and discoloured. It was not possible to say how the injuries had been inflicted. A heavy club of wood, or a broad bar of iron, or a chair – any large, heavy and obtuse weapon would have produced such results, if wielded by the hands of a very powerful man. No woman could have inflicted the blows with any weapon. The head of the deceased, when seen by witness, was entirely separated from the

THE MURDERS IN THE RUE MORGUE

body, and was also greatly shattered. The throat had evidently been cut with some very sharp instrument – probably with a razor.

Alexandre Etienne, surgeon, was called with M. Dumas, to view the bodies. Corroborated the testimony, and the opinions of M. Dumas.

Nothing further of importance was elicited, although several other persons were examined. A murder so mysterious, and so perplexing in all its particulars, was never before committed in Paris – if indeed a murder has been committed at all. The police are entirely at a loss – an unusual occurrence in affairs of this nature. There is not, however, the shadow of a clue apparent.

The evening edition of the paper stated that the greatest excitement still continued in the Quartier St Roch – that the premises in question had been care-fully re-searched, and fresh examinations of witnesses instituted, but all to no purpose. A postscript, however, mentioned that Adolphe Le Bon had been arrested and imprisoned – although nothing appeared to criminate him, beyond the facts already detailed.

Dupin seemed singularly interested in the progress of this affair – at least so I judged from his manner, for he made no comments. It was only after the announcement that Le Bon had been imprisoned that he asked me my opinion respecting the murders.

I could merely agree with all Paris in considering them an insoluble mystery. I saw no means by which it would be possible to trace the murderer.

'We must not judge of the means,' said Dupin, 'by this shell of an examination. The Parisian police, so much extolled for acumen, are cunning, but no more.

There is no method in their proceedings, beyond the method of the moment. They make a vast parade of measures; but, not unfrequently, these are so ill adapted to the objects proposed as to put us in mind of M. Jourdain's calling for his *robe-de-chambre – pour mieux entendre la musique*. The results attained by them are not unfrequently surprising, but, for the most part, are brought about by simple diligence and activity. When these qualities are unavailing, their schemes fail. Vidocq, for example, was a good guesser, and a persevering man. But, without educated thought, he erred continually by the very intensity of his investigations. He impaired his vision by holding the object too close. He might see, perhaps, one or two points with unusual clearness, but in so doing, he, necessarily, lost sight of the matter as a whole. Thus there is such a thing as being too profound. Truth is not always in a well. In fact, as regards the more important knowledge, I do believe that she is invariably superficial. The depth lies in the valleys where we seek her, and not upon the mountain-top where she is found. The modes and sources of this kind of error are well typified in the contemplation of the heavenly bodies. To look at a star by glances – to view it in a sidelong way, by turning towards it the exterior portions of the retina (more susceptible of feeble impressions of light than the interior), is to behold the star distinctly – is to have the best appreciation of its lustre – a lustre which grows dim just in proportion as we turn our vision *fully* upon it. A greater number of rays actually fall upon the eye in the latter case, but, in the former, there is the more refined capacity for comprehension. By undue profundity we perplex and enfeeble thought;

and it is possible to make even Venus herself vanish from the firmament by a scrutiny too sustained, too concentrated or too direct.

'As for these murders, let us enter into some examinations for ourselves, before we make up an opinion respecting them. An enquiry will afford us amusement' (I thought this an odd term, so applied, but said nothing), 'and, besides, Le Bon once rendered me a service for which I am not ungrateful. We will go and see the premises with our own eyes. I know G——, the Prefect of Police, and shall have no difficulty in obtaining the necessary permission.'

The permission was obtained, and we proceeded at once to the Rue Morgue. This is one of those miserable thoroughfares which intervene between the Rue Richelieu and the Rue St Roch. It was late in the afternoon when we reached it, as this quarter is at a great distance from that in which we resided. The house was readily found; for there were still many persons gazing up at the closed shutters, with an objectless curiosity, from the opposite side of the way. It was an ordinary Parisian house, with a gateway, on one side of which was a glazed watch-box, with a sliding panel in the window, indicating a *loge de concierge*. Before going in we walked up the street, turned down an alley, and then, again turning, passed in the rear of the building – Dupin, meanwhile, examining the whole neighbourhood, as well as the house, with a minuteness of attention for which I could see no possible object.

Retracing our steps, we came again to the front of the dwelling, rang, and having shown our credentials, were admitted by the agents in charge. We went upstairs – into the chamber where the body of Mlle

L'Espanaye had been found, and where both the deceased still lay. The disorders of the room had, as usual, been suffered to exist. I saw nothing beyond what had been stated in the *Gazette des Tribunaux*. Dupin scrutinised everything – not excepting the bodies of the victims. We then went into the other rooms, and into the yard, a gendarme accompanying us throughout. The examination occupied us until dark, when we took our departure. On our way home my companion stepped in for a moment at the office of one of the daily papers.

I have said that the whims of my friend were manifold, and that *je les ménageais* – for this phrase there is no English equivalent [perhaps, 'I humoured them with cautious respect]. It was his humour, now, to decline all conversation on the subject of the murders, until about noon the next day. He then asked me, suddenly, if I had observed anything *peculiar* at the scene of the atrocity.

There was something in his manner of emphasising the word 'peculiar', which caused me to shudder, without knowing why.

'No, nothing *peculiar*,' I said; 'nothing more, at least, than we both saw stated in the paper.'

'The *Gazette*,' he replied, 'has not entered, I fear, into the unusual horror of the thing. But dismiss the idle opinions of this print. It appears to me that this mystery is considered insoluble for the very reason which should cause it to be regarded as easy of solution – I mean for the *outré* character of its features. The police are confounded by the seeming absence of motive – not for the murder itself, but for the atrocity of the murder. They are puzzled, too, by the seeming impossibility of reconciling the voices heard in contention with the facts that no one was discovered upstairs but the assassinated Mlle L'Espanaye, and that there were no means of egress without the notice of the party ascending. The wild disorder of the room; the corpse thrust, with the head downward, up the chimney; the frightful mutilation of the body of the old lady; these considerations, with those just mentioned, and others which I need not mention, have sufficed to paralyse the powers, by putting completely at fault the boasted acumen of the government agents. They have fallen into the gross but common error of confounding the unusual with the abstruse. But it is by these deviations from the plane of the ordinary that reason feels its way, if at all, in its search for the true. In investigations such as we are now pursuing, it should not be so much asked "what has occurred?" as "what has occurred that has never occurred before?" In fact, the facility with which I shall arrive, or have arrived, at the solution of this mystery, is in the direct ratio of its apparent insolubility in the eyes of the police.'

I stared at the speaker in mute astonishment.

'I am now awaiting,' continued he, looking towards the door of our apartment – 'I am now awaiting a person who, although perhaps not the perpetrator of these butcheries, must have been in some measure implicated in their perpetration. Of the worst portion of the crimes committed, it is probable that he is innocent. I hope that I am right in this supposition; for upon it I build my expectation of reading the entire riddle. I look for the man here – in this room – every moment. It is true that he may not arrive; but the probability is that he will. Should he come, it will be necessary to detain him. Here are pistols; and we both know how to use them when occasion demands their use.'

I took the pistols, scarcely knowing what I did, or believing what I heard, while Dupin went on, very much as if in a soliloquy. I have already spoken of his abstract manner at such times. His discourse was addressed to myself; but his voice, although by no means loud, had that intonation which is commonly employed in speaking to someone at a great distance. His eyes, vacant in expression, regarded only the wall.

'That the voices heard in contention,' he said, 'by the party upon the stairs were not the voices of the women themselves was fully proved by the evidence. This relieves us of all doubt upon the question whether the old lady could have first destroyed the daughter, and afterwards have committed suicide. I speak of this point chiefly for the sake of method; for the strength of Mme L'Espanaye would have been utterly unequal to the task of thrusting her daughter's corpse up the chimney as it was found; and the nature of the wounds upon her own person entirely precludes the idea of self-destruction. Murder, then, has been committed by some third party; and the voices of this third party were those heard in contention. Let me now advert, not to the whole testimony respecting these voices, but to what was peculiar in that testimony. Did you observe anything peculiar about it?'

I remarked that, while all the witnesses agreed in supposing the gruff voice to be that of a Frenchman, there was much disagreement in regard to the shrill, or, as one individual termed it, the harsh voice.

'That was the evidence itself,' said Dupin, 'but it was not the peculiarity of the evidence. You have observed nothing distinctive. Yet there *was* something to be observed. The witnesses, as you remark, agreed about the gruff voice; they were here unanimous. But in regard to the shrill voice, the peculiarity is – not that they disagreed – but that, while an Italian, an Englishman, a Spaniard, a Hollander and a Frenchman attempted to describe it, each one spoke of it as that *of a foreigner*. Each is sure that it was not the voice of one of his own countrymen. Each likens it not to the voice of an individual of any nation with whose language he is conversant – but the converse. The Frenchman supposes it the voice of a Spaniard, and "might have distinguished some words *had he been acquainted with the Spanish*". The Dutchman maintains it to have been that of a Frenchman; but we find it stated that, "*not understanding French, this witness was examined through an interpreter*". The Englishman thinks it the voice of a German, and "*does not understand German*". The Spaniard "is sure" that it was that of an Englishman, but "judges by the intonation" altogether, "*as he has no knowledge of the English*". The Italian believes it the voice of a Russian, but "*has never conversed with a native of Russia*". A second Frenchman differs, moreover, with the first, and is positive that the voice was that of an Italian; but, *not being cognisant of that tongue*, is, like the Spaniard, "convinced by the intonation". Now, how strangely unusual must that voice have really been, about which such testimony as this *could* have been elicited! – in whose *tones*, even, denizens of the five great divisions of Europe could recognise nothing familiar! You will say that it might have been the voice of an Asiatic – of an African. Neither Asiatics nor Africans abound in Paris; but, without denying the inference, I will now merely call your attention to three points. The voice is termed by one witness "harsh rather than shrill". It is represented by two others to have been "quick and *unequal*". No words – no sounds resembling words – were by any witness mentioned as distinguishable.

'I know not,' continued Dupin, 'what impression I may have made, so far, upon your own understanding; but I do not hesitate to say that legitimate deductions even from this portion of the testimony – the portion respecting the gruff and shrill voices – are in themselves sufficient to engender a suspicion which should give direction to all further progress in the investigation of the mystery. I said "legitimate deductions"; but my meaning is not thus fully expressed. I designed to imply that the deductions are the *sole* proper ones, and that the suspicion arises *inevitably* from them as the single result. What the suspicion is, however, I will not say just yet. I merely wish you to bear in mind that, with myself, it was sufficiently forcible to give a definite form – a certain tendency – to my enquiries in the chamber.

'Let us now transport ourselves, in fancy, to this chamber. What shall we first seek here? The means of egress employed by the murderers. It is not too much to say that neither of us believes in preternatural events. Mme and Mlle L'Espanaye were not destroyed by spirits. The doers of the deed were material, and escaped materially. Then how? Fortunately, there is but one mode of reasoning upon the point, and that mode *must* lead us to a definite decision. Let us examine, each by each, the possible means of egress. It is clear that the assassins were in the room where Mlle L'Espanaye was found, or at least in the room adjoining, when the party ascended the stairs. It is, then, only from these two apartments that we have to seek issues. The police have laid bare the floors, the ceilings, and the masonry of the walls, in every direction. No *secret* issues could have escaped their vigilance. But, not trusting to *their* eyes, I examined with my own. There were, then, *no* secret issues. Both doors leading from the rooms into the passage were securely locked, with the keys inside. Let us turn to the chimneys. These, although of ordinary width for some eight or ten feet above the hearths, will not admit, throughout their extent, the body of a large cat. The impossibility of egress, by means already stated, being thus absolute, we are reduced to the windows. Through those of the front room no one could have escaped without notice from the crowd in the street. The murderers *must* have passed, then, through those of the back room. Now, brought to this conclusion in so unequivocal a manner as we are, it is not our part, as reasoners, to reject it on account of apparent impossibilities. It is only left for us to prove that these apparent "impossibilities" are, in reality, not such.

'There are two windows in the chamber. One of them is unobstructed by furniture, and is wholly visible. The lower portion of the other is hidden from view by the head of the unwieldy bedstead which is thrust close up against it. The former was found securely fastened from within. It resisted the utmost force of those who endeavoured to raise it. A large gimlet hole had been pierced in its frame to the left, and a very stout nail was found fitted therein, nearly to the head. Upon examining the other window, a similar nail was seen similarly fitted in it; and a vigorous attempt to raise this sash, failed also. The police were now entirely satisfied that egress had not been in these directions. And, *therefore*, it was thought a matter of supererogation to withdraw the nails and open the windows.

'My own examination was somewhat more particular, and was so for the reason I have just given – because here it was, I knew, that all apparent impossibilities *must* be proved to be not such in reality.

'I proceeded to think thus – *a posteriori*. The murderers *did* escape from one of these windows. This being so, they could not have re-fastened the sashes from the inside, as they were found fastened – the consideration which put a stop, through its obviousness, to the scrutiny of the police in this quarter. Yet the sashes *were* fastened. They *must*, then, have the power of fastening themselves. There was no escape from this conclusion. I stepped to the unobstructed casement, withdrew the nail with some difficulty, and attempted to raise the sash. It resisted all my efforts, as I had anticipated. A concealed spring must, I now knew, exist; and this corroboration of my idea convinced me that my premises, at least, were correct, however mysterious still appeared the circumstances attending the nails. A careful search soon brought to light the hidden spring. I pressed it, and, satisfied with the discovery, forbore to upraise the sash.

'I now replaced the nail and regarded it attentively. A person passing out through this window might have reclosed it, and the spring would have caught – but the nail could not have been replaced. The conclusion was plain, and again narrowed in the field of my investigations. The assassins *must* have escaped through the other window. Supposing, then, the springs upon each sash to be the same, as was probable, there *must* be found a difference between the nails, or at least between the modes of their fixture. Getting upon the sacking of the bedstead, I looked over the headboard minutely at the second casement. Passing my hand down behind the board, I readily discovered and pressed the spring, which was, as I had supposed, identical in character with its neighbour. I now looked at the nail. It was as stout as the other, and apparently fitted in the same manner – driven in nearly up to the head.

'You will say that I was puzzled; but, if you think so, you must have misunderstood the nature of the inductions. To use a sporting phrase, I had not been once "at fault". The scent had never for an instant been lost. There was no flaw in any link of the chain. I had traced the secret to its ultimate result – and that result was *the nail*. It had, I say, in every respect, the appearance of its fellow in the other window; but this fact was an absolute nullity (conclusive as it might seem to be) when compared with the consideration that here, at this point, terminated the clue. "There *must* be something wrong," I said, "about the nail." I touched it; and the head, with about a quarter of an inch of the shank, came off in my fingers. The rest of the shank was in the gimlet hole, where it had been broken off. The fracture was an old one (for its edges were incrusted with rust), and had apparently been accomplished by the blow of a hammer, which had partially embedded, in the top of the bottom sash, the head portion of the nail. I now carefully replaced this head portion in the indentation whence I had taken it, and the resemblance to a perfect nail was complete – the fissure was invisible. Pressing the spring, I gently raised the sash for a few inches; the head went up with it, remaining firm in its bed. I closed the window, and the semblance of the whole nail was again perfect.

'The riddle, so far, was now unriddled. The assassin had escaped through the window which looked upon the bed. Dropping of its own accord upon his exit (or perhaps purposely closed), it had become fastened by the spring; and it was the retention of this spring which had been mistaken by the police for that of the nail – further enquiry being thus considered unnecessary.

'The next question is that of the mode of descent. Upon this point I had been satisfied in my walk with you around the building. About five feet and a half from the casement in question there runs a lightning-rod. From this rod it would have been impossible for anyone to reach the window itself, to say nothing of entering it. I observed, however, that the shutters of the fourth storey were of the peculiar kind called by Parisian carpenters *ferrades* – a kind rarely employed at the present day, but frequently seen upon very old mansions at Lyons and Bordeaux. They are in the form of an ordinary door (a single, not a folding door), except that the lower half is latticed or worked in open trellis – thus affording an excellent hold for the hands. In the present instance these shutters are fully three feet and a half broad. When we saw them from the rear of the house, they were both about half open – that is to say, they stood off at right angles from the wall. It is probable that the police, as well as myself, examined the back of the tenement; but, if so, in looking at these *ferrades* in the line of their breadth (as they must have done), they did not perceive this great breadth itself, or, at all events, failed to take it into due consideration. In fact, having once satisfied themselves that no egress could have been made in this quarter, they would naturally bestow here a very cursory examination. It was clear to me, however, that the shutter belonging to the window at the head of the bed, would, if swung fully back to the wall, reach to within two feet of the lightning-rod. It was also evident that, by exertion of a very unusual degree of activity and courage, an entrance into the window, from the rod, might have been thus effected. By reaching to the distance of two feet and a half (we now suppose the shutter open to its whole extent) a robber might have taken a firm grasp upon the trellis-work. Letting go, then, his hold upon the rod, placing his feet securely against the wall, and springing boldly from it, he might have swung the shutter so as to close it, and, if we imagine the window open at the time, might even have swung himself into the room.

'I wish you to bear especially in mind that I have spoken of a *very* unusual degree of activity as requisite to success in so hazardous and so difficult a feat. It is my design to show you, first, that the thing might possibly have been accomplished; but, secondly and *chiefly*, I wish to impress upon your understanding the *very extraordinary* – the almost preternatural character of that agility which could have accomplished it.

'You will say, no doubt, using the language of the law, that "to make out my case", I should rather undervalue than insist upon a full estimation of the activity required in this matter. This may be the practice in law, but it is not the usage of reason. My ultimate object is only the truth. My immediate purpose is to lead you to place in juxtaposition that *very unusual* activity of which I have just spoken, with that *very peculiar* shrill (or harsh) and *unequal* voice, about whose nationality no two persons could be found to agree, and in whose utterance no syllabification could be detected.'

At these words a vague and half-formed conception of the meaning of Dupin flitted over my mind. I seemed to be upon the verge of comprehension, without power to comprehend – as men, at times, find themselves upon the brink of remembrance, without being able in the end, to remember. My friend went on with his discourse.

'You will see,' he said, 'that I have shifted the question from the mode of egress to that of ingress. It was my design to convey the idea that both were effected in the same manner, at the same point. Let us now revert to the interior of the room. Let us survey the appearances here. The drawers of the bureau, it is said, had been rifled, although many articles of apparel still remained within them. The conclusion here is absurd. It is a mere guess – a very silly one – and no more. How are we to know that the articles found in the drawers were not all these drawers had originally contained? Mme L'Espanaye and her daughter lived an exceedingly retired life – saw no company – seldom went out – had little use for numerous changes of habiliment. Those found were at least of as good quality as any likely to be possessed by these ladies. If a thief had taken any, why did he not take the best – why did he not take all? In a word, why did he abandon four thousand francs in gold to encumber himself with a bundle of linen? The gold *was* abandoned. Nearly the whole sum mentioned by M. Mignaud, the banker, was discovered, in bags, upon the floor. I wish you, therefore, to discard from your thoughts the blundering idea of *motive* engendered in the brains of the police by that portion of the evidence which speaks of money delivered at the door of the house. Coincidences ten times as remarkable as this (the delivery of the money, and murder committed within three days upon the party receiving it), happen to all of us every hour of our lives, without attracting even momentary notice. Coincidences, in general, are great stumbling-blocks in the way of that class of thinkers who have been educated to know nothing of the theory of probabilities – that theory to which the most glorious objects of human research are indebted for the most glorious of illustration. In the present instance, had the gold been gone, the fact of its delivery three days before would have formed something more than a coincidence. It would have been corroborative of this idea of motive. But, under the real circumstances of the case, if we are to suppose gold the motive of this outrage, we must also imagine the perpetrator so vacillating an idiot as to have abandoned his gold and his motive together.

'Keeping now steadily in mind the points to which I have drawn your attention – that peculiar voice, that unusual agility, and that startling absence of motive in a murder so singularly atrocious as this – let us glance at the butchery itself. Here is a woman strangled to death by manual strength, and thrust up a chimney, head downward. Ordinary assassins employ no such modes of murder as this. Least of all, do they thus dispose of the murdered. In the manner of thrusting the corpse up the chimney, you will admit that there was something *excessively outré* – something altogether irreconcilable with our common notions of human action, even when we suppose the actors the most depraved of men. Think, too, how great must have been that strength which could have thrust the body *up* such an aperture so forcibly that the united vigour of several persons was found barely sufficient to drag it *down*!

'Turn, now, to other indications of the employment of a vigour most marvellous. On the hearth were thick tresses – very thick tresses – of grey human hair. These had been torn out by the roots. You are aware of the great force necessary in tearing thus from the head even twenty or thirty hairs together. You saw the locks in question as well as myself. Their roots (a hideous sight!) were clotted with fragments of the flesh of the scalp – sure token of the prodigious power which had been exerted in uprooting perhaps half a million of hairs at a time. The throat of the old lady was not merely cut, but the head absolutely severed from the body: the instrument was a mere razor. I wish you also to look at the *brutal* ferocity of these deeds. Of the bruises upon the body of Mme L'Espanaye I do not speak. M. Dumas, and his worthy coadjutor M. Etienne, have pronounced that they were inflicted by some obtuse instrument; and so far these gentlemen are very correct. The obtuse instrument was clearly the stone pavement in the yard, upon which the victim had fallen from the window which looked in upon the bed. This idea, however simple it may now seem, escaped the police for the same reason that the breadth of the shutters escaped them – because, by the affair of the nails, their perceptions had been hermetically sealed against the possibility of the windows having ever been opened at all.

'If now, in addition to all these things, you have properly reflected upon the odd disorder of the chamber, we have gone so far as to combine the ideas of an agility astounding, a strength superhuman, a ferocity brutal, a butchery without motive, a *grotesquerie* in horror absolutely alien from humanity, and a voice foreign in tone to the ears of men of many nations, and devoid of all distinct or intelligible syllabification. What result, then, has ensued? What impression have I made upon your fancy?'

I felt a creeping of the flesh as Dupin asked me the question. 'A madman,' I said, 'has done this deed – some raving maniac escaped from a neighbouring Maison de Santé.'

'In some respects,' he replied, 'your idea is not irrelevant. But the voices of madmen, even in their wildest paroxysms, are never found to tally with that peculiar voice heard upon the stairs. Madmen are of some nation, and their language, however incoherent in its words, has always the coherence of syllabification. Besides, the hair of a madman is not such as I now hold in my hand. I disentangled this little tuft from the rigidly clutched fingers of Mme L'Espanaye. Tell me what you can make of it.'

'Dupin,' I said, completely unnerved; 'this hair is most unusual – this is no *human* hair.'

'I have not asserted that it is,' said he; 'but, before we decide this point, I wish you to glance at the little sketch I have here traced upon this paper. It is a facsimile drawing of what has been described in one portion of the testimony as "dark bruises, and deep indentations of fingernails", upon the throat of Mlle L'Espanaye, and in another (by Messrs Dumas and Etienne), as a "series of livid spots, evidently the impression of fingers".

'You will perceive,' continued my friend, spreading

out the paper upon the table before us, 'that this drawing gives the idea of a firm and fixed hold. There is no *slipping* apparent. Each finger has retained – possibly until the death of the victim – the fearful grasp by which it originally embedded itself. Attempt, now, to place all your fingers, at the same time, in the respective impressions as you see them.'

I made the attempt in vain.

'We are possibly not giving this matter a fair trial,' he said. 'The paper is spread out upon a plane surface; but the human throat is cylindrical. Here is a *billot* of wood, the circumference of which is about that of the throat. Wrap the drawing round it, and try the experiment again.'

I did so; but the difficulty was even more obvious than before. 'This,' I said, 'is the mark of no human hand.'

'Read now,' replied Dupin, 'this passage from Cuvier.'

It was a minute anatomical and generally descriptive account of the large fulvous orang-utan of the East Indian Islands. The gigantic stature, the prodigious strength and activity, the wild ferocity and the imitative propensities of these mammalia are sufficiently well known to all. I understood the full horrors of the murder at once.

'The description of the digits,' said I, as I made an end of reading, 'is in exact accordance with this drawing. I see that no animal but an orang-utan, of the species here mentioned, could have impressed the indentations, as you have traced them. This tuft of tawny hair, too, is identical in character with that of the beast of Cuvier. But I cannot possibly comprehend the particulars of this frightful mystery. Besides, there were *two* voices heard in contention, and one of them was unquestionably the voice of a Frenchman.'

'True; and you will remember an expression attributed almost unanimously, by the evidence, to this voice – the expression "Mon Dieu!" This, under the circumstances, has been justly characterised by one of the witnesses (Montani, the confectioner) as an expression of remonstrance or expostulation. Upon these two words, therefore, I have mainly built my hopes of a full solution of the riddle. A Frenchman was cognisant of the murder. It is possible – indeed it is far more than probable – that he was innocent of all participation in the bloody transactions which took place. The orang-utan may have escaped from him. He may have traced it to the chamber; but, under the agitating circumstances which ensued, he could never have recaptured it. It is still at large. I will not pursue these guesses – for I have no right to call them more – since the shades of reflection upon which they are based are scarcely of sufficient depth to be appreciable to my own intellect and since I could not pretend to make them intelligible to the understanding of another. We will call them guesses, then, and speak of them as such. If the Frenchman in question is indeed, as I suppose, innocent of this atrocity, this advertisement, which I left last night, upon our return home, at the office of *Le Monde* (a paper devoted to the shipping interest, and much sought by sailors), will bring him to our residence.'

He handed me a paper, and I read thus:

CAUGHT

In the Bois de Boulogne, early in the morning of the — inst. [the morning of the murder], a very

large, tawny orang-utan of the Bornese species.
The owner (who is ascertained to be a sailor,
belonging to a Maltese vessel), may have the
animal again, upon identifying it satisfactorily,
and paying a few charges arising from its capture
and keeping. Call at No. —, Rue —, Faubourg
St Germain – au troisième.

'How was it possible,' I asked, 'that you should
know the man to be a sailor, and belonging to a
Maltese vessel?'

'I do *not* know it,' said Dupin. 'I am not *sure* of it.
Here, however, is a small piece of ribbon, which from
its form, and from its greasy appearance, has evidently
been used in tying the hair in one of those long queues
of which sailors are so fond. Moreover, this knot is
one which few besides sailors can tie, and is peculiar
to the Maltese. I picked the ribbon up at the foot of
the lightning-rod. It could not have belonged to either
of the deceased. Now if, after all, I am wrong in my
induction from this ribbon, that the Frenchman was
a sailor belonging to a Maltese vessel, still I can have
done no harm in saying what I did in the advertisement. If I am in error, he will merely suppose that I
have been misled by some circumstance into which
he will not take the trouble to enquire. But if I am
right, a great point is gained. Cognisant although
innocent of the murder, the Frenchman will naturally
hesitate about replying to the advertisement – about
demanding the orang-utan. He will reason thus: "I
am innocent; I am poor; my orang-utan is of great
value – to one in my circumstances a fortune of itself –
why should I lose it through idle apprehensions of
danger? Here it is within my grasp. It was found in

the Bois de Boulogne – at a vast distance from the scene of that butchery. How can it ever be suspected that a brute beast should have done the deed? The police are at fault – they have failed to procure the slightest clue. Should they even trace the animal, it would be impossible to prove me cognisant of the murder, or to implicate me in guilt on account of that cognisance. Above all, *I am known*. The advertiser designates me as the possessor of the beast. I am not sure to what limit his knowledge may extend. Should I avoid claiming a property of so great value, which it is known that I possess, I will render the animal at least liable to suspicion. It is not my policy to attract attention either to myself or to the beast. I will answer the advertisement, get the orang-utan, and keep it close until this matter has blown over." '

At this moment we heard a step upon the stairs.

'Be ready,' said Dupin, 'with your pistols, but neither use them nor show them until at a signal from myself.'

The front door of the house had been left open, and the visitor had entered, without ringing, and advanced several steps upon the staircase. Now, however, he seemed to hesitate. Presently we heard him descending. Dupin was moving quickly to the door, when we again heard him coming up. He did not turn back a second time, but stepped up with decision, and rapped at the door of our chamber.

'Come in,' said Dupin, in a cheerful and hearty tone.

A man entered. He was a sailor, evidently – a tall, stout and muscular-looking person, with a certain dare-devil expression of countenance, not altogether unprepossessing. His face, greatly sunburnt, was more than half hidden by whisker and mustachio. He had with him a huge oaken cudgel, but appeared to be otherwise unarmed. He bowed awkwardly, and bade us 'good-evening', in French accents, which although somewhat Neufchâtelish were still sufficiently indicative of a Parisian origin.

'Sit down, my friend,' said Dupin. 'I suppose you have called about the orang-utan. Upon my word, I almost envy you the possession of him; a remarkably fine, and no doubt a very valuable animal. How old do you suppose him to be?'

The sailor drew a long breath, with the air of a man relieved of some intolerable burden, and then replied, in an assured tone, 'I have no way of telling – but he can't be more than four or five years old. Have you got him here?'

'Oh no; we had no conveniences for keeping him here. He is at a livery stable in the Rue Dubourg, just by. You can get him in the morning. Of course you are prepared to identify the property?'

'To be sure I am, sir.'

'I shall be sorry to part with him,' said Dupin.

'I don't mean that you should be at all this trouble for nothing, sir,' said the man. 'Couldn't expect it. Am very willing to pay a reward for the finding of the animal – that is to say, anything in reason.'

'Well,' replied my friend, 'that is all very fair, to be sure. Let me think! – what should I have? Oh! I will tell you. My reward shall be this. You shall give me all the information in your power about these murders in the Rue Morgue.'

Dupin said the last words in a very low tone, and very quietly. Just as quietly, too, he walked towards the door, locked it and put the key in his pocket. He then drew a pistol from his bosom, and placed it, without the least flurry, upon the table.

The sailor's face flushed up as if he were struggling with suffocation. He started to his feet and grasped his cudgel; but the next moment he fell back into his seat, trembling violently, and with the countenance of death itself. He spoke not a word. I pitied him from the bottom of my heart.

'My friend,' said Dupin, in a kind tone, 'you are alarming yourself unnecessarily – you are indeed. We mean you no harm whatever. I pledge you the honour of a gentleman, and of a Frenchman, that we intend you no injury. I perfectly well know that you are innocent of the atrocities in the Rue Morgue. It will not do, however, to deny that you are in some measure implicated in them. From what I have already said, you must know that I have had means of information about this matter – means of which you could never have dreamed. Now the thing stands thus. You have done nothing which you could have avoided – nothing, certainly, which renders you culpable. You were not even guilty of robbery, when you might have robbed with impunity. You have nothing to conceal. You have no reason for concealment. On the other hand, you are bound by every principle of honour to confess all you know. An innocent man is now imprisoned, charged with that crime of which you can point out the perpetrator.'

The sailor had recovered his presence of mind, in a great measure, while Dupin uttered these words; but his original boldness of bearing was all gone.

'So help me God,' said he, after a brief pause, 'I *will* tell you all I know about this affair; but I do not expect you to believe one half I say – I would be a fool indeed if I did. Still, I *am* innocent, and I will make a clean breast if I die for it.'

What he stated was, in substance, this. He had lately made a voyage to the Indian Archipelago. A party, of which he formed one, landed at Borneo, and passed into the interior on an excursion of pleasure. Himself and a companion had captured the orang-utan. This companion dying, the animal fell into his own exclusive possession. After great trouble, occasioned by the intractable ferocity of his captive during the home voyage, he at length succeeded in lodging it safely at his own residence in Paris, where, not to attract towards himself the unpleasant curiosity of his neighbours, he kept it carefully secluded, until such time as it should recover from a wound in the foot, received from a splinter on board ship. His ultimate design was to sell it.

Returning home from some sailors' frolic on the night, or rather in the morning of the murder, he found the beast occupying his own bedroom, into which it had broken from a closet adjoining, where it had been, as was thought, securely confined. Razor in hand, and fully lathered, it was sitting before a looking-glass, attempting the operation of shaving, in which it had no doubt previously watched its master through the keyhole of the closet. Terrified at the sight of so dangerous a weapon in the possession of an animal so ferocious, and so well able to use it, the man, for some moments, was at a loss what to do. He had been accustomed, however, to quiet the creature, even in its fiercest moods, by the use of a whip, and to this he now resorted. Upon sight of it, the orang-utan sprang at once through the door of the chamber, down the stairs, and thence, through a window, unfortunately open, into the street.

The Frenchman followed in despair; the ape, razor still in hand, occasionally stopping to look back and gesticulate at its pursuer, until the latter had nearly come up with it. It then again made off. In this manner the chase continued for a long time. The streets were profoundly quiet, as it was nearly three o'clock in the morning. In passing down an alley in the rear of the Rue Morgue, the fugitive's attention was arrested by a light gleaming from the open window of Mme L'Espanaye's chamber, in the fourth storey of her house. Rushing to the building, it perceived the lightning-rod, clambered up with inconceivable agility, grasped the shutter, which was thrown fully back against the wall, and, by its means, swung itself directly upon the headboard of the bed. The whole feat did not occupy a minute. The shutter was kicked open again by the orang-utan as it entered the room.

The sailor, in the meantime, was both rejoiced and perplexed. He had strong hopes of now recapturing the brute, as it could scarcely escape from the trap into which it had ventured, except by the rod, where it might be intercepted as it came down. On the other hand, there was much cause for anxiety as to what it might do in the house. This latter reflection urged the man still to follow the fugitive. A lightning-rod is ascended without difficulty, especially by a sailor; but, when he had arrived as high as the window, which lay far to his left, his career was stopped; the most that he could accomplish was to reach over so as to obtain a glimpse of the interior of the room. At this glimpse he nearly fell from his hold through excess of horror.

Now it was that those hideous shrieks arose upon the night, which had startled from slumber the inmates of the Rue Morgue. Mme L'Espanaye and her daughter, habited in their nightclothes, had apparently been occupied in arranging some papers in the iron chest already mentioned, which had been wheeled into the middle of the room. It was open, and its contents lay beside it on the floor. The victims must have been sitting with their backs towards the window; and, from the time elapsing between the ingress of the beast and the screams, it seems probable that it was not immediately perceived. The flapping-to of the shutter would naturally have been attributed to the wind.

As the sailor looked in, the gigantic animal had seized Mme L'Espanaye by the hair (which was loose, as she had been combing it), and was flourishing the razor about her face, in imitation of the motions of a barber. The daughter lay prostrate and motionless; she had swooned. The screams and struggles of the old lady (during which the hair was torn from her head) had the effect of changing the probably pacific purposes of the orang-utan into those of wrath. With one determined sweep of its muscular arm it nearly severed her head from her body. The sight of blood inflamed its anger into frenzy. Gnashing its teeth, and flashing fire from its eyes, it flew upon the body of the girl, and embedded its fearful talons in her throat, retaining its grasp until she expired. Its wandering and wild glances fell at this moment upon the head of the bed, over which the face of its master, rigid with horror, was just discernible. The fury of the beast, who no doubt bore still in mind the dreaded whip, was instantly converted into fear. Conscious of having deserved punishment, it seemed desirous of concealing its bloody deeds, and skipped about the chamber in an agony of nervous agitation; throwing down and breaking the furniture as it moved, and dragging the bed from the bedstead. In conclusion, it seized first the corpse of the daughter, and thrust it up the chimney, as it was found; then that of the old lady, which it immediately hurled through the window headlong.

As the ape approached the casement with its mutilated burden, the sailor shrank aghast to the rod, and rather gliding than clambering down it, hurried at once home – dreading the consequences of the butchery, and gladly abandoning, in his terror, all solicitude about the fate of the orang-utan. The words heard by the party upon the staircase were the Frenchman's exclamations of horror and affright, commingled with the fiendish jabberings of the brute.

I have scarcely anything to add. The orang-utan must have escaped from the chamber, by the rod, just before the breaking of the door. It must have closed the window as it passed through it. It was subsequently caught by the owner himself, who obtained for it a very large sum at the Jardin des Plantes. Le Bon was instantly released upon our narration of the circumstances (with some comments from Dupin) at the bureau of the Prefect of Police. This functionary, however well disposed to my friend, could not altogether conceal his chagrin at the turn which affairs had taken, and was fain to indulge in a sarcasm or two about the propriety of every person minding his own business.

'Let him talk,' said Dupin, who had not thought it necessary to reply. 'Let him discourse; it will ease his conscience. I am satisfied with having defeated him in his own castle. Nevertheless, that he failed in the solution of this mystery is by no means that matter for wonder which he supposes it; for, in truth, our friend the prefect is somewhat too cunning to be profound. In his wisdom is no *staying power*. It is all head and no body, like the pictures of the goddess Laverna – or, at best, all head and shoulders, like a codfish. But he is a good creature after all. I like him especially for one masterstroke of cant, by which he has attained his reputation for ingenuity. I mean the way he has *"de nier ce qui est, et d'expliquer ce qui n'est pas"* [to deny what is, and explain what is not].'*

---

* Rousseau, *La Nouvelle Héloïse*

ARTHUR B. REEVE

The Black Cross

'Censorship or no censorship, of course I won't
publish a word of that thing – but what do you make
of it, Kennedy?'

The managing editor of the *Star* shoved over at
Kennedy and myself, whom he had called urgently by
telephone one evening, a confidential tip that had been
sent in by messenger from the *Star* reporter assigned
to the army cantonment out at Camp Mahan, on
Long Island.

Something strange is going on under the surface
here [it read]. Wild rumours are about that the
hospital is full, that many of the officers, men and
even nurses are ill. Tonight I sent you a dispatch of
the death of Dr Dwyer, bacteriologist with the New
York Hospital unit here. The unconfirmed story is,
however, that he was murdered in the temporary
laboratory. Both Wade Martine and Dr Delano of
the Red Cross refuse absolutely to be interviewed
regarding the reported epidemic or the murder. I
believe the situation is really serious. Of course, not
a word of it has been put on the wire by anyone,
but you know how rapidly and how far such stories
spread. What shall I do?

Kennedy glanced up from the note. 'Epidemic –
murder,' he repeated. 'It looks very bad.'

'Indeed it does!' hastened the editor. 'Will you go

out there as the *Star*'s representative – not as a writer, but as this newspaper's agent for national defence, so to speak?'

'When can we get a train?' was Kennedy's laconic reply.

'Train be hanged. The service is wretched at night. I'll get you a car, and a fast one.'

The editor reached for his telephone before he had finished speaking, and in less than half an hour we found ourselves in a long speedster, crossing over the bridge to Long Island.

We swung into the motor parkway, and as the engine picked up speed I settled back in the seat, with one eye on the parkway as the beam of our lights unfolded it and the other eye on the speedometer wavering about the fifty-mile mark.

It was a long journey out to Camp Mahan, and, at this hour of the night, lonely. We passed scarcely a car. Mile after mile of the splendid road we reeled off. The farther we got away from the city the more sparsely settled was the country, until at last we came to the section where we passed scarcely a town, then not even a farmhouse for miles, nothing but the scrub-oaks and pines of the wastes in the centre of the island.

We were bowling along with a steady hum when suddenly, around a well-banked curve to the left, a car loomed up ahead. It seemed to be driving straight at us, its spotlight glaring full in Kennedy's eyes.

Craig pulled over as far on the high side of the curve as he could. The car swerved, just missing us as it banked on its own side of the road. As it flashed past I caught a glimpse for a fraction of a moment, in the light from the little bulb on its dashboard, of the face of a lone rider, a man, his features set as if intent solely on speed.

'Must be a matter of life or death for that fellow to be driving like that,' growled Kennedy, swinging back into the road and proceeding more cautiously.

We could not have gone a mile farther when the lights of another car gleamed fiercely at us. Kennedy hugged his own side of the road, but it seemed as though the lights were stationary.

As we passed slowly, we could see that this car was standing still. Beside it, with the hood over the engine raised, stood a girl, blinking into our lights until Craig dimmed them, and waving to us to stop.

There had been no house for miles. Here was a lady, alone, in distress. Kennedy yanked up on the emergency and we pulled aside, some yards past her. We got out and walked back.

'I was on my way to the city,' she explained, looking from us in pretty helplessness at the engine. 'My name is Sonia Strusky. I'm a Red Cross nurse at the camp.'

It seemed at first rather strange to me that a Red Cross nurse should be driving about the country in a not inexpensive car, but then, I reflected, many wealthy girls had gone into the Red Cross, so that it might not be so strange, after all.

Kennedy introduced himself and stuck his head under the hood, examining the engine. Ignition and carburation were all right. In fact, he seemed to be puzzled until, finally, he climbed behind the wheel and started to let in the clutch. Nothing happened.

'Can't I – go on?' she asked, as he got out and looked at the car again.

Craig shook his head. 'I'm afraid not. You've broken the clutch. You're from Camp Mahan, you say? We are on our way out there. I don't think there is a thing ahead of you for miles. But if you'll get in with us we'll be glad to take you back. Your car will have to be towed, anyhow. I think there's a tow-rope in my car.'

There was keen disappointment written on her face. But there was no other course open. She thanked us and accepted the offer, climbing in beside Kennedy, while I took the wheel of her car.

Our journey was made slowly and in comparative silence. Further than what she told us at the start, Sonia seemed to be very reticent about herself and her business.

As we drove along, I was wondering how she had come to grief, why she should have put such an unusual strain on the clutch, but to neither Kennedy nor myself did she at any time confide anything further; nevertheless she seemed to be a most attractive girl.

It was almost midnight when, after leaving the parkway and crossing a few miles of country road, we pulled up before a hotel a mile or so from the camp.

Sonia Strusky thanked us and flitted away to get someone to attend to her car and take it to the local garage, which, of course, was closed.

'For heaven's sake, Kennedy! You out here – and Jameson, too?'

We turned quickly, as we were mounting the hotel steps, at a familiar voice that greeted us from the shadows beside the porch. It was our old friend Burke of the Secret Service.

'I saw you drive up. Didn't recognise you and couldn't quite make up my mind whether to follow you or the girl. Where did you meet her?'

'On the parkway. We had just passed a fellow in a car going about sixty, I guess. She was a mile or two farther on, stalled – broken clutch.'

'A fellow in another car?' repeated Burke. 'What did he look like? Could you see him at all?'

As nearly as I could I described him, but it was mostly cap and coat that I had seen.

'Wade Martine – director of the Red Cross relief here – I'll bet,' returned Burke eagerly. 'She must have been trailing him and trying to keep up with him when she broke down.'

Accompanied by Burke, we walked inside. It was late and no one was around in the little lobby into which we went.

'What brings you out here?' parried Kennedy to Burke's further enquiry.

Burke looked about, saw no one, and lowered his voice. 'I've been assigned out here at the camp,' he whispered. 'It's not yet generally known, but the camp is greatly upset – wild rumours about the hospital being full – relatives and friends of the men coming out to see what is going on – and all that. Yesterday Dr Dwyer, the bacteriologist, died – very suddenly. Well – there's something suspicious about it.'

Burke checked himself before he told too much, even to us.

'You think he was killed?' queried Kennedy, evidently hoping to catch Burke off his guard with the surprise. 'Has Dr Delano or any of them admitted anything to you?'

'What?' returned Burke, shaking his head. 'You know about it? How do you know? How did you hear?'

'Never mind that, now,' Craig hastened. 'I'm out

here for the *Star*, with Jameson – not to write, you understand – but merely to help – if I can.'

'You can,' replied Burke fervidly. 'No, Dr Delano has had very little to say, even to us. Did you know that Dwyer had been shot with a pistol? That was how they came to send for me in the first place. My! but these army people are queer! After I get out here none of them seem to help me. Oh, say, what do you make of that?' he asked finally.

I looked. Burke was holding out in the palm of his hand a peculiar piece of gun-metal. It was cast in the form of a Maltese cross – perfectly blue-black and smooth. Kennedy took it and turned it over as he examined it. On the other side there was nothing either, except the simple number, '1402'.

'Where did you get it?' asked Kennedy.

'Directly after Dr Dwyer was shot in his laboratory, as nearly as I can determine,' replied Burke, 'a nurse, Thelma Dallinger, attempted suicide in the hospital.'

'Attempted suicide? How? Why?'

Burke shook his head again. 'Don't ask me. I have an operative from the service here, a woman, posing as a nurse with the others – Alda Anderson. It wasn't she who discovered Thelma unconscious – that was your friend, Sonia; but Alda was with her almost immediately afterwards. She found that thing on her.'

'What do you think it means?' I asked, still gazing at the peculiar cross.

Burke shook his head in perplexity. 'When Thelma was discovered, Alda says, she was delirious. Says it looked very much as though she had taken an overdose of morphine or opium – at least enough to make her see things, I mean. In her delirium she was constantly raving about the "Black Cross".'

I looked at Kennedy, but his face betrayed no comprehension. The words themselves, however, had an ominous sound.

'Did she overhear anything else?'

'No. One of the doctors took her in charge – Dr Godart. He quieted her. But it seemed as though he didn't want any of the others to hear a word. She isn't all right yet, but she isn't raving.'

'And is this Dr Godart taking charge of her?'

'Yes. He would let no one else do it – wouldn't let Delano or Martine even see her. Sonia wanted to do the nursing, but Alda was too clever for her and got in first. Still, that is about all she has accomplished. Both Thelma and Dr Godart will say nothing.'

'And the rest?'

'You mean Delano and Martine? Delano is in the sanitary service. I don't expect he knows much, anyhow. I don't think he and Dr Godart are – well, chums exactly. As for Martine, he seems to have been much upset by the death of Dr Dwyer. He hasn't said much, but I imagine that it was he whom you saw in the car going to the city. I thought perhaps he was going to beg a bacteriologist from one of the hospitals there. You know they're short, even in the city, now. Work at most of the research laboratories is practically stopped on account of the government's demand for experts. As for me, except for Alda Anderson I am playing a lone hand here. There's no one, Kennedy, could get at the truth of these things quicker than you could. Will you help?'

'That is what the *Star* sent us here for,' returned Craig simply. 'When can I see Miss Anderson?'

'The first thing in the morning. She is at the hospital. I will take you in.'

Kennedy was apparently quite gratified at this quick turn of events so soon after our arrival. The presence of Burke would give us a sort of official standing in the case now, which we had sorely lacked before.

'There's nothing we can accomplish tonight,' decided Kennedy finally. 'We're thoroughly tired. Let us bring fresh minds to bear on it in the morning.'

Early the following morning Kennedy lost no time in making his first visit to the camp hospital with Burke. Camp Mahan was a huge place, as indeed was necessary for the housing and training of some forty thousand men; it covered a couple of thousand acres, besides parades, manoeuvring-fields and rifle-ranges.

There were no tents in the camp. The men lived in two-storey wooden barracks a couple of hundred feet long, each with kitchen and mess-hall attached. All were electrically lighted, with running water and sewers, paved streets, stables, stores, amusements – a veritable city.

At one end we found the huge hospital building, and grouped about it the various administration buildings that had to do with the health of the encampment. As we entered the hospital, Burke summoned an orderly and dispatched him to bring Alda Anderson to meet us in a little private reception-room, that seeming to be the best way for us to get acquainted first-hand with the case before coming out into the open.

Alda Anderson proved to be a rather plain, ordinary-looking girl, though on closer study one found many striking features about her. It was some time before I realised that her plainness was in reality part of her make-up. Then I saw the fine artistic hand of Burke, for Burke's idea of a detective was someone who would not, above all else, attract attention.

'Is there anything new about Thelma?' enquired Burke, after our presence had been explained.

'Nothing since last night,' she replied. 'She seems to be very grateful for anything I do, but I fancy she is always on guard.'

'How about Dr Godart? Does he suspect you?'

'Not a bit. He thinks I am just like the other nurses – perhaps not so busy at gossip.' She laughed. 'I fancy, too, that he is constantly on guard also.'

'On guard against each other or against you?' asked Craig.

'Against everybody,' she returned, then leaned over and whispered, as though even the walls of the reception-room might overhear: 'You know Thelma was one of the most popular girls in the corps at the cantonment, I find. They say she was engaged to Wade Martine, of the Red Cross. But anyone can see that Dr Godart is really very much interested in her.'

'In love with her?' I hazarded.

'I should say so, though he tries hard not to betray it.'

Kennedy had glanced out into the hall, and motioned quietly to us to look down too. Some distance away, I could catch a glimpse of the girl we had towed back in the car the night before. She had stopped and was talking to a young surgeon, a rather striking man in his white linen suit which admirably set off his dark features.

'Who is that?' asked Kennedy.

'That is Dr Godart, with Sonia Strusky.'

'Yes? Who *is* this Sonia?'

Alda smiled. 'Her father is a well-to-do merchant in the city – used to be an importer, before the war. It's a rather interesting situation that you see there.

As nearly as I have been able to make it out since I
came here, both Dr Godart and Mr Martine have
been rivals for Thelma. Sonia – well, it is as you see.
She seems always to be around when Dr Godart is in
the hospital. There is no doubt that Sonia likes the
boys, but she seems to be just a bit more interested in
Dr Godart than the rest. He doesn't like it. Sometimes it seems to make him quite vexed. I don't think
he cares for her – if hoping for that is what brings her
about him so much. I think she'd have more success
if she cultivated some of the others. Just watch.'

Alda's eyes indicated another white-coated young
fellow, who was coming towards the pair in the hall.
'Dr Delano,' she whispered, 'who has charge of many
of the sanitary arrangements in the camp.'

As Delano bowed and paused, chatting, Godart
seized the opportunity to excuse himself, leaving
Sonia and Delano together. I could not notice any
less cordiality on the part of Sonia towards him,
however. It seemed that, like many young nurses,
she was fascinated by young doctors, especially if
they were good-looking and athletic. Together they
walked down the corridor. Once she turned, and I
felt that her quick glance had caught us watching.

'I think you'll find there is something very peculiar
in the relations of these people,' interposed Burke.
'From what I have observed, Dr Godart seems to
take every excuse to avoid Dr Delano, Mr Martine
and, in fact, all the rest. It's my opinion that Godart
is concealing something. We'll have to watch that
fellow. I want you to meet him.'

With Miss Anderson we moved out, now, into the
hall, and Burke steered us round a bend and up a
staircase towards which Godart had exited. A little

search and Burke succeeded in finding him and introducing us.

'How is Miss Dallinger this morning?' he enquired.

Godart seemed to be watching us furtively. 'Doing very well, I should say,' he returned.

'Have you any idea yet why she should have tried to commit suicide?' asked Burke, in the hope that a direct question might succeed where indirection had failed.

'Suicide?' parried Dr Godart quickly. 'I don't know of any suicide. Miss Dallinger, as nearly as I can determine, had a bad attack of some throat trouble – influenza, perhaps. She may have been in pain, may have taken an over-large dose of some drug to relieve it. That is all. At any rate, I have her in a private ward until I can determine what's the matter. We miss Dwyer in such things. You'll pardon me – I see I am due at the operating-room in a few minutes. Pleased to have met you,' to Kennedy. 'I'll see you again later, I trust?'

He was gone adroitly, while Burke looked at Craig enquiringly. 'Influenza – the deuce! He doesn't think there is anything serious – yet he has her isolated. Confound it! these people put nothing but obstacles in our way. They don't seem to realise that they are playing with fire. If it keeps up I shall go to the Surgeon-General about it.'

Someone had come to summon Alda to ward duty, and for a moment Burke walked along with her, asking questions in a low tone.

'I would like to meet Martine,' suggested Craig when Burke rejoined us.

Burke nodded, and with him we walked to the extreme end of the hospital buildings. Fortunately,

Martine was in his office, a perfectly appointed administrative bureau for the many activities that fell to his direction.

As we shook hands I caught the resemblance to the face I had seen in the car the night before. I thought, too, that he looked both tired and worried. There was every evidence in his eyes of having been up all night, and he received us with a sort of weary cordiality.

'Has anything been discovered about the – er – sudden death of Dr Dwyer?' enquired Burke.

If Martine had had any disposition to hide anything, he did not show it as Burke had hoped.

'Terrible! terrible!' he repeated, shaking his head, adding, 'to be struck down that way, when we so need him. Such a loss cannot easily be repaired, especially when the medical service is so short of bacteriologists already. If it had only been a surgeon – we have many doctors who have dabbled in surgery and are fit for everything up to major cases. Then, too, almost anyone of average intelligence can learn enough of camp sanitation to be useful in that field. But the trained bacteriologist takes years to develop. It has been a sad blow. I cannot seem to get anyone in the city immediately, either. I don't know what we shall do – what we shall do.'

We chatted for a few moments, but it was apparent that Martine had a great deal on his mind and was in no mood to prolong the conversation.

As we left his office we happened upon Sonia Strusky. I had the feeling that she had been watching us while we were not aware of it.

'Oh, good-morning!' she greeted, in apparent surprise. 'I don't believe that I properly thanked you last night in the excitement.'

'How is the car this morning?' asked Kennedy.

'The garage man has wired to the city for a new clutch and promises to have the car running again this afternoon. If you care to go, I think I might repay your help by driving you about the camp and showing you the points of interest.'

'I should be delighted,' promised Kennedy, much to my surprise, for I had a mounting suspicion of Sonia, especially now, since she had, evidently, been watching us in Martine's office.

She seemed delighted, and promised to let us know as soon as the car was fixed.

Kennedy's next move was to direct Burke to take us to Thelma Dallinger's ward, where we found that Alda Anderson had returned to duty.

As we entered we saw that Thelma, in health, must have been a very prepossessing young lady. Even now, as she lay ill in the plain and cheerless ward of the camp hospital, her face had an ethereal sweetness that showed the character of the girl.

Burke hung back, but Alda was quite equal to the occasion and hastily reassured Thelma that everything was all right and that a specialist from the city had called at the camp and wanted to see her.

She smiled wanly, but behind the languor I could see that the very mention of the word 'specialist' had aroused her attention and that she was studying Kennedy closely under her long, dark lashes.

Kennedy did not recur to the subject of how she had come to be in the ward, although just previously he had been talking in a low tone to Alda about her various symptoms and her condition. Instead, for some time he studied the face of the poor little nurse.

I was standing apart from Kennedy and Alda when I saw that he, in apparent nervousness, had begun fishing in his pockets, as though looking for something. Finally he drew out the black cross, and casually returned it to his pocket, as though that had not been what he was looking for.

The action had not escaped the quick glance of Thelma. Her pale face blanched even whiter. As she turned slightly I noticed for the first time that her head seemed to be drawn back rigidly.

Without a word, Craig reached for a packet of gauze that was lying on a little medicine-table. Hastily wrapping a piece of it about a glass tube that was standing in a tumbler of sterilised water, he bent over her.

'Would you please open your mouth – wide – Miss Dallinger?' he asked.

She obeyed mechanically, not taking her eyes from his face.

I saw that he was now passing the improvised swab about the posterior throat, as though trying to collect the secretions of both throat and nostrils.

As he withdrew the swab and carefully preserved the piece of gauze, the look on Thelma's face was startling – almost fearful. There was a mute appeal in her gaze. Her lips moved as though she was about to say something, but she checked it. Instead, she turned away and hid her face.

When she turned back I saw that the pillow was wet with tears. What had her struggle been about? What did it all mean? What was the secret that she held locked behind those tightened lips that only the delirium had opened?

A glance from Miss Anderson was sufficient hint to

Kennedy that the patient should not be disturbed further. Without a word, we withdrew.

In the hall again, Burke shot an enquiring look at Kennedy.

'Might I use the laboratory of Dr Dwyer?' asked Craig, ignoring the silent query. 'I should like to see it, anyway.'

Burke curbed his impatience, and, in a few minutes, after complying with some red-tape regulation or other, led the way to the laboratory.

No sooner had Kennedy entered it than one could see he felt at home, in spite of the tragic shooting that had occurred there the night before.

Seemingly oblivious to us, Kennedy stripped off his coat and immediately set to work. Though I had no great knowledge of the technique, I could see that he was preparing to make a culture of the secretions of Thelma's throat.

He looked over what was on a table and seemed mightily interested in what he found.

'I wonder if Dwyer suspected anything?' he muttered, half to himself, holding up a test-tube. 'Trypsin-agar extract – just what I need.'

'Suspected what?' interrupted Burke, who was growing nervous at what he considered Kennedy's cryptic actions.

The question went unanswered, as I knew it would, for Craig was not one to hazard guesses so long as he had within his power the discovery of facts.

I gazed about keenly. 'There seem to be windows on two sides that face the roads,' I commented, quite as much to divert Burke and save Kennedy annoyance as to satisfy my own curiosity.

'Yes. It's my theory,' said Burke, taking the hint,

'that the shot might have been fired at Dwyer from the road. If it came from a car, no one would be the wiser – a blown shoe, a backfire through the muffler – it might have passed for either.'

Kennedy by this time was so deeply engrossed in whatever investigation he was making that I hinted to Burke that we should leave him and perhaps continue our own investigations elsewhere.

We had scarcely left the door to the bacteriological laboratory when we ran across Dr Godart, bustling past. Evidently his business had not detained him long in the operating-room, if, indeed, he had had any. I glanced about. Martine's office was not far away, and he could have been there, or was he watching us? I had an uncomfortable feeling that the watchers were, in turn, watched, especially as Dr Godart seemed to ignore us, although only the greatest preoccupation would have excused his not recognising us.

Burke was making a great show of investigation, though I knew that in a case like this, involving, as it seemed, much that was scientific, he was far beyond his depth. We talked to a number of attendants about the camp, but all the time I knew that nothing would get us anywhere except Kennedy's work.

Accordingly, I was glad when sufficient time had elapsed to allow us to return to the laboratory.

We had come towards it from an angle different from that by which it was usually approached from the camp.

'What do you know about that?' exclaimed Burke, pulling me back from a corner we were turning.

As I drew back I had a chance to get just a glimpse of Dr Delano and Sonia Strusky. We did not, however, have to worry. The couple were too engrossed in each other to know that we were about.

'Little flirt!' commented Burke. 'I wonder if that is the right man that she has now? She seems to be after all of them. Why have they picked this place as their tryst?'

I glanced around cautiously; then an idea came to me. 'From where they are standing,' I whispered, 'it must be easy to see Kennedy at work in Dwyer's laboratory. Do you suppose the lovemaking is a cover?'

'It might have been possible to take a shot at Dr Dwyer through his window from this side,' pointed out Burke by way of reply.

I had a half-formed intention of stepping forward to see whether our sudden appearance might prove embarrassing to them, but before we could do so the couple had strolled off, passing very close to the laboratory window and, I noticed, glancing in.

A few moments later we rejoined Kennedy.

'Have you found anything yet?' I asked.

Kennedy glanced up, pausing in his work over a microscope. 'Yes,' he replied. 'Dr Godart is lying. Thelma Dallinger did attempt suicide. It is not a case of influenza, and he knows it.'

'What is it, then?' demanded Burke. 'What did she use?'

'I don't know what drug she used – opium, I think – but I don't care.'

'What have you found, then?' I asked.

Kennedy regarded us thoughtfully. 'I have found,' he replied slowly, 'in the naso-pharynx secretions what I suspected – germs of spotted fever, cerebro-spinal meningitis, which, as you know, is a disease peculiarly common among troops.'

The information came as a distinct shock, for I had heard much of the dreaded scourge. 'She has it?' I gulped.

Kennedy shook his head. 'Thelma is a meningococcus-carrier, as the doctors would call her – a person who, without having the disease, perhaps without knowing it, may spread it.'

'Isn't that – dangerous?' queried Burke.

'Rather,' replied Craig patiently. 'The fact is that there may be scores of carriers here by this time – first among the nurses, then among the men with whom they have come in contact. Every case is a carrier, in a sense. But the most dangerous are those who carry it without actually having the disease themselves.'

We had no chance to question him on the deeply ominous discovery, for the ringing of the telephone interrupted us. It was Sonia. She had not forgotten Kennedy's promise of the morning. The new clutch had arrived on an early train, had been put in, and she wanted to take us out that afternoon.

Kennedy agreed, though I must say I viewed Sonia's intimacy with alarm. I was frankly uncomfortable while she was about. I could not place her correctly, and, therefore, perhaps, I feared her. What was behind her intimacy? What did she expect to gain from us? Was she secretly working for someone else?

'Another thing,' resumed Kennedy, hanging up the receiver. 'I think I have established a motive for the killing of Dwyer. You see that?' he pointed out a package in a cabinet.

I nodded, and he went on: 'It is supposed to be a fresh shipment of the anti-meningitis serum to Dr Dwyer. I discovered it and have made a rather hasty, though conclusive, test. There's nothing in those tubes but coloured water. Someone has got in here and removed the real serum. Even the cure has been doctored.'

'What do you think of such a devilish thing?' gasped Burke. 'Who could do it?'

Kennedy regarded us thoughtfully. 'You recall the little piece of metal you gave me, Burke, with the number 1402?'

Burke nodded.

'Who is trying to save our men here and in the trenches?'

'The Red Cross,' replied Burke, uncomprehending.

'Who, then, more likely to fight us even in this humane field than the Black Cross?' he suggested.

Neither Burke nor I could reply as the fiendish ingenuity of the idea burned itself into our minds.

'And the number 1402,' continued Kennedy. 'Doesn't that suggest an identification tag to you?'

'You think Thelma might have been in this Black Cross – that she might have tried suicide because she was about to be discovered?' hurriedly deduced Burke.

'No, no,' corrected Kennedy, to whom jumping to hasty conclusions was a bugbear. 'I do not say that. She may have been a victim, a tool. Now that the thing is started, she is no longer necessary.'

'But the black cross itself – I mean that thing you have with the number stamped on it,' I persisted. 'How was it that that was found on her?'

'A question that must be answered,' granted Kennedy. 'When we find that out we shall be well on the way to solving the mystery.'

It was growing late, and we decided to return to our hotel for a hasty bite of lunch and to meet Sonia.

Like the hospital, which was a model in many respects, the hotel which the government had erected was well regulated and fully patronised by relatives and friends visiting the men.

Just at present there seemed to be an overflow of visitors, and on many of the faces it was easy to read anxiety. Whatever it was that was going on in the camp, I felt that it would not be possible much longer for the authorities to keep the lid on it.

Kennedy, Burke and I were joined at luncheon by Joyce, the *Star* reporter who had sent the confidential note that had resulted in bringing us out. Naturally Joyce was very curious to hear what we had discovered, but Kennedy maintained a strict reticence.

'Is it true that Thelma Dallinger is very ill?' he asked, with true reporter's persistence.

Again Kennedy ducked the question.

'Her mother is here – in the parlour with Mr Martine of the Red Cross,' volunteered Joyce. 'We tried to interview him, but he wouldn't talk. Say, Jameson, are we fellows never going to get a line of copy out of you, either?'

I could not help smiling. Military regulations irked Joyce, as they did all reporters, for if there is anything that a reporter loves to the point of desperation it is to be in the 'know'.

I shook my head deprecatingly towards Kennedy and Burke. Though he was giving out nothing, Kennedy was quite eager to absorb.

'Are they in there now?' he asked.

'Yes. Would you like to meet her?' volunteered Joyce, in the vain hope of picking up even a crumb of information.

'If they haven't gone,' Craig agreed.

Joyce was on his feet in a moment, anxious to be of service, and we followed him into the reception-room.

Mrs Dallinger was a nervous little woman, and it was evident that she had been greatly worried.

As Martine caught sight of us approaching, I could see that he was calling her attention to us, and a moment later, as we came up, he introduced us.

'Perhaps Professor Kennedy can tell you even more than I can,' he concluded, with an enquiring look at Craig.

Kennedy exchanged a glance with me, and I understood that he wanted to talk with Mrs Dallinger about her daughter, alone. Together we managed to contrive it, and left the others standing watching us as, one on either side, we walked out of the reception-room to the veranda with the old lady.

'Tell me, please,' she pleaded, 'is Thelma very badly? She will get well, won't she? Oh, this has been such a shock to me! Poor girl! poor little girl! What did she do it for, Professor Kennedy?'

'I cannot say,' replied Kennedy gently. 'All those questions are just the ones I want answered, too.'

'I have been to the hospital,' she went on frantically. 'I cannot get anything out of Dr Godart. Everything is so secret. Oh, this cruel, cruel war! If there is anything that takes my poor little girl from me I shall never forgive myself for letting her go in for this nursing.'

'Who is this Dr Godart?' asked Kennedy, leading the conversation. 'Has Thelma ever told you anything about him?'

'Not a word in her letters.'

'And Mr Martine?' continued Craig. 'What do you know of him?'

'Nothing but that he seems to be a very sympathetic young man,' she replied. 'I didn't even know, until I got here today, that Thelma was engaged.'

Though she did not say it in so many words, it was easy to see which of the two men had made the better impression on the future mother-in-law.

'You didn't know?' repeated Kennedy. 'Then she hasn't made you her confidante since she has been here?'

'No, but I could always trust my girl,' she said, with a pride that took no effort to show. 'Oh, Professor Kennedy, I am sure that when the truth is known things will look very differently for her from what they do now!'

'What did Dr Godart say?'

'Very little. He seemed to be afraid to talk. Oh, when I told Mr Martine that, he said that there was some rule doctors have that means they can't repeat what patients tell them in confidence; that perhaps that would account for it.'

'Yes, medical ethics,' agreed Kennedy.

'But he might have told *her mother*,' she reproached. 'Instead, he seemed to be afraid to talk to me.'

The poor woman was almost in tears. Kennedy hastened to promise that he would personally do all he could for Thelma, for outside we could see Sonia had come for us in her car and was waiting at the carriage entrance of the hotel.

For an hour or two we drove about the great wooden military city, really a series of villages, with miles of streets, for infantry, cavalry, artillery, machine-gun and aviation companies.

Nothing happened on the drive, and Sonia prattled on, relaying all the gossip of the encampment without telling anything that was of much assistance in incriminating those we were observing.

We were coming down the road behind the hospital and other buildings, past Martine's office, and on the side on which Burke and I had seen Delano and Miss Strusky in the morning.

Suddenly from the shrubbery across the road, and outside of the cantonment altogether, there came the crack of a gun, followed by a whir, a ping and a rip. It was a bullet that had passed through the top of the car, not two feet from where Craig was sitting.

Miss Strusky uttered a scream, and for the moment would have lost control of the car if Kennedy had not reached over and steadied the wheel.

'Who sent me that billet-doux?' he muttered, glancing up at the hole drilled in the leather top.

By the time we could stop there had been ample opportunity for the attacker to escape into the bushes from which he had fired.

None of us had an answer to Kennedy's question, although, as for myself, I wondered whether I might not have been right in my suspicions of Sonia. Had she led us into a trap? Of one thing I was now sure. Someone was trying to 'get' Kennedy as they had Dr Dwyer. Why? Was he making it too uncomfortable for someone? Who could it be?

The attack, however, seemed to decide Kennedy upon a certain course of action. Instead of returning directly to the laboratory, he asked Sonia to drive about a bit until they found Burke. She complied, though still nervous over what had happened. Burke was amazed at the attack and apparently eager to carry out the instructions Kennedy gave him.

Together, Kennedy, Sonia and I returned to the

laboratory, where, almost immediately, Kennedy set to work. Without explanation of any sort he prepared several swabs as carefully as he had done when he examined Thelma's throat.

The door opened and Alda Anderson entered, sent by Burke. It was evident no love was lost between the two women. However, Kennedy did not stop for that. Quickly he swabbed out the throats of both nurses and set to work studying the culture that he made.

The arrival of Dr Godart, rather surly at the peremptory orders of Burke, was followed by a repetition of the process on his throat. He would have liked to refuse, but as Burke walked in with Delano and Martine, he could hardly make a scene. Examination of Delano followed, and finally of Martine, who submitted like a good sport. The culture from each throat Kennedy carefully labelled and preserved.

As we all waited, no one said a word, although I could see that Kennedy was in his element. 'In this war,' he remarked casually, busying himself with his culture-tubes, slides and the microscope, 'as you all know, the medical profession has a part to play second to that of no other group. It is a branch of the service concerned almost wholly with the amelioration of the horrors of war. Anything, therefore, that strikes at it is most dastardly. Yet in this instance I have found that there is someone who is using the service to increase the already unspeakable horrors.' He turned from his work, adding forcefully, as all fixed their attention on him: 'Systematic bacteriological examination of the naso-pharynx of Thelma Dallinger – and others – has disclosed a condition that I would have pronounced unbelievable if I had not discovered it myself. Carriers of spotted fever, inoculated in some way, are being deliberately sent out to infect our men.'

Before anyone could question this startling accusation he went on to elaborate. 'We all know that of the acute infectious diseases none is more feared than epidemic meningitis, and justly so, for it is seriously destructive. Conditions in military camps and garrisons favour such outbreaks among soldiers, as has been shown repeatedly since a time seventy-five or eighty years ago when a regiment of infantry carried the pest from one end to the other of France. Already British and Canadian troops have had experiences with it. But here we have the thing purposely promoted.'

He paused a moment, then resumed: 'It is spread by contact with both sick and healthy carriers, but the latter are the more numerous. The presence of one carrier results in the infection of a large number. Link by link, a chain of carriers is established. It is this process that we must prevent. If you do not mind, I will ask you all to accompany Mr Burke and myself to the ward of Miss Dallinger. You need not fear – those of you who are not carriers – for I shall arrange nasal sprays and other means to stamp this thing out before it gets beyond control.'

Silently the group left the laboratory, and a few minutes later stood just inside the door of Thelma's room.

As the little nurse looked at them in wild surprise, Kennedy moved forward. 'Tell us, Thelma,' he asked, bending down, 'there is something that you know, that you fear. What was it you told Dr Godart in your delirium?'

Thelma seemed almost frantic with fright. A

struggle was going on in her mind, and now there was no one to whom to appeal. It seemed criminal to badger the poor girl in her weakened condition. And yet I knew that Kennedy would not have pursued the course unless it had been absolutely the only way.

'No – no!' she cried pitifully. 'If I tell, they will kill him, too – as they did Dr Dwyer!' She gazed about wildly, but there was no loophole of escape.

'Kill whom?' demanded Kennedy remorselessly.

It seemed as though the name was rung from her very soul by main force. He bent over and caught her eyes and held them.

'Bernard!' she whispered, as though hypnotised.

Delano turned to Dr Godart. 'You?' he demanded. 'Kill you?'

At the same time Sonia broke forward and, next to Craig, leaned over the now trembling Thelma. 'Then you – really – love *him*?'

She seemed to put an eager wistfulness into the words. Thelma's lips moved, but the answer was inaudible. It did not need to be heard.

'And your engagement to Mr Martine?'

'I did it to protect him.'

Burke had stepped forward too. 'Who will kill Godart?' he demanded harshly.

The same frightened look crossed Thelma's face. It was as though the words froze on her lips.

'Who?' he repeated.

An unnatural colour mounted to her cheeks. She lifted herself in the bed. 'The Black Cross!' she almost shouted, falling back, fainting.

The Black Cross! We stood aghast as we realised the truth – the depth of the conspiracy against our own Red Cross. Alda gently pushed us all aside and tried to revive the drooping girl.

'Deliberately,' rapped out Kennedy, turning from the bed, 'meningococcus-carriers have been sent out. Worst of all, the chosen carriers have been unsuspected and unsuspecting Red Cross nurses. The course of events was devilish – first the spreading of the disease, then, when it was in danger of being discovered and checked by Dr Dwyer, the killing of the man who might have stopped it. Let me tell you another refinement of the devilry. Whoever it was was amply protected by anti-meningococcus serum, stolen from those it might later cure. That is what Thelma Dallinger knew. The strain of it, the threat against Dr Godart, too, were too great for her.'

All eyes were fixed on Godart. Instead of hesitation and surliness now, there was a look of relief that spread over his face, as though the die were cast and events had relieved him of the burden of a terrible conflict.

'Yes,' he cried, 'what I learned in her delirium was a secret I could not divulge – or possess. I did not know what to do. Medical ethics said, "Keep it; it is her secret." Then, too, I received a threat that if I told it would mean her life. Love said, "Keep it." I hoped I could save her and end the thing, too. All the time patriotism was dinning in my ears, "Tell what you know." Was ever a doctor faced by a worse dilemma? Above all loomed the threat against her.'

Kennedy had pulled from his pocket and was holding up the peculiar black cross – with the side uppermost on which was stamped the number 1402.

'That's the thing!' exclaimed Godart, catching sight of it. 'It was that she raved about all the time. It was

an identification tag of some devilish secret order –
each member with his number. She had stolen it –
then came the threat, to both of us, for playing the
game as we had done.'

In a flash I saw it all, even down to the engagement
to the man Thelma suspected. Kennedy wheeled
about suddenly. Wade Martine – Martinka, a Prussian
Pole, as the papers we found on him proved – had
sunk back in his chair, his hand holding an empty vial
that he had raised to his lips.

Sonia leaned over and massaged Thelma's forehead as her eyes fluttered open. 'I didn't know you
suspected too,' she murmured. 'I thought I was alone
when I tried to follow him to New York. He must
have gone to warn the headquarters of his danger.'

There flickered for a moment a cynical smile over
the set face of the medical spy. Then it seemed as
if something seized the smile and congealed it,
mockingly.

' "Black Cross number 1402",' observed Kennedy
grimly, 'has done his bit for the "fatherland" and has
cheated both American court martial and firing-
squad.'

J. S. FLETCHER

The Mystery at Merrill's Mill

About half-past three o'clock of a spring afternoon in
the year 1897, a well-dressed, somewhat distinguished-
looking gentleman, bearded and spectacled, got out
of a private brougham at a point immediately opposite
the Otley Road entrance to Peel Park, in Bradford,
and, after bidding the coachman await his return,
walked on a little way and turned down Sydenham
Place. A close observer, watching him intently, would
have seen certain signs of mental uneasiness in this
man's face and manner.

As he walked along, glancing at the numbers of the
houses, he occasionally talked to himself in muttering
tones, and now and then he threw back his head with
a quick jerking movement, which seemed to indicate
distaste. Suddenly catching sight of the number of
which he was in search, he turned abruptly to the
door and knocked sharply upon it. A moment later
a middle-aged woman, stolid and unemotional in
appearance, opened the door a little way and looked
at the visitor enquiringly.

'Is Mr Dawe in?' asked the caller. Then, without
waiting for a reply, he added, impatiently, 'If he is,
tell him that Mr Abraham Merrill wants to see him –
at once.'

The woman, without further delay, opened the
door wide, silently inviting Mr Merrill to enter. She
stepped back, motioning him to walk into a small
parlour on the left-hand side of the narrow passage.

Mr Merrill walked in; the door closed behind him; the woman had gone away without a word.

Mr Merrill took off his hat, and, drawing out his handkerchief, wiped his forehead. He made a hasty step or two round the little room, glancing half carelessly, half interestedly at its belongings. It was certainly a curiously appointed room, he thought. There was a solid writing table, littered with books and papers, in the middle of the floor space; a businesslike-looking bureau in one corner; there was nothing in it suggestive of comfort or indolence save one easy-chair. The greater part of the walls was lined with books. Mr Merrill, having been in that room before, did not upon this occasion make any particular examination of them. A stranger, left there alone for the first time, would have noticed, however, that this somewhat large collection of volumes related almost entirely to criminology. Crime and criminals formed the subject of almost every book. Crime and criminals, too, were suggested by the curious contents of a large, glass-fronted cabinet which stood above the mantelpiece. Within it, arranged against a background of black velvet, was stored a collection of gruesome objects, all ticketed or labelled, every one of which was a memento of some famous crime.

Mr Merrill was gazing at these things when he heard the door open with an almost imperceptible sound. He turned to confront Archer Dawe – a man who, after long years of service in the employ of Merrill and Sons, had retired five years previously on a modest competency, and had since given himself up to the one hobby of his life – the study of crime and criminals. Archer Dawe was now aged sixty – a little, squat-figured man, who dressed, Sunday or weekday, in rusty black; was never seen, indoors or out, without a very high-crowned, wide-brimmed silk hat; and who wore old-fashioned stick-up collars, held tightly to his wizened throat by swathes of black neck-cloth. He was a notable figure enough, seen in this wise, and in company with a gamp-like umbrella which he always carried with him wherever he went, wet or fine; but few people noticed his garments when they had looked at his face. It was at most times more of a mask than a face: there was a high, bulging forehead; a small nose; a straight, hard line of a mouth; a square, determined jaw and chin. And deep-set in the general pallor of the face were two eyes – dark, inscrutable, steady as steel, with a curious penetrating light that seemed to burn far back in mysterious, unreachable recesses.

'Good-afternoon, Mr Abraham,' said Archer Dawe, in a voice as steady and cold as his eyes. 'It's been a grand day today, sir!'

Mr Merrill took a step towards his old employee.

'Archer,' he said, without ceremony, 'I want you to come down to the mill. There's – there's something happened.'

Archer Dawe, still watching his visitor, nodded his head without speaking.

'You know our old engine-house,' continued Mr Merrill. 'You know it was built before either you or I knew the place, and that's getting on for fifty years since – well, of course, it hasn't been in use since we built the new one last year, and we decided last week that we'd pull it down. There's been workmen at it ever since, and this last day or two they've been excavating the floor because I've a notion of putting the site to another use. Now, this afternoon, just after

I came back from lunching at the Liberal Club, my son Arthur came into the office to tell me that the men had come across something in the floor of the old place. Bones! Human bones!'

Mr Merrill wiped his forehead again. Archer Dawe, statue-like in his rigidity, stood watching and waiting, his face expressionless.

'In fact,' continued the mill-owner presently, 'they unearthed what was practically a skeleton. There were some bits of what one might take to be flesh about it, but it was – well – you'll see it. As soon as I saw what they'd come across I made every man that had seen it – there were only a few of them – promise to hold his tongue till I gave him leave to speak, and I had the place covered up, and left Arthur and the foreman in charge of it. I want you to come down and see it before we tell the police. It – well, it puzzles me, Archer.'

'Why, Mr Abraham?' asked Archer Dawe.

'Because, since that old engine-house was built by my father, it stands to reason that whoever buried that body there must have had access to it,' said Mr Merrill; 'and nobody could have had access to it but somebody employed about the place. And I've been wondering all the way up here from Valley Road whose body it can be, and who put it there?'

Archer Dawe opened the door of his little parlour and took down an old overcoat from a peg in the passage, 'I'm ready, Mr Abraham,' he said, possessing himself of his umbrella. 'I expect you've got the carriage somewhere about, sir?'

All the way to the mill Archer Dawe talked of anything but the matter in hand. He had been busy in his garden, he said, when Mr Merrill was announced, and he spoke with some pride of his prospects of early peas and potatoes. From that subject he turned to politics, and was deep in a burning question of the day when the brougham, at its owner's orders, stopped a little distance from the mill.

'I don't want any of the hands to think you're here for any special purpose, Archer,' said Mr Merrill. 'There's some of them, you know, have a bit of knowledge of your liking to ferret into things. We'll just stroll round in a casual way until we come to the spot.'

Anyone watching Mr Merrill and his ex-overlooker wandering about the mill yard would have thought that they were having a friendly chat about old times. They moved here and there in an apparently aimless fashion, until they came to the dismantled engine-house. Within its doorway young Mr Merrill and the labourers' foreman stood awaiting them.

'Send those two away,' said Archer Dawe, as they drew near. 'Let's have the place to ourselves.'

When the other two, at a word from the mill-owner, had gone, he and Archer Dawe stepped inside the old engine-house. The roof had already been stripped from the walls; the walls had been torn down to half their height. All around the bed in which the great driving wheel had once revolved the labourers had excavated a good deal of the floor space; at one point in these excavations a couple of packing sheets lay stretched across a cavity. Mr Merrill pointed to these and said, in a hushed voice: 'There it is!'

Archer Dawe laid down his umbrella and went across to the spot indicated by the mill-owner's outstretched finger. His face was as stolid and unemotional as ever as he drew the packing-sheets aside.

He gazed into the cavity for a moment, and then knelt down at its edge and peered more closely at all that was left of what had once been a living man.

Mr Merrill hovered in the background. A strong man; a man of iron will; a man of such strength of character that he had made himself prominent among equally clever men, and was at this time Member of Parliament for one of the divisions of his native town, he felt himself unable to look upon this grisly evidence of some long dead, unsuspected crime. He drew out a cigar-case, and began to smoke, watching the crouched figure in its rusty black clothes as it bent over the thing lying in the cavity.

As he watched he thought of all he remembered of Archer Dawe. The little man, always eccentric, always strange in his manner to folk who were not in his confidence, had entered the employ of Merrill and Sons just about the time that he, Abraham Merrill, had left school to come into the business. Archer Dawe had steadily won his way upwards until at last he had occupied a position of great trust. He had always been a quiet, reserved man; no one ever found him in clubs or public-houses; what he did with his spare time no one ever knew. But just before the time of his retirement a matter arose in the counting-house of the mill which required all the sagacity, all the untiring patience, all the pitiless insistence of a sleuth-hound to unravel. Archer Dawe, without a word to anybody, unravelled it, ran the criminal to earth and flung him out into the broad light of day, trembling and guilty. Then it came out that for years and years he had spent all his spare time engrossed in the subject of criminology, had watched and studied men, had compared, and classified, and analysed, and had invented a system of his own in the detection of crime which was soon to make his name a terror to evil-doers.

This was the man whom Mr Merrill watched with curiosity, and with a certain feeling of loathing as he kept away from the spot over which Archer Dawe was stooping. How could the man examine that dead thing with such cold-blooded earnestness? Bending over it, peering into its mysteries, actually touching it, fingering it, as if it were some mere anatomical specimen, and he a professor holding forth to a class! It seemed –

'Mr Abraham!'

Archer Dawe had turned round from the cavity and was looking earnestly at the mill-owner.

'Yes, Archer?'

'You haven't such a thing as a magnifying glass in the office, sir, have you? One of those that near-sighted folk use to read by?'

'Yes, we have,' answered the mill-owner. 'Do you want it?'

'If you please, sir.'

Mr Merrill left the dismantled engine-house with the alacrity of one who is only too glad to get out of a place in which he has no mind to stay.

'I'll bring it to you in a minute, Archer,' he threw over his shoulder.

Archer Dawe kept his keen eyes fastened on his erstwhile employer until Mr Merrill had quitted the place. Then, bending over the cavity again he whipped out a big coloured handkerchief from his pocket, snatched something from the thing which he had been inspecting, folded what he had snatched in the handkerchief, and restored the handkerchief to his pocket. He rose to his feet and walked a few yards in the direction of the door. As he walked he whistled a bar or two of a popular tune.

Mr Merrill came back with a reading-glass in his hand.

'Will that do?' he queried.

'That will do, sir,' replied Archer Dawe. 'Just a moment, Mr Abraham, and I shall have done all I want to do.'

He went back to the cavity, got down on his knees again, and made a show of using the reading-glass. Presently he rose and drew the packing-sheets over the thing which he had been inspecting.

Then, walking over to the door, where Mr Merrill stood watching him, he said: 'Mr Abraham, I want you to see that nothing is touched here until you hear from me. As I see things at present I think I can tell you something by this time tomorrow. Can you keep all quiet till then?'

'I don't think there'll be very much difficulty about that, Archer,' said the mill-owner. 'You mean that – '

'I mean that I don't want a soul to enter this place until I give you leave to let him,' replied Archer Dawe. 'Have you got a man that you can trust – a man that'll stop here all night and see that no one enters to find what is there?'

'Yes,' answered Mr Merrill, 'I have. Dick Row-botham's the man. And after that, Archer?'

'Wait and see, Mr Abraham,' said Archer Dawe.

Dick Rowbotham, night-watchman at the mill, lived in a cottage in the yard, immediately opposite the old engine-house. When Mr Merrill and Archer Dawe had seen and talked to him they went away to the mill-owner's private office. Mr Merrill produced a decanter of whisky, a syphon of soda and glasses. He motioned Archer Dawe to help himself and offered him his cigar-case. Archer Dawe mixed himself a drink and bit off the end of a cigar. He sat down, nursing his gamp-like umbrella upon his knees.

'Now, as regards this question of bimetallism, Mr Abraham?' he said. 'Now you're in Parliament, sir, you'll no doubt hear a good deal said by members on both sides of the House. Don't you think that – '

Not one word of opinion as to what he had seen in the dismantled engine-house could Mr Abraham Merrill get out of Archer Dawe that afternoon.

The little man drank two tumblers of whisky and soda and smoked two cigars and talked of various political and economic matters, but said nothing of the thing that lay, an unearthed witness of the past, under the packing-sheets which he had just replaced.

Next morning, Archer Dawe, having eaten his usual breakfast of bacon and eggs, set out, the gamp-like umbrella over his shoulder, the tall, rusty hat on the back of his head, for the Midland Railway station. There he took a third-class ticket for Ilkley. He was quite spry and active when he entered the train, but when he arrived at his destination and turned into Brook Street he had assumed the character of an oldish gentleman with a rather halting step and a very wheezy cough. And when he entered a barber's shop, for the purpose of being shaved, he had aged ten years since the previous evening. He had also developed the dialect of south-east Yorkshire, from which part, many a long year before, he had come to Bradford to earn his living.

'Theere's a gentleman named Mestur Oliver Wild-smith lives i' this here place, isn't theer?' he said to the barber as he handed over his twopence. 'A very well-to-do gentleman – I ewsed to wark for him at one time, a many year sin'.'

'Lives in one of those big houses up the Moor,' answered the barber. 'Aye, he's one of the big swells of the place, is Mr Wildsmith. Come back from South America with quite a big fortune, so they tell me.'

Archer Dawe made his way to Mr Wildsmith's house – a fine stone-built villa standing in its own grounds and overlooking the valley of the Wharfe. His step was very feeble, and his asthma – carefully assumed for the occasion – very bad, as he walked up the drive to the front door. He looked a weary, tired old man in the eyes of the smart serving-maid who opened the door to him. He looked still older, still feebler, when, after a brief interval, he was shown into Mr Wildsmith's presence.

Mr Oliver Wildsmith, a solid-faced fleshy man of about Archer Dawe's own age, sat in the midst of mahogany and scarlet leather, writing letters. He stared at the queer old figure in rusty black.

'Eh, dear, dear! Ye'll not remember me, Mestur Wildsmith, sir,' said Archer Dawe. 'I wor a hand at Merrill's Mill when ye wor t' heead engineer there – it'll be thirty years ago sin' you left us, sir! Benjyman Simpson my name is – many's the pipe o' 'bacca ye've given me in them days. Aye – I've left t' mill now, sir – I hev' a bit on a pension, like. I just come out for t' day to Eekla, like, and I heerd 'at you wor livin' here, sir, sin' you cam' back fro' South America wi' all that gre't fortune, so I says, "Nay," I says, "I'll go an' say how-do to Mestur Wildsmith." I'm gettin' an owd man, sir – aye, sure-ly.'

'Sit you down – sit you down,' said the man at the

desk. 'Dear me! one of Merrill's old workmen, are you? Aye, it's a long time ago, is that. Why, I'm past sixty myself. Here, you must have a drink. Benjamin Simpson, isn't it? Well, I don't remember you, Benjamin, but old friends are old friends. I've been out of England a good many years, so I haven't had much chance of seeing many yet.'

He went over to a sideboard and came back with a glass of whisky and water for his visitor. Archer Dawe bowed his respect.

'Aye, I mind you well – well indeed, sir – theer wor you an' your brother Edward, as wor your assistant i' t' engineerin'. He wor a fine young feller, wor Mestur Ned – theer wor a young lady up Manningham way, 'at he wor varry sweet on. He went off varry sudden to Canyda, did Mestur Ned, didn't he, sir?'

The heavy-faced man at the mahogany desk frowned. 'Yes,' he said. 'He emigrated to Canada, did my brother.'

'An' niver cam' back to t' owd country,' sighed the visitor. 'Dear-a-dear! It's a strange thing, is life. I did hear, sir, 'at you married t' young lady 'at Mestur Ned wor to hev' married – but, of course, he never cam' back no more. I hope your missus is i' good health, sir.'

'My wife is dead,' said the man at the desk shortly.

'Is sha now?' said the visitor, in tones of deep commiseration. 'Deary me! Well, it's a vale o' tears, is this here. But you'll have childer, no doubt, Mestur Wildsmith?'

'We had no children,' answered Mr Wildsmith, still more shortly. 'Here, would you like to smoke a cigar?'

'Thenkin' you kindly, sir. Ah, a deal of changes there is i' this life! Now, you wouldn't think it, sir, but do you know 'at they're pullin' down t' owd engine-house at Merrill's Mill?'

'Oh – are they?'

'Aye, and rivin' t' floor up an' all! Excavatin' it. An' it's a strange thing what they find under floors when they rive 'm up – it is!'

The man at the mahogany desk was sitting back staring in a strange, inquisitive fashion at his visitor.

The visitor, shaking his old head from side to side, rambled on: 'Aye, they fun' a skellinton under t' floor ther' yisterda' – a reyt skellinton! Ye mus' ha' walked over that there skellinton many a time when ye wor engineer, Mestur Wildsmith! Did ye niver notice nowt?'

'I? Not I, man! A skeleton? Why, whose could it be – there?'

'Nay, ye're axin summat! But – '

The visitor was seized by a bad attack of coughing. He set down his glass on the edge of the mahogany desk and fumbled in his old coat for his handkerchief. But instead of using the handkerchief, he suddenly produced something from its folds and held that something, laid on the palm of his own right hand, before the other man's eyes. A human hand! – dried, withered, little more than bone – the second finger missing, and on the fourth a ring, of curious and exceptional device. And as he thus held it, Archer Dawe, old and doddering no longer, spoke.

'Whose hand is that?'

Oliver Wildsmith half-rose, gasped, caught at his throat, fell – inert, limp.

Archer Dawe went across the room and rang the bell, rang it twice, loudly.

'Look to your master,' he said, as the servants came

running into the room. 'He's in a fit. And send for a doctor.'

Then he walked out of the house – walked swiftly, and with a strong man's determination, to the police-station and the post-office.

MAURICE LEBLANC

The Mysterious Railway Passenger

I had sent my motor car to Rouen by road on the previous day. I was to meet it by train, and go on to some friends, who have a house on the Seine

A few minutes before we left Paris my compartment was invaded by seven gentlemen, five of whom were smoking. Short though the journey by the fast train be, I did not relish the prospect of taking it in such company, the more so as the old-fashioned carriage had no corridor. I therefore collected my overcoat, my newspapers and my railway guide and sought refuge in one of the neighbouring compartments.

It was occupied by a lady. At the sight of me, she made a movement of vexation which did not escape my notice, and leaned towards a gentleman standing on the footboard – her husband, no doubt, who had come to see her off. The gentleman took stock of me, and the examination seemed to conclude to my advantage; for he whispered to his wife and smiled, giving her the look with which we reassure a frightened child. She smiled in her turn, and cast a friendly glance in my direction, as though she suddenly realised that I was one of those well-bred men with whom a woman can remain locked up for an hour or two in a little box six feet square without having anything to fear.

Her husband said to her: 'You must not mind, darling, but I have an important appointment and I cannot wait.'

He kissed her affectionately and went away. His wife blew him some discreet little kisses through the window and waved her handkerchief.

Then the guard's whistle sounded, and the train started.

At that moment, and in spite of the warning shouts of the railway officials, the door opened and a man burst into our carriage. My travelling companion, who was standing up and arranging her things in the rack, uttered a cry of terror and dropped down upon the seat.

I am no coward – far from it; but I confess that these sudden incursions at the last minute are always annoying. They seem so ambiguous, so unnatural. There must be something behind them, else . . .

The appearance of the newcomer, however, and his bearing were such as to correct the bad impression produced by the manner of his entrance. He was neatly, almost smartly, dressed; his tie was in good taste, his gloves clean; he had a powerful face . . . But, speaking of his face, where on earth had I seen it before? For I had seen it: of that there was no possible doubt; or at least, to be accurate, I found within myself that sort of recollection which is left by the sight of an oft-seen portrait of which one has never beheld the original. And at the same time I felt the uselessness of any effort of memory that I might exert, so inconsistent and vague was that recollection.

But when my eyes reverted to the lady I sat astounded at the pallor and disorder of her features. She was staring at her neighbour – he was seated on the same side of the carriage – with an expression of genuine affright, and I saw one of her hands steal trembling towards a little travelling-bag that lay on

the cushion a few inches from her lap. She ended by
taking hold of it and nervously drawing it to her.

Our eyes met, and I read in hers so great an amount
of uneasiness and anxiety that I could not help saying:
'I hope you are not unwell, madame . . . Would you
like me to open the window?'

She made no reply, but, with a timid gesture, called
my attention to the individual beside her. I smiled as
her husband had done, shrugged my shoulders, and
explained to her by signs that she had nothing to fear,
that I was there and that, besides, the gentleman in
question seemed quite harmless.

Just then he turned towards us, contemplated us,
one after the other, from head to foot, and then
huddled himself into his corner, and made no further
movement.

A silence ensued; but the lady, as though she had
summoned up all her energies to perform an act of
despair, said to me, in a hardly audible voice: 'You
know he is in our train.'

'Who?'

'Why, he . . . he himself . . . I assure you.'

'Whom do you mean?'

'Arsène Lupin!'

She had not removed her eyes from the passenger,
and it was at him rather than at me that she flung the
syllables of that alarming name.

He pulled his hat down upon his nose. Was this to
conceal his agitation, or was he merely preparing to
go to sleep?

I objected.

'Arsène Lupin was sentenced yesterday, in his
absence, to twenty years' penal servitude. It is not
likely that he would commit the imprudence of

showing himself in public today. Besides, the news-papers have discovered that he has been spending the winter in Turkey ever since his famous escape from the Santé.'

'He is in this train,' repeated the lady, with the ever more marked intention of being overheard by our companion. 'My husband is a deputy prison-governor, and the station-inspector himself told us that they were looking for Arsène Lupin.'

'That is no reason why . . .'

'He was seen at the booking-office. He took a ticket for Rouen.'

'It would have been easy to lay hands upon him.'

'He disappeared. The ticket-collector at the door of the waiting-room did not see him; but they thought that he must have gone round by the suburban plat-forms and stepped into the express that leaves ten minutes after us.'

'In that case, they will have caught him there.'

'And supposing that, at the last moment, he jumped out of that express and entered this, our own train . . . as he probably . . . as he most certainly did?'

'In that case they will catch him here; for the porters and the police cannot have failed to see him going from one train to the other, and, when we reach Rouen, they will net him finely.'

'Him? Never! He will find some means of escaping again.'

'In that case I wish him a good journey.'

'But think of all that he may do in the meantime!'

'What?'

'How can I tell? One must be prepared for any-thing.'

She was greatly agitated; and, in point of fact, the

situation, to a certain degree, warranted her nervous state of excitement. Almost in spite of myself, I said: 'There are such things as curious coincidences, it is true . . . But calm yourself. Admitting that Arsène Lupin is in one of these carriages, he is sure to keep quiet, and, rather than bring fresh trouble upon himself, he will have no other idea than that of avoiding the danger that threatens him.'

My words failed to reassure her. However she said no more, fearing, no doubt, lest I should think her troublesome.

As for myself, I opened my newspapers and read the reports of Arsène Lupin's trial. They contained nothing that was not already known, and they interested me but slightly. Moreover, I was tired, I had had a poor night; I felt my eyelids growing heavy, and my head began to nod.

'But surely, sir, you are not going to sleep?'

The lady snatched my paper from my hands, and looked at me with indignation.

'Certainly not,' I replied. 'I have no wish to.'

'It would be most imprudent,' she said.

'Most,' I repeated.

And I struggled hard, fixing my eyes on the landscape, on the clouds that streaked the sky. But soon all this became confused in space, the image of the excited lady and the drowsy man was obliterated in my mind, and I was filled with the great, deep silence of sleep.

It was soon made agreeable by light and incoherent dreams, in which a being who played the part and bore the name of Arsène Lupin occupied a certain place. He turned and shifted on the horizon, his back laden with valuables, clambering over walls and stripping country-houses of their contents.

But the outline of this being, who had ceased to be Arsène Lupin, grew more distinct. He came towards me, grew bigger and bigger, leaped into the carriage with incredible agility, and fell full upon my chest.

A sharp pain . . . a piercing scream . . . I awoke. The man, my fellow-traveller, with one knee on my chest, was clutching my throat.

I saw this very dimly, for my eyes were shot with blood. I also saw the lady in a corner writhing in a violent fit of hysterics. I did not even attempt to resist. I should not have had the strength for it had I wished to: my temples were throbbing, I choked . . . my throat rattled . . . Another minute . . . and I should have been suffocated.

The man must have felt this. He loosened his grip. Without leaving hold of me, with his right hand he stretched a rope, in which he had prepared a slipknot, and with a quick turn tied my wrists together. In a moment I was bound, gagged – rendered motionless and helpless.

And he performed this task in the most natural manner in the world, with an ease that revealed the knowledge of a master, of an expert in theft and crime. Not a word, not a fevered movement. Sheer coolness and audacity. And there lay I on the seat, roped up like a mummy – I, Arsène Lupin!

It was really ridiculous. And notwithstanding the seriousness of the circumstances I could not but appreciate and almost enjoy the irony of the situation. Arsène Lupin 'done' like a novice, stripped like the first-comer! For of course the scoundrel relieved me of my pocketbook and purse! Arsène Lupin victimised in his turn – duped and beaten! What an adventure!

There remained the lady. He took no notice of her at all. He contented himself with picking up the wrist-bag that lay on the floor and checking on the jewels, the purse, the gold and silver knicknacks which it contained. The lady opened her eyes, shuddered with fright, took off her rings and handed them to the man as though she wished to spare him any superfluous exertion. He took the rings, and looked at her: she fainted away.

Then, calm and silent as before, without troubling about us further, he resumed his seat, lit a cigarette and abandoned himself to a careful scrutiny of the treasures which he had captured, the inspection of which seemed to satisfy him completely.

I was much less satisfied. I am not speaking of the twelve thousand francs of which I had been unduly plundered: this was a loss which I accepted only for the time; I had no doubt that those twelve thousand francs would return to my possession after a short interval, together with the exceedingly important papers which my pocketbook contained: plans, estimates, specifications, addresses, lists of correspondents, letters of a coin-promising character. But, for the moment, a more immediate and serious care was worrying me: what was to happen next?

As may be readily imagined, the excitement caused by my passing through the Gare St-Lazare had not escaped me. As I was going to stay with friends who knew me by the name of Guillaume Berlat, and to whom my resemblance to Arsène Lupin was the occasion of many a friendly jest, I had not been able to disguise myself after my wont, and my presence had been discovered. Moreover, a man, doubtless Arsène Lupin, had been seen to rush from the express into the fast train. Hence it was inevitable and fated that the commissary of police at Rouen, warned by telegram, would await the arrival of the train, assisted by a respectable number of constables, question any suspicious passengers and proceed to make a minute inspection of the carriages.

All this I had foreseen, and had not felt greatly excited about it; for I was certain that the Rouen police would display no greater perspicacity than the Paris police, and that I should have been able to pass unperceived: was it not sufficient for me, at the wicket, carelessly to show my deputy's card, thanks to which I had already inspired the ticket-collector at St-Lazare with every confidence? But how things had changed since then! I was no longer free. It was impossible to attempt one of my usual moves. In one of the carriages the commissary would discover the Sieur Arsène Lupin, whom a propitious fate was sending to him bound hand and foot, gentle as a lamb, packed up complete. He had only to accept delivery, just as you receive a parcel addressed to you at a railway station, a hamper of game or a basket of vegetables and fruit.

And to avoid this annoying catastrophe, what could I do, entangled as I was in my bonds?

And the train was speeding towards Rouen, the next and the only stopping-place; it rushed through Vernon, through St-Pierre . . .

I was puzzled also by another problem in which I was not so directly interested, but the solution of which aroused my professional curiosity: What were my fellow-traveller's intentions?

If I had been alone he would have had ample time to alight quite calmly at Rouen. But the lady? As soon as the carriage door was opened the lady, meek and quiet as she sat at present, would scream, and throw herself about, and cry for help!

Hence my astonishment. Why did he not reduce her to the same state of powerlessness as myself, which would have given him time to disappear before his twofold misdeed was discovered?

He was still smoking, his eyes fixed on the view outside, which a hesitating rain was beginning to streak with long, slanting lines. Once, however, he turned round, took up my railway guide, and consulted it.

As for the lady, she made every effort to continue fainting, so as to quiet her enemy. But a fit of coughing, produced by the smoke, gave the lie to her pretended swoon.

Myself, I was very uncomfortable, and had pains all over my body. And I thought . . . I planned.

Pont-de-l'Arche . . . Oissel . . . The train hurried on, glad, drunk with speed . . . St-Etienne . . .

At that moment the man rose and took two steps towards us, to which the lady hastened to reply with a new scream and a genuine fainting fit.

But what could his object be? He lowered the window on our side. The rain was now falling in torrents, and he made a movement of annoyance at having neither umbrella nor overcoat. He looked up at the rack: the lady's *en-tout-cas* was there; he took it. He also took my overcoat and put it on.

We were crossing the Seine. He turned up his trousers, and then, leaning out of the window, raised the outer latch.

Did he mean to fling himself on the permanent way? At the rate at which we were going it would have been certain death. We plunged into the tunnel pierced under the Côte Ste-Catherine. The man opened the door, and with one foot, felt for the step. What madness! The darkness, the smoke, the din – all combined to give a fantastic appearance to any such attempt. But suddenly the train slowed up, the Westinghouse brakes counteracted the movement of the wheels. In a minute the pace from fast became normal, and decreased still more. Without a doubt there was a gang at work repairing this part of the tunnel; this would necessitate a slower passage of the trains, for some days perhaps, and the man knew it.

He had only, therefore, to put his other foot on the step, climb down to the footboard, and walk away quietly, not without first closing the door, and throwing back the latch.

He had scarcely disappeared when the smoke showed whiter in the daylight. We emerged into a valley. One more tunnel, and we should be at Rouen.

The lady at once recovered her wits, and her first care was to bewail the loss of her jewels. I gave her a beseeching glance. She understood, and relieved me of the gag which was stifling me. She wanted also to unfasten my bonds, but I stopped her.

'No, no; the police must see everything as it was. I want them to be fully informed as regards that blackguard's actions.'

'Shall I pull the alarm-signal?'

'Too late. You should have thought of that while he was attacking me.'

'But he would have killed me! Ah, sir, didn't I tell you that he was travelling by this train? I knew him at once, by his portrait. And now he's taken my jewels!'

'They'll catch him, have no fear.'

'Catch Arsène Lupin! Never.'

'It all depends on you, madame. Listen. When we arrive be at the window, call out, make a noise. The police and porters will come up. Tell them what you have seen in a few words: the assault of which I was the victim, and the flight of Arsène Lupin. Give his description: a soft hat, an umbrella – yours – a grey frock-overcoat . . . '

'Yours,' she said.

'Mine? No, his own. I didn't have one.'

'I thought that he had none either when he got in.'

'He must have had . . . unless it was a coat which someone left behind in the rack. In any case, he had it when he got out, and that is the essential thing . . . A grey frock-overcoat, remember . . . Oh, I was forgetting . . . tell them your name to start with. Your husband's functions will stimulate the zeal of all those men.'

We were arriving. She was already leaning out of the window. I resumed, in a louder, almost imperious voice, so that my words should sink into her brain: 'Give my name also, Guillaume Berlat. If necessary, say you know me . . . That will save time . . . we must hurry on the preliminary enquiries . . . the important thing is to catch Arsène Lupin . . . with your jewels . . . You quite understand, don't you? Guillaume Berlat, a friend of your husband's.'

'Quite . . . Guillaume Berlat.'

She was already calling out and gesticulating. Before the train had come to a standstill a gentleman climbed in, followed by a number of other men. The critical hour was at hand.

Breathlessly the lady exclaimed: 'Arsène Lupin . . . he attacked us . . . he has stolen my jewels . . . I am

Madame Renaud . . . my husband is a deputy prison-governor . . . Ah, here's my brother, Georges Andelle, manager of the Credit Rouennais . . . What I want to say is . . .'

She kissed a young man who had just come up, and who exchanged greetings with the commissary. She continued, weeping: 'Yes, Arsène Lupin . . . He flew at this gentleman's throat in his sleep . . . Monsieur Berlat, a friend of my husband's.'

'But where is Arsène Lupin?'

'He jumped out of the train in the tunnel, after we had crossed the Seine.'

'Are you sure it was he?'

'Certain. I recognised him at once. Besides, he was seen at the Gare St-Lazare. He was wearing a soft hat . . .'

'No; a hard felt hat, like this,' said the commissary, pointing to my hat.

'A soft hat, I assure you,' repeated Madame Renaud, 'and a grey frock-overcoat.'

'Yes,' muttered the commissary; 'the telegram mentions a grey frock-overcoat with a black velvet collar.'

'A black velvet collar, that's it!' exclaimed Madame Renaud, triumphantly.

I breathed again. What a good, excellent friend I had found in her!

Meanwhile the policemen had released me from my bonds. I bit my lips violently till the blood flowed. Bent in two, with my handkerchief to my mouth, as seems proper to a man who has long been sitting in a constrained position, and who bears on his face the blood-stained marks of a gag, I said to the commissary, in a feeble voice: 'Sir, it was Arsène Lupin, there is no doubt of it . . . You can catch him if you hurry . . . I think I may be of some use to you . . .'

The coach, which was needed for the inspection by the police, was slipped. The remainder of the train went on towards Le Havre. We were taken to the station-master's office through the crowd of onlookers who filled the platform.

Just then I felt a hesitation. I must make some excuse to absent myself, find my motor car, and be off. It was dangerous to wait. If anything happened, if a telegram came from Paris, I was lost.

Yes; but what about my robber? Left to my own resources, in a district with which I was not very well acquainted, I could never hope to come up with him.

'Bah!' I said to myself. 'Let us risk it, and stay. It's a difficult hand to win, but a very amusing one to play. And the stakes are worth the trouble.'

And as we were being asked provisionally to repeat our depositions, I exclaimed: 'Mr Commissary, Arsène Lupin is getting a start on us. My motor is waiting for me in the yard. If you will do me the pleasure to accept a seat in it, we will try . . . '

The commissary gave a knowing smile.

'It's not a bad idea . . . such a good idea, in fact, that it's already being carried out.'

'Oh!'

'Yes; two of my officers started on bicycles . . . some time ago.'

'But where to?'

'To the entrance to the tunnel. There they will pick up the clues and the evidence, and follow the track of Arsène Lupin.'

I could not help shrugging my shoulders.

'Your two officers will pick up no clues and no evidence.'

'Really!'

'Arsène Lupin will have arranged that no one should see him leave the tunnel. He will have taken the nearest road, and from there . . .'

'From there made for Rouen, where we shall catch him.'

'He will not go to Rouen.'

'In that case, he will remain in the neighbourhood, where we shall be even more certain . . .'

'He will not remain in the neighbourhood.'

'Oh! Then where will he hide himself?'

I took out my watch.

'At this moment Arsène Lupin is hanging about the station at Darnétal. At ten-fifty – that is to say, in twenty-two minutes from now – he will take the train which leaves Rouen from the Gare du Nord for Amiens.'

'Do you think so? And how do you know?'

'Oh, it's very simple. In the carriage Arsène Lupin consulted my railway guide. What for? To see if there was another line near the place where he disappeared, a station on that line, and a train which stopped at that station. I have just looked at the guide myself, and learned what I wanted to know.'

'Upon my word, sir,' said the commissary, 'you possess marvellous powers of deduction. What an expert you must be!'

Dragged on by my certainty, I had blundered by displaying too much cleverness. He looked at me in astonishment, and I saw that a suspicion flickered through his mind. Only just, it is true; for the photographs dispatched in every direction were so unlike, represented an Arsène Lupin so different from the one that stood before him, that he could not possibly recognise the original in me. Nevertheless, he was troubled, restless, perplexed.

There was a moment of silence. A certain ambiguity and doubt seemed to interrupt our words. A shudder of anxiety passed through me.

Was luck about to turn against me? Mastering myself, I began to laugh.

'Ah well, there's nothing to sharpen one's wits like the loss of a pocketbook and the desire to find it again. And it seems to me that, if you will give me two of your men, the three of us might, perhaps . . .'

'Oh, please, Mr Commissary,' exclaimed Madame Renaud, 'do what Monsieur Berlat suggests.'

My kind friend's intervention turned the scale. Uttered by her, the wife of an influential person, the name of Berlat became mine in reality, and conferred upon me an identity which no suspicion could touch. The commissary rose.

'Believe me, Monsieur Berlat, I shall be only too pleased to see you succeed. I am as anxious as yourself to have Arsène Lupin arrested.'

He accompanied me to my car. He introduced two of his men to me: Honoré Massol and Gaston Delivet. They took their seats. I placed myself at the wheel. My chauffeur started the engine. A few seconds later we had left the station. I was saved.

I confess that as we dashed in my powerful 35-hp Moreau-Lepton along the boulevards that skirt the old Norman city I was not without a certain sense of pride. The engine hummed harmoniously. The trees sped behind us to right and left. And now, free and out of danger, I had nothing to do but to settle my own little private affairs with the cooperation of two worthy representatives of the law. Arsène Lupin was going in search of Arsène Lupin!

Ye humble mainstays of the social order of things, Gaston Delivet and Honoré Massol, how precious was your assistance to me! Where should I have been without you? But for you, at how many crossroads should I have taken the wrong turning! But for you, Arsène Lupin would have gone astray and the other escaped!

But all was not over yet. Far from it. I had first to capture the fellow and next to take possession, myself, of the papers of which he had robbed me. At no cost must my two satellites be allowed to catch a sight of those documents, much less lay hands upon them. To make use of them and yet act independently of them was what I wanted to do; and it was no easy matter.

We reached Darnétal three minutes after the train had left. I had the consolation of learning that a man in a grey frock-overcoat with a black velvet collar had got into a second-class carriage with a ticket for Amiens. There was no doubt about it: my first appearance as a detective was a promising one.

Delivet said: 'The train is an express, and does not stop before Monterolier-Buchy, in nineteen minutes from now. If we are not there before Arsène Lupin he can go on towards Amiens, branch off to Cleres, and from there make for Dieppe or Paris.'

'How far is Monterolier?'

'Fourteen miles and a half.'

'Fourteen miles and a half in nineteen minutes . . . We shall be there before he is.'

It was a stirring race. Never had my trusty Moreau-

Lepton responded to my impatience with greater ardour and regularity. It seemed to me as though I communicated my wishes to her directly, without the intermediary of levers or handles. She shared my desires. She approved of my determination. She understood my animosity against that blackguard Arsène Lupin. The scoundrel! The sneak! Should I get the best of him? Or would he once more baffle authority, that authority of which I was the incarnation?

'Right!' cried Delivet . . . 'Left! . . . Straight ahead! . . . ' We skimmed the ground. The milestones looked like little timid animals that fled at our approach.

And suddenly at the turn of a road a cloud of smoke – the north express!

For half a mile it was a struggle side by side – an unequal struggle, of which the issue was certain – we beat the train by twenty lengths.

In three seconds we were on the platform in front of the second class. The doors were flung open. A few people stepped out. My thief was not among them. We examined the carriages. No Arsène Lupin.

'By Jove!' I exclaimed, 'he must have recognised me in the motor while we were going alongside the train, and jumped!'

The guard of the train confirmed my supposition. He had seen a man scrambling down the embankment at two hundred yards from the station.

'There he is! . . . Look! . . . At the level crossing!'

I darted in pursuit, followed by my two satellites, or, rather, by one of them; for the other, Massol, turned out to be an uncommonly fast sprinter, gifted with both speed and staying power. In a few seconds the distance between him and the fugitive was greatly diminished. The man saw him, jumped a hedge, and scampered off towards a slope, which he climbed. We saw him, farther still, entering a little wood.

When we reached the wood we found Massol waiting for us. He had thought it no use to go on, lest he should lose us.

'You were quite right, my dear fellow,' I said. 'After a run like this our friend must be exhausted. We've got him.'

I examined the skirts of the wood while thinking how I could best proceed alone to arrest the fugitive, in order myself to effect certain recoveries which the law, no doubt, would only have allowed after a number of disagreeable enquiries. Then I returned to my companions.

'Look here, it's very easy. You, Massol, take up your position on the left. You, Delivet, on the right. From there you can watch the whole rear of the wood, and he can't leave it unseen by you except by this hollow, where I shall stand. If he does not come out, I'll go in and force him back towards one or the other of you. You have nothing to do, therefore, but wait. Oh, I was forgetting: in case of alarm, I'll fire a shot.'

Massol and Delivet moved off, each to his own side. As soon as they were out of sight I made my way into the wood with infinite precautions, so as to be neither seen nor heard. It consisted of close thickets, contrived for the shooting, and intersected by very narrow paths, in which it was only possible to walk by stooping, as though in a leafy tunnel.

One of these ended in a glade, where the damp grass showed the marks of footsteps. I followed them, taking care to steal through the underwood. They led me to the bottom of a little mound, crowned by a tumbledown lath-and-plaster hovel.

'He must be there,' I thought. 'He has selected a good observation post.'

I crawled close up to the building. A slight sound warned me of his presence and, in fact, I caught sight of him through an opening; with his back turned towards me.

Two bounds brought me upon him. He tried to point the revolver which he held in his hand. I did not give him time, but pulled him to the ground in such a way that his two arms were twisted and caught under him, while I held him pinned down with my knee upon his chest.

'Listen to me, old chap,' I whispered in his ear. 'I am Arsène Lupin. You've got to give me back, this minute and without any fuss, my pocketbook and the lady's wrist-bag . . . in return for which I'll save you from the clutches of the police and enrol you among my friends. Which is it to be: yes or no?'

'Yes,' he muttered.

'That's right. Your plan of this morning was cleverly thought out. We shall be good friends.'

I got up. He fumbled in his pocket, fetched out a great knife, and tried to strike me with it.

'You ass!' I cried.

With one hand I parried the attack. With the other I caught him a violent blow on the carotid artery, the blow which is known as 'the carotid hook'. He fell back stunned.

In my pocketbook I found my papers and banknotes. I took his own out of curiosity. On an envelope addressed to him I read his name: Pierre Onfrey.

I gave a start. Pierre Onfrey, the perpetrator of the

murder in the Rue Lafontaine at Auteuil! Pierre
Onfrey, the man who had cut the throats of Madame
Delbois and her two daughters. I bent over him.
Yes, that was the face which, in the railway-carriage,
had aroused in me the memory of features which I
had seen before.

But time was passing. I placed two hundred-franc
notes in an envelope, with a visiting-card bearing
these words:

Arsène Lupin to his worthy assistants, Honoré
Massol and Gaston Delivet, with his best thanks.

I laid this where it could be seen, in the middle of
the room. Beside it I placed Madame Renaud's wrist-
bag. Why should it not be restored to the kind friend
who had rescued me? I confess, however, that I took
from it everything that seemed in any way interesting,
leaving only a tortoiseshell comb, a stick of lip-salve
and an empty purse. Business is business, when all is
said and done! And, besides, her husband followed
such a disreputable occupation! . . .

There remained the man. He was beginning to
move. What was I to do? I was not qualified either to
save or to condemn him.

I took away his weapons, and fired my revolver in
the air.

'That will bring the two others,' I thought. 'He
must find a way out of his own difficulties. Let fate
take its course.'

And I went down the hollow road at a run.

Twenty minutes later a cross-road which I had
noticed during our pursuit brought me back to my car.

At four o'clock I telegraphed to my friends from
Rouen that an unexpected incident compelled me to

put off my visit. Between ourselves, I greatly fear that, in view of what they must now have learned, I shall be obliged to postpone it indefinitely. It will be a cruel disappointment for them!

By six o'clock I had returned to Paris by L'Isle-Adam, Enghien and the Porte Bineau.

I gathered from the evening papers that the police had at last succeeded in capturing Pierre Onfrey.

The next morning – why should we despise the advantages of intelligent advertisement? – the *Echo de France* contained the following sensational paragraph:

Yesterday, near Buchy, after a number of incidents, Arsène Lupin effected the arrest of Pierre Onfrey. The Auteuil murderer had robbed a lady of the name of Renaud, the wife of a deputy prison-governor, in the train between Paris and Le Havre. Arsène Lupin has restored to Madame Renaud the wrist-bag which contained her jewels and has generously rewarded the two detectives who assisted him in the matter of this dramatic arrest.

EDGAR WALLACE

The Mind-Reader

'There is no police force in the world that can counter
the intelligent law-breaker,' wrote that remarkable
man Len Witlon, in an article he once contributed to
the American press, 'providing he lays his plans carefully and skilfully and carries them through without
deviation.'

Len Witlon knew five languages perfectly, and
had friends and sometimes confederates in at least a
dozen European prisons. He himself had certainly
been under detention, but had never been dis-
honoured by a conviction.

You met him at the American bar of Claridge's in
Paris, or dining at Armonvillier; occasionally he took
a cure at Vichy or Baden-Baden – there were certain
mud baths in Czechoslovakia that he visited regularly.
He was a vain and brilliant man, very jealous of his
reputation for gallantry.

To be successful in robbery one must be something of a psychologist. It is not sufficient to know
where material danger is to be found: one must be
able to read the mind of one's opponent. That is
the art of generalship: success comes when the
operator combines with his powers of organisation
a loyal and unswerving loyalty to his comrades.

Inspector O. Rater read this interesting article so
often that he could almost quote it word for word. He

had cut out the article soon after its publication, had pasted it in an exercise book against the day when Len would commence operations in England.

'Tell that friend of yours,' said the Orator, to a familiar of the great man, 'that if he ever puts his nose inside of London he won't be giving interviews for fourteen years.'

One day Len took up the challenge . . .

A policeman came through Burford Square at a leisurely pace, moving towards the corner of Canford Street. He had arranged with the constable patrolling the next beat to meet him there at eleven and finish the interrupted story of a brother-in-law's short-comings, and the problem of the wife and three children who had been left unsupported by the afore-said brother-in-law's hasty departure for Canada.

He came to the rendezvous at almost the same moment as his mate appeared. And the serial was continued: ' . . . "Well," I says to my sister, "you've only got yourself to blame . . . " '

He stopped dead.

The scream came from one of the dark houses of the square, and not very far away.

'Murder . . . murder!'

The two police officers were already running . . . On the doorstep of No. 95 a girl was standing. They saw the white of her nightgown in the dim light of a street lamp.

'Help . . . please! Oh, thank God you've come!'

She retreated before them through the open door into the dark hall.

'I heard him scream . . . and the struggle . . . and I tried to get into his room . . . '

She had been feeling for the switch, and she found

it. A big glass lantern suspended from the high ceiling glowed with a golden light.

'What is it, miss? Which room?'

Her trembling fingers pointed to the stairway.

She was very pretty, though as white as chalk, the officer observed.

'Put a coat on the lady, Harry' – he indicated a little alcove where hats and coats were hanging. 'Now, miss, you'll have to show us the room.'

She shook her head; her eyes were wide with horror.

'No, no, no! I can't . . . It is the first landing – the room overlooking the square – '

The two uniformed men raced up the stairs; as they reached the first landing, a light came on, probably controlled from the hall below, for there was a push-button switch on the wall of the landing and nobody could have touched that. Facing them was a polished mahogany door with an ornamental gilt and enamelled doorknob.

PC Simpson (he of the wronged sister) turned the knob. The door was locked from the inside. He shook the knob vigorously and called out: 'Open this door!'

A futile invitation, and laughable in any other state of affairs. More futile, since now when he turned the knob the door opened.

It was a large room, running the whole width of the house. Light came from a crystal chandelier. PC Simpson saw a big gilt and mahogany writing-table; behind that was a carved marble fireplace, and on the white hearth an electric fire glowed redly. Until they passed round the table, they did not see the quiet figure that lay, face upwards. It was in evening dress; one hand gripped the edge of the marble curb that surrounded the fireplace; the other was half-raised, as though to ward off a blow.

'He's dead – shot . . . look!'

Simpson's companion pointed to the patch of blood above the heart.

PC Simpson stared down at the victim of his first murder, all too aware of the tremendous importance of this to him and to his career; he had a confused memory of instructions he had received as to what a policeman should do in such circumstances.

'Don't let nobody come in,' he said huskily, and gaped round the room. A long window was open – he stepped out on to a balcony, flashing his electric lamp along the rails.

A rope was knotted to the balcony rail and trailing down – as he saw by the rays of his lamp – to the front steps. It had not been there when they had come in or they must have knocked against it.

'He's got away since we came in, Harry. Come down with me!'

They flew down the stairs on their way to the silent square; they did not see the girl; she must have gone to her room.

The front door was closed. PC Simpson jerked at it with confidence, but this door did not open. He twisted the handle and pulled again, but it was a very heavy door, steel-lined, and did not budge.

'It's been double-locked on the inside,' he said, exasperated. 'That girl must have done it, Harry. Go and see her and get the key.'

Harry tried the nearest door; that was locked, and the second door was locked, but the door leading into the back of the house was open. It took him down to a kitchen, and his electric lamp showed him yet another door – wide open. Though it was the garage and the big gates leading to the mews were swinging idly in the breeze.

He went back to report to his companion.

'You wait here,' said PC Simpson; he flew down the kitchen stairs, and in a few seconds was in the mews.

With shaking hand he dragged his police whistle from his pocket and sent out a shrill summons, then circumnavigated the house in time to see three policemen running, and ahead of them a stolid, tall figure.

Inspector Rater had business of his own in the neighbourhood that night, but had surrendered all other interests at the alarm. Breathlessly the policeconstable told his story as he half-ran, half-walked back to the mews.

'All right, all right,' said the Orator impatiently. 'One of you fellows stand in front of these doors and don't move.'

He followed Simpson into the house and up to the ground floor. Harry the policeman stood rigidly to attention at the foot of the stairs.

'Where's the lady? Have you seen her?'

Harry had not seen her or heard her. He ventured the suggestion that she must be 'in a faint', for he was a family man, and knew the effects of such events upon the weak frame of womanhood.

The Orater was halfway up the stairs, and missed the plausible explanation.

'That's the room, sir.'

Inspector Rater turned the handle and pushed.

'Locked,' he said and, stooping, squinted through the keyhole.

He could see that the door to the balcony was open, and asked a question.

'I left it like that, sir. There was a rope tied to the rails of the balcony. The man who done it must have got out that way, sir – '

'Lend your shoulders to the door,' said the Orator.

Two strong men pushed together – and again. The lock broke with a snap, the door flew open . . .

'Where's your body?'

PC Simpson stared: where the dead man had lain there was no dead man. The room was entirely empty.

The Orater looked at the policeman, at the floor and then at the window; and then his mind instantly moved to the house of the Marquis Parello, which was on the opposite side of the square. He thought of the Marquis Parello naturally for two reasons: the first was that Len Witlon was in town, and the second that in the Marquis's house, in a safe, and not a very safe safe, were four packets of cut emeralds that had arrived in London a few days before. They were in transit to an illustrious person in Italy who had a passion for emeralds, and had been purchased in the Argentine at great cost. The Marquis had notified the police, and Mr O. Rater had thought it desirable to station a uniformed constable before and another behind the house. He knew the names of those constables, and, leaning over the balcony, he addressed the small gathering of police officers on the pavement below.

'Is Walton here?'

'Yes, sir,' said a voice.

'And Martin?'

'Yes, sir,' said another voice.

'Then,' asked the Orator gently, 'why the hell *are* you here?'

He was in haste, because he knew just how quickly

Len Witlon worked. He did not wait for the door to be opened, but slid down the rope on to the steps, and minutes later was knocking at the door of the Marquis Perello's house. He knocked for a very long time. The Marquis and his wife were at the theatre. The three maidservants were locked in a room upstairs. The armed valet who kept guard over the safe was found bludgeoned in the drawing-room, and the safe was open.

'He worked four-handed,' observed the Orator philosophically.

Len Witlon invariably worked four-handed, so the Orator had made no great discovery. And after a job was done the four would separate and leave England by various routes. There was, for example, a steamer that went from Dundee to Holland, and yet another that sailed from Plymouth to one of the French ports – Len never made the mistake of following the beaten track. His methods were unique: nobody but Len would have taken a furnished house in Burford Square and staged an elaborate murder mystery in order to bring all the police in the neighbourhood running to that one particular spot and leave unguarded the place he wished to burgle.

A search of the house revealed nothing of value except that in the fireplace of the dining-room were a number of burnt papers, and a little slip printed in red which was only half-burnt. It had apparently to do with passengers and guides and the difficulties of Customs. He put the little slip in his pocket very carefully and sent forth widespread enquiries. The only clue he had – and that came to him the next morning – was from a constable of the City Police who, standing at the junction of Queen Victoria Street and Cannon Street, had seen a car in which was a woman. He was not even certain it was a woman, but she had that appearance, for her head and the upper part of her body were enclosed in a frock. She was, in point of fact, at the moment he saw her, engaged in slipping on a dress.

Cannon Street Station drew blank; no woman had arrived in a car at that hour. She had obviously gone east of Cannon Street.

The Orator was something of a psychologist himself. He knew Witlon's method's, and knew that that gallant gentleman would first assure himself that his beautiful lady confederate was safe. He interviewed PC Simpson, a crestfallen and resentful man, from whom his first murder had been ruthlessly snatched.

'Yes, sir, she talked with a sort of foreign accent.'

'I want you to remember every word she said, Simpson,' said the Orator gently.

PC Simpson thought very hard, trying to coax, by a vigorous massaging of his head, the half-forgotten facts of the conversation.

'I can't remember anything she said, sir. The only thing that struck me as curious was that while she was a-moaning and a-groaning she had her eye on her wristwatch. I saw her look twice.'

'The time was about eleven, I think?'

The constable thought it was a little later.

'To me,' said the Orator, 'it is as clear as daylight.'

When PC Simpson had gone, the Orator took from an envelope the little half-burned slip of printed paper that had been found in the grate of the dining-room, and reconstructed it . . .

Early one morning, somewhere in the Bay of Biscay, a British destroyer came up over the horizon behind the slow-moving steamship *Emil* and signalled the captain to stop. The *Emil* was a small ship that carried a large number of pleasure-seeking passengers to the Moroccan ports and Madeira. She had left London at midnight on the night of the robbery, and the pretty Anglo-Spanish girl who had already become the belle of the ship had joined the *Emil* just before she cast off from one of the London docks. Miss Avilez protested vigorously against her arrest, but rather blotted her copybook by attempting to throw a small package overboard – a piece of extravagance on her part, since the package contained seventeen perfectly cut emeralds, none of which was under ten carats.

The matron who looked after her on the destroyer brought her to London and to Mr Rater. She replied to all his questions with the hauteur proper to a daughter of hidalgos.

The next morning there appeared in the London press a communication very carefully composed by the Orator himself. He wrote at greater length than he spoke.

Part of the proceeds of the Burford Square robbery have been recovered by the arrest of a woman calling herself Inez Avilez. It appears that the leader of the gang responsible for this cleverly planned robbery, while he was careful of his own skin, had not only sent the woman on a route where she could be easily traced, but had left evidence – possibly with the idea of using her as a decoy to draw attention from himself – to her destination.

On the day following the pretty Anglo-Spaniard's conviction (she was a British subject from Gibraltar), a second inspired paragraph appeared:

This woman was deliberately sacrificed by the man who planned the robbery, and goes to prison to bear the punishment for his crime.

It was a clumsily written paragraph, and there were several sub-editors who would have liked to alter it a little, but the Orator knew his man, though he might not have recognised Mr Len Witlon if he had seen him pacing the floor of his expensive suite in Aix, crazily incoherent, planning vengeance for the insult he had suffered.

'I've got Witlon,' reported the Orator laconically.

And yet his superiors knew there was nothing in the world to associate Witlon with the robbery. He had his perfectly turned alibis, and witnesses to prove his presence in France at the hour the emeralds were stolen.

'I'm a mind-reader, too,' said the Orator, when they asked him for an explanation; 'and just at this moment I'm reading Witlon's. What he's saying about me at this minute is enough to make me turn in my grave. Only I'm not dead.'

Mr Len Witlon had a brilliant associate, one John B. Stimmings, who came at the request of his master to Aix, not knowing the condition of Mr Len Witlon's mind.

'Too bad about Inez,' said Mr Stimmings as he came into the ornate sitting-room and closed the door. 'Clever kid that. I'll bet this man Rater framed up something on her – '

'This man Rater couldn't frame a picture,' spluttered Len, his ordinarily good-looking face swollen and purple with anger. 'Rater! They call him the Orater, don't they! I'll make him talk! Look at this!'

He slammed down two press cuttings before his visitor. 'He couldn't get anything on me. The Sureté came after me the next morning, and there was I snug in bed in my villa at Auteuil.'

'Up in Paris,' said John B., 'they talk about asking you to leave France – '

'Leave nothing! They know I wouldn't touch a thing in France. I'm going to England to see this Rater fellow.'

Mr Stimmings looked at him curiously,

'Count me out,' he said. 'Take one ticket – single. You're going dippy.'

The absurdity of the very suggestion that it was not a brilliant idea brought a fleeting smile to the angry man.

'Listen! You know me! I know just what that fellow's thinking. I've got right behind the thing he calls his mind. John, do you remember when I went after the Infanta's pearls and then went back to Madrid four days after? Did anybody know me or recognise me? I'm going to show you my biggest bit of work.'

He might have added his ugliest, for in a tempestuous and sleepless night he had designed a crime that had no equal in his brilliant record.

A week later there arrived in London an elderly English gentleman who gave his name at the best London hotel as Colonel Pershin. He had a British passport and was apparently a fussy, rather quick-tempered man, who had a special business in life. He stayed at the Wheetham Hotel, which was at once the most obscure and the most fashionable in London, and he read the newspapers with great industry.

A few days after his arrival Mr Rater received a scented letter. It was written by a lady who signed herself 'One Who Knows', and it ran:

If you wish to know where the rest of the Parello emeralds are to be found, I can tell you. I want you to promise me that I shall not be arrested, but knowing that a police officer cannot make any such promises, I cannot ask you to put that into writing. I shall come to Scotland Yard at 8 o'clock on Saturday evening. Will you be in your room?

The Orator read and reread the communication. Where women were concerned he believed in miracles. And yet he was satisfied in his mind that behind the letter was the inspiration of Mr Witlon. For a long, long time he stood by his window looking on to the Embankment, staring at the river, and thinking himself into the mind of his enemy.

There was at the Yard at this time a most unpopular Assistant Commissioner, who did not like the Orator. Major Dawlton had had his police training in India. He was an incurable theorist, and had a weakness for interfering with his executive. He summoned the Orator into his office.

'Come, come, Mr Rater,' he said, a little pompously, 'this won't do at all. Here are emeralds of an enormous value stolen under the eyes of the police, after you had been specifically instructed to protect their owner! Have you seen this morning's newspapers?'

'I can't read' – said the Orator wearily, and waited long enough for the Assistant Commissioner to get apoplectic before he concluded – 'newspapers when I have got work on hand.'

'It is a scandal, Mr Rater. Really, I am ashamed to meet my friends at the club. They are constantly asking me why we don't get detectives in from outside. And I think it would be an excellent scheme.'

'You don't want detectives, you want mind-readers to deal with Witlon,' said the Orator again.

'Stuff and nonsense!' said Major Dawlton.

It was a very peaceful Saturday afternoon at Scotland Yard. The day was warm and the double windows that shut out the noises of the Thames Embankment were wide open. Sunshine bathed the deserted wharves and warehouses that form so fine a skyline on the southern bank and laid on the river a sheet of fretted gold.

The tramway-cars were more or less empty, the promenade given over to leisurely sightseeing folk who had brought their children for a stroll.

Inspector Rater took of his pince-nez with a sigh, folded the letter he had been reading and returned it to its envelope. He gazed pensively through the open window. A tug drawing a string of barges was moving slowly upstream. Timber barges stacked high with planks of yellow pine. On the Embankment a few loungers leaned over the parapet.

He turned his head as the door opened and Major Dawlton came in. Without a word he handed the letter to his superior. The Major fixed his eyeglass, read and sneered.

'That, I suppose, is the art of criminal detection,' he said, with heavy irony – the Orator was very unpopular at that moment. 'Half the good work at Scotland Yard is done by informers. I should like to see this woman when she comes.'

'If she comes,' said the Orator softly.

'You think it is a hoax? I don't agree. It is probably some jealous confederate who has been badly treated. These scraps of information have come to the Yard every day since I have been here.'

'They have come every day I've been here,' said the Orator, 'and that's seventeen years.'

The Major snorted under this implication of his inexperience.

'She won't come, but he will.'

'Witlon? Rubbish! He's in France. That sort of scoundrel is not going to put his nose into this country, and if he did we've sufficient evidence to convict him of simple larceny. I'll be here at eight o'clock this evening.'

'Make it a quarter to,' suggested the Orator, venom in his eye, 'if you must come – which I don't advise.'

Major Dawlton, sitting in the office chair, yawned.

'She's sold you,' he said.

'I told you not to come,' said Mr Rater.

He stood with his back to the wall, regarding the Assistant Commissioner thoughtfully.

The Major looked at his watch. 'I'll give her another quarter of an hour – '

Whee-e-smack! Something whizzed past him; he felt the disturbance of the air, and turning his startled head, saw the glass of a framed photograph splinter into fragments.

There was no sound of a shot – no report.

He was on his feet in an instant and ran to the window.

Something struck the sill on which his hand rested,

ripped a jagged wound in the stone and brought down the plaster from the ceiling.

'I'd keep away from that window,' said the Orator gently. 'They tell me he's a wonderful rifle shot, but I thought he'd operate from the Council building. The barge was certainly a brilliant idea.'

Major Dawlton's face was white as death.

'Shooting!' he gasped. 'At me!'

'At me,' said the Orator pensively. 'I hope those fellows have located him. I should think they have.'

As he spoke he saw two motor-launches filled with men speed out from the cover of the parapet; they were making for the barge.

'That's all right,' said the Orator. 'Now we've got something to charge him with.'

'They were shooting at me!' squeaked the Major.

'I told you not to come,' said Mr Rater, but the joy in his eyes belied his tone of sympathy.

'The general idea was a good one,' said the Orator to the Chief Commissioner. 'Witlon knew my weakness for fresh air, and he must have made a reconnaissance and seen how easy it was to look into my room when the window was open. Oh, yes, I knew he was in England– one of my men picked up his trail when he landed at Southampton from Le Havre.'

The Chief Commissioner's stern gaze was fixed on the Orator. 'But you didn't dream he'd be shooting into your room, or you wouldn't have allowed the Major to come?' he said.

The Orator did not answer immediately. Then he sighed.

'I suppose I wouldn't,' he said.

G. K. CHESTERTON

The Invisible Man

In the cool blue twilight of two steep streets in Camden
Town, the shop at the corner, a confectioner's,
glowed like the butt of a cigar. One should rather
say, perhaps, like the butt of a firework, for the light
was of many colours and some complexity, broken
up by many mirrors and dancing on many gilt and
gaily-coloured cakes and sweetmeats. Against this
one fiery glass were glued the noses of many
guttersnipes, for the chocolates were all wrapped in
those red and gold and green metallic colours which
are almost better than chocolate itself; and the huge
white wedding-cake in the window was somehow at
once remote and satisfying, just as if the whole North
Pole were good to eat. Such rainbow provocations
could naturally collect the youth of the neighbourhood up to the ages of ten or twelve. But this corner
was also attractive to youth at a later stage; and a
young man, not less than twenty-four, was staring
into the same shop window. To him, also, the shop
was of fiery charm, but this attraction was not wholly
to be explained by chocolates; which, however, he
was far from despising.

He was a tall, burly, red-haired young man, with a
resolute face but a listless manner. He carried under
his arm a flat, grey portfolio of black-and-white
sketches, of the sort he had sold with more or less
success to publishers ever since his uncle (who was an
admiral) had disinherited him for Socialism, because

of a lecture which he had delivered against that economic theory. His name was John Turnbull Angus.

Entering at last, he walked through the confectioner's shop to the back room, which was a sort of pastry-cook restaurant, merely raising his hat to the young lady who was serving there. She was a dark, elegant, alert girl in black, with a high colour and very quick, dark eyes; and after the ordinary interval she followed him into the inner room to take his order.

His order was evidently a usual one. 'I want, please,' he said with precision, 'one halfpenny bun and a small cup of black coffee.' An instant before the girl could turn away he added, 'Also, I want you to marry me.'

The young lady of the shop stiffened visibly and said, 'Those are jokes I don't allow.'

The red-haired young man lifted grey eyes of an unexpected gravity. 'Really and truly,' he said, 'the emotion I feel is serious – as serious as the halfpenny bun. It is expensive, like the bun; one pays for it. It is indigestible, like the bun. It hurts.'

The young lady had never taken her dark eyes off him, but seemed to be studying him with almost tragic exactitude. At the end of her scrutiny she wore something like the shadow of a smile, and she sat down in a chair.

'Don't you think,' observed Angus, absently, 'that it's rather cruel to eat these halfpenny buns? They might grow up into penny buns. I shall give up these brutal sports when we are married.'

The dark young lady rose from her chair and walked to the window, evidently in a state of strong but not unsympathetic cogitation. When at last she swung round again with an air of resolution she was bewildered to observe that the young man was

carefully laying out on the table various objects from
the shop-window. They included a pyramid of highly
coloured sweets, several plates of sandwiches, and
the two decanters containing that mysterious port
and sherry which are peculiar to pastry-cooks. In the
middle of this neat arrangement he had carefully let
down the enormous load of white sugared cake which
had been the huge ornament of the window.

'What on earth are you doing?' she asked.

'Duty, my dear Laura,' he began.

'Oh, for the Lord's sake, stop a minute,' she cried,
'and don't talk to me in that way. I mean, what is all
that?'

'A ceremonial meal, Miss Hope.'

'And what is that?' she asked impatiently, pointing
to the mountain of sugar.

'The wedding-cake, Mrs Angus,' he said.

The girl marched to that article, removed it with
some clatter, and put it back in the shop window; she
then returned, and, putting her elegant elbows on the
table, regarded the young man not unfavourably but
with considerable exasperation.

'You don't give me any time to think,' she said.

'I'm not such a fool,' he answered; 'that's my
Christian humility.'

She was still looking at him; but she had grown
considerably graver behind the smile.

'Mr Angus,' she said steadily, 'before there is a
minute more of this nonsense I must tell you something about myself as shortly as I can.'

'Delighted,' replied Angus gravely. 'You might
tell me something about myself, too, while you are
about it.'

'Oh, do hold your tongue and listen,' she said. 'It's

nothing that I'm ashamed of, and it isn't even anything that I'm specially sorry about. But what would you say if there were something that is no business of mine and yet is my nightmare?'

'In that case,' said the man seriously, 'I should suggest that you bring back the cake.'

'Well, you must listen to the story first,' said Laura, persistently. 'To begin with, I must tell you that my father owned the inn called the Red Fish at Ludbury, and I used to serve people in the bar.'

'I have often wondered,' he said, 'why there was a kind of a Christian air about this one confectioner's shop.'

'Ludbury is a sleepy, grassy little hole in the Eastern Counties, and the only kind of people who ever came to the Red Fish were occasional commercial travellers, and for the rest, the most awful people you can see, only you've never seen them. I mean little, loungy men, who had just enough to live on and had nothing to do but lean about in bar-rooms and bet on horses, in bad clothes that were just too good for them. Even these wretched young rotters were not very common at our house; but there were two of them that were a lot too common – common in every sort of way. They both lived on money of their own, and were wearisomely idle and over-dressed. But yet I was a bit sorry for them, because I half believe they slunk into our little empty bar because each of them had a slight deformity; the sort of thing that some yokels laugh at. It wasn't exactly a deformity either; it was more an oddity. One of them was a surprisingly small man, something like a dwarf, or at least like a jockey. He was not at all jockeyish to look at, though; he had a round black head and a well-trimmed black beard, bright eyes like a bird's; he jingled money in his pockets; he jangled a great gold watch-chain; and he never turned up except dressed just too much like a gentleman to be one. He was no fool though, though a futile idler; he was curiously clever at all kinds of things that couldn't be the slightest use; a sort of impromptu conjuring; making fifteen matches set fire to each other like a regular firework; or cutting a banana or some such thing into a dancing doll. His name was Isidore Smythe; and I can see him still, with his little dark face, just coming up to the counter, making a jumping kangaroo out of five cigars.

'The other fellow was more silent and more ordinary; but somehow he alarmed me much more than poor little Smythe. He was very tall and slight, and light-haired; his nose had a high bridge, and he might almost have been handsome in a spectral sort of way; but he had one of the most appalling squints I have ever seen or heard of. When he looked straight at you, you didn't know where you were yourself, let alone what he was looking at. I fancy this sort of disfigurement embittered the poor chap a little; for while Smythe was ready to show off his monkey tricks anywhere, James Welkin (that was the squinting man's name) never did anything except soak in our bar parlour, and go for great walks by himself in the flat, grey country all round. All the same, I think Smythe, too, was a little sensitive about being so small, though he carried it off more smartly. And so it was that I was really puzzled, as well as startled, and very sorry, when they both offered to marry me in the same week.

'Well, I did what I've since thought was perhaps a silly thing. But, after all, these freaks were my friends in a way; and I had a horror of their thinking I refused them for the real reason, which was that they were so impossibly ugly. So I made up some gas of another sort, about never meaning to marry anyone who hadn't carved his way in the world. I said it was a point of principle with me not to live on money that was just inherited like theirs. Two days after I had talked in this well-meaning sort of way, the whole trouble began. The first thing I heard was that both of them had gone off to seek their fortunes, as if they were in some silly fairy tale.

'Well, I've never seen either of them from that day to this. But I've had two letters from the little man called Smythe, and really they were rather exciting.'

'Ever heard of the other man?' asked Angus.

'No, he never wrote,' said the girl, after an instant's hesitation. 'Smythe's first letter was simply to say that he had started out walking with Welkin to London; but Welkin was such a good walker that the little man dropped out of it, and took a rest by the roadside. He happened to be picked up by some travelling show, and partly because he was nearly a dwarf, and partly because he was really a clever little wretch, he got on quite well in the showbusiness, and was soon sent up to the Aquarium, to do some tricks that I forget. That was his first letter. His second was much more of a startler, and I only got it last week.'

The man called Angus emptied his coffee-cup and regarded her with mild and patient eyes. She had on her lips a slight twist of laughter as she resumed, 'I suppose you've seen on the hoardings all about this "Smythe's Silent Service"? If not you must be the only person that hasn't. Oh, I don't know much about it, it's some clockwork invention for doing all the housework by machinery. You know the sort of thing: "Press a Button – A Butler Who Never Drinks". "Turn a Handle – Ten Housemaids Who Never Flirt". You must have seen the advertisements. Well, whatever these machines are, they are making pots of money; and they are making it all for that little imp whom I knew down in Ludbury. I can't help feeling pleased the poor little chap has fallen on his feet; but the plain fact is, I'm in terror of his turning up any minute and telling me he's carved his way in the world – as he certainly has.'

'And the other man?' repeated Angus with a sort of obstinate quietude.

Laura Hope got to her feet suddenly. 'My friend,' she said, 'I think you are a witch. Yes, you are quite right. I have not seen a line of the other man's writing; and I have no more notion than the dead of what or where he is. But it is of him that I am frightened. It is he who is all about my path. It is he who has half driven me mad. Indeed, I think he has driven me mad; for I have felt him where he could not have been, and I have heard his voice when he could not have spoken.'

'Well, my dear,' said the young man, cheerfully, 'if he were Satan himself, he is done for now you have told somebody. One goes mad all alone, old girl. But when was it you fancied you felt and heard our squinting friend?'

'I heard James Welkin laugh as plainly as I hear you speak,' said the girl, steadily. 'There was nobody there, for I stood just outside the shop at the corner, and could see down both streets at once. I had forgotten how he laughed, though his laugh was as odd as his squint. I had not thought of him for nearly a year. But it's a solemn truth that a few seconds later the first letter came from his rival.'

'Did you ever make the spectre speak or squeak, or anything?' asked Angus, with some interest.

Laura suddenly shuddered, and then said, with an unshaken voice, 'Yes. Just when I had finished reading the second letter from Isidore Smythe announcing his success. Just then, I heard Welkin say, "He shan't have you, though." It was quite plain, as if he were in the room. It is awful, I think I must be mad.'

'If you really were mad,' said the young man, 'you would think you must be sane. But certainly there seems to me to be something a little rum about this unseen gentleman. Two heads are better than one – I spare you allusions to any other organs and really, if you would allow me, as a sturdy, practical man, to bring back the wedding-cake out of the window – '

Even as he spoke, there was a sort of steely shriek in the street outside, and a small motor, driven at devilish speed, shot up to the door of the shop and stuck there. In the same flash of time a small man in a shiny top hat stood stamping in the outer room.

Angus, who had hitherto maintained hilarious ease from motives of mental hygiene, revealed the strain of his soul by striding abruptly out of the inner room and confronting the newcomer. A glance at him was quite sufficient to confirm the savage guesswork of a man in love. This very dapper but dwarfish figure, with the spike of black beard carried insolently forward, the clever unrestful eyes, the neat but very nervous fingers, could be none other than the man just described to him: Isidore Smythe, who made dolls out of banana skins and matchboxes; Isidore Smythe, who made millions out of undrinking butlers and unflirting housemaids of metal. For a moment the two men, instinctively understanding each other's air of possession, looked at each other with that curious cold generosity which is the soul of rivalry.

Mr Smythe, however, made no allusion to the ultimate ground of their antagonism, but said simply and explosively, 'Has Miss Hope seen that thing on the window?'

'On the window?' repeated the staring Angus.

'There's no time to explain other things,' said the small millionaire shortly. 'There's some tomfoolery going on here that has to be investigated.'

He pointed his polished walking-stick at the window, recently depleted by the bridal preparations of Mr Angus; and that gentleman was astonished to see along the front of the glass a long strip of paper pasted, which had certainly not been on the window when he looked through it some time before. Following the energetic Smythe outside into the street, he found that some yard and a half of stamp paper had been carefully gummed along the glass outside, and on this was written in straggly characters, 'If you marry Smythe, he will die.'

'Laura,' said Angus, putting his big red head into the shop, 'you're not mad.'

'It's the writing of that fellow Welkin,' said Smythe gruffly. 'I haven't seen him for years, but he's always bothering me. Five times in the last fortnight he's had threatening letters left at my flat, and I can't even find out who leaves them, let alone if it is Welkin himself. The porter of the flats swears that no suspicious characters have been seen, and here he has pasted up a sort of dado on a public shop window, while the people in the shop –'

'Quite so,' said Angus modestly, 'while the people in the shop were having tea. Well, sir, I can assure you I appreciate your common sense in dealing so directly with the matter. We can talk about other things afterwards. The fellow cannot be very far off yet, for I swear there was no paper there when I went last to the window, ten or fifteen minutes ago. On the other hand, he's too far off to be chased, as we don't even know the direction. If you'll take my advice, Mr Smythe, you'll put this at once in the hands of some energetic enquiry man, private rather than public. I know an extremely clever fellow, who has set up in business five minutes from here in your car. His name's Flambeau, and though his youth was a bit stormy, he's a strictly honest man now, and his brains are worth money. He lives in Lucknow Mansions, Hampstead.'

'That is odd,' said the little man, arching his black eyebrows. 'I live, myself, in Himalaya Mansions, round the corner. Perhaps you might care to come with me; I can go to my rooms and sort out these queer Welkin documents, while you run round and get your friend the detective.'

'You are very good,' said Angus politely. 'Well, the sooner we act the better.'

Both men, with a queer kind of impromptu fairness, took the same sort of formal farewell of the lady, and both jumped into the brisk little car. As Smythe took the handles and they turned the great corner of the street, Angus was amused to see a gigantesque poster of 'Smythe's Silent Service', with a picture of a huge headless iron doll, carrying a saucepan with the legend, 'A Cook Who is Never Cross.'

'I use them in my own flat,' said the little black-bearded man, laughing, 'partly for advertisements, and partly for real convenience. Honestly, and all above board, those big clockwork dolls of mine do bring your coals or claret or a timetable quicker than any live servants I've ever known, if you know which knob to press. But I'll never deny, between ourselves, that such servants have their disadvantages, too.

'Indeed?' said Angus; 'is there something they can't do?'

'Yes,' replied Smythe coolly; 'they can't tell me who left those threatening letters at my flat.'

The man's motor was small and swift like himself; in fact, like his domestic service, it was of his own invention. If he was an advertising quack, he was one who believed in his own wares. The sense of something tiny and flying was accentuated as they swept up long white curves of road in the dead but open daylight of evening. Soon the white curves came sharper and dizzier; they were upon ascending spirals, as they say in the modern religions. For, indeed, they were cresting a corner of London which is almost as precipitous as Edinburgh, if not quite so picturesque. Terrace rose above terrace, and the special tower of flats they sought, rose above them all to almost Egyptian height, gilt by the level sunset. The change, as they turned the corner and entered the crescent known as Himalaya Mansions, was as abrupt as the opening of a window; for they found that pile of flats sitting above London as above a green sea of slate. Opposite to the mansions, on the other side of the gravel crescent, was a bushy enclosure more like a steep hedge or dyke than a garden, and some way below that ran a strip of artificial water, a sort of canal, like the moat of that embowered fortress. As the car swept round the crescent it passed, at one corner, the stray stall of a man selling chestnuts; and right away at the other end of the curve, Angus could see a dim blue policeman walking slowly. These were the only human shapes in that high suburban solitude; but he had an irrational sense that they expressed the speechless poetry of London. He felt as if they were figures in a story.

The little car shot up to the right house like a bullet, and shot out its owner like a bombshell. He was immediately enquiring of a tall commissionaire in shining braid and a short porter in shirt sleeves whether anybody or anything had been seeking his apartments. He was assured that nobody and nothing had passed these officials since his last enquiries; whereupon he and the slightly bewildered Angus were shot up in the lift like a rocket, till they reached the top floor.

'Just come in for a minute,' said the breathless Smythe. 'I want to show you those Welkin letters. Then you might run round the corner and fetch your friend.' He pressed a button concealed in the wall, and the door opened of itself.

It opened on a long, commodious ante-room, of which the only arresting features, ordinarily speaking, were the rows of tall half-human mechanical figures that stood up on both sides like tailors' dummies. Like tailors' dummies they were headless; and like tailors' dummies they had a handsome unnecessary humpiness in the shoulders, and a pigeon-breasted protuberance of chest; but barring this, they were not much more like a human figure than any automatic machine at a station that is about the human height. They had two great hooks like arms, for carrying trays; and they were painted pea-green, or vermilion, or black for convenience of distinction; in every other way they were only automatic machines and nobody would have looked twice at them. On this occasion, at least, nobody did. For between the two rows of these domestic dummies lay something more interesting than most of the mechanics of the world. It was a white, tattered scrap of paper scrawled with red ink; and the agile inventor had snatched it up almost as soon as the door flew open. He handed it to Angus without a word. The red ink on it actually was not dry, and the message ran, 'If you have been to see her today, I shall kill you.'

There was a short silence, and then Isidore Smythe said quietly, 'Would you like a little whisky? I rather feel as if I should.'

'Thank you; I should like a little Flambeau,' said Angus, gloomily. 'This business seems to me to be getting rather grave. I'm going round at once to fetch him.'

'Right you are,' said the other, with admirable cheerfulness. 'Bring him back here as quick as you can.'

As Angus closed the front door behind him he saw Smythe push a button, and one of the clockwork images glided from its place and slid along a groove in the floor carrying a tray with syphon and decanter. There did seem something a trifle weird about leaving the little man alone among those dead servants, who were coming to life as the door closed.

Six steps down from Smythe's landing the man in shirt sleeves was doing something with a pail. Angus stopped to extract a promise, fortified with a prospective bribe, that he would remain in that place until the return with the detective, and would keep count of any kind of stranger coming up those stairs. Dashing down to the front hall, Angus then laid similar charges of vigilance on the commissionaire at the front door, from whom he learned the simplifying circumstances that there was no back door. Not content with this, he captured the floating policeman and induced him to stand opposite the entrance and watch it; and finally paused an instant for a pennyworth of chestnuts, and an enquiry as to the probable length of the merchant's stay in the neighbourhood.

The chestnut seller, turning up the collar of his coat, told him he should probably be moving shortly, as he thought it was going to snow. Indeed, the evening was growing grey and bitter, but Angus, with all his eloquence, proceeded to nail the chestnut man to his post.

'Keep yourself warm on your own chestnuts,' he said earnestly. 'Eat up your whole stock; I'll make it worth your while. I'll give you a sovereign if you'll wait here till I come back, and then tell me whether any man, woman or child has gone into that house where the commissionaire is standing.'

He then walked away smartly, with a last look at the besieged tower.

'I've made a ring round that room, anyhow,' he said. 'They can't all four of them be Mr Welkin's accomplices.'

Lucknow Mansions were, so to speak, on a lower platform of that hill of houses, of which Himalaya Mansions might be called the peak. Mr Flambeau's semi-official flat was on the ground floor, and presented in every way a marked contrast to the American machinery and cold hotel-like luxury of the flat of the Silent Service. Flambeau, who was a friend of Angus, received him in an artistic rococo den behind his office, of which the ornaments were sabres, harquebuses, Eastern curiosities, flasks of Italian wine, savage cooking-pots, a plumy Persian cat and a small dusty-looking Roman Catholic priest, who looked particularly out of place.

'This is my friend Father Brown,' said Flambeau. 'I've often wanted you to meet him. Splendid weather, this; a little cold for southerners like me.'

'Yes, I think it will keep clear,' said Angus, sitting down on a violet-striped Eastern ottoman.

'No,' said the priest quietly, 'it has begun to snow.'

And, indeed, as he spoke, the first few flakes, foreseen by the man of chestnuts, began to drift across the darkening windowpane.

'Well,' said Angus heavily. 'I'm afraid I've come on business, and rather jumpy business at that. The fact is, Flambeau, within a stone's throw of your house is a fellow who badly wants your help; he's perpetually being haunted and threatened by an invisible enemy – a scoundrel whom nobody has even seen.' As Angus proceeded to tell the whole tale of Smythe and Welkin, beginning with Laura's story, and going on with his own, the supernatural laugh at the corner of two empty streets, the strange distinct words spoken in an empty room, Flambeau grew more and more vividly concerned, and the little priest seemed to be left out of it, like a piece of furniture. When it came to the scribbled stamp-paper pasted on the window, Flambeau rose, seeming to fill the room with his huge shoulders.

'If you don't mind,' he said, 'I think you had better tell me the rest on the nearest road to this man's house. It strikes me, somehow, that there is no time to be lost.'

'Delighted,' said Angus, rising also, 'though he's safe enough for the present, for I've set four men to watch the only hole to his burrow.'

They turned out into the street, the small priest trundling after them with the docility of a small dog. He merely said, in a cheerful way, like one making conversation, 'How quick the snow gets thick on the ground.'

As they threaded the steep side streets already powdered with silver, Angus finished his story; and by the time they reached the crescent with the towering flats, he had leisure to turn his attention to the four sentinels. The chestnut seller, both before and after receiving a sovereign, swore stubbornly that he had watched the door and seen no visitor enter. The policeman was even more emphatic. He said he had had experience of crooks of all kinds, in top hats and in rags; he wasn't so green as to expect suspicious characters to look suspicious; he looked out for anybody, and, so help him, there had been nobody. And when all three men gathered round the gilded commissionaire, who still stood smiling astride of the porch, the verdict was more final still.

'I've got a right to ask any man, duke or dustman, what he wants in these flats,' said the genial and gold-laced giant, 'and I'll swear there's been nobody to ask since this gentleman went away.'

The unimportant Father Brown, who stood back, looking modestly at the pavement, here ventured to say meekly, 'Has nobody been up and down the steps, then, since the snow began to fall? It began while we were all round at Flambeau's.'

'Nobody's been in here, sir, you can take it from me,' said the official, with beaming authority.

'Then I wonder what that is?' said the priest, and stared at the ground blankly like a fish.

The others all looked down also; and Flambeau used a fierce exclamation and a French gesture. For it was unquestionably true that down the middle of the entrance guarded by the man in gold lace, actually between the arrogant, stretched legs of that colossus, ran a stringy pattern of grey footprints stamped upon the white snow.

'God!' cried Angus involuntarily, 'the Invisible Man!'

Without another word he turned and dashed up the stairs, with Flambeau following; but Father Brown still stood looking about him in the snow-clad street as if he had lost interest in his query.

Flambeau was plainly in a mood to break down the door with his big shoulders; but the Scotchman, with more reason, if less intuition, fumbled about on the frame of the door till he found the invisible button; and the door swung slowly open.

It showed substantially the same serried interior; the hall had grown darker, though it was still struck here and there with the last crimson shafts of sunset, and one or two of the headless machines had been moved from their places for this or that purpose, and stood here and there about the twilit place. The green and red of their coats were all darkened in the dusk; and their likeness to human shapes slightly increased by their very shapelessness. But in the middle of them all, exactly where the paper with the red ink had lain, there lay something that looked like red ink spilt out of its bottle. But it was not red ink.

With a French combination of reason and violence
Flambeau simply said, 'Murder!' and, plunging into
the flat, had explored every corner and cupboard of it
in five minutes. But if he expected to find a corpse he
found none. Isidore Smythe was not in the place,
either dead or alive. After the most frantic search
the two men met each other in the outer hall, with
streaming faces and staring eyes. 'My friend,' said
Flambeau, talking French in his excitement, 'not only
is your murderer invisible, but he makes invisible also
the murdered man.'

Angus looked round at the dim room full of
dummies, and in some Celtic corner of his Scotch
soul a shudder started. One of the life-size dolls
stood immediately overshadowing the bloodstain,
summoned, perhaps, by the slain man an instant
before he fell. One of the high-shouldered hooks that
served the thing for arms, was a little lifted, and Angus
had suddenly the horrid fancy that poor Smythe's
own iron child had struck him down. Matter had
rebelled, and these machines had killed their master.
But even so, what had they done with him?

'Eaten him?' said the nightmare at his ear; and he
sickened for an instant at the idea of rent, human
remains absorbed and crushed into all that acephalous
clockwork.

He recovered his mental health by an emphatic
effort, and said to Flambeau, 'Well, there it is. The
poor fellow has evaporated like a cloud and left a red
streak on the floor. The tale does not belong to this
world.'

'There is only one thing to be done,' said Flambeau,
'whether it belongs to this world or the other. I must
go down and talk to my friend.'

They descended, passing the man with the pail, who again asseverated that he had let no intruder pass, down to the commissionaire and the hovering chestnut man, who rigidly reasserted their own watchfulness. But when Angus looked round for his fourth confirmation he could not see it, and called out with some nervousness, 'Where is the policeman?'

'I beg your pardon,' said Father Brown; 'that is my fault. I just sent him down the road to investigate something – that I just thought worth investigating.'

'Well, we want him back pretty soon,' said Angus abruptly, 'for the wretched man upstairs has not only been murdered, but wiped out.'

'How?' asked the priest.

'Father,' said Flambeau, after a pause, 'upon my soul I believe it is more in your department than mine. No friend or foe has entered the house, but Smythe is gone, as if stolen by the fairies. If that is not supernatural, I – '

As he spoke they were all checked by an unusual sight; the big blue policeman came round the corner of the crescent, running. He came straight up to Brown.

'You're right, sir,' he panted, 'they've just found poor Mr Smythe's body in the canal down below.'

Angus put his hand wildly to his head. 'Did he run down and drown himself?' he asked.

'He never came down, I'll swear,' said the constable, 'and he wasn't drowned either, for he died of a great stab over the heart.'

'And yet you saw no one enter?' said Flambeau in a grave voice.

'Let us walk down the road a little,' said the priest. As they reached the other end of the crescent he observed abruptly, 'Stupid of me! I forgot to ask the policeman something. I wonder if they found a light-brown sack.'

'Why a light-brown sack?' asked Angus, astonished.

'Because if it was any other coloured sack, the case must begin over again,' said Father Brown; 'but if it was a light-brown sack, why, the case is finished.'

'I am pleased to hear it,' said Angus with hearty irony. 'It hasn't begun, so far as I am concerned.'

'You must tell us all about it,' said Flambeau, with a strange heavy simplicity, like a child.

Unconsciously they were walking with quickening steps down the long sweep of road on the other side of the high crescent, Father Brown leading briskly, though in silence. At last he said with an almost touching vagueness, 'Well, I'm afraid you'll think it so prosy. We always begin at the abstract end of things, and you can't begin this story anywhere else.

'Have you ever noticed this – that people never answer what you say? They answer what you mean – or what they think you mean. Suppose one lady says to another in a country house, "Is anybody staying with you?" The lady doesn't answer, "Yes; the butler, the three footmen, the parlourmaid, and so on," though the parlourmaid may be in the room, or the butler behind her chair. She says, "There is nobody staying with us," meaning nobody of the sort you mean. But suppose a doctor enquiring into an epidemic asks, "Who is staying in the house?" then the lady will remember the butler, the parlourmaid, and the rest. All language is used like that; you never get a question answered literally, even when you get it answered truly. When those four quite honest men said that no man had gone into the Mansions, they did not really mean that no man had gone into them. They meant no man whom they could suspect of being your man. A man did go into the house, and did come out of it, but they never noticed him.'

'An invisible man?' enquired Angus, raising his red eyebrows.

'A mentally invisible man,' said Father Brown.

A minute or two passed before he resumed in the same unassuming voice, like a man thinking his way, 'Of course, you can't think of such a man, until you do think of him. That's where his cleverness comes in. But I came to think of him through two or three little things in the tale Mr Angus told us. First, there was the fact that this Welkin went for long walks. And then there was the vast lot of stamp paper on the window. And then, most of all, there were the two things the young lady said – things that couldn't be true. Don't get annoyed,' he added hastily, noting a sudden movement of the Scotchman's head; 'she thought they were true. A person can't be quite alone in a street a second before she receives a letter. She can't be quite alone in a street when she starts reading a letter just received. There must be somebody pretty near her; he must be mentally invisible.'

'Why must there be somebody near her?' asked Angus.

'Because,' said Father Brown, 'barring carrier-pigeons, somebody must have brought her the letter.'

'Do you really mean to say,' asked Flambeau, with energy, 'that Welkin carried his rival's letters to his lady?'

'Yes,' said the priest. 'Welkin carried his rival's letters to his lady. You see, he had to.'

'Oh, I can't stand much more of this,' exploded

Flambeau. 'Who is this fellow? What does he look like? What is the usual get-up of a mentally invisible man?'

'He is dressed rather handsomely in red, blue and gold,' replied the priest promptly with precision, 'and in this striking, and even showy, costume he entered Himalaya Mansions under eight human eyes; he killed Smythe in cold blood, and came down into the street again carrying the dead body in his arms – '

'Reverend sir,' cried Angus, standing still, 'are you raving mad, or am I?'

'You are not mad,' said Brown, 'only a little un-observant. You have not noticed such a man as this, for example.'

He took three quick strides forward, and put his hand on the shoulder of an ordinary passing postman who had bustled by them unnoticed under the shade of the trees.

'Nobody ever notices postmen somehow,' he said thoughtfully; 'yet they have passions like other men, and even carry large bags where a small corpse can be stowed quite easily.'

The postman, instead of turning naturally, had ducked and tumbled against the garden fence. He was a lean fair-bearded man of very ordinary appearance, but as he turned an alarmed face over his shoulder, all three men were fixed with an almost fiendish squint.

Flambeau went back to his sabres, purple rugs and Persian cat, having many things to attend to. John Turnbull Angus went back to the lady at the shop, with whom that imprudent young man contrives to be extremely comfortable. But Father Brown walked those snow-covered hills under the stars for many hours with a murderer, and what they said to each other will never be known.

SAPPER

The Horror at Staveley Grange

'A fact pointing in a certain direction is just a fact; two
pointing in the same direction become a coincidence;
three – and you begin to get into the regions of
certainty. But you must be very sure of your facts.'

Thus ran Ronald Standish's favourite dictum, and
it was the astonishing skill with which he seemed to
be able to sort out the facts that mattered from the
mass of irrelevant detail, and having sorted them out,
to interpret them correctly, that had earned him his
reputation as a detective of quite unusual ability.

There is no doubt that had he been under the
necessity of earning his own livelihood, he would
have risen to a very high position at Scotland Yard;
or, if he had chosen to set up on his own, that his
career would have been assured. But not being under
any such necessity, his gifts were known only to a
small circle of friends and acquaintances. Moreover,
he was apt to treat the matter as rather a joke – as an
interesting recreation more than a serious business.
He regarded it in much the same light as solving a
chess problem or an acrostic.

In appearance he was about as unlike the con-
ventional detective as it is possible to be. Of medium
height, he was inclined to be thickset. His face was
ruddy, with a short, closely-clipped moustache – and
in his eyes there shone a perpetual twinkle. In fact,
most people on first meeting him took him for an

army officer. He was a first-class man to hounds, and an excellent shot; a cricketer who might easily have become first class, had he devoted enough time to it, and a scratch golfer. And last, but not least, he was a man of very great personal strength without a nerve in his body.

This, then, was the man who sat opposite to me in a first-class carriage of a Great Western express on the way to Devonshire. On the spur of the moment that morning, I had rung him up at his club in London – on the spur of the moment, he had thrown over a week's cricket and arranged to come with me to Exeter. And now that we were actually in the train, I began to wonder if I had brought him on a wild-goose chase. I took the letter out of my pocket – the letter that was the cause of our journey, and read it through once again.

DEAR TONY, I am perfectly distracted with worry and anxiety. I don't know whether you saw it in the papers, and it's such ages since we met, but I'm engaged to Billy Mansford. And we're in the most awful trouble. Haven't you got a friend or someone you once told me about who solves mysteries and things? Do, for pity's sake, get hold of him and bring him down here to stay. I'm nearly off my head with it all. Your distracted MOLLY

I laid the letter on my knee and stared out of the window. Somehow or other I couldn't picture pretty little Molly Tremayne, the gayest and most feckless girl in the world, as being off her head over anything. And having only recently returned from Brazil I had not heard of her engagement – nor did I know anything about the man she was engaged to. But as I say,

I rang up Standish on the spur of the moment, and a little to my surprise he had at once accepted.

He leant over at that moment and took the letter off my knee.

'The Old Hall,' he remarked thoughtfully. Then he took a large-scale ordnance map from his pocket and began to study it. 'Three miles approximately from Staveley Grange.'

'Staveley Grange,' I said, staring at him. 'What has Staveley Grange got to do with the matter?'

'I should imagine – everything,' he answered. 'You've been out of the country, Tony, and so you're a bit behindhand. But you may take it from me that it was not the fact that your Molly was distracted that made me give up an excellent I Zingari tour. It was the fact that she is engaged to Mr William Mansford.'

'Never heard of him,' I said. 'Who and what is he?'

'He is the younger and only surviving son of the late Mr Robert Mansford,' he answered thoughtfully. 'Six months ago the father was alive – also Tom, the elder son. Five months ago the father died; two months ago Tom died. And the circumstances of their deaths were, to put it mildly, peculiar.'

'Good heavens!' I cried, 'this is all news to me.'

'Probably,' he answered. 'The matter attracted very little attention. But you know my hobby, and it was the coincidence of the two things that attracted my attention. I only know, of course, what appeared in the papers – and that wasn't very much. Mansford senior and both his sons had apparently spent most of their lives in Australia. The two boys came over with the Anzacs, and a couple of years or so after the war they all decided to come back to England. And so he bought Staveley Grange. He had gone out a poor man of distinctly humble origin: he returned as a wealthy Australian magnate. Nine months after he stepped into the house he was found dead in his bed in the morning by the butler. He was raised up on his pillows and he was staring fixedly at a top corner of the room by one of the windows. And in his hand he held the speaking-tube which communicated with the butler's room. A post-mortem revealed nothing, and the verdict was that he had died of heart failure. In view of the fact that most people do die of heart failure, the verdict was fairly safe.'

Ronald Standish lit a cigarette.

'That was five months ago. Two months ago, one of the footmen coming in in the morning was horrified to find Tom sprawling across the rail at the foot of the bed – stone dead. He had taken over his father's room, and had retired the previous night in the best of health and spirits. Again there was a post-mortem – again nothing was revealed. And again the same verdict was given – heart failure. Of course, the coincidence was commented on in the press, but there the matter rested, at any rate as far as the newspapers were concerned. And therefore that is as much as I know. This letter looks as if further developments were taking place.'

'What an extraordinary affair,' I remarked, as he finished. 'What sort of men physically were the father and Tom?'

'According to the papers,' answered Standish, 'they were two singularly fine specimens. Especially Tom.'

Already we were slowing down for Exeter, and we began gathering our suitcases and coats preparatory to alighting. I leant out of the window as we ran into the station, having wired Molly our time of arrival, and there she was sure enough, with a big, clean-cut man standing beside her, who, I guessed, must be her fiancé. So, in fact, it proved, and a moment or two later we all walked out of the station together towards the waiting motor car. And it was as I passed the ticket collector that I got the first premonition of trouble. Two men standing on the platform, who looked like well-to-do farmers, whispered together a little significantly as Mansford passed them, and stared after him with scarcely veiled hostility in their eyes.

On the way to the Old Hall, I studied him under cover of some desultory conversation with Molly. He was a typical Australian of the best type: one of those open-air, clear-eyed men who came over in their thousands to Gallipoli and France. But it seemed to me that his conversation with Ronald was a little forced; underlying it was a vague uneasiness – a haunted fear of something or other. And I thought he was weighing-up my friend with a kind of desperate hope tinged with disappointment, as if he had been building on Ronald's personality and now was unsatisfied.

That some such idea was in Molly's mind I learned as we got out of the car. For a moment or two we were alone, and she turned to me with a kind of desperate eagerness.

'Is he very clever, Tony – your friend? Somehow I didn't expect him to look quite like that!'

'You may take it from me, Molly,' I said reassuringly, 'that there are very few people in Europe who can see farther into a brick wall than Ronald. But he knows nothing, of course, as to what the trouble is – any more than I do. And you mustn't expect him to work miracles.'

'Of course not,' she answered. 'But oh! Tony – it's – it's – damnable.'

We went into the house and joined Standish and Mansford, who were in the hall.

'You'd like to go up to your rooms,' began Molly, but Ronald cut her short with a grave smile.

'I think, Miss Tremayne,' he said quietly, 'that it will do you both good to get this little matter off your chests as soon as possible. Bottling things up is no good, and there's some time yet before dinner.'

The girl gave him a quick smile of gratitude and led the way across the hall.

'Let's go into the billiard room,' she said. 'Daddy is pottering round the garden, and you can meet him later. Now, Bill,' she continued, when we were comfortably settled, 'tell Mr Standish all about it.'

'Right from the very beginning, please,' said Ronald, stuffing an empty pipe in his mouth. 'The reasons that caused your father to take Staveley Grange and everything.'

Bill Mansford gave a slight start.

'You know something about us already then.'

'Something,' answered Ronald briefly. 'I want to know all.'

'Well,' began the Australian, 'I'll tell you all I know. But there are many gaps I can't fill in. When we came back from Australia two years ago, we naturally gravitated to Devonshire. My father came from these parts, and he wanted to come back after his thirty years' absence. Of course he found everything changed, but he insisted on remaining here and we set about looking for a house. My father was a wealthy man – very wealthy, and his mind was set on getting something good. A little pardonable vanity perhaps – but having left England practically penniless to return almost a millionaire, he was determined to get what he wanted regardless of cost. And it was after we had been here about six months that Staveley Grange came quite suddenly on to the market. It happened in rather a peculiar way. Some people of the name of Bretherton had it, and had been living here for about three years. They had bought it, and spent large sums of money on it; introduced a large number of modern improvements, and at the same time preserved all the old appearance. Then, as I say, quite suddenly, they left the house and threw it on the market.

'Well, it was just what we wanted. We all went over it, and found it even more perfect than we had anticipated. The man who had been butler to the Brethertons was in charge, and when we went over, he and his wife were living there alone. We tried to pump them as to why the Brethertons had gone, but they appeared to know no more than we did. The butler – Templeton – was a charming old bird with side-whiskers; his wife, who had run the kitchen, was a rather timorous-looking little woman – but a damned good cook.

'Anyway, the long and short of it was, we bought the place. The figure was stiff, but my father could afford it. And it was not until we had bought it, that we heard in a roundabout way the reason for the Brethertons' departure. It appeared that old Mrs Bretherton woke up one night in screaming hysterics, and alleged that a dreadful thing was in the room with her. What it was she wouldn't say, except to babble foolishly about a shining, skinny hand that had touched her. Her husband and various maids came rushing in, and of course the room was empty. There was nothing there at all. The fact of it was that the old lady had had lobster for dinner – and a nightmare afterwards. At least,' added Mansford slowly, 'that's what we thought at the time.'

He paused to light a cigarette.

'Well – we gathered that nothing had been any good. Templeton proved a little more communicative once we were in, and from him we found out that in spite of every argument and expostulation on the part of old Bretherton the old lady flatly refused to live in the house for another minute. She packed up her boxes and went off the next day with her maid to some hotel in Exeter, and nothing would induce her to set foot inside the house again. Old Bretherton was livid.'

Mansford smiled grimly.

'But – he went, and we took the house. The room that old Mrs Bretherton had had was quite the best bedroom in the house, and my father decided to use it as his own. He came to that decision before we knew anything about this strange story, though even if we had, he'd still have used the room. My father was not the man to be influenced by an elderly woman's indigestion and subsequent nightmare. And when bit by bit we heard the yarn, he merely laughed, as did my brother and myself.

'And then one morning it happened. It was Templeton who broke the news to us with an ashen face, and his voice shaking so that we could hardly make out what he said. I was shaving at the time, I remember, and when I'd taken in what he was trying to say, I rushed along the passage to my father's room with the soap still lathered on my chin. The poor old man was sitting up in bed propped against the pillows. His left arm was flung half across his face as if to ward off something that was coming; his right hand was grasping the speaking-tube beside the bed. And in his wide-open, staring eyes was a look of dreadful terror.'

He paused as if waiting for some comment or question, but Ronald still sat motionless, with his empty pipe in his mouth.

And after a while Mansford continued: 'There was a post-mortem, as perhaps you may have seen in the papers, and they found my father had died from heart failure. But my father's heart, Mr Standish, was as sound as mine, and neither my brother nor I were satisfied. For weeks he and I sat up in that room, taking it in turns to go to sleep, to see if we could see anything – but nothing happened. And at last we began to think that the verdict was right, and that the poor old man had died of natural causes. I went back to my own room, and Tom – my brother – stayed on in my father's room. I tried to dissuade him, but he was an obstinate fellow, and he had an idea that if he slept there alone he might still perhaps get to the bottom of it. He had a revolver by his side, and Tom was a man who could hit the pip out of the ace of diamonds at ten yards. Well, for a week nothing happened. And then one night I stayed chatting with him for a few moments in his room before going to bed. That was the last time I saw him alive. One of the footmen came rushing in to me the next morning, with a face like a sheet – and before he spoke I knew what must have happened. It was perhaps a little foolish of me – but I dashed past him while he was still stammering at the door – and went to my brother's room.'

'Why foolish?' said Standish quietly.

'Some people at the inquest put a false construction on it,' answered Mansford steadily. 'They wanted to know why I made that assumption before the footman told me.'

'I see,' said Standish. 'Go on.'

'I went into the room, and there I found him. In one hand he held the revolver, and he was lying over the rail at the foot of the bed. The blood had gone to his head, and he wasn't a pretty sight. He was dead, of course – and once again the post-mortem revealed nothing. He also was stated to have died of heart failure. But he didn't, Mr Standish.' Mansford's voice shook a little. 'As there's a God above, I swear Tom never died of heart failure. Something happened in that room – something terrible occurred there which killed my father and brother as surely as a bullet through the brain. And I've *got* to find out what it was: I've *got* to, you understand – because' – and here his voice faltered for a moment, and then grew steady again – 'because there are quite a number of people who suspect me of having murdered them both.'

'Naturally,' said Standish, in his most matter-of-fact tone. 'When a man comes into a lot of money through the sudden death of two people, there are certain to be lots of people who will draw a connection between the two events.'

He stood up and faced Mansford.

'Are the police still engaged on it?'

'Not openly,' answered the other. 'But I know they're working at it still. And I can't and won't marry Molly with this cloud hanging over my head. I've got to disprove it.'

'Yes, but, my dear, it's no good to me if you

disprove it by being killed yourself,' cried the girl. Then she turned to Ronald. 'That's where we thought that perhaps you could help us, Mr Standish. If only you can clear Bill's name, why – '

She clasped her hands together beseechingly, and Standish gave her a reassuring smile.

'I'll try, Miss Tremayne – I can't do more than that. And now I think we'll get to business at once. I want to examine that bedroom.'

Ronald Standish remained sunk in thought during the drive to Staveley Grange. Molly had not come with us, and neither Mansford nor I felt much inclined for conversation. He, poor devil, kept searching Ronald's face with a sort of pathetic eagerness, almost as if he expected the mystery to be already solved.

And then, just as we were turning into the drive, Ronald spoke for the first time. 'Have you slept in that room since your brother's death, Mansford?'

'No,' answered the other, a little shamefacedly. 'To tell the truth, Molly extracted a promise from me that I wouldn't.'

'Wise of her,' said Standish tersely, and relapsed into silence again.

'But you don't think – ' began Mansford.

'I think nothing,' snapped Standish, and at that moment the car drew up at the door.

It was opened by an elderly man with side-whiskers, whom I placed as the butler – Templeton. He was a typical, old-fashioned manservant of the country-house type, and he bowed respectfully when Mansford told him what we had come for.

'I am thankful to think there is any chance, sir, of

clearing up this terrible mystery,' he said earnestly.
'But I fear, if I may say so, that the matter is beyond
earthly hands.' His voice dropped, to prevent the two
footmen overhearing. 'We have prayed, sir, my wife
and I, but there are more things in heaven and earth
than we can account for. You wish to go to the room,
sir? It is unlocked.'

He led the way up the stairs and opened the door.

'Everything, sir, is as it was on the morning when
Mr Tom – er – died. Only the bedclothes have been
removed.'

He bowed again and left the room, closing the
door.

'Poor old Templeton,' said Mansford. 'He's convinced that we are dealing with a ghost. Well, here's
the room, Standish – just as it was. As you see, there's
nothing very peculiar about it.'

Ronald made no reply. He was standing in the
centre of the room taking in the first general impression
of his surroundings. He was completely absorbed, and
I made a warning sign to Mansford not to speak. The
twinkle had left his eyes: his expression was one of
keen concentration. And, after a time, knowing the
futility of speech, I began to study the place on my
own account.

It was a big, square room, with a large double bed
of the old-fashioned type. Over the bed was a canopy,
made fast to the two bedposts at the head, and
supported at the foot by two wires running from the
two corners of the canopy to two staples let into the
wall above the windows. The bed itself faced the
windows, of which there were two, placed sym-
metrically in the wall opposite, with a writing-table in
between them. The room was on the first floor in the

centre of the house, and there was thus only one outside wall – that facing the bed. A big open fireplace and a wash-hand basin with water laid on occupied most of one wall; two long built-in cupboards filled up the other. Beside the bed, on the fireplace side, stood a small table, with a special clip attached to the edge for the speaking-tube. In addition there stood on this table a thing not often met with in a private house in England. It was a small, portable electric fan, such as one finds on board ship or in the tropics.

There were two or three easy-chairs standing on the heavy-pile carpet, and the room was lit by electric light. In fact the whole tone was solid comfort, not to say luxury; it looked the last place in the world with which one would have associated anything ghostly or mysterious.

Suddenly Ronald Standish spoke.

'Just show me, will you, Mansford, as nearly as you can, exactly the position in which you found your father.'

With a slight look of repugnance, the Australian got on to the bed.

'There were bedclothes, of course, and pillows which are not here now, but allowing for them, the poor old man was hunched up somehow like this. His knees were drawn up, the speaking-tube was in his hand, and he was staring towards that window.'

'I see,' said Standish. 'The window on the right as we look at it. And your brother, now. When he was found he was lying over the rail at the foot of the bed. Was he on the right side or the left?'

'On the right,' said Mansford, 'almost touching the upright.'

Once again Standish relapsed into silence and

stared thoughtfully round the room. The setting sun was pouring in through the windows, and suddenly he gave a quick exclamation. We both glanced at him and he was staring up at the ceiling with a keen, intent look on his face. The next moment he had climbed on to the bed, from where, standing up, he examined the two wire stays which supported the canopy. He touched each of them in turn, and began to whistle under his breath. It was a sure sign that he had stumbled on something, but I knew him far too well to make any comment at that stage of the proceedings.

'Very strange,' he remarked at length, getting down and lighting a cigarette.

'What is?' asked Mansford eagerly.

'The vagaries of sunlight,' answered Standish, with an enigmatic smile. He was pacing up and down the room smoking furiously, only to stop suddenly and stare again at the ceiling.

'It's the clue,' he said slowly. 'It's the clue to everything. It must be. Though what that everything is I know no more than you. Listen, Mansford, and pay careful attention. This trail is too old to follow: in sporting parlance the scent is too faint. We've got to get it renewed: we've got to get your ghost to walk again. Now I've only the wildest suspicions to go on, but I have a feeling that that ghost will be remarkably shy of walking if there are strangers about. I'm just gambling on one very strange fact – so strange as to make it impossible to be an accident. When you go downstairs I shall adopt the role of advising you to have this room shut up. You will laugh at me, and announce your intention of sleeping in this room tonight. You will insist on clearing this matter up.

Tony and I will go, and we shall return later to the grounds, where I see there is some very good cover. You will come to bed here – you will get into bed and switch out the light. You will give it a quarter of an hour, and then you will drop out of the window and join us. And we shall see if anything happens.'

'But if we're all outside, how can we?' cried Mansford.

Standish smiled grimly. 'You may take it from me,' he remarked, 'that if my suspicions are correct the ghost will leave a trail. And it's the trail I'm interested in – not the ghost. Let's go and don't forget your part.'

'But, my God! Standish – can't you tell me a little more?'

'I don't know any more to tell you,' answered Standish gravely. 'All I can say is – as you value your life, don't fall asleep in this room. And don't breathe a word of this conversation to a soul.'

Ten minutes later he and I were on our way back to the Old Hall. True to his instructions Mansford had carried out his role admirably as we came down the stairs and stood talking in the hall. He gave it to be understood that he was damned if he was going to let things drop; that if Standish had no ideas on the matter – well, he was obliged to him for the trouble he had taken – but from now on he was going to take the matter into his own hands. And he proposed to start that night. He had turned to one of the footmen standing by, and had given instructions for the bed to be made up, while Ronald had shrugged his shoulders and shaken his head.

'Understandable, Mansford,' he remarked, 'but unwise. My advice to you is to have that room shut up.'

And the old butler, shutting the door of the car, had fully agreed.

'Obstinate, sir,' he whispered, 'like his father. Persuade him to have it shut up, sir – if you can. I'm afraid of that room – afraid of it.'

'You think something will happen tonight, Ronald,' I said as we turned into the Old Hall.

'I don't know, Tony,' he said slowly. 'I'm utterly in the dark – utterly. And if the sun hadn't been shining today while we were in that room, I shouldn't have even the faint glimmer of light I've got now. But when you've got one bit of a jigsaw, it saves trouble to let the designer supply you with a few more.'

And more than that he refused to say. Throughout dinner he talked cricket with old Tremayne: after dinner he played him at billiards. And it was not until eleven o'clock that he made a slight sign to me, and we both said good-night.

'No good anyone knowing, Tony,' he said as we went upstairs. 'It's an easy drop from my window to the ground. We'll walk to Staveley Grange.'

The church clock in the little village close by was striking midnight as we crept through the under-growth towards the house. It was a dark night – the moon was not due to rise for another three hours – and we finally came to a halt behind a big bush on the edge of the lawn from which we could see the house clearly. A light was still shining from the windows of the fatal room, and once or twice we saw Mansford's shadow as he undressed. Then the light went out, and the house was in darkness; the vigil had begun.

For twenty minutes or so we waited, and Standish began to fidget uneasily.

'Pray heavens he hasn't forgotten and gone to

sleep,' he whispered to me, and even as he spoke he gave a little sigh of relief. A dark figure was lowering itself out of the window, and a moment or two later we saw Mansford skirting the lawn. A faint hiss from Standish and he'd joined us under cover of the bush.

'Everything seemed perfectly normal,' he whispered. 'I got into bed as you said – and there's another thing I did too. I've tied a thread across the door, so that if the ghost goes in that way we'll know.'

'Good,' said Standish. 'And now we can compose ourselves to wait. Unfortunately we mustn't smoke.'

Slowly the hours dragged on, while we took it in turns to watch the windows through a pair of night glasses. And nothing happened – absolutely nothing. Once it seemed to me as if a very faint light – it was more like a lessening of the darkness than an actual light – came from the room, but I decided it must be my imagination. And not till nearly five o'clock did Standish decide to go into the room and explore. His face was expressionless: I couldn't tell whether he was disappointed or not. But Mansford made no effort to conceal his feelings: frankly he regarded the whole experiment as a waste of time.

And when the three of us had clambered in by the window he said as much.

'Absolutely as I left it,' he said. 'Nothing happened at all.'

'Then, for heaven's sake, say so in a whisper,' snapped Standish irritably, as he clambered on to the bed. Once again his objective was the right hand wire stay of the canopy, and as he touched it he gave a quick exclamation. But Mansford was paying no attention: he was staring with puzzled eyes at the electric fan by the bed.

'Now who the devil turned that on,' he muttered. 'I haven't seen it working since the morning Tom died.' He walked round to the door. 'Say, Standish – that's queer. The thread isn't broken – and that fan wasn't going when I left the room.'

Ronald Standish looked more cheerful.

'Very queer,' he said. 'And now I think, if I was you, I'd get into that bed and go to sleep – first removing the thread from the door. You're quite safe now.'

'Quite safe,' murmured Mansford. 'I don't understand.'

'Nor do I – as yet,' returned Standish. 'But this I will tell you. Neither your father nor your brother died of heart failure, through seeing some dreadful sight. They were foully murdered, as in all probability you would have been last night had you slept in this room.'

'But who murdered them, and how and why?' said Mansford dazedly.

'That is just what I'm going to find out,' answered Standish grimly.

As we came out of the breakfast-room at the Old Hall three hours later, Standish turned away from us. 'I'm going into the garden to think,' he said. 'I have a sort of feeling that I'm not being very clever. For the life of me at the moment I cannot see the connection between the canopy wire that failed to shine in the sunlight, and the electric fan that was turned on so mysteriously. I am going to sit under that tree over there. Possibly the link may come.'

He strolled away, and Molly joined me. She was looking tired and *distraite*, as she slipped her hand through my arm.

'Has he found out anything, Tony?' she asked eagerly. 'He seemed so silent and preoccupied at breakfast.'

'He's found out something, Molly,' I answered guardedly, 'but I'm afraid he hasn't found out much. In fact, as far as my brain goes it seems to me to be nothing at all. But he's an extraordinary fellow,' I added, reassuringly.

She gave a little shudder and turned away.

'It's too late, Tony,' she said miserably. 'Oh! if only I'd sent for you earlier. But it never dawned on me that it would come to this. I never dreamed that Bill would be suspected. He's just telephoned through to me: that horrible man McIver – the Inspector from Scotland Yard – is up there now. I feel that it's only a question of time before they arrest him. And though he'll get off – he must get off if there's such a thing as justice – the suspicion will stick to him all his life. There will be brutes who will say that failure to prove that Bill did it is a very different matter from proving that he didn't. But I'm going to marry him all the same, Tony – whatever he says. Of course, I suppose you know that he didn't get on too well with his father?'

'I didn't,' I answered. 'I know nothing about him except just what I've seen.'

'And the other damnable thing is that he was in some stupid money difficulty. He'd backed a bill or something for a pal and was let down, which made his father furious. Of course there was nothing in it, but the police got hold of it – and twisted it to suit themselves.'

'Well, Molly, you may take it from me,' I said reassuringly, 'that Ron Standish is certain he had nothing to do with it.'

'That's not much good, Tony,' she answered with a twisted smile. 'So am I certain, but I can't *prove* it.'

With a little shrug of her shoulders she turned and went indoors, leaving me to my own thoughts. I could see Standish in the distance, with his head enveloped in a cloud of smoke, and after a moment's indecision I started to stroll down the drive towards the lodge. It struck me that I would do some thinking on my own account, and see if by any chance I could hit on some solution which would fit the facts. And the more I thought the more impossible did it appear: the facts at one's disposal were so terribly meagre.

What horror had old Mansford seen coming at him out of the darkness which he had tried to ward off even as he died? And was it the same thing that had come to his elder son, who had sprung forward revolver in hand, and died as he sprang? And again, who had turned on the electric fan? How did that fit in with the two deaths? No one had come in by the door on the preceding night; no one had got in by the window. And then suddenly I paused, struck by a sudden idea. Staveley Grange was an old house – early sixteenth century; just the type of house to have secret passages and concealed entrances . . . There must be one into the fatal room: it was obvious.

Through that door there had crept some dreadful thing – some man, perhaps, and if so the murderer himself – disguised and dressed up to look awe-inspiring. Phosphorus doubtless had been used – and phosphorus skilfully applied to a man's face and clothes will make him sufficiently terrifying at night to strike terror into the stoutest heart. Especially someone just awakened from sleep. That faint luminosity which we thought we had seen the preceding night was accounted for, and I almost laughed at dear old Ronald's stupidity in not having looked for a secret entrance. I was one up on him this time.

Mrs Bretherton's story came back to me – her so-called nightmare – in which she affirmed she had been touched by a shining skinny hand. Shining – here lay the clue – the missing link. The arm of the murderer only was daubed with phosphorus; the rest of his body was in darkness. And the terrified victim waking suddenly would be confronted with a ghastly shining arm stretched out to clutch his throat.

A maniac probably – the murderer: a maniac who knew the secret entrance to Staveley Grange: a homicidal maniac – who had been frightened in his foul work by Mrs Bretherton's shrieks, and had fled before she had shared the same fate as the Mansfords. Then and there I determined to put my theory in front of Ronald. I felt that I'd stolen a march on him this time at any rate.

I found him still puffing furiously at his pipe, and he listened in silence while I outlined my solution with a little pardonable elation.

'Dear old Tony,' he said as I finished. 'I congratulate you. The only slight drawback to your idea is that there is no secret door into the room.'

'How do you know that?' I cried. 'You hardly looked.'

'On the contrary, I looked very closely. I may say that for a short while I inclined to some such theory as the one you've just put forward. But as soon as I saw that the room had been papered I dismissed it at once. As far as the built-in cupboard was concerned, it was erected by a local carpenter quite recently, and any secret entrance would have been either blocked over or opened up. Besides McIver has been in charge of this case – Inspector McIver from Scotland Yard. Now he and I have worked together before, and I have the very highest opinion of his ability. His powers of observation are extraordinary, and if his powers of deduction were as high he would be in the very first flight. Unfortunately he lacks imagination. But what I was leading up to was this. If McIver failed to find a secret entrance, it would be so much waste of time looking for one oneself. And if he had found one, he wouldn't have been able to keep it dark. We should have heard about it sharp enough.'

'Well, have you got any better idea?' I said, a little peevishly. 'If there isn't any secret door, how the deuce was that fan turned on?'

'There is such a thing as a two-way switch,' murmured Ronald mildly. 'That fan was not turned on from inside the room; it was turned on from somewhere else. And the person who turned it on was the murderer of old Mansford and his son.'

I stared at him in amazement.

'Then all you've got to do,' I cried excitedly, 'is to find out where the other terminal of the two-way switch is? If it's in someone's room you've got him.'

'Precisely, old man. But if it's in a passage, we haven't. And here, surely, is McIver himself. I wonder how he knew I was here?'

I turned to see a short thickset man approaching us over the lawn.

'He was up at Staveley Grange this morning,' I said. 'Mansford telephoned through to Molly.'

'That accounts for it then,' remarked Standish, waving his hand at the detective. 'Good-morning, Mac.'

'Morning, Mr Standish,' cried the other. 'I've just heard that you're on the track, so I came over to see you.'

'Splendid,' said Standish. 'This is Mr Belton – a great friend of mine – who is responsible for my giving up a good week's cricket and coming down here. He's a friend of Miss Tremayne's.'

McIver looked at me shrewdly.

'And therefore of Mr Mansford's, I see.'

'On the contrary,' I remarked, 'I never met Mr Mansford before yesterday.'

'I was up at Staveley Grange this morning,' said McIver, 'and Mr Mansford told me you'd all spent the night on the lawn.'

I saw Standish give a quick frown, which he instantly suppressed.

'I trust he told you that in private, McIver.'

'He did. But why?'

'Because I want it to be thought that he slept in that room,' answered Standish. 'We're moving in deep waters, and a single slip at the present moment may cause a very unfortunate state of affairs.'

'In what way?' grunted McIver.

'It might frighten the murderer,' replied Standish. 'And if he is frightened, I have my doubts if we shall ever bring the crime home to him. And if we don't bring the crime home to him, there will always be people who will say that Mansford had a lot to gain by the deaths of his father and brother.'

'So you think it was murder?' said McIver slowly, looking at Standish from under his bushy eyebrows.

Ronald grinned. 'Yes, I quite agree with you on that point.'

'I haven't said what I think!' said the detective.

'True, McIver – perfectly true. You have been the soul of discretion. But I can hardly think that Scotland Yard would allow themselves to be deprived of your valuable services for two months while you enjoyed a rest cure in the country. Neither a ghost nor two natural deaths would keep you in Devonshire.'

McIver laughed shortly.

'Quite right, Mr Standish. I'm convinced it's murder: it must be. But frankly speaking, I've never been so absolutely floored in all my life. Did you find out anything last night?'

Standish lit a cigarette.

'Two very interesting points – two extremely interesting points, I may say, which I present to you free, gratis and for nothing. One of the objects of oil is to reduce friction, and one of the objects of an electric fan is to produce a draught. And both these profound facts have a very direct bearing on . . . ' He paused and stared across the lawn. 'Hello! here is our friend Mansford in his car. Come to pay an early call, I suppose.'

The Australian was standing by the door talking to his fiancée, and after a glance in their direction, McIver turned back to Ronald.

'Well, Mr Standish, go on. Both those facts have a direct bearing on – what?'

But Ronald Standish made no reply. He was staring fixedly at Mansford, who was slowly coming towards us talking to Molly Tremayne. And as he came closer, it struck me that there was something peculiar about his face. There was a dark stain all round his mouth, and every now and then he pressed the back of his hand against it as if it hurt.

'Well, Standish,' he said with a laugh, as he came

up, 'here's a fresh development for your ingenuity. Of course,' he added, 'it can't really have anything to do with it, but it's damned painful. Look at my mouth.'

'I've been looking at it,' answered Ronald. 'How did it happen?'

'I don't know. All I can tell you is that about an hour ago it began to sting like blazes and turn dark red.'

And now that he had come closer, I could see that there was a regular ring all round his mouth, stretching up almost to his nostrils and down to the cleft in his chin. It was dark and angry looking, and was evidently paining him considerably.

'I feel as if I'd been stung by a family of hornets,' he remarked. 'You didn't leave any infernal chemical in the telephone, did you, Inspector McIver?'

'I did not,' answered the detective stiffly, to pause in amazement as Standish uttered a shout of triumph.

'I've got it!' he cried. 'The third point – the third elusive point. Did you go to sleep this morning as I suggested, Mansford?'

'No, I didn't,' said the Australian, looking thoroughly mystified. 'I sat up on the bed puzzling over that darned fan for about an hour, and then I decided to shave. Well, the water in the tap wasn't hot, so – '

'You blew down the speaking-tube to tell someone to bring you some,' interrupted Standish quietly.

'I did,' answered Mansford. 'But how the devil did you know?'

'Because one of the objects of a speaking-tube, my dear fellow, is to speak through. Extraordinary how that simple point escaped me. It only shows, McIver, what I have invariably said: the most obvious points are the ones which most easily elude us. Keep your most private papers loose on your writing-table, and your most valuable possessions in an unlocked drawer, and you'll never trouble the burglary branch of your insurance company.'

'Most interesting,' said McIver with ponderous sarcasm. 'Are we to understand, Mr Standish, that you have solved the problem?'

'Why, certainly,' answered Ronald, and Mansford gave a sharp cry of amazement. 'Oil reduces friction, an electric fan produces a draught, and a speaking-tube is a tube to speak through secondarily; primarily, it is just – a tube. For your further thought, McIver, I would suggest to you that Mrs Bretherton's digestion was much better than is popularly supposed, and that a brief perusal of some chemical work, bearing in mind Mr Mansford's remarks that he felt as if he'd been stung by a family of hornets, would clear the air.'

'Suppose you cease jesting, Standish,' said Mansford a little brusquely. 'What exactly do you mean by all this?'

'I mean that we are up against a particularly clever and ingenious murderer,' answered Standish gravely. 'Who he is – I don't know; why he's done it – I don't know; but one thing I do know – he is a very dangerous criminal. And we want to catch him in the act. Therefore, I shall go away today; McIver will go away today; and you, Mansford, will sleep in that room again tonight. And this time, instead of you joining us on the lawn – we shall all join you in the room. Do you follow me?'

'I follow you,' said Mansford excitedly. 'And we'll catch him in the act.'

'Perhaps,' said Standish quietly. 'And perhaps we

may have to wait a week or so. But we'll catch him, provided no one says a word of this conversation.'

'But look here, Mr Standish,' said McIver peevishly, 'I'm not going away today. I don't understand all this rigmarole of yours, and . . . '

'My very good Mac,' laughed Standish, 'you trot away and buy a ticket to London. Then get out at the first stop and return here after dark. And I'll give you another point to chew the cud over. Mrs Bretherton was an elderly and timorous lady, and elderly and timorous ladies, I am told, put their heads under the bedclothes if they are frightened. Mr Mansford's father and brother were strong virile men, who do not hide their heads under such circumstances. They died, and Mrs Bretherton lived. Think it over – and bring a gun tonight.'

For the rest of the day we saw no sign of Ronald Standish. He had driven off in the Tremaynes' car to the station, and had taken McIver with him. And there we understood from the chauffeur they had both taken tickets to London and left the place. Following Ronald's instructions, Mansford had gone back to Staveley Grange, and announced the fact of their departure, at the same time stating his unalterable intention to continue occupying the fatal room until he had solved the mystery. Then he returned to the Old Hall, where Molly, he and I spent the day, racking our brains in futile endeavours to get to the bottom of it.

'What beats me,' said Mansford, after we had discussed every conceivable and inconceivable possibility, 'is that Standish can't know any more than we do.

We've both seen exactly what he's seen; we both know the facts just as well as he does. We're neither of us fools, and yet he can see the solution – and we can't.'

'It's just there that he is so wonderful,' I answered thoughtfully. 'He uses his imagination to connect what are apparently completely disconnected facts. And you may take it from me, Mansford, that he's very rarely wrong.'

The Australian pulled at his pipe in silence.

'I think we'll find out everything tonight,' he said at length. 'Somehow or other I've got great faith in that pal of yours. But what is rousing my curiosity almost more than how my father and poor old Tom were murdered is who did it? Everything points to it being someone in the house – but in heaven's name, who? I'd stake my life on the two footmen – one of them came over with us from Australia. Then there's that poor old boob Templeton – who wouldn't hurt a fly – and his wife, and the other women servants, who, incidentally, are all new since Tom died. It beats me – beats me utterly.'

For hours we continued the unending discussion, while the afternoon dragged slowly on. At six o'clock Mansford rose to go: his orders were to dine at home. He smiled reassuringly at Molly, who clung to him nervously; then with a cheerful wave of his hand he vanished down the drive. My orders were equally concise: to dine at the Old Hall, wait there until it was dark, and then make my way to the place where Standish and I had hidden the previous night.

It was not till ten that I deemed it safe to go; then slipping a small revolver into my pocket, I left the house by a side door and started on my three-mile walk.

As before, there was no moon, and in the shadow of the undergrowth I almost trod on Ronald before I saw him.

'That you, Tony?' came his whisper, and I lay down at his side. I could dimly see McIver a few feet away. Then once again began the vigil. It must have been about half-past eleven that the lights were switched on in the room, and Mansford started to go to bed. Once he came to the window, and leaned out, seeming to stare in our direction; then he went back inside, and we could see his shadow as he moved about. And I wondered if he was feeling nervous.

At last the light went out, and almost at once Standish rose. 'There's no time to lose,' he muttered. 'Follow me – and not a sound.'

Swiftly we crossed the lawn and clambered up the old buttressed wall to the room above. I heard Ronald's whispered greeting to Mansford, who was standing by the window in his pyjamas, and then McIver joined us, blowing slightly. Climbing walls was not a common form of exercise as far as he was concerned.

'Don't forget,' whispered Standish again, 'not a sound, not a whisper. Sit down and wait.'

He crossed to the table by the bed – the table on which stood the motionless electric fan. Then he switched on a small electric torch, and we watched him eagerly as he took up the speaking-tube. From his pocket he extracted what appeared to be a hollow tube some three inches long, with a piece of material attached to one end. This material he tied carefully round the end of the speaking-tube, thereby forming a connection between the speaking-tube and the short metal tube he had removed from his pocket. And finally he placed a cork very lightly in position at the other end of the metal cylinder. Then he switched off his torch and sat down on the bed. Evidently his preparations were complete; there was nothing to do now but wait.

The ticking of the clock on the mantelpiece sounded incredibly loud in the utter silence of the house. One o'clock had struck – then half-past – when suddenly there came a faint pop from near the bed which made me jump violently. I heard Ronald draw in his breath sharply and craned forward to see what was happening. There came a gentle rasping noise, as Standish lit his petrol cigarette lighter. It gave little more light than a flickering glimmer, but it was just enough for me to see what he was doing. He was holding the flame to the end of the hollow tube, in which there was no longer a cork. The little pop had been caused by the cork blowing out. And then to my amazement a blue flame sprang from the end of the tube and burnt steadily. It burnt with a slight hiss, like a bunsen burner in a laboratory – and it gave about the same amount of light. One could just see Ronald's face looking white and ghostly; then he pulled the bed curtain round the table, and the room was in darkness once again.

McIver was sitting next to me and I could hear his hurried breathing over the faint hiss of the hidden flame. And so we sat for perhaps ten minutes, until a board creaked in the room above us.

'It's coming now,' came in a quick whisper from Ronald. 'Whatever I do – don't speak, don't make a sound.'

I make no bones about it – my heart was going in

great sickening thumps. I've been in many tight corners in the course of my life, but this silent room had got my nerves stretched to the limit. And I don't believe McIver was any better. I know I bore the marks of his fingers on my arm for a week after.

'My God! look,' I heard him breathe, and at that moment I saw it. Up above the window on the right had appeared a faint luminous light, in the centre of which was a hand. It wasn't an ordinary hand – it was a skinny, claw-like talon, which glowed and shone in the darkness. And even as we watched it, it began to float downwards towards the bed. Steadily and quietly it seemed to drift through the room – but always towards the bed. At length it stopped, hanging directly over the foot of the bed and about three feet above it.

The sweat was pouring off my face in streams, and I could see young Mansford's face in the faint glow of that ghastly hand, rigid and motionless with horror. Now for the first time he knew how his father and brother had died – or he would know soon. What was this dismembered talon going to do next? Would it float forward to grip him by the throat – or would it disappear as mysteriously as it had come?

I tried to picture the dreadful terror of waking up suddenly and seeing this thing in front of one in the darkened room; and then I saw that Ronald was about to do something. He was kneeling on the bed examining the apparition in the most matter-of-fact way, and suddenly he put a finger to his lips and looked at us warningly. Then quite deliberately he hit at it with his fist, gave a hoarse cry and rolled off the bed with a heavy thud.

He was on his feet in an instant, again signing to us imperatively to be silent, and we watched the thing swinging backwards and forwards as if it was on a string. And now it was receding – back towards the window and upwards just as it had come, while the oscillations grew less and less, until at last it had vanished completely and the room once more was in darkness save for the faint blue flame which still burnt steadily at the end of the tube.

'My God!' muttered McIver next to me, as he mopped his brow with a handkerchief, only to be again imperatively silenced by a gesture from Standish. The board creaked in the room above us, and I fancied that I heard a door close very gently; then all was still once more.

Suddenly with disconcerting abruptness the blue flame went out, almost as if it had been a gas jet turned off. And simultaneously a faint whirring noise and a slight draught on my face showed that the electric fan had been switched on. Then we heard Ronald's voice giving orders in a low tone. He had switched on his torch, and his eyes were shining with excitement.

'With luck we'll get the last act soon,' he muttered. 'Mansford, lie on the floor, as if you'd fallen off the bed. Sprawl; sham dead and don't move. We three will be behind the curtain in the window. Have you got handcuffs, Mac?' he whispered as we went to our hiding place. 'Get 'em on as soon as possible, because I'm inclined to think that our bird will be dangerous.'

McIver grunted, and once again we started to wait for the unknown. The electric fan still whirred, and looking through the window I saw the first faint streaks of dawn. And then suddenly Standish gripped my arm; the handle of the door was being turned. Slowly it opened, and someone came in shutting it cautiously behind him. He came round the bed, and paused as he got to the foot. He was crouching – bent almost double – and for a long while he remained motionless. And then he began to laugh, and the laugh was horrible to hear. It was low and exulting – but it had a note in it which told its own story. The man who crouched at the foot of the bed was a maniac.

'On him,' snapped Ronald, and we sprang forward simultaneously. The man snarled and fought like a tiger – but madman though he was he was no match for the four of us. Mansford had sprung to his feet the instant the fight started, and in a few seconds we heard the click of McIver's handcuffs. It was Standish who went to the door and switched on the light, so that we could see who it was. And the face of the handcuffed man, distorted and maniacal in its fury, was the face of the butler Templeton.

'Pass the handcuffs round the foot of the bed, McIver,' ordered Standish, 'and we'll leave him here. We've got to explore upstairs now.'

McIver slipped off one wristlet, passed it round the upright of the bed and snapped it closed again. Then the four of us dashed upstairs.

'We want the room to which the speaking-tube communicates,' cried Standish, and Mansford led the way. He flung open a door, and then with a cry of horror stopped dead in the doorway.

Confronting us was a wild-eyed woman, clad only in her nightdress. She was standing beside a huge glass retort, which bubbled and hissed on a stand in the centre of the room. And even as we stood there she snatched up the retort with a harsh cry, and held it above her head.

'Back,' roared Standish, 'back for your lives.'

But it was not necessary. Somehow or other the retort dropped from her hands and smashed to pieces on her own head. And a scream of such mortal agony rang out as I have never heard and hope never to hear again. Nothing could be done for her; she died in five minutes, and of the manner of the poor demented thing's death it were better not to write. For a large amount of the contents of the retort was hot sulphuric acid.

'Well, Mansford,' said Standish a few hours later, 'your ghost is laid, your mystery is solved, and I think I'll be able to play in the last match of that tour after all.'

We were seated in the Old Hall dining-room after an early breakfast and Mansford turned to him eagerly. 'I'm still in the dark,' he said. 'Can't you explain?'

Standish smiled. 'Don't see it yet? Well – it's very simple. As you know, the first thing that struck my eye was that right-hand canopy wire. It didn't shine in the sun like the other one, and when I got up to examine it, I found it was coated with dried oil. Not one little bit of it – but the whole wire. Now that was very strange – very strange indeed. Why should that wire have been coated with oil – and not the other? I may say at once that I had dismissed any idea of psychic phenomena being responsible for your father's and brother's deaths. That such things exist we know – but they don't *kill* two strong men.

'However, I was still in the dark; in fact, there was only one ray of light. The coating of that wire with oil was *so* strange, that of itself it established with practical certainty the fact that a human agency was at work. And before I left the room that first afternoon I was certain that that wire was used to introduce something into the room from outside. The proof came the next morning. Overnight the wire had been dry; the following morning there was wet oil on it. The door was intact; no one had gone in by the window; and, further, the fan was going. Fact number two. Still, I couldn't get the connection. I admit that the fact that the fan was going suggested some form of gas – introduced by the murderer, and then removed by him automatically. And then you came along with your mouth blistered. You spoke of feeling as if you'd been stung by a hornet, and I'd got my third fact. To get it presupposed a certain knowledge of chemistry. Formic acid – which is what a wasp's sting consists of – can be used among other things for the manufacture of carbon monoxide. And with that the whole diabolical plot was clear. The speaking-tube was the missing link through which carbon monoxide was poured into the room, bringing with it traces of the original ingredients which condensed on the mouthpiece. Now, as you may know, carbon monoxide is lighter than air, and is a deadly poison to breathe. Moreover, it leaves no trace – certainly no obvious trace. So before we went into the room last night, I had decided in my own mind how the murders had taken place. First, from right under the sleeper's nose a stream of carbon monoxide was discharged which I rendered harmless by igniting. The canopy helped to keep it more or less confined, but since it was lighter than air, something was necessary to make the sleeper awake and sit up. That is precisely what your father and brother did when they saw the phosphorescent hand – and they died at once. Mrs Bretherton hid her face and lived. Then the fan was turned on – the carbon monoxide was gradually expelled from the room, and in the morning no trace remained. If it failed one night it could be tried again the next until it succeeded. Sooner or later that infernal hand travelling on a little pulley wheel on the wire and controlled from above by a long string, would wake the sleeper – and then the end – or the story of a ghost.'

He paused and pressed out his cigarette.

'From the very first also I had suspected Templeton. When you know as much of crime as I do – you're never surprised at anything. I admit he seemed the last man in the world who would do such a thing – but there are more cases of Jekyll and Hyde than we even dream of. And he and his wife were the only connecting links in the household staff between you and the Brethertons. That Mrs Templeton also was mad had not occurred to me, and how much she was his assistant or his dupe we shall never know. She has paid a dreadful price, poor soul, for her share of it; the mixture that broke over her was hot concentrated sulphuric acid mixed with formic acid. Incidentally, from enquiries made yesterday, I discovered that Staveley Grange belonged to a man named Templeton some forty years ago. This man had an illegitimate son, whom he did not provide for – and it may be that Templeton the butler is that son – gone mad. Obsessed with the idea that Staveley Grange should be his perhaps – who knows? No man can read a madman's mind.'

He lit another cigarette and rose.

'So I can't tell you why. How you know; and who;

why must remain a mystery for ever. And now I think I can just catch my train.'

'Yes, but wait a moment,' cried Mansford. 'There are scores of other points I'm not clear on.'

'Think 'em out for yourself, my dear fellow,' laughed Ronald. 'I want to make a few runs tomorrow.'

ERNEST BRAMAH

The Curious Circumstances
of the Two Left Shoes

At the time when the Enderleighs lost their silver the
Monkey Burglar was at the height of his fame. The
Monkey Burglar, should you by this date have forgotten, was the one who invariably gained access by
leaping from a tree on to an upper-storey window-sill.
So strong was habit that there were said to be cases of
the Monkey Burglar going through this performance
at houses where the front door stood open, or where a
builder's ladder, left in position overnight, was reared
against the very point he gained by the more
sensational flight. During the thick of the burglary
season that year each number of *Punch* regularly
contained one or more jokes about the Monkey; no
pantomime was complete without a few references to
him; and the burgled invariably tried to claim distinction as authentic victims. In this, the press, to do
it justice, worthily seconded their endeavours.

The Enderleighs lived near Silver Park at that time,
in one of the old-fashioned cottages that have long
delightful gardens running down to the river's edge.
They were a young couple, setting themselves a very
moderate standard until the day when Enderleigh's
wonderful qualities should be suitably recognised by
a partnership. In the meanwhile he was something
exceptionally responsible but not so exceptionally
rewarded in connection with a firm of estate agents

and surveyors. Max Carrados had heard of him
favourably from one or two friends and was not
unwilling to put business in the young man's way.
An opportunity came when the blind criminologist
had, as trustee, to deal with an estate down in
Warwickshire. He ascertained that Enderleigh was
not debarred from doing work on his own account,
and gave him a commission to inspect the property
and make a general report. Business being slack,
there was no difficulty in arranging a few days' leave
of absence from the office, and the proposal was
gratefully accepted.

On his return – he had conscientiously managed to
cover the ground within two days – Enderleigh looked
in at The Turrets before proceeding home and found
Mr Carrados at leisure.

'I thought that I would leave the report with you
now,' he explained, 'in case you cared to glance over
it and ask me about any details while it's all fresh in
my mind. I wrote up my notes in the train on the way
back.'

'Good man,' smiled Carrados, accepting the docket.
'I should have liked you to stay while we discussed the
matter, but I am afraid that someone else has a prior
lien on your time.'

'In what way?'

'A few hours ago Mrs Enderleigh rang me up on
the phone, and there is what I might describe as a
standing order for you to communicate with her from
here at the earliest moment.'

'Good heavens!' exclaimed Enderleigh in some
trepidation. 'What's up, I wonder? Nothing wrong
that you know of?'

'Nothing at all,' replied Carrados with reassuring

unconcern. 'Your wife was in exceptional spirits, I gathered, but somewhat cryptical. However, there is the means of setting your mind at rest,' and he indicated the instrument. 'I'll leave you to it.'

'Please don't go.' Enderleigh seemed to be toying with the moment as if rather unwilling to set his mind at rest. 'I was startled for a second, but if my wife herself spoke to you there can't be anything much the matter. The fact is,' he confided with a certain shy complacency, 'she has been getting rather fanciful of late – not an unusual phase of the situation, I understand.'

Mr Carrados murmured his discreet congratulations, and his visitor summed up enough indifference to make the call.

'Holy Moses!' the blind man heard him mutter, and there followed a rapid fusillade of 'How?' and 'When?' and 'What?' and 'You don't mean it!' all indicating consternation and surprise, as long as the colloquy lasted.

'Here's a pretty go,' announced Mr Enderleigh, hanging up the receiver. 'We've been burgled!'

'The deuce!' exclaimed Carrados sympathetically. 'I hope your wife isn't much upset?'

'No, I don't think so. In fact, she seems rather set up, because some of our neighbours were robbed in a very commonplace way lately, and she's determined that this must have been the authentic Monkey.'

'Much taken?'

'Apparently the silver chest and nothing else. Myra rather fancied that I would call here on my way from something I had said – that's why she rang you up – and she wants me to go straight on. I hope you don't mind?'

'Of course not. I had hoped that you would keep me company for an hour or two, but that's out of the question now . . . I'll tell you what, though: I will make a bargain with you. Stay another fifteen minutes, in which we can have a snack of some kind in place of dinner. In the meanwhile I will have a car got out that will land you at your place quicker than any other way you could go; and in return you shall invite me to inspect the depredation.'

'That's certainly a bargain from my side of the transaction,' replied Enderleigh. 'If it isn't putting you out, I'll accept like a shot.'

'Not a bit,' declared his host with more than polite formality. He moved across to the house telephone and quickly distributed the necessary orders. 'I love anything that comes suddenly along. It may be the beginning of who knows what adventure.'

'Well, as to that, of course there are two sides,' said the domesticated Enderleigh. 'This is quite sudden enough for me and I certainly don't love it.'

Carrados was as good as his literal word, and fifteen minutes after he had spoken the lean form of his speedy Redshank car glided down the drive into the high road and then stretched out for Silver Park.

'Now that it's come to this, I may as well tell you about our silver,' explained Mr Enderleigh to his companion, on a confidential impulse. 'We happen to have rather a lot – more than people in our modest way generally sport, I mean. Myra's father was a fruit-grower and won a lot of cups and plates in his time. I used to be something of a runner and I amassed a few more, and when we got married our friends showered cruets and cake baskets down on us galore. The consequence is that there was a solid half-hundredweight of the metal reposing in a specially made case in the dining-room at Homecroft. Of course it ought to have been kept at the bank, and at first it was, but Myra liked to see an assortment out on the sideboard, so that it got to be a nuisance sending it backwards and forwards. Then I said that if we had it in the house it ought to be kept up in the bedroom for safety, and Myra found that she couldn't even lift the chest and decided that it would be too inconvenient to have it there. What with one thing and another, the confounded silver got to become a bit of a sore point between us – it brought on the first unpleasantness we had. Then, as bad luck would have it, just when I was leaving the other morning to go on this job we must needs get arguing about it again. I suggested that as there would be only two women alone in the house – herself and the servant – it would be safer if I carried the box up and hid it under the bed. Myra – God know why – retorted that if the silver was the danger-point it wasn't very kind to want to put it just under where she would be. One silly word led to another until I finally went off saying that I wished the damned stuff was at the bottom of the river.'

'You seem to have got the next thing to what you asked for then,' remarked Carrados. 'The silver apparently won't trouble you again.' But Enderleigh demurred at this cheerful summary and shook his head.

'Oh, yes,' he replied, 'but when you wish a thing like that you don't really mean that you want it to happen.'

'You are insured, I suppose?'

'Only partly, I'm afraid, because the value of the silver now exceeds the percentage allowed. And of course a lot of the things have associations, although there is nothing of antique value. I'm really wondering how Myra will take it when the excitement wears off.'

But so far the excitement was on, and she welcomed them radiantly, albeit a shade mystified that Mr Carrados should have chosen that moment to pay his call. It does not say much for the criminal expert's sense of publicity that neither his host nor hostess had the faintest idea of his uncanny reputation. To them he was simply the rich blind man who seemed as though he might be useful to Guy.

'But isn't it a shame, Mr Carrados?' she cooed, when the first round of wonder and exclamation had been gone through. 'Sergeant Lapworth declares that it can't possibly be the Monkey Burglar. And I was so relying on that to squelch the Higgses with.'

Carrados divined an exchange of private glances, expostulatory from the husband, playfully defiant on her part.

'I have met Sergeant Lapworth once or twice and he seemed to know his work,' said the visitor. 'Did he say why it couldn't be?'

'Well, the only way they could have got in was by the side door. No fastenings have been forced or windows opened. And the Monkey wouldn't ever dream of using a side door.'

'But how on earth could they do that?' demanded Enderleigh. 'I mean without using force. Chloe fastens the door at night, doesn't she?'

'I'll show you if you don't mind accompanying me to the nether regions,' said the light-hearted girl. 'Chloe only locks the door it seems – the bolts are too stiff to work – and Sergeant Lapworth says that these people – he's almost sure he knows the gang –

have all manner of ingenious tools. There's a sort of pincers that you catch hold of a key with from the other side and turn it quite easily. You can see that the lock has been oiled to make it go.'

'You found the door unlocked this morning?'

'No – I don't know. I never thought of that. But I suppose they could just as easily lock it again to cover their tracks, and as it happened it was not until this afternoon that I missed the silver chest. Then there are footprints on the flower bed from the gate to the side door. He found those as well. It's most wildly exciting discovering clues; I've been looking for some all the afternoon, but so far without success.'

'Come on then,' suggested Enderleigh. 'You have a lamp or candle, I suppose?'

'Yes. Do you care to see our private morgue, Mr Carrados – oh, I am sorry: I forgot!'

'That's very nice of you – to forget,' smiled the blind man. 'It shows that I'm not so helpless after all. Certainly I should like to come; I'm as keen on clues as you are.'

The side door was the chief point of interest. It opened on to the garden from the scullery. The scullery – a dank and forbidding chamber that almost justified its epithet – in turn led into the kitchen, and the kitchen into the hall. But there were other ways of getting about, for it was an old house with many passages and on various levels. Most of the rooms appeared to have at least two doors. 'I think that the man who built it must have been fond of French farces,' remarked Mr Enderleigh, pointing out this feature.

But even at the side door there was very little to see, the Enderleigh burglary being chiefly remarkable for its negative features. There was the oiled lock, and the key bore certain recent scratches, and that was all.

'If the bolts had been shot this would never have happened,' said the master of the house. 'Perhaps in future – '

'But the bolts can't be stirred, dear,' protested Myra. 'I've tried myself until my poor thumbs are nearly dislocated. And everyone says that if burglars want to get in they will, even if they have to come down the chimney.'

'I think the bolts might move if they were simply oiled,' suggested Carrados. 'The level is all right, you see.'

'Chloe,' called out Mr Enderleigh – the kitchen door stood open – 'is there any oil about?'

A young girl in cap and apron – a girl of quite unusual prettiness – appeared at the door.

'Oil, sir?' she repeated faintly, and she continued to look from one to another of them as though something was amiss.

'Yes, oil – ordinary oil – the sort you oil with, you know. There must be some about somewhere.'

'Oh, yes – for the sewing machine,' she replied, and disappeared to return with it in a moment.

'Now a feather.'

The girl's eyes shot to a bucket holding kitchen refuse that stood beneath the sink; then rose to the level again as she continued to stand there.

'Feathers: in the middle dresser drawer, Chloe,' prompted her mistress tartly. 'Bless me,' she confided to the others, 'the girl's going dotty, I believe. Over-excitement isn't good for our poor sex.'

'Now we want a chair or something for the top bolt,' said Enderleigh.

'I think I can do it without, if you will allow me,' put in Carrados. 'I fancy that I am just a few inches to the good in that respect.'

'But really, Mr Carrados,' protested the lady, 'won't you get it on your clothes – or something?'

'That is only a matter of carelessness, not vision,' replied Carrados. He gave the feather a dexterous turn in the neck of the bottle to remove the excess of oil before he withdrew it. 'Children have the keenest sight, Mrs Enderleigh, and yet look how they drop the jam about!'

'It's quite marvellous,' she murmured, watching him apply the oil and then work the action until the bolt slid easily.

'Not so much as you might think,' he assured her. 'Frequently you are indebted to other senses when you think you are using your eyes, and they get all the credit. Several men have told me that they always close their eyes when they are doing certain delicate adjustments.'

'I once knew a lady who always shut her eyes before she fired a gun off,' contributed Enderleigh. 'Yet she was fond of shooting, and often hit things.'

'Dogs or keepers?' enquired Myra politely.

Certainly the burglary did not seem to have damped anyone's spirits. Presently they went out to look at the incriminating footprints – 'viewing the body', Myra called it – by candlelight, until they were tired of striking matches and the friendly darkness put Carrados at liberty to go down on hands and knees and touch the well-marked impressions with his eerily perceptive fingers in his own peculiar way.

'What's this – snowing?' Enderleigh had exclaimed as he opened the door to lead the way into the garden.

A sprinkling of white showed on the bare earth before them.

'Goose!' retorted Myra fondly, 'it's lime, of course. Old Benjamin – he's a sort of local unhandyman, Mr Carrados, whom Guy employs one day a week to sit in the garden and smoke shag – put it on only yesterday. He said the soil was too "thodden" for bulbs: it's always too something for Ben.'

'It came in useful, all the same,' said her husband. 'You see, the lime being crushed down in the footprints shows that they were made after it was put there. That's important.'

'Lapworth the Sleuth had already diagnosed that, O Fountain of Wisdom,' mocked his wife. She leaned forward and struck him lightly on the arm. 'You're it! Race you to the river, Guy!'

'Ssh!' warned Enderleigh with a nod towards their guest.

'Go, children – run,' urged Carrados benignly. 'I will follow at a pace more suited to my years.'

'Hold up!' cried Myra, limping into a walk before they were fairly off. 'I forgot; my feet are as soft as mush today. Besides, I oughtn't to now.'

'No, of course you oughtn't to,' said Guy severely. 'And we oughtn't to leave Mr Carrados like that. God knows what sort of a lunatic asylum he'll think he's dropped on.'

'Never mind: I got you away. Just one, Guy. And don't worry about him. He said his ears, but he meant his eyes, of course: his ears are sharp enough. That old man wouldn't take any harm if you put him down in the middle of a sawmill.'

'Old!' exclaimed Mr Enderleigh indignantly. 'Great Scott! What next?'

They walked back to meet the advancing Carrados, and then they all strolled soberly down to the extremity of the garden and stood contemplating the slow, muddy river before they turned back again.

'You take Mr Carrados into the dining-room, Guy,' said Myra, hastening on ahead as they neared the house. 'I'm going up to change my shoes – these are soaked.'

'Yes, my lady, you are pretty high up already, I'm afraid,' apostrophised her husband as they followed. 'That's the way of it, Mr Carrados. I shall think myself lucky if she isn't down below zero before the night is out.'

'I've taken hot water up to the spare room, sir,' said Chloe, as they passed her in the hall.

They washed their hands leisurely and went down to the dining-room. The maid had lit the lamp and was replenishing the fire. Still Mrs Enderleigh did not appear. A few minutes passed rather flatly. Enderleigh made a half-hearted show of asking his guest if he was fond of this and that, but Carrados divined his vague uneasiness and soon they both frankly waited.

'Guy,' said a queer little voice just outside the door which had been left slightly ajar – 'do you mind coming here a minute.'

Enderleigh threw a quick, enquiring look across, and the blind man – informed by what sense, who shall say? – nodded mute assent. Then the door closed and Carrados slowly turned his face to the four points of the room.

It was perhaps five minutes later that Enderleigh returned. He came thoughtfully across the room and stood close to his guest's chair.

'It's just as I was afraid,' he said, pitching his voice

cautiously. 'Myra is now at a very minus stage indeed. And a curious thing – curious and trivial, and yet, I must admit, extraordinary – has happened to upset her. It's mixed up with one or two other matters, and I suppose that this burglary also – although that has nothing to do with it – has helped to put the emotional screw on. If you care to hear I will tell you with pleasure, especially as you have seen how bright she was a few minutes ago, but I don't want to bore you.'

'Go on,' said Carrados. 'Curious and trivial things that are extraordinary have never bored me yet.'

'Well, you shall judge. I indicated, over at your place, that we are expecting our little household to be increased in the course of a few months. Not unnaturally, Myra has to pass through a variety of new emotions on the subject, and she also has an unfortunate misgiving. It happened that her father was born club-footed and his father was disfigured in the same way. Of course, we tell her that it's all nonsense, but there is undeniably an element of heredity in that sort of thing, and she knows it well enough. Just now she is doubly prone to take notice of any kind of suggestion or premonition that may come along, especially on that one unlucky possibility. You heard her say that she was going up to change her shoes? Well, this is what has happened: she went upstairs, kicked off her wet shoes, and proceeded to pull on another pair. They are shoes that she has worn quite comfortably at intervals for the past few weeks, but now one – the right foot – would not go on. Thinking nothing of it, she picked up a shoe-lift and tried again. Still it refused to accommodate, and then she went to the light and looked more closely . . . It wasn't likely to fit, Carrados, for the extraordinary

thing is that those shoes, which she has worn quite
easily and naturally a dozen times in the last few
weeks, are both for the left foot!'

There was a rattle of cups and glasses as the
attractive maid nearly dropped the tray she was
bringing in. Enderleigh looked sharply round, but
the girl kept her face averted and quickly went out
again.

'There's another who's certainly got the jumps,'
said her master. 'But about those shoes. Of course it's
ridiculous, but you see the inference? In each fore-
running case it was the right foot that was wrong, and
so poor Myra is miraculously endowed with two left
shoes at this moment as a sort of admonition than an
ordinary right will not be needed . . . But you don't
see anything in it, I expect?'

'On the contrary,' replied Carrados slowly, 'I see so
much in it – so many thousand possibilities, all wrong
but one – that I should like to go up into a very large,
perfectly bare attic, lit by several twenty-thousand-
candle-power arc-lamps, and there meditate.'

'And the nearest thing I can offer you,' said Enderleigh, 'is the coal cellar. It's roomy as such places go
and certainly practically empty now. For the rest – '
He found the pleasantry difficult to sustain.

'So,' continued the blind man seriously, 'we must
still proceed on directly material lines. I should very
much like to handle the pair of shoes that has caused
the trouble. Do you think Mrs Enderleigh would
allow me?'

'Why not?' assented the lady's husband. 'I'll go and
get them.'

He went, and returned almost immediately – but
empty-handed.

'She's coming down now. Much better,' he whispered in the voice of a conspirator. 'Bringing them.' And almost at his heels a sobered Myra reappeared.

'I'm a hopeless little rabbit, Mr Carrados,' she apologised. 'Please don't say anything nice about it, because I am.'

'Rabbit!' ejaculated her natural protector loyally; 'rabbit! Why, Mr Carrados, that – that sylph has the heart of a – a – well, I'm not strong on the faunas, but of whatever is the antithesis of rabbit.'

'That would be a ferret, wouldn't it?' asked Myra in her funny way. 'What a sad flatterer you are, Guy!'

'Go on,' said Guy happily. 'So long as you can laugh –'

She waved a reassuring hand to him across the room as she addressed their guest again.

'Of course, I know that he has told you all about it, Mr Carrados,' she said. 'Because when I taxed him he began by saying, "I only just – " Here is the mystery.'

It was a pair of pretty bronze shoes, neat yet not fragile, that she put into the blind man's hands. He held them one by one, and as his long, delicately formed fingers brushed across their surface the two watchers received a curious impression of seeing something read.

'I shouldn't mind – I shouldn't mind the shoes a particle,' declared Myra – she felt compelled to speak to break the almost hypnotic quest of those under-standing hands – 'though, of course, they're no earthly use. But for weeks I've been wearing them all right, and now I know perfectly well that I couldn't. There's something wrong with me somewhere, don't you see?'

'But, dearest,' pleaded Guy soothingly, 'there's some perfectly simple explanation if only we could see it. Why, only just now you said that your feet were tender. That's probably it. You've got them sore, and so you can't put on the shoe. If they were all right you'd jump into them and not notice that anything was the matter, just as you have been doing up to now.'

'Don't talk tommy, Guy!' she exclaimed half wrathfully. 'As if I could possibly put on two left shoes without knowing it, even if I could get them on. And yet,' she wailed, 'I *have* been putting them on – that's the horrible thing about it.'

Carrados had apparently finished his scrutiny, for he was listening to this exchange with his usual benign complacency, and as he listened he absently rubbed his nose gently with the polished toe of one shoe.

'Set your mind at rest, Mrs Enderleigh,' he remarked quietly, as he offered her the other one. 'There is nothing wrong. You have never worn that shoe.'

'I have never worn it?'

'Neither you nor anybody else. The shoe has not been worn.'

'But look at the wear,' she persisted, displaying the scarified sole. 'Look at this worn lace.'

'The lace, yes,' he admitted, with unshaken confidence. 'But not the shoe.'

'But how can you possibly know that?'

'In exactly the same way that I could oil the bolt – by using other powers than that of sight.'

'Do you mean – ' began Enderleigh, but Carrados interrupted him with uplifted hand.

'If I may suggest, please don't say anything more

about the shoes just yet. At this moment Sergeant Lapworth has come to the door and your servant is admitting him. Let us hear what he has to say.'

Myra and Guy exchanged looks of bewilderment – almost of alarm – and then the girl's face cleared.

'Yes,' she exclaimed, 'I had forgotten to tell you. He did say that he would look in again after you got back, Guy.'

'If you please, m'm,' said Chloe at the door, 'there's the detective here again, and he would like to see the master if it's convenient.'

'Quite right,' replied Myra. 'Show him in here.'

Sergeant Lapworth was a plain-clothes man of the local staff. If he had a fault it was that of giving the impression of knowing more than he would tell, a suggestion that resulted in people sometimes finding him less omniscient in the end than they had expected. The Enderleighs were rather surprised at the sudden respect that came over him when he recognised their blind visitor.

'One or two small matters I thought I'd like to see you about, sir,' he said, addressing Mr Enderleigh. 'Those footprints by the side gate. I understand that no one came along that way between the time your gardener put the lime there yesterday and my seeing them this afternoon?'

'That is quite right,' agreed Myra. 'We allow the milkman to come in at the front gate and go to the side door, to save him carrying his can right round the other way. No one else came; I asked Chloe particularly.'

'You see the point, sir?' continued the sergeant, directing his voice at Mr Carrados this time. 'Whoever left those footprints is the man we want to put our hands on. We should like him to account for his movements last night at all events. Old Ben certainly never made those prints, sir. Now, I wonder,' the sergeant's voice became softly speculative as he leisurely felt in one or two pockets and finally produced a neat paper template of a boot, 'I wonder if this suggests anything to either of you?"

Myra shook her head and passed the paper on to Enderleigh.

'It's a man's boot, I suppose,' she said. 'It is broader than a woman's and the heel is twice as large. But it's much smaller than any of yours, Guy.'

'Lord, yes,' he agreed. 'I'm miles beyond that.'

'Perhaps,' continued Sergeant Lapworth, becoming almost dreamy in his quiet detachment, 'perhaps this might help you more if you should ever have seen the original.' It was a small fancy button that he mysteriously produced this time from the Aladdin's cave among his garments.

Myra's spirits went up. 'What a splendid clue, Mr Lapworth!' she exclaimed. 'Where did you find it?'

'I don't want anything said about it just yet,' he stipulated. 'As a matter of fact I picked it up in your scullery this afternoon.'

'It is a boot button, I suppose?' questioned Enderleigh. 'It strikes me as rather dressy.'

'It is the top of a pearl boot button undoubtedly, I should say,' pronounced the sergeant. 'One of those metal-shanked things that they wire into the boot nowadays. First question is, Does it belong to anyone of the house? I dare say you have plenty of pairs of fancy boots and shoes in use or put by, but it isn't a button that you would readily forget.'

Myra breathlessly agreed that if she had had boot

buttons like that she would never have forgotten it, and added that if Guy had appeared with them she could never have forgiven it – a sotto-voce effort that elicited nothing more than an anxious look from her husband.

'And how about the young person in the kitchen?' suggested Lapworth.

'I know Chloe's boots, and it certainly doesn't come from there,' replied Chloe's mistress. 'However, you had better ask her, to make sure. Shall I ring now?'

'Don't trouble,' he replied, with a quite spontaneous glance towards the decanters on the table, as he returned the precious relic to its hiding-place. 'I can have a word with her as I go out. Now as regards the silver. Your good lady said that you would be able to make me out a list, sir.'

'Of course,' assented Enderleigh; 'that's got to be done, hasn't it? And then there'll be the insurance people. And then a young man introducing himself as "The Press". I'll tell you what, sergeant, this being burgled isn't such a soft thing after all.'

'I don't know, sir. It strikes me that you have come off uncommonly lightly, seeing as how things were. No mess, no breakages, no odds and ends from every room that you can't remember until it's too late to claim. Just one big lot taken clean.'

'It would be about as much as he could take, anyway,' said the owner. 'I shouldn't like to heft that case far.' He casually indicated the group of liquors. 'What shall it be, sergeant?'

'I'll leave that to you, sir,' said the sergeant modestly. 'Yes, it would be a tidy load. I don't know that I ever remember a case being taken before. Reckon they had a car somewhere near.'

'Anyway, nothing was overlooked,' said Myra. 'There were some tankards out on the sideboard here, and three dozen spoons of various sizes in the drawer, and they went too. I put them –'

'You put them what?' prompted her husband, for Myra had stopped as though she had said her say.

'I haven't the faintest notion, dear,' she replied frankly. 'To tell the truth I think I was half asleep. Put what what?'

'Well, I think I'll be getting on along, sir,' said Lapworth, reading in this a pretty obvious hint. 'As soon as we hear from you –'

'Nonsense,' interposed Enderleigh, rather put out at the turn; 'have another first,' and he refilled the not altogether inflexible sergeant's glass.

There was a hesitating knock at the door and Chloe entered with a card.

'Please, m'm,' said the girl – Mrs Enderleigh happened to be seated nearest to her – 'there's a gentleman would like to see the master for a minute.'

' "Wich" – "Mr William Wich",' read Myra. 'Isn't there a Lady Wich a few houses away?'

'Trefusis is the house of Lady Wich, madam,' volunteered Lapworth. 'There is a Mr William, the son.'

'I'd better go out and see what it is,' said Enderleigh. 'Probably only a minute – excuse me, won't you?'

For so short a gap it did not seem worth while discovering a topic of conversation, and so no one broke the minute's silence. If they had spoken their thoughts the exchange would have been something after this fashion: 'I wonder if Lady Wich ever intends to call – city knight's widow, I suppose. Now will Mr

Carrados go when the fat sergeant leaves, or does he expect that we have proper supper?'

'Bit of a card this Mr Willie Wich from what I hear. Old party keeps him in pretty tight by all accounts. Larky; girls. Damn fine stuff this Scotch here. Wonder if it'd be all right, if he does give the nod again, for me to – '

'She must stand five feet five – possibly six. At that, with the tread she has, she will take a 4 to 5. Yes, under any vigorous exercise she might reasonably split a pliant 3. There were certainly two definable personal exudations about the other shoe, and associable with them syringa – that's the girl – and cheiranthus – this one.'

The door opened and Enderleigh entered, then standing aside he waited for someone else.

'Rather curious,' he announced. 'Mr Wich has come to give us some information about our friend last night; so as we are all here – my wife, Mr Wich; Mr Carrados; Sergeant Lapworth.'

'It's really from my mother, you know,' said the dapper youth who followed the host in. 'She's a frightful invalid – heart and all that – so she sent me to tell you. We only just heard of what had happened: beastly shame – '

'We didn't know that you'd be interested,' ventured Myra graciously.

'Eh? Oh, I mean rotten luck being burgled like that. Well, it seems that last night the mater was having a bad turn and she had to get up and sit at the open window to have air. That's how it takes her. It seems that from her bedroom window one can see most of your garden – we live a couple of houses along: Trefusis, you know – and as she sat there she

distinctly saw someone go down your garden towards
the river and disappear among the trees. She says she
wasn't taking much notice of it at the time, because
there was no reason why there should be anything
wrong in that, and it being dark she didn't see a lot,
and she was feeling pretty washed out as well. But
she did notice that it seemed to be a figure carrying
something large and heavy, and when she heard of
this she thought you'd better know.'

'It's most awfully good of Lady Wich to send,'
gushed Myra; 'and of you to come. We are just
celebrating the event with frugal hospitality. Will you
drink the toast "Our Absent Friend" in whisky, port
or coffee, Mr Wich?'

'Eh? Oh, I don't mind. The first for choice, thank
you.'

'The river,' mused Lapworth. 'That's certainly an
idea now; we couldn't find any fresh wheel-tracks
down the side road here. A boat waiting, that makes
sense. What time about would this be, sir?'

'Oh, about half-past twelve, she said.'

'Ah!' The sergeant continued to regard Mr Wich
with an air of distant speculation while at the same
time his hand went mechanically to his mysterious
pocket. 'I suppose you didn't by any chance happen
to be in the neighbourhood yourself at about that
hour, sir?'

The perfect respect of the tone could not wholly
disguise a certain significance in the question, and
Willie Wich looked up to meet the sergeant's eyes
on level terms. Enderleigh also found something
arresting in the sudden tension that seemed to have
involved two of his guests, while Carrados continued
to gaze into unseen space with the faint half-smile of

placid contemplation. Myra alone appeared to have no interest in the passage, and her face was turned away, but her lips were tight pressed to hold back a cry of generous warning and her heart was thudding like an engine beat, for in a flash her eyes had followed Lapworth's and in a flash had seen on her spruce guest's extended foot a boot with identical pearl buttons, of which the upper one was missing.

The gap between the question and the answer was almost as long as it takes to tell of it, for with their eyes meeting Wich paused to consider his reply as though a thought urged caution.

'What do you quite mean by that?' he asked guardedly. 'You know, of course, that I live in the neighbourhood. Do you mean, was I at home?'

'Not exactly, sir,' replied the sergeant. 'You might have been passing this very house on your way home and thought you saw or heard something suspicious here and come nearer to investigate. Or you might have had a dog stray into this garden and come in to call it back, or a dozen things. What I should like to know is, did you come into this house or garden last night for any purpose?'

'I did not,' said Wich, his face relaxing into something like an amused grin. 'What is more, sergeant, I have never before been in this house or garden in the course of my long and industrious life.'

'That's quite definite, sir,' Lapworth admitted. 'In the circumstances, would you mind stating where you were between the hours of eleven last night and two o'clock this morning?'

To those who knew him pretty well young Mr Wich was something of a puzzle, and they complained that you never knew how he would take it

and whether the fellow was quite the fool he sometimes seemed.

' "In the circumstances", sergeant, seems to imply
the existence of certain conditions of which I have no
knowledge,' he now replied. 'Should I ever find myself in the dock of the Old Bailey, charged with the
murder of a constable, or before the Surrey Petty
Sessions accused of appropriating Mr Enderleigh's
ancestral plate, either of those eventualities would
constitute an aggregation of circumstances that would
enforce my acquiescence. At present I fail to see any
reason why I should render an account of my trivial
life and movements.'

Sergeant Lapworth took out an irreproachably
white pocket handkerchief and wiped his face
profusely.

'Very good, sir,' he remarked with dark significance. 'Should you have any objection to my comparing this form' – here the sergeant dramatically
produced his first exhibit – 'with the boots you are
now wearing?'

'Not the least,' replied the buoyant young man,
raising his right foot to facilitate the operation;
'though I must protest against the attention thus
gratuitously directed to my very unprepossessing
footwear. Anything to assist the legitimate ends of
justice. But not,' he added severely, 'of mere vulgar
curiosity.'

Without deigning to reply, Sergeant Lapworth went
down on one knee and from that position fitted the
paper impression against the proffered boot. It was at
once plain to everyone that the two outlines coincided
perfectly. But an even more significant piece of
evidence was to emerge, for as the sergeant performed

this office he slyly inserted a fingernail into the angle of the instep and an appreciable sprinkling of white-peppered soil fell down into his hand.

'I must call your attention, sir, to the fact that this earth from your boot appears to correspond with the soil of the garden here.'

'I say!' exclaimed Mr Wich aghast, 'I am sorry, Mrs Enderleigh – bringing stuff like that into your pretty room!' Then with a bright look of toleration, 'But I expect you know what servants are!'

'Lastly,' said Sergeant Lapworth, with admirable composure in spite of a rather flushed complexion, 'I shall be glad if you will look at this button which corresponds exactly with those on your boot, where one is missing.'

'Thank you,' replied young Mr Wich, passing it back again; it's very good of you to have kept it for me, but it's really no use. It isn't a button you sew on, but one of those metal-shanked affairs and the shank is broken.'

'Then I understand, sir, that you decline to assist us with any information?'

'Oh, no, you don't, sergeant – not if you understand the common or vernacular tongue, that is,' retorted his antagonist. 'So far, what I have declined is to give an account of my movements on the strength of an old button hypothetically lost at some time from my boot and a little piece of paper traced to measure. It may be the law that I have to if anyone shows me those: I must look that up. But you may remember that the only reason for my being here was to bring you information.'

'Oh, yes,' exclaimed Myra, completely won over by the suspect's ready nonchalance, 'we are all sure that

Mr Wich is quite all right, Sergeant Lapworth. Aren't we, Guy?'

'Mrs Enderleigh,' put in Wich, gazing at her with melancholy admiration, 'before I go I must unburden my mind, and I'm afraid you may think very poorly of me in consequence. I did not purloin your silver and I have not the faintest idea who did. Goodbye.'

'Must you really go?' she asked. 'Please be sure and thank Lady Wich from me, won't you? And any Thursday.'

'If you would be so kind as to help a blind man to his car, Mr Wich,' interposed Carrados, and Enderleigh found his own proffered services quietly brushed aside.

'You don't say you are!' exclaimed Wich. 'I never tumbled to it. And that's your little jigger waiting then? I'm looking forward to something on four wheels myself, but so far I have to be content with two.'

'It's hardly worth while offering you a lift,' said Carrados, when they were in the road, 'but if you don't mind I should like to walk with you as far as your gate.'

'Right-o,' said Mr Wich, wondering who this queer customer who had made up to him might be. 'Lovely night, isn't it? What about your car?'

'It will follow presently; my driver understands. I have been trying to think where we have met before. Are you by any chance the Wich who made forty-nine for The Rest against Lord's Schools five years ago?'

'Oh, I say!' exclaimed his companion, becoming quite boyishly shy at the reference to this exploit. 'You don't mean to say that you remember that? Were you at Lord's?'

236

'Yes. I am fond of the minor fixtures; I can hear more play in them than often comes out in first-class matches. We did not speak, but you passed, and I thought I recognised your step again. A Winchester fellow was commenting on the game for me. You were given run out.'

'You must simply be a walking *Wisden*, sir,' said Wich, brimming with admiration. And then with a curious intonation in his voice he added, 'But why "given"?'

'I remember some reference to it . . . Were you out?'

'As a matter of fact I was not,' he admitted.

'I don't think you made any fuss about it – quarrelled with the umpire or groused about the pavilion?'

'Well, should I be likely? . . . It was cricket.'

'Yes . . . And now about this business?'

They had reached the gate of Trefusis, but the young man made no movement towards it, and presently they fell to walking slowly on again.

'That isn't so easy. Not by a long, long way. I was taken by surprise, I must admit; I hadn't a notion that there'd be any trace. Of course it would have been simple enough to tell the sergeant how it came about, if that was all.'

'You mean the lady in the case; or shall we say the girl in the shoes?'

'Partly; and then there is my mother. She would certainly have a heart attack if she found that William had been taking her neighbour's hand-maiden out to midnight carnivals and other forms of penance.'

'Is that quite – cricket?'

'Not absolutely MCC, perhaps, but it isn't to be inferred that I had the inklingest of who she was at

237

first. And Chloe really is an awfully pretty girl, you know. What has she let out?'

'Nothing at all, so far as I am aware.'

'Then how on earth do you come to know of her – and the shoes?'

'Very much, I suppose, in the same way that Sergeant Lapworth has come to know of you and the boot – because the traces are so obvious.'

'I must say I think Chloe was a bit of a mutt to walk on the flower bed and then leave a button somewhere about. She might have learned better than that from the pictures surely.'

'Chloe naturally had not foreseen that the escapade would coincide with a burglary. But I would not be too ready to blame her, my young friend,' advised Carrados dryly. 'The most disastrous blunder of all was made by someone else.'

'That's a straight one,' said Mr Wich. 'What did I do?'

'Suppose you tell me about it?' suggested Mr Carrados. 'Under the seal of confidence.'

'I don't mind. I was going to see a lawyer first thing tomorrow to find out what I'd better do to circumvent the forces of law and order. Perhaps you could advise me?'

'Perhaps I could,' admitted Carrados. 'At all events I will.'

'There really isn't very much to tell,' said young Mr Wich pensively. 'I happened to be on the river alone a few months ago when I noticed a dazzling creature watching my feeble efforts from the bank. To have a nearer look I landed and asked her if she was not, excuse me, Miss Prendergast? She said no, but, how curious, she had been almost sure that I was

THE TWO LEFT SHOES

a certain Mr Johnson. This constituting a deputy introduction on established lines I prevailed upon the bright vision to go for a short cruise and even to accept some slight refreshment of a light and portable nature.

'Under the auspices of the gods the idyll proceeded with exemplary propriety to run its normal course. So far as I was concerned, the chief attraction was the extreme likelihood of detection and the certainty that everyone concerned would impute the very worst motives to my conduct when they did find out.

'On our usual "evening" last week I was indulging the delightful being's passion for a harmless beverage known as Tango Teaser when she espied a handbill announcing a cheap fancy dance at one of the public halls a few miles away and artlessly exclaimed: ' "I should love to go to one of those."

'Of course there was only one humanly possible reply to a heart-cry like that, and I gallantly made it.

' "And I should love to take you. Why not?"

'To this she said that it was absolutely impossible and we fell to making the arrangements. She was to creep out quietly by a side door after the others had gone to bed, lock the door after her and bring the key, and meet me at our usual trysting place – a spot a few hundred yards from our respective abodes. I would be there with my iron steed, and on the pillion thereof would whirl her into fairyland.

'Everything went off as per schedule. The only contretemps was that Chloe – have I mentioned that the heroine was Chloe, by the way? – ripped one of her shoes across and thus passed automatically into the retired list. I confess that I was surprised at the consternation the mishap occasioned the sweet chit,

239

and then she told me. Ashamed at the deficiency of her own pedal outfit, she had surreptitiously "borrowed" a pair belonging to her mistress. Detection would now inevitably follow, disgrace, possibly dismissal. Sighs, tears – heavens! – reproaches. Again I did the insane chivalrous thing and swore to replace the shoe within twelve hours or perish.'

'The rest is obvious. Chloe knew where they had been bought – a shop in Oxford Street – and I was to hie me off at dawn and duplicate them. As there would be the business of counterfeiting the necessary "wear", it would be simpler to concentrate on only one, and this I was to put into a clump of ivy on the garden's side wall. But when it came to parting a difficulty arose: it was essential for me to have the split shoe as a pattern; I could not allow the fair penitent to walk stocking-footed along the stony road; and it wasn't wise to risk being seen together any nearer our houses. The simple way out was for me to lend her one of mine, and this I recovered from the ivy clump when I put in the replacement shoe. And there, Mr Carrados, you have the whole egg in a nutshell.'

'Everything went off all right then?' enquired Carrados maliciously.

'Like a clock. I obtained the exact thing in the exact size, scrubbed it down to the exact appearance of the other and put in the old lace. The superfluous shoe was flung over into an orchard somewhere Isleworth way. There was nothing much in all that. But now you see why it was impossible to satisfy Sergeant Lapworth's inopportune curiosity.'

'You may perhaps find it difficult to satisfy one or two other people as well. Did Chloe say anything when she let you in just now?'

'Why, yes; it struck me as ungracious at the time. The angel looked at me very weirdly and just said "Idiot!" I thought she must be overwrought.'

'I think it very likely. I told you that there had been other blunders besides Chloe's. What she wished to indicate by a single appropriate word, my budding Lothario, was that you had thrown away the wrong shoe, with the consequence that Mrs Enderleigh is now on the verge of hysterics at an apparent miracle.'

'No!' exclaimed Wich incredulously, 'I could not. And yet, surely . . . Oh, good Lord, I did! I kept them to make a pair – the new one and the other, instead of . . . Well, I am a prize fathead! What will happen now?'

'What? Why the extreme probability that you have had your trouble for nothing and that Chloe will be sacked after all.'

'Oh, I don't think that – not after seeing Mrs Enderleigh. You and Chloe both misjudge her strangely. She seems the jolliest sort of girl to me. I bet she'll understand.'

'I'll bet she will,' assented Carrados grimly. 'And when she understands that her pretty servant has been wearing her things, sneaking out at night (to say nothing about giving burglars the chance of sneaking in) to foot it at dance-halls with the young spark from next-door-but-one, you may not find her quite so sympathetic as she was half an hour ago. If she doesn't take the opportunity of calling upon Lady Wich about it I'm badly out.'

'It's a mug's business,' said Mr Wich with a qualmish note in his voice. 'What had I better do?'

'What you had better do is to leave it in my hands and agree to my condition.'

'What condition?'

'That you never go gallivanting with Chloe again. You both "don't mean anything", but suppose you did happen to get the girl discharged with a very dubious character? Should you see any alternative to behaving either as a fool or a knave to put it right?'

'Whew!' exclaimed Mr Wich, easing the collar against his neck, 'that's heart-to-heart stuff. Well, if you can bring it off I'm good for my part. Chloe certainly is a dazzling thing, but, strictly between ourselves, her mind is little more than an assortment of obsolete film captions.'

When Mr Enderleigh returned from business the next day Myra greeted him with a subdued note. It was plain that the excitement had quite worn off.

'If Mr Carrados is really going to be useful to you, Guy, of course I shall do my best to amuse him. But I wonder all the same if he is going to make a practice of dropping in every evening.'

'How so?' demanded Guy.

'He rang me up this afternoon and hoped that we should both be in later as he would like to call. I had to say we should be charmed.'

'Just as well you did, my lady,' remarked Guy. 'Do you know that quite important people have a most extraordinary opinion of the man, and I am told that Scotland Yard will do anything to oblige him. That's what I've come across today.'

'My gracious!' said Myra, deeply impressed; 'it's just as well I fawned. Talking about police, I met

Sergeant Lapworth in the road this morning and he seemed very odd. He said they had received instructions to go slow in taking any steps.'

'That ought to suit them down to the ground,' suggested Guy pessimistically. 'We don't look like seeing any of our plate again, old girl.'

'I don't know, Guy. It struck me that Sergeant Lapworth knew more than he would tell. He said that they expected developments.'

'It used to be "were investigating a clue",' said the unimpressed gentleman.

Mrs Enderleigh had named nine o'clock as a convenient hour and with the busy man's punctuality nine o'clock found Mr Carrados walking up the Homecraft garden path. Looking out, the lady of the house felt a pleasant access of importance, arising from the notable proportions of the car waiting at her gate.

'How nice of you to come again!' she exclaimed playfully. 'After the alarms and excursions of yesterday I hardly dared to hope it.'

'Oh, yes,' he replied prosaically, 'your husband and I have some small business details to discuss.'

'Of course,' she assented quickly. 'I am going to leave you at it.'

'But first,' he continued, 'I have a bargain to offer you.'

'Offer me? How exciting! Whatever can it be?'

'You really want to get your silver back again?'

'Why, naturally. Guy tells me that we shall only receive about half the value the way our policy goes – isn't that so, Guy?'

'I'm afraid it is,' admitted her husband.

'And that's only money. To both of us many of the things are priceless.'

'While you have no particular affection for that odd pair of shoes?'

'Shoes? Oh, *those*! How ridiculous, Mr Carrados! You are not coming like an up-to-date genie to offer silver plates for old shoes, are you?'

'You have guessed. But there's always a catch about these attractive bargains, you remember. If you agree to let the shoes go, everything connected with them goes also. You have no curiosity, make no enquiries, entertain no suspicions: it is to be as though they and all that appertains to them had never been.'

'I wonder if I understand?' mused Myra with a sharp little look in his direction.

'I think you do,' replied Carrados. 'You are – forgive the homely phrase – no fool, Mrs Enderleigh. If you do not quite understand yet it's only because you have not had time to think about it. You soon would.'

'All right; I'll take it,' said Myra, with a very sporting air.

'But do you mean that you actually know now where the silver is?' demanded Enderleigh.

'I know where the silver is,' Carrados admitted.

'Where?' exclaimed two simultaneous voices.

'When you went off a few days ago, you expressed a wish as to where it might be, Mr Enderleigh, didn't you?'

'What was that?' asked Myra, from whose mind the malediction had apparently faded. Her husband, on the contrary, remembered very well and he coloured at the recollection.

'I am sorry to be reminded of that,' he said moodily. 'Something happened to put me out, Myra, and in a moment of irritation, without meaning it, I said

244

I wished the stuff at the bottom of the river. That's all.'

'Yes; that's the way with you impulsive people, as we genii are always finding. You want a thing and then discover that you don't. Well, my friend, you have got your wish, willy-nilly. The stuff is at the bottom of the river.'

'What a lark!' exclaimed the lady.

'The burglars dropped it or hid it there?' said her husband, keenly intrigued. 'How on earth did you find that out?'

'The burglars had nothing to do with it, because there was no burglar – no burglary,' was the reply.

'Oh, but I say! Besides, it's gone. No, Mr Carrados! And then the side-door key, you know.'

'Hush!' said Carrados mysteriously. 'That doesn't count. The side-door key went, according to our bargain, with the shoes.'

'Very well,' acquiesced Myra, with something very like a giggle, 'but if there was no burglar how did the silver get into the river?'

'How?' Carrados raised an accusing finger and slowly brought it dead level on his hostess. 'How? Behold the culprit! You, my dear lady, threw it there!'

Moved by a common impulse Guy and Myra came slowly to their feet. Looking at Max Carrados's quietly smiling face it seemed impossible to believe that he – to doubt that he – to know what to think.

'I – threw – it – there?' articulated Myra queerly.

'You deliberately cast the "damned stuff" in. Rising in the dead of night, without staying to put on slippers or to cover those inadequate garments that are no longer the prerogative of my sex, you crept down, carefully replaced the silver lying about, took up the burden, let yourself out by the french window in the drawing-room, crossed the lawn, reached the silent river, and with a sigh of relief at accomplishing so meritorious a task, tipped the whole bag of tricks into the water. All in a profound sleep, of course. By the way, I hope your feet are better today?'

Myra sat down again with a strange look in her eyes.

'But I could not – I could not even move the box,' she whispered.

'Not when you are awake,' he replied, becoming grave again. 'And do you know why that is? It is because you know that you cannot, and so, your slavish body assenting, you really cannot. But in your sleep you do not know it; your unbound mind admits no limits, and so – '

'Do you know,' interposed Enderleigh sagely, 'I've heard something like that several times lately. I suppose there may be something in it after all.'

'Anyway,' said Mr Carrados, 'there is one thing you can congratulate yourself on. A wife who carries out her husband's slightest wish even in her sleep is a woman in a thousand.'

ARTHUR CONAN DOYLE

The Dancing Men

Holmes had been seated for some hours in silence with his long thin back curved over a chemical vessel in which he was brewing a particularly malodorous product. His head was sunk upon his breast, and he looked from my point of view like a strange, lank bird, with dull grey plumage and a black topknot.

'So, Watson,' said he, suddenly, 'you do not propose to invest in South African securities?'

I gave a start of astonishment. Accustomed as I was to Holmes's curious faculties, this sudden intrusion into my most intimate thoughts was utterly inexplicable.

'How on earth do you know that?' I asked.

He wheeled round upon his stool, with a steaming test-tube in his hand and a gleam of amusement in his deep-set eyes.

'Now, Watson, confess yourself utterly taken aback,' said he.

'I am.'

'I ought to make you sign a paper to that effect.'

'Why?'

'Because in five minutes you will say that it is all so absurdly simple.'

'I am sure that I shall say nothing of the kind.'

'You see, my dear Watson' – he propped his test-tube in the rack and began to lecture with the air of a professor addressing his class – 'it is not really difficult to construct a series of inferences, each dependent upon its predecessor and each simple in itself. If, after doing so, one simply knocks out all the central inferences and presents one's audience with the starting-point and the conclusion, one may produce a startling, though possibly a meretricious, effect. Now, it was not really difficult, by an inspection of the groove between your left forefinger and thumb, to feel sure that you did *not* propose to invest your small capital in the goldfields.'

'I see no connection.'

'Very likely not; but I can quickly show you a close connection. Here are the missing links of the very simple chain: 1. You had chalk between your left finger and thumb when you returned from the club last night. 2. You put chalk there when you play billiards to steady the cue. 3. You never play billiards except with Thurston. 4. You told me four weeks ago that Thurston had an option on some South African property which would expire in a month, and which he desired you to share with him. 5. Your cheque-book is locked in my drawer, and you have not asked for the key. 6. You do not propose to invest your money in this manner.'

'How absurdly simple!' I cried.

'Quite so!' said he, a little nettled. 'Every problem becomes very childish when once it is explained to you. Here is an unexplained one. See what you can make of that, friend Watson.' He tossed a sheet of paper upon the table and turned once more to his chemical analysis.

I looked with amazement at the absurd hieroglyphics upon the paper.

'Why, Holmes, it is a child's drawing,' I cried.

'Oh, that's your idea!'

'What else should it be?'

'That is what Mr Hilton Cubitt, of Ridling Thorpe Manor, Norfolk, is very anxious to know. This little conundrum came by the first post, and he was to follow by the next train. There's a ring at the bell, Watson. I should not be very much surprised if this were he.'

A heavy step was heard upon the stairs, and an instant later there entered a tall, ruddy, clean-shaven gentleman, whose clear eyes and florid cheeks told of a life led far from the fogs of Baker Street. He seemed to bring a whiff of his strong, fresh, bracing, east-coast air with him as he entered. Having shaken hands with each of us, he was about to sit down when his eye rested upon the paper with the curious markings which I had just examined and left upon the table.

'Well, Mr Holmes, what do you make of these?' he cried. 'They told me that you were fond of queer mysteries, and I don't think you can find a queerer one than that. I sent the paper on ahead so that you might have time to study it before I came.'

'It is certainly rather a curious production,' said Holmes. 'At first sight it would appear to be some childish prank. It consists of a number of absurd little figures dancing across the paper upon which they are drawn. Why should you attribute any importance to so grotesque an object?'

'I never should, Mr Holmes. But my wife does. It is frightening her to death. She says nothing, but I can see terror in her eyes. That's why I want to sift the matter to the bottom.'

Holmes held up the paper so that the sunlight shone full upon it. It was a page torn from a notebook. The markings were done in pencil, and ran in this way:

Holmes examined it for some time, and then, folding it carefully up, he placed it in his pocket-book.

'This promises to be a most interesting and unusual case,' said he. 'You gave me a few particulars in your letter, Mr Hilton Cubitt, but I should be very much obliged if you would kindly go over it all again for the benefit of my friend, Dr Watson.'

'I'm not much of a storyteller,' said our visitor, nervously clasping and unclasping his great, strong hands. 'You'll just ask me anything that I don't make clear. I'll begin at the time of my marriage last year; but I want to say first of all that, though I'm not a rich man, my people have been at Ridling Thorpe for a matter of five centuries, and there is no better-known family in the county of Norfolk. Last year I came up to London for the Jubilee, and I stopped at a boarding-house in Russell Square, because Parker, the vicar of our parish, was staying in it. There was an American young lady there – Patrick was the name – Elsie Patrick. In some way we became friends, until before my month was up I was as much in love as a man could be. We were quietly married at a registry office, and we returned to Norfolk a wedded couple. You'll think it very mad, Mr Holmes, that a man of a good old family should marry a wife in this fashion, knowing nothing of her past or of her people; but if you saw her and knew her it would help you to understand.

'She was very straight about it, was Elsie. I can't say that she did not give me every chance of getting out of it if I had wished to do so. "I have had some very disagreeable associations in my life," said she; "I wish to forget all about them. I would rather never allude to the past, for it is very painful to me. If you take me, Hilton, you will take a woman who has nothing that she need be personally ashamed of; but you will have to be content with my word for it, and to allow me to be silent as to all that passed up to the time when I became yours. If these conditions are too hard, then go back to Norfolk and leave me to the lonely life in which you found me." It was only the day before our wedding that she said those very words to me. I told her that I was content to take her on her own terms, and I have been as good as my word.

'Well, we have been married now for a year, and very happy we have been. But about a month ago, at the end of June, I saw for the first time signs of trouble. One day my wife received a letter from America. I saw the American stamp. She turned deadly white, read the letter, and threw it into the fire. She made no allusion to it afterwards, and I made none, for a promise is a promise; but she has never known an easy hour from that moment. There is always a look of fear upon her face – a look as if she were waiting and expecting. She would do better to trust me. She would find that I was her best friend. But until she speaks I can say nothing. Mind you, she is a truthful woman, Mr Holmes, and whatever trouble there may have been in her past life it has been no fault of hers. I am only a simple Norfolk squire, but there is not a man in England who ranks his family honour more highly than I do. She knows it well, and she knew it well before she married me. She would never bring any stain upon it – of that I am sure.

'Well, now I come to the queer part of my story. About a week ago – it was the Tuesday of last week – I found on one of the window-sills a number of absurd little dancing figures, like these upon the paper. They were scrawled with chalk. I thought that it was the stable-boy who had drawn them, but the lad swore he knew nothing about it. Anyhow, they had come there during the night. I had them washed out, and I only mentioned the matter to my wife afterwards. To my surprise she took it very seriously, and begged me if any more came to let her see them. None did come for a week, and then yesterday morning I found this paper lying on the sundial in the garden. I showed it to Elsie, and down she dropped in a dead faint. Since then she has looked like a woman in a dream, half dazed, and with terror always lurking in her eyes. It was then that I wrote and sent the paper to you, Mr Holmes. It was not a thing that I could take to the police, for they would have laughed at me, but you will tell me what to do. I am not a rich man; but if there is any danger threatening my little woman I would spend my last copper to shield her.'

He was a fine creature, this man of the old English soil, simple, straight and gentle, with his great, earnest blue eyes and broad, comely face. His love for his wife and his trust in her shone in his features. Holmes had listened to his story with the utmost attention, and now he sat for some time in silent thought.

'Don't you think, Mr Cubitt,' said he, at last, 'that your best plan would be to make a direct appeal to your wife, and to ask her to share her secret with you?'

Hilton Cubitt shook his massive head.

'A promise is a promise, Mr Holmes. If Elsie wished

to tell me she would. If not, it is not for me to force her confidence. But I am justified in taking my own line – and I will.'

'Then I will help you with all my heart. In the first place, have you heard of any strangers being seen in your neighbourhood?'

'No.'

'I presume that it is a very quiet place. Any fresh face would cause comment?'

'In the immediate neighbourhood, yes. But we have several small watering-places not very far away. And the farmers take in lodgers.'

'These hieroglyphics have evidently a meaning. If it is a purely arbitrary one it may be impossible for us to solve it. If, on the other hand, it is systematic, I have no doubt that we shall get to the bottom of it. But this particular sample is so short that I can do nothing, and the facts which you have brought me are so indefinite that we have no basis for an investigation. I would suggest that you return to Norfolk, that you keep a keen lookout, and that you take an exact copy of any fresh dancing men which may appear. It is a thousand pities that we have not a reproduction of those which were done in chalk upon the window-sill. Make a discreet enquiry also as to any strangers in the neighbourhood. When you have collected some fresh evidence come to me again. That is the best advice which I can give you, Mr Hilton Cubitt. If there are any pressing fresh developments I shall be always ready to run down and see you in your Norfolk home.'

The interview left Sherlock Holmes very thoughtful, and several times in the next few days I saw him take the slip of paper from his notebook and look long and earnestly at the curious figures inscribed

VINTAGE DETECTIVE STORIES

upon it. He made no allusion to the affair, however, until one afternoon a fortnight or so later. I was going out when he called me back.

'You had better stay here, Watson.'

'Why?'

'Because I had a wire from Hilton Cubitt this morning – you remember Hilton Cubitt, of the dancing men? He was to reach Liverpool Street at one-twenty. He may be here at any moment. I gather from his wire that there have been some new incidents of importance.'

We had not long to wait, for our Norfolk squire came straight from the station as fast as a hansom could bring him. He was looking worried and depressed, with tired eyes and a lined forehead.

'It's getting on my nerves, this business, Mr Holmes,' said he, as he sank, like a wearied man, into an armchair. 'It's bad enough to feel that you are surrounded by unseen, unknown folk, who have some kind of design upon you; but when, in addition to that, you know that it is just killing your wife by inches, then it becomes as much as flesh and blood can endure. She's wearing away under it – just wearing away before my eyes.'

'Has she said anything yet?'

'No, Mr Holmes, she has not. And yet there have been times when the poor girl has wanted to speak, and yet could not quite bring herself to take the plunge. I have tried to help her; but I dare say I did it clumsily, and scared her off from it. She has spoken about my old family, and our reputation in the county, and our pride in our unsullied honour, and I always felt it was leading to the point; but somehow it turned off before we got there.'

'But you have found out something for yourself?'

'A good deal, Mr Holmes. I have several fresh dancing men pictures for you to examine, and, what is more important, I have seen the fellow.'

'What, the man who draws them?'

'Yes, I saw him at his work. But I will tell you everything in order. When I got back after my visit to you, the very first thing I saw next morning was a fresh crop of dancing men. They had been drawn in chalk upon the black wooden door of the tool-house, which stands beside the lawn in full view of the front windows. I took an exact copy, and here it is.' He unfolded a paper and laid it upon the table. Here is a copy of the hieroglyphics:

'Excellent!' said Holmes. 'Excellent! Pray continue.'

'When I had taken the copy I rubbed out the marks; but two mornings later a fresh inscription had appeared. I have a copy of it here.'

Holmes rubbed his hands and chuckled with delight. 'Our material is rapidly accumulating,' said he.

'Three days later a message was left scrawled upon paper, and placed under a pebble upon the sundial. Here it is. The characters are, as you see, exactly the same as the last one. After that I determined to lie in wait; so I got out my revolver and I sat up in my study, which overlooks the lawn and garden. About two in the morning I was seated by the window, all being dark save for the moonlight outside, when I heard steps behind me, and there was my wife in her dressing-gown. She implored me to come to bed. I told her frankly that I wished to see who it was that played such absurd tricks upon us. She answered that it was some senseless practical joke, and that I should not take any notice of it.

' "If it really annoys you, Hilton, we might go and travel, you and I, and so avoid this nuisance."

' "What, be driven out of our own house by a practical joker?" said I. "Why, we should have the whole county laughing at us."

' "Well, come to bed," said she, "and we can discuss it in the morning."

'Suddenly, as she spoke, I saw her white face grow whiter yet in the moonlight, and her hand tightened upon my shoulder. Something was moving in the shadow of the tool-house. I saw a dark, creeping figure which crawled round the corner and squatted in front of the door. Seizing my pistol I was rushing out, when my wife threw her arms round me and held me with convulsive strength. I tried to throw her off, but she clung to me most desperately. At last I got clear, but by the time I had opened the door and reached the house the creature was gone. He had left a trace of his presence, however, for there on the door was the very same arrangement of dancing men which had already twice appeared, and which I have copied on that paper. There was no other sign of the fellow anywhere, though I ran all over the grounds. And yet the amazing thing is that he must have been there all the time, for when I examined the door again in the morning he had scrawled some

more of his pictures under the line which I had
already seen.'

'Have you that fresh drawing?'

'Yes; it is very short, but I made a copy of it, and
here it is.'

Again he produced a paper. The new dance was in
this form:

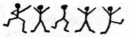

'Tell me,' said Holmes – and I could see by his eyes
that he was much excited – 'was this a mere addition
to the first, or did it appear to be entirely separate?'

'It was on a different panel of the door.'

'Excellent! This is far the most important of all
for our purpose. It fills me with hopes. Now, Mr
Hilton Cubitt, please continue your most interesting
statement.'

'I have nothing more to say, Mr Holmes, except
that I was angry with my wife that night for having
held me back when I might have caught the skulking
rascal. She said that she feared that I might come to
harm. For an instant it had crossed my mind that
perhaps what she really feared was that *he* might come
to harm, for I could not doubt that she knew who this
man was and what he meant by these strange signals.
But there is a tone in my wife's voice, Mr Holmes,
and a look in her eyes which forbid doubt, and I am
sure that it was indeed my own safety that was in her
mind. There's the whole case, and now I want your
advice as to what I ought to do. My own inclination is
to put half a dozen of my farm lads in the shrubbery,
and when this fellow comes again to give him such a
hiding that he will leave us in peace for the future.'

'I fear it is too deep a case for such simple remedies,' said Holmes. 'How long can you stay in London?'

'I must go back today. I would not leave my wife alone all night for anything. She is very nervous and begged me to come back.'

'I dare say you are right. But if you could have stopped I might possibly have been able to return with you in a day or two. Meanwhile you will leave me these papers, and I think that it is very likely that I shall be able to pay you a visit shortly and to throw some light upon your case.'

Sherlock Holmes preserved his calm professional manner until our visitor had left us, although it was easy for me, who knew him so well, to see that he was profoundly excited. The moment that Hilton Cubitt's broad back had disappeared through the door my comrade rushed to the table, laid out all the slips of paper containing dancing men in front of him, and threw himself into an intricate and elaborate calculation. For two hours I watched him as he covered sheet after sheet of paper with figures and letters, so completely absorbed in his task that he had evidently forgotten my presence. Sometimes he was making progress and whistled and sang at his work; sometimes he was puzzled, and would sit for long spells with a furrowed brow and a vacant eye. Finally he sprang from his chair with a cry of satisfaction, and walked up and down the room rubbing his hands together. Then he wrote a long telegram upon a cable form. 'If my answer to this is as I hope, you will have a very pretty case to add to your collection, Watson,' said he. 'I expect that we shall be able to go down to Norfolk tomorrow, and to take our friend some very definite news as to the secret of his annoyance.'

I confess that I was filled with curiosity, but I was aware that Holmes liked to make his disclosures at his own time and in his own way; so I waited until it should suit him to take me into his confidence.

But there was a delay in that answering telegram, and two days of impatience followed, during which Holmes pricked up his ears at every ring of the bell. On the evening of the second there came a letter from Hilton Cubitt. All was quiet with him, save that a long inscription had appeared that morning upon the pedestal of the sundial. He enclosed a copy of it, which is here reproduced:

Holmes bent over this grotesque frieze for some minutes, and then suddenly sprang to his feet with an exclamation of surprise and dismay. His face was haggard with anxiety.

'We have let this affair go far enough,' said he. 'Is there a train to North Walsham tonight?'

I turned up the timetable. The last had just gone.

'Then we shall breakfast early and take the very first in the morning,' said Holmes. 'Our presence is most urgently needed. Ah! here is our expected cablegram. One moment, Mrs Hudson; there may be an answer. No, that is quite as I expected. This message makes it even more essential that we should not lose an hour in letting Hilton Cubitt know how matters stand, for it is a singular and a dangerous web in which our simple Norfolk squire is entangled.'

So, indeed, it proved, and as I come to the dark conclusion of a story which had seemed to me to be only childish and bizarre I experience once again the dismay and horror with which I was filled. Would that I had some brighter ending to communicate to my readers, but these are the chronicles of fact, and I must follow to their dark crisis the strange chain of events which for some days made Ridling Thorpe Manor a household word through the length and breadth of England.

We had hardly alighted at North Walsham, and mentioned the name of our destination, when the station-master hurried towards us. 'I suppose that you are the detectives from London?' said he.

A look of annoyance passed over Holmes's face.

'What makes you think such a thing?'

'Because Inspector Martin from Norwich has just passed through. But maybe you are the surgeons. She's not dead – or wasn't by last accounts. You may be in time to save her yet – though it be for the gallows.'

Holmes's brow was dark with anxiety.

'We are going to Ridling Thorpe Manor,' said he, 'but we have heard nothing of what has passed there.'

'It's a terrible business,' said the station-master. 'They are shot, both Mr Hilton Cubitt and his wife. She shot him and then herself – so the servants say. He's dead and her life is despaired of. Dear, dear, one of the oldest families in the county of Norfolk, and one of the most honoured.'

Without a word Holmes hurried to a carriage, and during the long seven miles' drive he never opened his mouth. Seldom have I seen him so utterly despondent. He had been uneasy during all our journey from town, and I had observed that he had turned over the morning papers with anxious attention; but now this sudden realisation of his worst fears left him in a blank melancholy. He leaned back in his seat, lost in gloomy speculation. Yet there was much around to interest us, for we were passing through as singular a country-side as any in England, where a few scattered cottages represented the population of today, while on every hand enormous square-towered churches bristled up from the flat, green landscape and told of the glory and prosperity of old East Anglia. At last the violet rim of the German Ocean appeared over the green edge of the Norfolk coast, and the driver pointed with his whip to two old brick and timber gables which projected from a grove of trees. 'That's Ridling Thorpe Manor,' said he.

As we drove up to the porticoed front door I observed in front of it, beside the tennis lawn, the black tool-house and the pedestalled sundial with which we had such strange associations. A dapper little man, with a quick, alert manner and a waxed moustache, had just descended from a high dog-cart. He introduced himself as Inspector Martin, of the Norfolk Constabulary, and he was considerably astonished when he heard the name of my companion.

'Why, Mr Holmes, the crime was only committed at three this morning. How could you hear of it in London and get to the spot as soon as I?'

'I anticipated it. I came in the hope of preventing it.'

'Then you must have important evidence of which we are ignorant, for they were said to be a most united couple.'

'I have only the evidence of the dancing men,' said Holmes. 'I will explain the matter to you later. Meanwhile, since it is too late to prevent this tragedy, I am very anxious that I should use the knowledge which I possess in order to ensure that justice is done. Will you associate me in your investigation, or will you prefer that I should act independently?'

'I should be proud to feel that we were acting together, Mr Holmes,' said the inspector, earnestly.

'In that case I should be glad to hear the evidence and to examine the premises without an instant of unnecessary delay.'

Inspector Martin had the good sense to allow my friend to do things in his own fashion, and contented himself with carefully noting the results. The local surgeon, an old, white-haired man, had just come down from Mrs Hilton Cubitt's room, and he reported that her injuries were serious, but not necessarily fatal. The bullet had passed through the front of her brain, and it would probably be some time before she could regain consciousness. On the question of whether she had been shot or had shot herself he would not venture to express any decided opinion. Certainly the bullet had been discharged at very close quarters. There was only the one pistol found in the room, two barrels of which had been emptied. Mr Hilton Cubitt had been shot through the heart. It was equally conceivable that he had shot her and then himself, or that she had been the criminal, for the revolver lay upon the floor midway between them.

'Has he been moved?' asked Holmes.

'We have moved nothing except the lady. We could not leave her lying wounded upon the floor.'

'How long have you been here, doctor?'

'Since four o'clock.'

'Anyone else?'

'Yes, the constable here.'

'And you have touched nothing?'

'Nothing.'

'You have acted with great discretion. Who sent for you?'

'The housemaid, Saunders.'

'Was it she who gave the alarm?'

'She and Mrs King, the cook.'

'Where are they now?'

'In the kitchen, I believe.'

'Then I think we had better hear their story at once.'

The old hall, oak-panelled and high-windowed, had been turned into a court of investigation. Holmes sat in a great, old-fashioned chair, his inexorable eyes gleaming out of his haggard face. I could read in them a set purpose to devote his life to this quest until the client whom he had failed to save should at last be avenged. The trim Inspector Martin, the old, grey-headed country doctor, myself and a stolid village policeman made up the rest of that strange company.

The two women told their story clearly enough. They had been aroused from their sleep by the sound of an explosion, which had been followed a minute later by a second one. They slept in adjoining rooms, and Mrs King had rushed in to Saunders. Together they had descended the stairs. The door of the study was open and a candle was burning upon the table. Their master lay upon his face in the centre of the room. He was quite dead. Near the window his wife was crouching, her head leaning against the wall. She was horribly wounded, and the side of her face was red with blood. She breathed heavily, but was incapable of saying anything. The passage, as well as the room, was full of smoke and the smell of powder. The window was certainly shut and fastened upon the inside. Both women were positive upon the point. They had at once sent for the doctor and for the constable. Then, with the aid of the groom and the stable-boy, they had conveyed their injured mistress to her room. Both she and her husband had occupied the bed. She was clad in her dress – he in his dressing-gown, over his night clothes. Nothing had been moved in the study. So far as they knew there had never been any quarrel between husband and wife. They had always looked upon them as a very united couple.

These were the main points of the servants' evidence. In answer to Inspector Martin they were clear that every door was fastened upon the inside, and that no one could have escaped from the house. In answer to Holmes they both remembered that they were conscious of the smell of powder from the moment that they ran out of their rooms upon the top floor. 'I commend that fact very carefully to your attention,' said Holmes to his professional colleague. 'And now I think that we are in a position to undertake a thorough examination of the room.'

The study proved to be a small chamber, lined on three sides with books, and with a writing-table facing an ordinary window, which looked out upon the garden. Our first attention was given to the body of the unfortunate squire, whose huge frame lay stretched across the room. His disordered dress showed that he had been hastily aroused from sleep. The bullet had been fired at him from the front, and had remained in his body after penetrating the heart. His death had

certainly been instantaneous and painless. There was
no powder-marking either upon his dressing-gown
or on his hands. According to the country surgeon
the lady had stains upon her face, but none upon her
hands.

'The absence of the latter means nothing, though its
presence may mean everything,' said Holmes. 'Unless
the powder from a badly-fitting cartridge happens to
spurt backwards, one may fire many shots without
leaving a sign. I would suggest that Mr Cubitt's body
may now be removed. I suppose, doctor, you have not
recovered the bullet which wounded the lady?'

'A serious operation will be necessary before that
can be done. But there are still four cartridges in
the revolver. Two have been fired and two wounds
inflicted, so that each bullet can be accounted for.'

'So it would seem,' said Holmes. 'Perhaps you can
account also for the bullet which has so obviously
struck the edge of the window?'

He had turned suddenly, and his long thin finger
was pointing to a hole which had been drilled right
through the lower window-sash about an inch above
the bottom.

'By George!' cried the inspector. 'How ever did
you see that?'

'Because I looked for it.'

'Wonderful!' said the country doctor. 'You are
certainly right, sir. Then a third shot has been fired,
and therefore a third person must have been present.
But who could that have been and how could he
have got away?'

'That is the problem which we are now about
to solve,' said Sherlock Holmes. 'You remember,
Inspector Martin, when the servants said that on

leaving their room they were at once conscious of a smell of powder I remarked that the point was an extremely important one?'

'Yes, sir; but I confess I did not quite follow you.'

'It suggested that at the time of the firing the window as well as the door of the room had been open. Otherwise the fumes of powder could not have been blown so rapidly through the house. A draught in the room was necessary for that. Both door and window were only open for a very short time, however.'

'How do you prove that?'

'Because the candle has not guttered.'

'Capital!' cried the inspector. 'Capital!'

'Feeling sure that the window had been open at the time of the tragedy I conceived that there might have been a third person in the affair, who stood outside this opening and fired through it. Any shot directed at this person might hit the sash. I looked, and there, sure enough, was the bullet mark!'

'But how came the window to be shut and fastened?'

'The woman's first instinct would be to shut and fasten the window. But, hello! what is this?'

It was a lady's handbag which stood upon the study table – a trim little handbag of crocodile-skin and silver. Holmes opened it and turned the contents out. There were twenty fifty-pound notes of the Bank of England, held together by an india-rubber band – nothing else.

'This must be preserved, for it will figure in the trial,' said Holmes, as he handed the bag with its contents to the inspector. 'It is now necessary that we should try to throw some light upon this third bullet, which has clearly, from the splintering of the wood, been fired from inside the room. I should like to see Mrs King, the cook, again . . . You said, Mrs King, that you were awakened by a *loud* explosion. When you said that, did you mean that it seemed to you to be louder than the second one?'

'Well, sir, it wakened me from my sleep, and so it is hard to judge. But it did seem very loud.'

'You don't think that it might have been two shots fired almost at the same instant?'

'I am sure I couldn't say, sir.'

'I believe that it was undoubtedly so. I rather think, Inspector Martin, that we have now exhausted all that this room can teach us. If you will kindly step round with me, we shall see what fresh evidence the garden has to offer.'

A flower bed extended up to the study window, and we all broke into an exclamation as we approached it. The flowers were trampled down, and the soft soil was imprinted all over with footmarks. Large, masculine feet they were, with peculiarly long, sharp toes. Holmes hunted about among the grass and leaves like a retriever after a wounded bird. Then, with a cry of satisfaction, he bent forward and picked up a little brazen cylinder.

'I thought so,' said he; 'the revolver had an ejector, and here is the third cartridge. I really think, Inspector Martin, that our case is almost complete.'

The country inspector's face had shown his intense amazement at the rapid and masterful progress of Holmes's investigation. At first he had shown some disposition to assert his own position; but now he was overcome with admiration and ready to follow without question wherever Holmes led.

'Whom do you suspect?' he asked.

'I'll go into that later. There are several points in this problem which I have not been able to explain to you yet. Now that I have got so far I had best proceed on my own lines, and then clear the whole matter up once and for all.'

'Just as you wish, Mr Holmes, so long as we get our man.'

'I have no desire to make mysteries, but it is impossible at the moment of action to enter into long and complex explanations. I have the threads of this affair all in my hand. Even if this lady should never recover consciousness we can still reconstruct the events of last night and ensure that justice be done. First of all I wish to know whether there is any inn in this neighbourhood known as "Elrige's"?'

The servants were cross-questioned, but none of them had heard of such a place. The stable-boy threw a light upon the matter by remembering that a farmer of that name lived some miles off in the direction of East Ruston.

'Is it a lonely farm?'

'Very lonely, sir.'

'Perhaps they have not heard yet of all that happened here during the night?'

'Maybe not, sir.'

Holmes thought for a little and then a curious smile played over his face.

'Saddle a horse, my lad,' said he. 'I shall wish you to take a note to Elrige's Farm.'

He took from his pocket the various slips of the dancing men. With these in front of him he worked for some time at the study table. Finally he handed a note to the boy, with directions to put it into the hands of the person to whom it was addressed, and especially to answer no questions of any sort which might be put to him. I saw the outside of the note, addressed in straggling, irregular characters, very unlike Holmes's usual precise hand. It was consigned to Mr Abe Slaney, Elrige's Farm, East Ruston, Norfolk.

'I think, inspector,' Holmes remarked, 'that you would do well to telegraph for an escort, as, if my calculations prove to be correct, you may have a particularly dangerous prisoner to convey to the county gaol. The boy who takes this note could no doubt forward your telegram. If there is an afternoon train to town, Watson, I think we should do well to take it, as I have a chemical analysis of some interest to finish, and this investigation draws rapidly to a close.'

When the youth had been dispatched with the note, Sherlock Holmes gave his instructions to the servants. If any visitor were to call asking for Mrs Hilton Cubitt no information should be given as to her condition, but he was to be shown at once into the drawing-room. He impressed these points upon them with the utmost earnestness. Finally, he led the way into the drawing-room with the remark that the business was now out of our hands, and that we must while away the time as best we might until we could see what was in store for us. The doctor had departed to his patients, and only the inspector and myself remained.

'I think that I can help you to pass an hour in an interesting and profitable manner,' said Holmes, drawing his chair up to the table and spreading out in front of him the various papers upon which were recorded the antics of the dancing men. 'As to you, friend Watson, I owe you every atonement for having allowed your natural curiosity to remain so long unsatisfied. To you, inspector, the whole incident may appeal as a remarkable professional study. I must tell you first of all the interesting circumstances connected with the previous consultations which Mr Hilton Cubitt has had with me in Baker Street.' He then shortly recapitulated the facts which have already been recorded. 'I have here in front of me these singular productions, at which one might smile had they not proved themselves to be the forerunners of so terrible a tragedy. I am fairly familiar with all forms of secret writings, and am myself the author of a trifling monograph upon the subject, in which I analyse one hundred and sixty separate ciphers; but I confess that this is entirely new to me. The object of those who invented the system has apparently been to conceal that these characters convey a message, and to give the idea that they are the mere random sketches of children.

'Having once recognised, however, that the symbols stood for letters, and having applied the rules which guide us in all forms of secret writings, the solution was easy enough. The first message submitted to me was so short that it was impossible for me to do more than to say with some confidence that the symbol stood for E. As you are aware, E is the most common letter in the English alphabet, and it predominates to so marked an extent that even in a short sentence one would expect to find it most often. Out of fifteen symbols in the first message four were the same, so it was reasonable to set this down as E. It is true that in some cases the figure was bearing a flag and in some cases not, but it was probable from the way in which the flags were distributed that they were used to break the sentence up into words. I accepted this as a hypothesis, and noted that E was represented by .

'But now came the real difficulty of the enquiry. The order of the English letters after E is by no means well marked, and any preponderance which may be shown in an average of a printed sheet may be reversed in a single short sentence. Speaking roughly, T, A, O, I, N, S, H, R, D and L are the numerical order in which letters occur; but T, A, O and I are very nearly abreast of each other, and it would be an endless task to try each combination until a meaning was arrived at. I, therefore, waited for fresh material. In my second interview with Mr Hilton Cubitt he was able to give me two other short sentences and one message, which appeared – since there was no flag – to be a single word. Here are the symbols. Now, in the single word I have already got the two Es coming second and fourth in a word of five letters. It might be "sever", or "lever" ' or "never". There can be no question that the latter as a reply to an appeal is far the most probable, and the circumstances pointed to its being a reply written by the lady. Accepting it as correct, we are now able to say that the symbols stand respectively for N, V and R.

'Even now I was in considerable difficulty, but a happy thought put me in possession of several other letters. It occurred to me that if these appeals came, as I expected, from someone who had been intimate with the lady in her early life, a combination which contained two Es with three letters between might very well stand for the name "ELSIE". On examination I found that such a combination formed the termination of the message which was three times repeated. It was certainly some appeal to "Elsie". In this way I had got my L, S and I. But what appeal could it be? There were only four letters in the word which preceded "Elsie", and it ended in E. Surely the word must be "COME". I tried all other four letters ending in E, but could find none to fit the case. So now I was in possession of C, O and M, and I was in a position to attack the first message once more, dividing it into words and putting dots for each symbol which was still unknown. So treated it worked out in this fashion:

·M ·ERE ··E SL·NE·

'Now the first letter *can* only be A, which is a most useful discovery, since it occurs no fewer than three times in this short sentence, and the H is also apparent in the second word. Now it becomes:

AM HERE A·E SLANE·

Or, filling in the obvious vacancies in the name:

AM HERE ABE SLANEY

I had so many letters now that I could proceed with considerable confidence to the second message, which worked out in this fashion:

A· ELRI·ES

Here I could only make sense by putting T and G for the missing letters and assuming that the name was that of some house or inn at which the writer was staying.'

Inspector Martin and I had listened with the utmost

interest to the full and clear account of how my friend had produced results which had led to so complete a command over our difficulties.

'What did you do then, sir?' asked the inspector.

'I had every reason to suppose that this Abe Slaney was an American, since Abe is an American contraction, and since a letter from America had been the starting-point of all the trouble. I had also every cause to think that there was some criminal secret in the matter. The lady's allusions to her past and her refusal to take her husband into her confidence both pointed in that direction. I therefore cabled to my friend Wilson Hargreave of the New York Police Bureau, who has more than once made use of my knowledge of London crime. I asked him whether the name of Abe Slaney was known to him. Here is his reply: "The most dangerous crook in Chicago." On the very evening upon which I had his answer Hilton Cubitt sent me the last message from Slaney. Working with known letters it took this form:

ELSIE ·RE·ARE TO MEET THY GO·

The addition of two Ps and a D completed a message which showed me that the rascal was proceeding from persuasion to threats, and my knowledge of the crooks of Chicago prepared me to find that he might very rapidly put his words into action. I at once came to Norfolk with my friend and colleague, Dr Watson, but, unhappily, only in time to find that the worst had already occurred.'

'It is a privilege to be associated with you in the handling of a case,' said the inspector, warmly. 'You will excuse me, however, if I speak frankly to you. You are only answerable to yourself, but I have to answer to my superiors. If this Abe Slaney, living at Elrige's, is indeed the murderer, and if he has made his escape while I am seated here, I should certainly get into serious trouble.'

'You need not be uneasy. He will not try to escape.'

'How do you know?'

'To fly would be a confession of guilt.'

'Then let us go to arrest him.'

'I expect him here every instant.'

'But why should he come?'

'Because I have written and asked him.'

'But this is incredible, Mr Holmes! Why should he come because you have asked him? Would not such a request rather rouse his suspicions and cause him to fly?'

'I think I have known how to frame the letter,' said Sherlock Holmes. 'In fact, if I am not very much mistaken, here is the gentleman himself coming up the drive.'

A man was striding up the path which led to the door. He was a tall, handsome, swarthy fellow, clad in a suit of grey flannel, with a panama hat, a bristling black beard and a great, aggressive hooked nose, and he flourished a cane as he walked. He swaggered up the path as if the place belonged to him, and we heard his loud, confident peal at the bell.

'I think, gentlemen,' said Holmes, quietly, 'that we had best take up our position behind the door. Every precaution is necessary when dealing with such a fellow. You will need your handcuffs, inspector. You can leave the talking to me.'

We waited in silence for a minute – one of those minutes which one can never forget. Then the door opened and the man stepped in. In an instant Holmes clapped a pistol to his head and Martin slipped the handcuffs over his wrists. It was all done so swiftly and deftly that the fellow was helpless before he knew that he was attacked. He glared from one to the other of us with a pair of blazing black eyes. Then he burst into a bitter laugh.

'Well, gentlemen, you have the drop on me this time. I seem to have knocked up against something hard. But I came here in answer to a letter from Mrs Hilton Cubitt. Don't tell me that she is in this? Don't tell me that she helped to set a trap for me?'

'Mrs Hilton Cubitt was seriously injured and is at death's door.'

The man gave a hoarse cry of grief which rang through the house.

'You're crazy!' he cried, fiercely. 'It was he that was hurt, not she. Who would have hurt little Elsie? I may have threatened her, God forgive me, but I would not have touched a hair of her pretty head. Take it back – you! Say that she is not hurt!'

'She was found badly wounded by the side of her dead husband.'

He sank with a deep groan on to the settee and buried his face in his manacled hands. For five minutes he was silent. Then he raised his face once more, and spoke with the cold composure of despair.

'I have nothing to hide from you, gentlemen,' said he. 'If I shot the man he had his shot at me, and there's no murder in that. But if you think I could have hurt that woman, then you don't know either me or her. I tell you there was never a man in this world loved a woman more than I loved her. I had a right to her. She was pledged to me years ago. Who was this Englishman that he should come between

275

us? I tell you that I had the first right to her, and that I was only claiming my own.'

'She broke away from your influence when she found the man that you are,' said Holmes, sternly. 'She fled from America to avoid you, and she married an honourable gentleman in England. You dogged her and followed her and made her life a misery to her in order to induce her to abandon the husband whom she loved and respected in order to fly with you, whom she feared and hated. You have ended by bringing about the death of a noble man and driving his wife to suicide. That is your record in this business, Mr Abe Slaney, and you will answer for it to the law.'

'If Elsie dies I care nothing what becomes of me,' said the American. He opened one of his hands and looked at a note crumpled up in his palm. 'See here, mister,' he cried, with a gleam of suspicion in his eyes, 'you're not trying to scare me over this, are you? If the lady is hurt as bad as you say, who was it that wrote this note?' He tossed it forward on to the table.

'I wrote it to bring you here.'

'You wrote it? There was no one on earth outside the Joint who knew the secret of the dancing men. How came you to write it?'

'What one man can invent another can discover,' said Holmes. 'There is a cab coming to convey you to Norwich, Mr Slaney. But, meanwhile, you have time to make some small reparation for the injury you have wrought. Are you aware that Mrs Hilton Cubitt has herself lain under grave suspicion of the murder of her husband, and that it was only my presence here and the knowledge which I happened to possess which has saved her from the accusation? The least that you owe her is to make it clear to the whole world that she was in no way, directly or indirectly, responsible for his tragic end.'

'I ask nothing better,' said the American. 'I guess the very best case I can make for myself is the absolute naked truth.'

'It is my duty to warn you that it will be used against you,' cried the inspector, with the magnificent fair-play of the British criminal law.

Slaney shrugged his shoulders.

'I'll chance that,' said he. 'First of all, I want you gentlemen to understand that I have known this lady since she was a child. There were seven of us in a gang in Chicago, and Elsie's father was the boss of the Joint. He was a clever man, was old Patrick. It was he who invented that writing, which would pass as a child's scrawl unless you just happened to have the key to it. Well, Elsie learned some of our ways; but she couldn't stand the business, and she had a bit of honest money of her own, so she gave us all the slip and got away to London. She had been engaged to me, and she would have married me, I believe, if I had taken over another profession; but she would have nothing to do with anything on the cross. It was only after her marriage to this Englishman that I was able to find out where she was. I wrote to her, but got no answer. After that I came over, and, as letters were no use, I put my messages where she could read them.

'Well, I have been here a month now. I lived in that farm, where I had a room down below, and could get in and out every night, and no one the wiser. I tried all I could to coax Elsie away. I knew that she read the messages, for once she wrote an answer under one of them. Then my temper got the better of me, and I began to threaten her. She sent me a letter then, imploring me to go away and saying that it would break her heart if any scandal should come upon her husband. She said that she would come down when her husband was asleep at three in the morning, and speak with me through the end window, if I would go away afterwards and leave her in peace. She came down and brought money with her, trying to bribe me to go. This made me mad, and I caught her arm and tried to pull her through the window. At that moment in rushed the husband with his revolver in his hand. Elsie had sunk down upon the floor, and we were face to face. I was heeled also, and I held up my gun to scare him off and let me get away. He fired and missed me. I pulled off almost at the same instant, and down he dropped. I made away across the garden, and as I went I heard the window shut behind me. That's God's truth, gentlemen, every word of it, and I heard no more about it until that lad came riding up with a note which made me walk in here, like a jay, and give myself into your hands.'

A cab had driven up while the American had been talking. Two uniformed policemen sat inside. Inspector Martin rose and touched his prisoner on the shoulder.

'It is time for us to go.'

'Can I see her first?'

'No, she is not conscious. Mr Sherlock Holmes, I only hope that if ever again I have an important case I shall have the good fortune to have you by my side.'

We stood at the window and watched the cab drive away. As I turned back my eye caught the pellet of paper which the prisoner had tossed upon the table. It was the note with which Holmes had decoyed him.

'See if you can read it, Watson,' said he, with a smile.

It contained no word, but this little line of dancing men:

'If you use the code which I have explained,' said Holmes, 'you will find that it simply means, "Come here at once." I was convinced that it was an invitation which he would not refuse, since he could never imagine that it could come from anyone but the lady. And so, my dear Watson, we have ended by turning the dancing men to good when they have so often been the agents of evil, and I think that I have fulfilled my promise of giving you something unusual for your notebook. Three-forty is our train, and I fancy we should be back in Baker Street for dinner.'

Only one word of epilogue. The American, Abe Slaney, was condemned to death at the winter assizes at Norwich; but his penalty was changed to penal servitude in consideration of mitigating circumstances, and the certainty that Hilton Cubitt had fired the first shot. Of Mrs Hilton Cubitt I only know that I have heard she recovered entirely, and that she still remains a widow, devoting her whole life to the care of the poor and to the administration of her husband's estate.

VICTOR WHITECHURCH

Sir Gilbert Murrell's Picture

The affair of the goods truck on the Didcot and
Newbury branch of the Great Western Railway was
of singular interest, and found a prominent place in
Thorpe Hazell's notebook. It was owing partly to
chance, and partly to Hazell's sagacity, that the main
incidents in the story were discovered, but he always
declared that the chief interest to his mind was the
unique method by which a very daring plan was
carried out.

He was staying with a friend at Newbury at the
time, and had taken his camera down with him, for he
was a bit of an amateur photographer as well as book-
lover, though his photos generally consisted of trains
and engines. He had just come in from a morning's
ramble with his camera slung over his shoulder, and
was preparing to partake of two plasmon biscuits,
when his friend met him in the hall.

'I say, Hazell,' he began, 'you're just the fellow they
want here.'

'What's up?' asked Hazell, taking off his camera
and commencing some 'exercises'.

'I've just been down to the station. I know the
station-master very well, and he tells me an awfully
queer thing happened on the line last night.'

'Where?'

'On the Didcot branch. It's a single line, you know,
running through the Berkshire Downs to Didcot.'

Hazell smiled, and went on whirling his arms round

his head. 'Kind of you to give me the information,' he said, 'but I happen to know the line. But what's occurred?'

'Well, it appears a goods-train left Didcot last night bound through to Winchester, and that one of the waggons never arrived here at Newbury.'

'Not very much in that,' replied Hazell, still at his 'exercises', 'unless the waggon in question was behind the brake and the couplings snapped, in which case the next train along might have run into it.'

'Oh no. The waggon was in the middle of the train.'

'Probably left in a siding by mistake,' replied Hazell.

'But the station-master says that all the stations along the line have been wired to, and that it isn't at any of them.'

'Very likely it never left Didcot.'

'He declares there is no doubt about that.'

'Well, you begin to interest me,' replied Hazell, stopping his whirligigs and beginning to eat his plasmon. 'There may be something in it, though very often a waggon is mislaid. But I'll go down to the station.'

'I'll go with you, Hazell, and introduce you to the station-master. He has heard of your reputation.'

Ten minutes later they were in the station-master's office, Hazell having re-slung his camera.

'Very glad to meet you,' said that functionary, 'for this affair promises to be mysterious. *I* can't make it out at all.'

'Do you know what the truck contained?'

'That's just where the bother comes in, sir. It was valuable property. There's a loan exhibition of pictures at Winchester next week, and this waggon was bringing down some of them from Leamington. They belong

281

to Sir Gilbert Murrell – three of them I believe – large pictures, and each in a separate packing-case.'

'H'm – this sounds very funny. Are you *sure* the truck was on the train?'

'Simpson, the brakesman, is here now, and I'll send for him. Then you can hear the story in his own words.'

So the goods-guard appeared on the scene. Hazell looked at him narrowly, but there was nothing suspicious in his honest face.

'I know the waggon was on the train when we left Didcot,' he said in answer to enquiries, 'and I noticed it at Upton, the next station, where we took a couple off. It was the fifth or sixth in front of my brake. I'm quite certain of that. We stopped at Compton to take up a cattle-truck, but I didn't get out there. Then we ran right to Newbury, without stopping at the other stations, and then I discovered that the waggon was not on the train. I thought very likely it might have been left at Upton or Compton by mistake, but I was wrong, for they say it isn't there. That's all I know about it, sir. A rum go, ain't it?'

'Extraordinary!' exclaimed Hazell. 'You must have made a mistake.'

'No, sir, I'm sure I haven't.'

'Did the driver of the train notice anything?'

'No, sir.'

'Well, but the thing's impossible,' said Hazell. 'A loaded waggon couldn't have been spirited away. What time was it when you left Didcot?'

'About eight o'clock sir.'

'Ah! – quite dark. You noticed nothing along the line?'

'Nothing, sir.'

'You were in your brake all the time, I suppose?'

'Yes, sir – while we were running.'

At this moment there came a knock at the station-master's door and a porter entered.

'There's a passenger train in just from the Didcot branch,' said the man, 'and the driver reports that he saw a truck loaded with packing-cases in Churn siding.'

'Well, I'm blowed!' exclaimed the brakesman. 'Why, we ran through Churn without a stop – trains never do stop there except in camp time.'

'Where is Churn?' asked Hazell, for once at a loss.

'It's merely a platform and a siding close to the camping ground between Upton and Compton,' replied the station-master, 'for the convenience of troops only, and very rarely used, except in the summer, when soldiers are encamped there.'

'I should very much like to see the place, and as soon as possible,' said Hazell.

'So you shall,' replied the station-master. 'A train will soon start on the branch. Inspector Hill shall go with you, and instruction shall be given to the driver to stop there, while a return train can pick you both up.'

In less than an hour Hazell and Inspector Hill alighted at Churn. It is a lonely enough place, situated in a vast, flat basin of the Downs, scarcely relieved by a single tree, and far from all human habitation, with the exception of a lonely shepherd's cottage some half a mile away.

The 'station' itself is only a single platform, with a shelter and a solitary siding, terminating in what is know in railway language as a 'dead-end' – that is, as in this case, wooden buffers to stop any trucks. This siding runs off the single line of rail at points from the Didcot direction of the line.

And in this siding was the lost truck, right against the 'dead-end', filled with three packing-cases and labelled 'Leamington to Winchester, via Newbury'. There could be no doubt about it at all. But how it had got there from the middle of a train running through without a stop was a mystery even to the acute mind of Thorpe Hazell.

'Well,' said the inspector, when they had gazed long enough at the truck, 'we'd better have a look at the points. Come along.'

There is not even a signal-box at this primitive station. The points are actuated by two levers in a ground frame, standing close by the side of the line, one lever unlocking and shifting the same points.

'How about these points?' said Hazell as they drew near. 'You only use them so occasionally that I suppose they are kept out of action?'

'Certainly,' replied the inspector. 'A block of wood is bolted down between the point rail and the main rail, fixed as a wedge – ah! there it is, you see, quite untouched; and the levers themselves are locked – here's the keyhole in the ground frame. This is the strangest thing I've ever come across, Mr Hazell.'

Thorpe Hazell stood looking at the points and levers, sorely puzzled. They *must* have been worked to get that truck in the siding, he knew well. But how?

Suddenly his face lit up. Oil evidently had been used to loosen the nut of the bolt that fixed the wedge of wood. Then his eyes fell on the handle of one of the two levers, and a slight exclamation of joy escaped him.

'Look,' said the inspector at that moment, 'it's impossible to pull them off,' and he stretched out his hand towards a lever. To his astonishment Hazell seized him by the collar and dragged him back before he could touch it.

'I beg you pardon,' he exclaimed, 'hope I've not hurt you, but I want to photograph those levers first, if you don't mind.'

The inspector watched him rather sullenly as he fixed his camera on a folding tripod stand he had with him, only a few inches from the handle of one of the levers, and took two very careful photographs of it.

'Can't see the use of that, sir,' growled the inspector. But Hazell vouchsafed no reply.

'Let him find it out for himself,' he thought.

Then he said aloud: 'I fancy they must have had that block out, inspector – and it's evident the points must have been set to get the truck where it is. How it was done is a problem, but, if the doer of it was anything of a regular criminal, I think we might find *him*.'

'How?' asked the puzzled inspector.

'Ah,' was the response, 'I'd rather not say at present. Now, I should very much like to know whether those pictures are intact?'

'We shall soon find that out,' replied the inspector, 'for we'll take the truck back with us.' And he commenced undoing the bolt with a spanner, after which he unlocked the levers. 'H'm – they work pretty freely,' he remarked as he pulled one.

'Quite so,' said Hazell, 'they've been oiled recently.'

There was an hour or so before the return train would pass, and Hazell occupied it by walking to the shepherd's cottage.

'I am hungry,' he explained to the woman there, 'and hunger is Nature's dictate for food. Can you oblige me with a couple of onions and a broomstick?'

And she talks today of the strange man who 'kept a swingin' o' that there broomstick round 'is 'ead and then eat them onions as solemn as a judge'.

The first thing Hazell did on returning to Newbury was to develop his photographs. The plates were dry enough by the evening for him to print one or two photos on gaslight-paper and to enclose the clearest of them with a letter to a Scotland Yard official whom he knew, stating that he would call for an answer as he intended returning to town in a couple of days.

The following evening he received a note from the station-master, which read:

DEAR SIR – I promised to let you know if the pictures in the cases on that truck were in any way tampered with. I have just received a report from Winchester by which I understand that they have been unpacked and carefully examined by the Committee of the Loan Exhibition. The Committee are perfectly satisfied that they have not been damaged or interfered with in any way, and that they have been received just as they left the owner's hands.

We are still at a loss to account for the running of the waggon on to the Churn siding or to explain the object of it. An official has been down from Paddington, and, at his request, we are not making the affair public – the goods having arrived in safety. I am sure you will observe confidence in this matter.

'More mysterious than ever,' said Hazell to himself, 'I can't understand it at all.'

The next day he called at Scotland Yard and saw the official. 'I've had no difficulty with your little matter, you'll be glad to hear,' he said. 'We looked up our records and very soon spotted the man.'

'Who is he?'

'His real name is Edgar Jeffreys, but we know him under several aliases. He's served four sentences for burglary and robbery – the latter a daring theft from a train, so he's in your line, Mr Hazell. What's he been up to, and how did you get that print?'

'Well,' replied Hazell, 'I don't quite know yet what he's been doing. But I should like to be able to find him if anything turns up. Never mind how I got the print – the affair is quite a private one at present, and nothing may come of it.'

The official wrote an address on a bit of paper and handed it to Hazell.

'He's living there just now, under the name of Allen. We keep such men in sight, and I'll let you know if he moves.'

When Hazell opened his newspaper the following morning he gave a cry of joy. And no wonder, for this is what he saw:

MYSTERY OF A PICTURE
Sir Gilbert Murrell and the Winchester
Loan Exhibition: An Extraordinary Charge

The Committee of the Loan Exhibition of Pictures to be opened next week at Winchester are in a state of very natural excitement brought about by a strange charge that has been made against them by Sir Gilbert Murrell.

Sir Gilbert, who lives at Leamington, is the owner of several very valuable pictures, among them being the celebrated *The Holy Family* by Vélazquez. This picture, with two others, was dispatched by him from Leamington to be exhibited at Winchester, and yesterday he journeyed to that city in order to make himself satisfied with the hanging arrangements, as he had particularly stipulated that *The Holy Family* was to be placed in a prominent position.

The picture in question was standing on the floor of the gallery, leaning against a pillar, when Sir Gilbert arrived with some representatives of the Committee. Nothing occurred till he happened to walk behind the canvas, when he astounded those present by saying that the picture was not his at all, declaring that a copy had been substituted, and stating that he was absolutely certain on account of certain private marks of his at the back of the canvas, which were quite indecipherable, and which were now missing. He admitted that the painting itself in every way resembled his picture, and that it was the cleverest forgery he had every seen; but a very painful scene took place, the Committee stating that the picture had been received by them from the railway company just as it stood.

At present the whole affair is a mystery, but Sir Gilbert insisted most emphatically to our correspondent, who was able to see him, that the picture was certainly not his, and said that, as the original is extremely valuable, he intends holding the Committee responsible for the substitution which, he declares, has taken place.

It was evident to Hazell that the papers had not, as yet, got hold of the mysterious incident at Churn. As a matter of fact, the railway company had kept that affair strictly to themselves, and the Committee knew nothing of what had happened on the line.

But Hazell saw that enquiries would be made, and determined to probe the mystery without dealy. He saw at once that if there was any truth in Sir Gilbert's story the substitution had taken place in that lonely siding at Churn. He was staying at his London flat, and five minutes after he had read the paragraph had called a hansom and was being hurried off to a friend of his who was well known in art circles as a critic and art historian.

'I can tell you exactly what you want to know,' said he, 'for I've only just been looking it up, so as to have an article in the evening papers on it. There was a famous copy of the picture of Vélazquez, and there is said to have been a controversy among the respective owners as to which was the genuine one – just as there is today about a Madonna belonging to a gentleman at St Moritz but which a Vienna gallery also claims to possess.

'However, in the case of *The Holy Family* the dispute was ultimately settled once and for all years ago, and, undoubtedly, Sir Gilbert Murrell held the genuine picture. What became of the copy no one knows. For twenty years all trace of it has been lost. There – that's all I can tell you. I shall pad it out a bit in my article, and I must get to work on it as once. Goodbye!'

'One moment – where was the copy last seen?'

'Oh! the old Earl of Ringmere had it last, but when he knew it to be a forgery he is said to have sold it for a mere song, all interest in it being lost, you see.'

'Let me see, he's a very old man, isn't he?'

'Yes – nearly eighty – perfect enthusiast on pictures still though.'

'Only *said* to have sold it,' muttered Hazell to himself, as he left the house; 'that's very vague – and there's no knowing what these enthusiasts will do when they're really bent on a thing. Sometimes they lose all sense of honesty. I've known fellows actually rob a friend's collections of stamps or butterflies. What if there's something in it? By George, what an awful scandal there would be. It seems to me that if such a scandal were prevented I'd be thanked all round. Anyhow, I'll have a shot at it on spec. And I *must* find out how that truck was run off the line.'

When once Hazell was on the track of a railway mystery he never let a moment slip by. In an hour's time, he was at the address given him at Scotland Yard. On his way there he took a card from his case – a blank one – and wrote on it, 'From the Earl of Ringmere'. This he put into an envelope.

'It's a bold stroke,' he said to himself, 'but, if there's anything in it, it's worth trying.'

So he asked for Allen. The woman who opened the door looked at him suspiciously, and said she didn't think Mr Allen was in.

'Give him this envelope,' replied Hazell. In a couple of minutes she returned, and asked him to follow her.

A short, wiry man, with sharp, evil-looking eyes, stood in the room waiting for him and looking at him suspiciously.

'Well,' he snapped, 'what is it – what do you want?'

'I come on behalf of the Earl of Ringmere. You will know that when I mention Churn,' replied Hazell, playing his trump card boldly.

'Well,' went on the man, 'what about that?'

Hazell wheeled round, locked the door suddenly,

put the key in his pocket, and then faced his man. The latter darted forward, but Hazell had a revolver pointing at him in a twinkling.

'You're a detective!'

'No, I'm not – I told you I came on behalf of the Earl – that looks like hunting up matters for his sake, doesn't it?'

'What does the old fool mean?' asked Jeffreys.

'Oh! I see you know all about it. Now listen to me quietly, and you may come to a little reason. You changed that picture at Churn the other night.'

'You seem to know a lot about it,' sneered the other, but less defiantly.

'Well, I do – but not quite all. You were foolish to leave your traces on that lever, eh?'

'How did I do that?' exclaimed the man, giving himself away.

'You'd been dabbling about with oil, you see, and you left your thumbprint on the handle. I photographed it, and they recognised it at Scotland Yard. Quite simple.'

Jeffreys swore beneath his breath.

'I wish you'd admit you've been involved,' I said.

'If I have, I'm not going to take any risks. I told the old man so. He's worse than I am – he put me up to getting the picture. Let him takes his chance when it comes out. I suppose he wants to keep his name out of if – that's why you're here.'

'You're not quite right. Now, just listen to me. You're a villain, and you deserve to suffer; but I'm acting in a purely private capacity, and I fancy if I can get the original picture back to its owner that it will be better for all parties to hush this affair up. Has the old Earl got it?'

'No, not yet,' admitted the other, 'he was too artful. But he knows where it is, and so do I.'

'Ah – now you're talking sense! Look here! You make a clean breast of it, and I'll take it down on paper you shall swear to the truth of your statement before the Commissioner for Oaths – he need not see the actual confession. I shall hold this in case it is necessary; but, if you help me to get the picture back to Sir Gilbert, I don't think it will be.'

After a little more conversation, Jeffreys explained. Before he did so, however, Hazell had taken a bottle of milk and a hunch of wholemeal bread from his pocket, and calmly proceeded to perform 'exercises' and then to eat his 'lunch' while Jeffreys told the story.

'It was the old Earl who did it. How he got hold of me doesn't matter; perhaps I got hold of him – maybe I put him up to it – but that's not the question. He'd kept that forged picture of his in a lumber room for years, but he always had his eye on the genuine one. He paid a long price for the forgery, and he got to think that he *ought* to have the original. But there, he's mad on pictures.

'Well, as I say, he kept the forgery out of sight and let folk think he'd sold it, but all the time he was in hopes of getting it changed somehow for the original.

'Then I came along and undertook the job for him. There were three of us in it, for it was a ticklish business. We found out by what train the picture was to travel – that was easy enough. I got hold of a key to unlock the ground frame, and the screwing off of the bolt was a mere nothing. I oiled the points well so that the thing should work as I wanted it to.

'One pal was with me – in the siding, ready to clap

on the side-brake when the truck was running in. I
was to work the points, and my other pal, who had
the most awkward job of all, was on the goods train –
under a tarpaulin in a truck. He had two lengths of
very stout rope with a hook at each end of them.

'When the train left Upton, he started his job. Goods
trains travel very slowly, and there was plenty of time.
Counting from the back brake-van, the truck we
wanted to run off was No. 5. First he hooked No. 4
truck to No. 6, fixing the hook at the side of the end
of both trucks, and having the slack in his hand,
coiled up.

'Then, when the train ran down a bit of a decline,
he uncoupled No. 5 from No. 4, standing on No. 5 to
do it. That was easy enough, for he'd taken a coupling
staff with him; then he paid out the slack till it was
tight. Next he hooked the second rope from No. 5 to
No. 6, uncoupled No. 5 from No. 6, and paid out the
slack of the second rope.

'Now you can see what happened. The last few
trucks of the train were being drawn by a long rope
reaching from No. 4 to No. 6, and leaving a space in
between. In the middle of this space No. 5 ran,
drawn by a short rope from No. 6. My pal stood on
No. 6, with a sharp knife in his hand.

'The rest was easy. I held the lever, close by the
side of the line, coming forward to it as soon as the
engine passed. The instant the space appeared after
No. 6 I pulled it over, and No. 5 took the siding
points, while my pal cut the rope at the same moment.

'Directly the truck had run by and off I reversed
the lever so that the rest of the train following took
the main line. There is a decline before Compton, and
the last four trucks came running down to the

main body of the train, while my pal hauled in the slack and finally coupled No. 4 to No. 6 when they came together. He jumped from the train as it ran very slowly into Compton. That's how it was done.'

Hazell's eyes sparkled.

'It's the cleverest thing I've heard of on the line,' he said.

'Think so? Well, it wanted some handling. The next thing was to unscrew the packing-case, take the picture out of the frame and put the forgery we'd bought with us in its place. That took us some time, but there was no fear of interruption in that lonely part. Then I took the picture off – rolling it up first – and hid it. The old Earl insisted on this. I was to tell him where it was, then he was going to wait for a few weeks and get it himself.'

'Where did you hide it?'

'You're sure you're going to hush this up?'

'You'd have been in charge long ago if I were not.'

'Well, there's a path from Churn to East Ilsley across the downs, and on the right hand of that path is an old sheep well – quite dry. It's down there. You can easily find the string if you look for it – fixed near the top.'

Hazell took down the man's confession, which was duly attested. His conscience told him that perhaps he ought to have taken stronger measures.

'I told you I was merely a private individual,' said Hazell to Sir Gilbert Murrell. 'I have acted in a purely private capacity in bringing you your picture.'

Sir Gilbert looked from the canvas to the calm face of Hazell.

'Who are you, sir?' he asked.

'Well, I rather aspire to be a book-collector;

you may have read my little monogram on *Jacobean Bindings*?'

'No,' said Sir Gilbert, 'I have not had that pleasure. But I must enquire further into this. How did you get this picture? Where was it – and who – ?'

'Sir Gilbert,' broke in Hazell, 'I could tell you the whole truth, of course. I am not in any way to blame myself. By chance, as much as anything else, I discovered how your picture had been stolen and where it was.'

'But I want to know all about it. I shall prosecute – I – '

'I think not. Now, do you remember where the forged picture was seen last?'

'Yes; the Earl of Ringmere had it – he sold it.'

'Did he?'

'Eh?'

'What if he kept it all this time?' said Hazell, with a peculiar look.

There was a long silence.

'Good heavens!' exclaimed Sir Gilbert at length. 'You don't mean *that*. Why, he has one foot in the grave – a very old man – I was dining with him only a fortnight ago.'

'Ah! Well, I think you are content now, Sir Gilbert?'

'It is terrible – terrible! I have the picture back, but I wouldn't have the scandal known for worlds.'

'It never need be,' replied Hazell. 'You will make it all right with the Winchester people?'

'Yes – yes – even if I have to admit I was mistaken, and let the forgery stay through the exhibition.'

'I think that would be the best way,' replied Hazell, who never regretted his action.

'Of course, Jeffreys ought to have been punished,'

he said to himself; 'but it was a clever idea – a clever idea!'

'May I offer you some lunch?' asked Sir Gilbert.

'Thank you; but I am a vegetarian, and – '

'I think my cook could arrange something; let me ring.'

'It is very good of you, but I ordered a dish of lentils and a salad at the station restaurant. But if you will allow me just to go through my physical-training ante-luncheon exercises here, it would save me the trouble of a more or less public display at the station.'

'Certainly,' replied the rather bewildered baronet; whereupon Hazell threw off his coat and commenced whirling his arms like a windmill.

'Digestion should be considered *before* a meal,' he explained.

MRS HENRY WOOD

The Ebony Box

1

In one or two of the papers already written for you, I have spoken of 'Lawyer Cockermuth', as he was usually styled by his fellow-townspeople at Worcester. I am now going to tell of something that happened in his family – that actually did happen and is no invention of mine.

Lawyer Cockermuth's house stood in Foregate Street. He had practised in it for a good many years; he had never married, and his sister lived with him. She had been christened Betty; it was a more common name in those days than it is in these. There was a younger brother named Charles. They were tall, wiry men with long arms and legs. John, the lawyer, had a smiling, homely face; Charles was handsome, but given to being choleric.

Charles had served in the militia once, and had been ever since called Captain Cockermuth. When only twenty-one he married a young lady with a good bit of money; he had also a small income of his own; so he abandoned the law, to which he had been bred, and lived as a gentleman in a pretty little house on the outskirts of Worcester. His wife died in the course of a few years leaving him with one child, a son, named Philip. The interest of Mrs Charles Cockermuth's money would be enjoyed by her husband until his death, and then would go to Philip.

When Philip left school he was articled to his uncle, Lawyer Cockermuth, and took up his abode with him. Captain Cockermuth (who was of a restless disposition and fond of roving) gave up his house then and went travelling about. Philip Cockermuth was a very nice steady young fellow, and his father was liberal to him in the way of pocket-money, allowing him a guinea a week. Every Monday morning Lawyer Cockermuth handed (for his brother) to Philip a guinea in gold; the coin being in use then. Philip spent most of this in books, but he saved some of it; and by the time he was of age he had sixty golden guineas put aside in a small round box of carved ebony. 'What are you going to do with it, Philip?' asked Miss Cockermuth, as he brought it down from his room to show her. 'I don't know what yet, Aunt Betty,' said Philip, laughing. 'I call it my nest-egg.'

He carried the little black box (the sixty guineas quite filled it) again to his chamber and put it back into one of the pigeon-holes of the old-fashioned bureau which stood in the room, where he always kept it, and left it there, locking the bureau as usual. After that time, Philip put his spare money, now increased by a salary, into the Old Bank; and it chanced that he did not again look at the ebony box of gold, never supposing but that it was safe in its hiding-place. On the occasion of his marriage, some years later, he laughingly remarked to Aunt Betty that he must now take his box of guineas into use; and he went up to fetch it. The box was not there.

Consternation ensued. The family flocked upstairs; the lawyer, Miss Betty and the captain – who had come to Worcester for the wedding, and was staying in the house – one and all put their hands into the deep, dark pigeon-holes, but failed to find the box. The captain, hot-tempered man, flew into a passion and swore over it; Miss Betty shed tears; Lawyer Cockermuth, always cool and genial, shrugged his shoulders and absolutely joked. None of them could form the slightest notion as to how the box had gone or who was likely to have taken it, and it had to be given up as a bad job.

Philip was married the next day, and left his uncle's house for good, having taken one out Barbourne way. Captain Cockermuth felt very sore about the loss of the box; he strode about Worcester talking of it, and swearing that he would send the thief to Botany Bay if he could find him.

A few years more yet, and poor Philip became ill. Ill of the disorder which had carried off his mother – decline. When Captain Cockermuth heard that his son was lying sick, he being (as usual) on his travels, he hastened to Worcester and took up his abode at his brother's – always his home on these visits. The disease was making very quick progress indeed; it was what is called 'rapid decline'. The captain called in all the famed doctors of the town – if they had not been called before: but there was no hope.

The day before Philip died, his father spoke to him about the box of guineas. It had always seemed to the captain that Philip must have, or ought to have, *some* notion of how it went. And he put the question to him again, solemnly, for the last time.

'Father,' said the dying man – who retained all his faculties and his speech to the very end – 'I declare to you that I have none. I have never been able to set up any idea at all upon the loss, or attach suspicion to a soul, living or dead. The two maids were honest;

they would not have touched it; the clerks had no opportunity of going upstairs. I had always kept the key safely, and you know that we found the lock of the bureau had not been tampered with.'

Poor Philip died. His widow and four children went to live at a pretty cottage in Malvern Link – upon a hundred pounds a year, supplied to her by her father-in-law. Mr Cockermuth added the best part of another hundred. These matters settled, Captain Cockermuth set off on his rovings again, considering himself hardly used by fate at having his limited income docked of nearly half its value. And yet some more years passed on.

This much has been by way of introduction to what has to come. It was best to give it.

Mr and Mrs Jacobson, our neighbours at Dyke Manor, had a whole colony of nephews, what with brothers' sons and sisters' sons; of nieces also; batches of them would come over in relays to stay at Elm Farm, which had no children of its own. Samson Dene was the favourite nephew of all; his mother was sister to Mr Jacobson, his father was dead. Samson Reginald Dene he was christened, but most people called him 'Sam'. He had been articled to the gentleman who took to his father's practice: a lawyer in a village in Oxfordshire. Later, he had gone to a firm in London for a year, had passed, and then came down to his uncle at Elm Farm, asking what he was to do next. For, upon his brother-in-law's death, Mr Jacobson had taken upon himself the expenses of Sam, his eldest son.

'Want to know what you are to do now, eh?' cried old Jacobson, who was smoking his evening pipe by the wide fire of the dark-wainscoted, handsome dining-parlour, one evening in February. He was a tall, portly man with a fresh-coloured, healthy face; and not, I dare say, far off sixty years old. 'What would you like to do? – what is your own opinion upon it, Sam?'

'I should like to set up in practice for myself, uncle.'

'Oh, indeed! In what quarter of the globe, pray?'

'In Worcester. I have always wished to practise at Worcester. It is the assize town; I don't care for pettifogging places: one can't get on in them.'

'You'd like to emerge all at once into a full-blown lawyer there? That's your notion, is it, Sam?'

Sam made no answer. He knew by the tone his notion was being laughed at.

'No, my lad. When you have been in some good office for another year or two maybe, then you might think about setting up. The office can be in Worcester if you like.'

'I am hard upon twenty-three, Uncle Jacobson. I have as much knowledge of law as I need.'

'And as much steadiness also, perhaps?' said old Jacobson.

Sam turned as red as the table-cover. He was a frank-looking, slender young fellow of middle height, with fine wavy hair almost a gold colour and worn of a decent length. The present fashion – to be cropped as if you were a prison-bird and to pretend to like it so – was not favoured by gentlemen in those days.

'You may have been acquiring a knowledge of law in London, Sam; I hope you have; but you've been kicking up your heels over it. What about those sums of money you've more than once got out of your mother?'

Sam's face was a deeper red that the cloth now. 'Did she tell you of it, uncle?' he gasped.

'No, she didn't; she cares too much for her graceless son to betray him. I chanced to hear of it, though.'

'One has to spend so much in London,' murmured Sam, in lame apology.

'I dare say! In my past days, sir, a young man had to cut his coat according to his cloth. We didn't rush into all kinds of random games and then go out to our fathers or mothers to help us out of them. Which is what you've been doing, my gentleman.'

'Does aunt know?' burst out Sam in a fright, as a step was heard on the stairs.

'I've not told her,' said Mr Jacobson, listening – 'she is gone into the kitchen. How much is it that you've left owing in London, Sam?'

Sam nearly choked. He did not perceive this was just a random shot: he was wondering whether magic had been at work.

'Left owing in London?' stammered he.

'That's what I asked. How much? And I mean to know. 'Twon't be of any use your fencing about the bush. Come! tell it in a lump.'

'Fifty pounds would cover it all, sir,' said Sam, driven by desperation into the avowal.

'I want the truth, Sam.'

'That is the truth, uncle, I put it all down in a list before leaving London; it comes to about fifty pounds.'

'How could you be so wicked as to contract it?'

'There has not been much wickedness about it,' said Sam miserably, 'indeed there hasn't. One gets drawn into expenses unconsciously in the most extraordinary manner up in London. Uncle Jacobson, you may believe me or not, when I say that until I added it up, I did not think it amounted to twenty pounds in all.'

'And then you found it to be fifty! How do you propose to pay this?'

'I intend to send it up by instalments, as I can.'

'Instead of doing which, you'll get into deeper debt at Worcester. If it's Worcester you go to.'

'I hope not, uncle. I shall do my best to keep out of debt. I mean to be steady.'

Mr Jacobson filled a fresh pipe, and lighted it with a spill from the mantelpiece. He did not doubt the young fellow's intentions; he only doubted his resolution.

'You shall go into some lawyer's office in Worcester for two years, Sam, when we shall see how things turn out,' said he presently. 'And, look here, I'll pay these debts of yours myself, provided you promise me not to get into trouble again. There, no more' – interrupting Sam's grateful looks – 'your aunt's coming in.'

Sam opened the door for Mrs Jacobson. A little pleasant-faced woman in a white net cap, with small flat silver curls under it. She carried a small basket lined with blue silk, in which lay her knitting.

'I've been looking to your room, my dear, to see that all's comfortable for you,' she said to Sam, as she sat down by the table and the candles. 'That new housemaid of ours is not altogether to be trusted. I suppose you've been telling your uncle all about the wonders of London?'

'And something else, too,' put in old Jacobson gruffly. 'He wanted to set up in practice for himself at Worcester: off-hand, red-hot!'

'Oh dear!' said Mrs Jacobson.

'That's what the boy wanted, nothing less. No. Another year or two's work in some good house, to acquire stability and experience, and then he may talk about setting up. It will be all for the best, Sam; trust me.'

'Well, uncle, perhaps it will.' It was of no use for him to say perhaps it won't: he could not help himself. But it was a disappointment.

Mr Jacobson walked over to Dyke Manor the next day, to consult the Squire as to the best lawyer to place Sam with, himself suggesting their old friend Cockermuth. He described all Sam's wild ways (it was how he put it) in that dreadful place, London, and the money he had wasted amidst its snares. The Squire took up the matter with his usual hearty sympathy, and quite agreed that no practitioner in the law could be so good for Sam as John Cockermuth.

John Cockermuth proved to be agreeable. He was getting to be an elderly man then, but was active as ever, saving when a fit of the gout took him. He received young Dene in his characteristically cheery manner, upon the day appointed for his entrance, and assigned him his place in the office next to Mr Parslet. Parslet had been there more than twenty years; he was, so to say, at the top and tail of all the work that went on in it, but he was not a qualified solicitor. Samson Dene was qualified, and could therefore represent Mr Cockermuth before the magistrates and what not, of which the old lawyer expected to find the benefit.

'Where are you going to live?' he questioned of Sam that first morning.

'I don't know yet, sir. Mr and Mrs Jacobson are about the town now, I believe, looking for lodgings for me. Of course they couldn't let *me* look; they'd think I should be taken in,' added Sam.

'Taken in and done for,' laughed the lawyer. 'I

should not wonder but Mr Parslet could accommodate you. Can you, Parslet?'

Mr Parslet looked up from his desk, his thin cheeks flushing. He was small and slight, with weak brown hair, and had a patient, sad sort of look in his face and in his meek, dark eyes.

James Parslet was one of those men who are said to spoil their own lives. Left alone early, he was looked after by a bachelor uncle, a minor canon of the cathedral, who perhaps tried to do his duty by him in a mild sort of manner. But young Parslet liked to go his own ways, and they were not very good ways. He did not stay at any calling he was put to, trying first one and then another; either the people got tired of him, or he of them. Money (when he got any) burnt a hole in his pocket, and his coats grew shabby and his boots dirty. 'Poor Jamie Parslet! how he has spoilt his life!' cried the town, shaking its pitying head at him; and thus things went on till he grew to be nearly thirty years of age. Then, to the public astonishment, Jamie pulled up. He got taken on by Lawyer Cockermuth as copying clerk, at twenty shillings a week, married and became as steady as Old Time. He had been nothing but steady from that day to this, had forty shillings a week now, instead of twenty, and was ever a meek, subdued man, as if he carried about with him a perpetual repentance for the past, regret for the life that might have been. He lived in Edgar Street, which is close to the cathedral, as everyone knows, Edgar Tower being at the top of it. An old gentleman attached to the cathedral had lodged in his house for ten years, occupying the drawing-room floor; he had recently died, and hence Lawyer Cockermuth's suggestion.

Mr Parslet looked up. 'I should be happy to, sir,' he said; 'if our rooms suited Mr Dene. Perhaps he would like to look at them?'

'I will,' said Sam. 'If my uncle and aunt do not fix on any for me.'

Is there any subtle mesmeric power, I wonder, that influences things unconsciously? Curiously to say, at this very moment Mr and Mrs Jacobsen were looking at these identical rooms. They had driven into Worcester with Sam very early indeed, so as to have a long day before them, and when breakfast was over at the inn, took the opportunity, which they very rarely got, of slipping into the cathedral to hear the beautiful ten o'clock service. Coming out the cloister way when it was over, and so down Edgar Street, Mrs Jacobson espied a card in a window with 'Lodgings' on it. 'I wonder if they would suit Sam?' she cried to her husband. 'Edgar Street is a nice, wide, open street, and quiet. Suppose we look at them?'

A young servant-maid, called by her mistress 'Sally', answered the knock. Mrs Parslet, a capable, bustling woman of ready speech and good manners, came out of the parlour, and took the visitors to the floor above. They liked the rooms and they liked Mrs Parslet; they also liked the rooms and they liked the moderate rent asked, for respectable country people in those days did not live by shaving one another; and when it came out that the house's master had been clerk to Lawyer Cockermuth for twenty years, they settled the matter off-hand, without the ceremony of consulting Sam. Mrs Jacobson looked upon Sam as a boy still. Mr Jacobson might have done the same but for the debts made in London.

And all this, you will say, has been yet more explanation; but I could not help it. The real thing begins now, with Sam Dene's sojourn in Mr Cockermuth's office and his residence in Edgar Street.

The first Sunday of his stay there, Sam went out to attend the morning service in the cathedral, congratulating himself that that grand office stood so conveniently near, and looking, it must be confessed, a bit of a dandy, for he had put a little bunch of spring violets into his coat, and 'buttonholes' were quite out of the common way then. The service began with the Litany, the earlier service of prayers having been held at eight o'clock. Sam Dene has not yet forgotten that day, for it is no imaginary person I am telling you of, and never will forget it. The Reverend Allen Wheeler chanted, and the prebendary in residence (Somers Cocks) preached. While wondering when the sermon (a very good one) would be over, and thinking it rather prosy, after the custom of young men, Sam's roving gaze was drawn to a young lady sitting in the long seat opposite to him on the other side of the choir, whose whole attention appeared to be given to the preacher, to whom her head was turned. It is a nice face, thought Sam; such a sweet expression in it. It really was a nice face, rather pretty, gentle and thoughtful, a patient look in the dark brown eyes. She had on a well-worn dark silk and a straw bonnet; all very quiet and plain; but she looked very much of a lady. Wonder if she sits there always? thought Sam.

Service over, he went home, and was about to turn the handle of the door to enter (looking another way) when he found it turned for him by someone who was behind and had stretched out a hand to do it. Turning quickly, he saw the same young lady.

'Oh, I beg your pardon,' said Sam, all at sea; 'did you wish to come in here?'

'If you please,' she answered – and her voice was sweet and her manner modest.

'Oh,' repeated Sam, rather taken aback at the answer. 'You did not want me, did you?'

'Thank you, it is my home,' she said.

'Your home?' stammered Sam, for he had not seen the ghost of anyone in the house yet, saving his landlord and landlady and Sally. 'Here?'

'Yes. I am Maria Parslet.'

He stood back to let her enter; a slender, gentle girl of middle height; she looked about eighteen, Sam thought (she was that and two years on to it), and he wondered where she had been hidden. He had to go out again, for he was invited to dine at Lawyer Cockermuth's, so he saw no more of the young lady that day; but she kept dancing about in his memory. And somehow she so fixed herself in it, and as the time went on so grew in it, and at last so filled it, that Sam may well hold that day as a marked day – the one that introduced him to Maria Parslet. But that is anticipating.

On the Monday morning all his ears and eyes were alert, listening and looking for Maria. He did not see her; he did not hear a sound of her. By degrees he got to learn that the young lady was resident teacher in a ladies' school hard by; and that she was often allowed to spend the whole day at home on Sundays. One Sunday evening he ingeniously got himself invited to take tea in Mrs Parslet's parlour, and thus became acquainted with Maria; but his opportunities for meeting her were rare.

There's not much to tell of the first twelve-month.

It passed in due course. Sam Dene was fairly steady. He made a few debts, as some young men, left to themselves, can't help making – at least, they'd tell you they can't. Sundry friends of Sam's in Worcester knew of this, and somehow it reached Mr Cockermuth's ears, who gave Sam a word of advice privately.

This was just as the first year expired. According to agreement, Sam had another year to stay. He entered upon it with inward gloom. On adding up his scores, which he deemed it as well to do after his master's lecture, he again found that they amounted to far more than he had thought for, and how he should contrive to pay them out of his own resources he knew no more than the man in the moon. In short he could not do it; he was in a fix, and lived in perpetual dread of its coming to the ears of his Uncle Jacobson.

The spring assize, taking place early in March, was just over; the judges had left the town for Stafford, and Worcester was settling down again to quietness. Miss Cockermuth gave herself and her two handmaidens a week's rest – assize time being always a busy and bustling period at the lawyer's, no end of chance company looking in – and then the house began its spring cleaning, a grand institution with our good grandmothers, often lasting a couple of weeks. This time, at the lawyer's house, it was to be a double bustle, for visitors were being prepared for.

It had pleased Captain Cockermuth to write word that he should be at home for Easter; upon which, the lawyer and his sister decided to invite Philip's widow and her children also to spend it with them; they knew Charles would be pleased. Easter Day was very early indeed that year, falling at the end of March.

To make clearer what's coming, the house had

better have a word or two of description. You entered from the street into a wide passage; no steps. On the left was the parlour and general sitting-room; in which all meals were usually taken. It was a long, low room, its two rather narrow windows looking upon the street, the back of the room being a little dark. Opposite the door was the fireplace. On the other side of the passage, facing the parlour-door, was the door that opened to the two rooms (one front, one back) used as the lawyer's offices. The kitchens and staircase were at the back of the passage, a garden lying beyond; and there was a handsome drawing-room on the first floor, not much used.

The house, I say, was in a commotion with the spring cleaning, and the other preparations. To accommodate so many visitors required contrivance: a bed-room for the captain, a bedroom for his daughter-in-law, two bedrooms for the children. Mistress and maids held momentous consultations together.

'We have decided to put the three little girls in Philip's old room, John,' said Miss Betty to her brother, as they sat in the parlour after dinner on the Monday evening of the week preceding Passion Week; 'and little Philip can have the small room off mine. We shall have to get in a child's bed, though; I can't put the three little girls in one bed; they might get fighting. John, I do wish you'd sell that old bureau for what it will fetch.'

'Sell the old bureau!' exclaimed Mr Cockermuth.

'I'm sure I should. What good does it do? Unless that bureau goes out of the room, we can't put the extra bed in. I've been in there half the day with Susan and Ann, planning and contriving, and we find it can't be done any way. Do let Ward take it away,

John; there's no place for it in the other chambers. He'd give you a fair price for it, I dare say.'

Miss Betty had never cared for this piece of furniture, thinking it more awkward than useful; she looked eagerly at her brother, awaiting his decision. She was the elder of the two; tall, like him; but while he maintained his thin, wiry form, just the shape of an upright gas-post with arms, she had grown stout with no shape at all. Miss Betty had dark, thick eyebrows and an amiable red face. She wore a 'front' of brown curls with a high and dressy cap perched above it. This evening her gown was of soft twilled shot-green silk, a white net kerchief was crossed under its body, and she had on a white muslin apron.

'I don't mind,' assented the lawyer, as easy in disposition as Miss Betty was; 'there's no point in keeping it that I know of. Send for Ward and ask him, if you like, Betty.'

Ward, a carpenter and cabinet-maker, who had a shop in the town and sometimes bought second-hand things, was sent for by Miss Betty on the following morning and he agreed, after some chaffering, to buy the old bureau. It was the bureau from which Philip's box of gold had disappeared – but I dare say you have understood that. In the midst of all this stir and clatter, just as Ward betook himself away after con-cluding the negotiation, and the maids were hard at work above stairs with mops and pails and scrubbing-brushes, the first advance-guard of the visitors un-expectedly walked in: Captain Cockermuth.

Miss Betty sat down in an access of consternation. She could do nothing but stare. He had not been expected for a week yet; there was nothing ready and nowhere to put him.

'I wish you'd take to behaving like a rational being, Charles!' she exclaimed. 'We are all in a mess; the rooms upside down and the bedside carpets hanging out at the windows.'

Captain Cockermuth said he did not care for bedside carpets, he could sleep anywhere – on the brewhouse bench, if she liked.

He quite approved of selling the old bureau, when told it was going to be done.

Ward had appointed five o'clock that evening to fetch it away. They were about to sit down to dinner when he came, five o'clock being the hour for late dinner then in ordinary life. Ward had brought a man with him and they went upstairs.

Miss Betty, as carver, sat at the top of the diningtable, her back to the windows, the lawyer in his place at the foot, Charles between them facing the fire. Miss Betty was cutting off the first joint of a loin of veal when the bureau was heard coming down the staircase with much bumping and noise.

Mr Cockermuth stepped out of the dining-room to look on. The captain followed: being a sociable man with his fellow-townspeople, he went to ask Ward how he did.

The bureau came down safely, and was lodged at the foot of the stairs; the man wiped his hot face, while Ward spoke with Captain Cockermuth. It seemed quite a commotion in the usually quiet dwelling. Susan, a jug of ale in her hand, which she had been to the cellar to draw, stood looking on from the passage; Mr Dene and a younger clerk, coming out of the office just then to leave for the evening, turned to look on also.

'I suppose there's nothing in here, sir?' cried Ward, returning to business and the bureau.

'Nothing, I believe,' replied Mr Cockermuth.

'Nothing at all,' called out Miss Betty through the open parlour-door. 'I emptied the drawers this morning.'

Ward, a cautious man and honest, drew back the lid and put his hand in succession into the pigeon-holes, which had not been used since Philip's time. There were twelve of them; three above, and three below on each side, and a little drawer that locked in the middle. 'Hello!' cried Ward, when his hand was in the depth of one of them: 'here's something.'

And he drew forth the lost box. The little ebony box with all the gold in it.

Well now, that was a strange thing, Worcester thinks so – those people who are still living to remember it – to this day. How it was that the box had appeared to be lost and was searched for in vain over and over again, by poor Philip and others; and how it was that it was now recovered in this easy and natural manner, was never explained or accounted for. Ward's opinion was that the box must have been put in, side upwards, that it had in some way stuck to the back of the deep, narrow pigeon-hole, which just about held the box in width, that those who had searched took the box for the back of the hole when their fingers touched it, and that the bumping of the bureau now in coming downstairs had dislodged the box and brought it forward. As a maker of bureaux, Ward's opinion was listened to with deference. Anyway, it was a sort of theory, serving passably well in the absence of any other. But who knew? All that was certain about it was the fact: the loss and the recovery after many years. It happened just as here described, as I have already said.

Sam Dene had never heard of the loss. Captain Cockermuth perfectly beside himself with glee, explained it to him. Sam laughed as he touched with his forefinger the closely packed golden guineas, lying here so snug and safe, offered his congratulations, and walked home to tea.

It chanced that on that especial Tuesday evening matters were at sixes and sevens in the Parslets' house. Sally had misbehaved herself and was discharged in consequence; and the servant engaged in her place, who was to have arrived that afternoon, had not made her appearance When Sam entered, Maria came out of the parlour, a pretty blush upon her face. And to Sam the unexpected sight of her (it was not often he got a chance of it) and the blush and the sweet eyes came like a gleam of Eden, for he had grown to love her dearly. Not that he had owned it to himself yet.

Maria explained. Her school had broken up for the Easter holidays earlier than it ought, one of the girls showing symptoms of measles; and her mother had gone out to see what had become of the new servant, leaving a request that Mr Dene would take his tea with them in the parlour that evening, as there was no one to wait on him.

Nothing loth, you may be sure, Mr Dene accepted the invitation, running up to wash his hands and give a look at his hair, and running down in a trice. The tea-tray stood in readiness on the parlour-table, Maria sitting behind it. Perhaps she had given a look at *her* hair, for it was quite more lovely, Sam thought, more soft and silken than any hair he had even seen. The little copper kettle sang away on the hob by the fire.

'Will papa be long, do you know?' began Maria

demurely, feeling shy and self-conscious at being thus thrown alone into Sam's company. 'I had better not make the tea until he comes in.'

'I don't know at all,' answered Sam. 'He went out on some business for Mr Cockermuth at half-past four, and was not back when I left. Such a curious thing has just happened up there, Miss Parslet!'

'Indeed! What is it?'

Sam entered on the narrative. Maria, who knew all about the strange loss of the box, grew quite excited as she listened. 'Found!' she exclaimed. 'Found in the same bureau! And all the golden guineas in it!'

'Every one,' said Sam: 'as I take it. They were packed right up to the top!'

'Oh, what a happy thing!' repeated Maria, in a fervent tone that rather struck Sam, and she clasped her fingers into one another, as one sometimes does in pleasure or in pain.

'Why do you say that, Miss Parslet?'

'Because papa – but I do not think I ought to tell you,' added Maria, breaking off abruptly.

'Oh, yes you may. I am quite safe, even if it's a secret. Please do.'

'Well,' cried the easily persuaded girl, 'papa has always had an uncomfortable feeling upon him ever since the loss. He feared that some people, knowing he was not well off, might think perhaps it was he who had stolen upstairs and taken it.'

Sam laughed at that.

'He has never *said* so, but somehow we have seen it, my mother and I. It was altogether so mysterious a loss, you see, affording no clue as to *when* it occurred, that people were ready to suspect anything, however improbable. Oh, I am thankful it is found!'

The kettle went on singing, the minutes went on flitting, and still nobody came. Six o'clock struck out from the cathedral as Mr Parslet entered. Had the two been asked the time, they might have said it was about a quarter-past five. Golden hours fly quickly; fly on angels' wings.

Now it chanced that while they were at tea, a creditor of Sam's came to the door, one Jonas Badger. Sam went to him and the colloquy that ensued might be heard in the parlour. Mr Badger said (in quite a fatherly way) that he really could not be put off any longer with promises; if his money was not repaid to him before Easter he should be obliged to take steps about it; should write to Mr Jacobson, of Elm Farm, to begin with. Sam returned to the tea-table with a wry face.

Soon after that, Mrs Parslet came in. The delinquent servant in her rear. Next, a friend of Sam's called, Austin Chance, whose father was a solicitor in good practice in the town. The two young men, who were very intimate and often together, went up to Sam's room above.

'I say, my good young friend,' began Chance, in a tone that might be taken for jest or earnest, 'don't you go and get into any entanglement in that quarter.'

'What d'you mean now?' demanded Sam, turning the colour of the rising sun.

'I mean Maria Parslet,' said Austin Chance, laughing. 'She's a deuced nice girl; I know that; just the one a fellow might fall in love with unawares. But it wouldn't do, Dene.'

'Why wouldn't it do?'

'Oh, come now, Sam, you know it wouldn't. Parslet is only a working clerk at Cockermuth's.'

'I should like to know what has put the thought in your head?' contended Sam. 'You had better put it out again. I've never told you I was falling in love with her; or told herself, either. Mrs Parslet would be about me, I expect, if I did. She looks after her as one looks after gold.'

'Well, I found you in their room, having tea with them, and – '

'It was quite by accident, an exceptional thing,' interrupted Sam.

'Well,' replied Austin, 'you need not put your back up, old fellow; a friendly warning does no harm. Talking of good, Dene, I've done my best to get up the twenty pounds you wanted to borrow of me, and I can't do it. I'd let you have it with all my heart if I could; but I find I am harder up than I thought for.'

Which was all true. Chance was as good-natured a young man as ever lived, but at this early stage of his life he made more debts than he could pay.

'Badger has just been here, whining and covertly threatening,' said Sam. 'I am to pay up in a week, or he'll make me pay – and tell my uncle, he says, to begin with.'

'Hypocritical old skinflint!' ejaculated Chance, himself sometimes in the hands of Mr Badger – a worthy gentleman who did a little benevolent usury in a small and quiet way, and took delight in accommodating safe young men.

A story was whispered that young M., desperately hard-up, borrowed two pounds from him one Saturday night, undertaking to repay it, with two pounds added on for interest, that day month; and when the day came and M. had not got the money, or was at all likely to get it, he carried off a lot of his mother's plate under his coat to the pawnbroker's.

'And there's more besides Badger's that is pressing,' went on Dene. 'I must get money from somewhere, or it will play the very deuce with me. I wonder whether Charley Hill could lend me any?'

'Don't much think so. You might ask him. Money seems scarce with Hill always. Has a good many ways for it, I fancy.'

'Talking of money, Chance, a lot has been found at Cockermuth's today. A box full of guineas that has been lost for years.'

Austin Chance stared. 'You don't mean that box of guineas that mysteriously disappeared in Philip's time?'

'Well, they say so. It is a small, round box of carved ebony, and it is stuffed to the brim with old guineas. Sixty of them, I hear.'

'I can't believe it's true; that *that's* found.'

'Not believe it's true, Chance! Why, I saw it. Saw the box found, and touched the guineas with my fingers. It has been hidden in an old bureau all the time,' added Sam, and he related the particulars of the discovery.

'What an extraordinary thing!' exclaimed young Chance: 'The queerest start I ever heard of.' And he fell to musing.

But the 'queer start', as Mr Austin Chance was pleased to designate the resuscitation of the box, did not prove to be a lucky one.

The sun shone brightly on Foregate Street, but did not yet touch the front windows on Lawyer Cockermuth's side of it. Miss Betty Cockermuth sat near one of them in the parlour, spectacles on nose, hard at work unpicking the braid of some very old woollen curtains, green once, but now faded to a sort of dingy brown. It was Wednesday morning, the day following the wonderful event of finding the box, lost so long, full of its golden guineas. In truth, no one thought of it as anything less than marvellous.

The house-cleaning, in preparation for Easter and Easter's visitors, was in full flow today, and would be for more than a week to come; the two maids were hard at it above. Ward, who did not disdain to labour with his own hands, was at the house, busy at some mysterious business in the brew-house, coat off, shirt-sleeves stripped up to elbow, plunging at that moment something or other into the boiling water of the furnace.

'How I could have let them remain up so long in this state, I can't think,' said Miss Betty to herself, arresting her employment, scissors in hand, to regard the dreary curtains. She had drawn the table towards her from the middle of the room, and the heavy work was upon it.

Susan came in to impart some domestic news. 'Ward says there's rare talk in the town about the finding of that box, missis,' cried she, when she had concluded it. 'My, how bad them curtains look, now they're down!'

Servants were on more familiar terms with their

mistress in those days without meaning, or showing, any disrespect; identifying themselves, as it were, with the family and its interests. Susan, a plump, red-cheeked young woman turned thirty, had been house-maid in her present place for seven years. She had promised a baker's headman to marry him, but never could be got to fix the day. In winter she'd say to him, 'Wait till summer;' and when summer came, she'd say, 'Wait till winter.' Miss Betty commended her prudence.

'Yes,' said she now, in answer to the girl, 'I've been wondering how we could have kept them up so long; they are not fit for much, I'm afraid, save the rag-bag. Chintz will make the room look much nicer.'

As Susan left the parlour, Captain Cockermuth entered it, a farmer with him who had come in from Hallow to the Wednesday market. The captain's delighted excitement at the finding of the box had not at all subsided; he had dreamt of it, he talked of it, he pinned every acquaintance he could pick up this morning and brought him in to see the box of gold. Independently of its being a very great satisfaction to have had the old mysterious loss cleared up, the sixty guineas would be a huge boon to the captain's pocket.

'But how was it that none of you ever found it, if it remained all this while in the pigeon-hole?' cried the wondering farmer, bending over the little round box of guineas, which the captain placed upon the table open, the lid by its side.

'Well, we didn't find it, that's all I know; or poor Philip, either,' said Captain Cockermuth.

The farmer took his departure. As the captain was showing him to the front-door, another gentleman came bustling in. It was Thomas Chance, the lawyer, father of the young man who had been the previous night with Samson Dene. He and Lawyer Cockermuth were engaged together just then in some complicated, private and very disagreeable business, each acting for a separate client, who were the defendant against a great wrong – or what they thought was one.

'Come in, Chance, and take a look at my box of guineas, resuscitated from the grave,' cried the captain, joyously. 'You can go into the office afterwards.'

'Well, I've hardly time this morning,' answered Mr Chance, turning, though, into the parlour and shaking hands with Miss Betty. 'Austin told me it was found.'

Now it happened the Lawyer Cockermuth came then into the parlour himself, to get something from his private desk-table which stood there. When the box had been discussed, Mr Chance took a letter from his pocket and placed it in his brother practitioner's hands.

'What do you think of that?' he asked. 'I got it by post this morning.'

'Think! why, that it is of vital importance,' said Mr Cockermuth when he had read it.

'Yes; not doubt of that. But what is to be our next move in answer to it?' asked the other.

Seeing they were plunging into business, the captain strolled away to the front-door, which stood open all day, for the convenience of those coming to the office, and remained there whistling, his hands in his pockets, on the lookout for somebody else to bring in. He had put the lid on the box of guineas, and left the box on the table.

'I should like to take a copy of the letter,' said Mr Cockermuth to the other lawyer.

'Well, you can take it,' answered Chance. 'Mind

who does it, though – Parselt, or somebody else that's confidential. Don't let it go into the office.'

'You are wanted, sir,' said Mr Dene, from the door.

'Who is it?' asked his master.

'Mr Chamberlain. He says he is in a hurry.'

'I'm coming. Here, Dene!' he called out as the latter was turning away and young Dene came back again.

'Sit down here, now, and take a copy of this letter,' cried the lawyer, rapidly drawing out and opening the little writing-desk table that stood against the wall at the back of the room. 'Here's pen, ink and paper, all ready: the letter is confidential, you perceive.'

He went out of the room as he spoke, Mr Chance with him; and Sam Dene sat down to commence his task, after exchanging a few words with Miss Betty, with whom he was on good terms.

'Charles makes as much fuss over this little box as if it were filled with diamonds from Golconda, instead of guineas,' remarked she, pointing with her scissors to the box, which stood near her on the table, to direct the young man's attention to it.

'I don't know how many folks he has not brought in already to have a look at it.'

'Well, it was a capital find, Miss Betty; one to be proud of,' answered Sam, settling to his work.

For some little time nothing was heard but the scratching of Mr Dene's pen and the clicking of Miss Betty's scissors. Her task was nearing completion. A few minutes more, and the last click was given, the last bit of the braid was off. 'And I'm glad of it,' cried she aloud, flinging the end of the curtain on the top of the rest.

'This braid will do again for something or other,'

considered Miss Betty, as she began to wind it upon an old book. 'It was put on fresh only three or four years ago. Well brushed, it will look almost like new.'

Again Susan opened the door. 'Miss Betty, here's the man come with the chintz: five or six rolls of it for you to choose from,' cried she. 'Shall he come in here?'

Miss Betty was about to say yes, but stopped and said no, instead. The commotion of holding up the chintzes to the light, to judge of their different merits, might disturb Mr Dene; and she knew better than to interrupt business.

'Let him take them to the room where they are to hang, Susan; we can judge best there.'

Tossing the braid to Susan, who stood waiting at the door, Miss Betty hastily took up her curtains, and Susan held the door open for her mistress to pass through.

Choosing chintz for window-curtains takes some time, as everybody knows whose fancy is erratic. And how long Miss Betty and Susan and the young man from the chintz-mart had been doubting and deciding and doubting again, did not quite appear, when Captain Cockermuth's voice was heard ascending from below.

'Betty! Are you upstairs, Betty?'

'Yes, I'm here,' she called back, crossing to the door to speak. 'Do you want me, Charles?'

'Where have you put the box?'

'What box?'

'The box of guineas.'

'It is on the table.'

'It is not on the table. I can't see it anywhere.'

'It was on the table when I left the parlour. I did

323

not touch it. Ask Mr Dene where it is: I left him there.'

'Mr Dene's not here. I wish you'd come down.'

'Very well; I'll come in a minute or two,' concluded Miss Betty, going back to the chintzes.

'Why, I saw that box on the table as I shut the door after you had come out, ma'am,' observed Susan, who had listened to the colloquy.

'So did I,' said Miss Betty; 'it was the very last thing my eyes fell on. If young Mr Dene finished what he was about and left the parlour, I dare say he put the box up somewhere for safety. I think, Susan, we must fix upon this light pea-green with the rose-buds running up it. It matches the paper, and the light coming through it takes quite a nice shade.'

A little more indecision yet; and yet a little more, as to whether the curtains should be lined, or not, and then Miss Cockermuth went downstairs. The captain was pacing the passage to and fro impatiently.

'Now then, Betty, where's my box?'

'But how am I to know where the box is, Charles, if it's not on the table?' she remonstrated, turning into the parlour, where two friends of the captain's waited to be regaled with the sight of the recovered treasure. 'I had to go upstairs with the young man who brought the chintzes; and I left the box here' – indicating the exact spot on the table. 'It was where you left it yourself. I did not touch it at all.'

She shook hands with the visitors. Captain Cockermuth looked gloomy – as if he were at sea and had lost his reckoning.

'If you had to leave the room, why didn't you put the box up?' asked he. 'A box full of guineas shouldn't be left alone in an empty room.'

'But Mr Dene was in the room; he sat at the desk there, copying a letter for John. As to why didn't I put the box up, it was not my place to do so that I know of. You were about yourself, Charles – only at the front-door, I suppose.'

Captain Cockermuth was aware that he had not been entirely at the front-door. Two or three times he had crossed over to hold a chat with acqaintances on the other side the way; had strolled with one of them nearly up to Salt Lane and back. Upon catching hold of these two gentlemen, now brought in, he had found the parlour empty of occupants and the box not to be seen.

'Well, this is a nice thing – that a man can't put his hand upon his own property when he wants to, or hear where it is!' grumbled he. 'And what business on earth had Dene to meddle with the box?'

'To put it in safety – if he did meddle with it – and a sensible thing to do,' retorted Miss Betty, who did not like to be scolded unjustly. 'Just like you, Charles, making a fuss over nothing! Why don't you go and ask young Dene where it is?'

'Young Dene is not in. And John's not in. Nobody is in but Parslet; and he does not know anything about it. I must say, Betty, you manage the house nicely!' concluded the captain, ironically, giving way to his temper.

This was, perhaps the reader may think, com-motion enough 'over nothing', as Miss Betty put it. But it was not much compared with the commotion which set in later. When Mr Cockermuth came in, he denied all knowledge of it, and Sam Dene was impatiently waited for.

It was past two o'clock when he returned, for he

had been home to dinner. The good-looking young
fellow turned in at the front door with a fleet step, and
encountered Captain Cockermuth, who attacked him
hotly, demanding what he had done with the box.

'Ah,' said Sam, lightly and coolly, 'Parslet said you
were looking for it.' Mr Parslet had in fact mentioned
it at home over his dinner.

'Well, where is it?' said the captain. 'Where did you
put it?'

'I?' cried young Dene. 'Not anywhere. Should I be
likely to touch the box, sir? I saw the box on the table
while I was copying a letter for Mr Cockermuth; that's
all I know of it.'

The captain turned red, and pale, and red again.
'Do you mean to tell me to my face, Mr Dene, that
the box is *gone*?'

'I'm sure I don't know,' said Sam in the easiest of
all easy tones. 'It seems to be gone.'

The box was gone. Gone once more with all its
golden guineas. It could not be found anywhere – in
the house or out of the house, upstairs or down. The
captain searched frantically, the others helped him,
but no trace of it could be found.

At first it was impossible to believe it. That this
selfsame box should mysteriously have vanished a
second time seemed to be too marvellous for fact.
But it was true.

Nobody would admit a share in the responsibility.
The captain left the box safe amidst (as he put it) a
room full of people: Miss Betty considered that she
left it equally safe, with Mr Dene seated at the writing-
table, and the captain dodging (as *she* put it) in and
out. Mr Cockermuth had not entered the parlour
since he left it, when called to Mr Chamberlain,

with whom he had gone out. Sam Dene reiterated that he had not meddled with the box; no, nor thought about it.

Sam's account, briefly given, was this. After finishing copying the letter, he closed the little table-desk and pushed it back to its place against the wall, and then carried the letter and the copy into the office. Finding Mr Cockermuth was not there, he locked them up in his own desk, having to go to the Guildhall upon some business. The business there took up some time, in fact until past one o'clock, and he then went home to dinner.

'And did you consider it right, Sam Dene, to leave a valuable box like that on the table, unguarded?' demanded Captain Cockermuth, as they all stood together in the parlour; the captain had been looking so fierce and speaking so sharply that it might be thought he was taking Sam for the thief, off-hand.

'To tell the truth, captain, I never thought of the box,' answered Sam. 'I might not have noticed that the box was in the room at all but for Miss Betty's drawing my attention to it. After that, I grew so much interested in the letter I was copying (for I know all about the cause, as Mr Cockermuth is aware, and it was curious news) that I forgot everything else.

Lawyer Cockermuth nodded to confirm this. The captain went on: 'Betty drew your attention to it, did she? Why did she draw it? In what way?'

'Well, she remarked that you made as much fuss over that box as if it were filled with diamonds,' replied the young man, glad to pay out the captain for his angry and dictatorial tone. But the captain was in truth beginning to entertain a very ominous suspicion.

'Do you wish to deny, Samson Dene, that my sister

Betty left that box on the table when she quitted the room?'

'Why, who does?' cried Sam. 'When Miss Betty says she left the box on the table, of course she did leave it. She must know. Susan, it seems also saw that it was left there.'

'And you could see that box of guineas standing stark staring on the table, and come out of the room and leave it to its fate!' foamed the captain. 'Instead of giving me a call to say nobody was on guard here!'

'I didn't see it,' returned Sam. 'There's no doubt it was there, but I did not see it. I never looked towards the table as I came out, that I know of. The table, as I dare say you remember, was not in its usual place; it was up there by the window. The box had gone clean out of my thoughts.'

'Well, Mr Dene, my impression is *that you have got the box*,' cried the angry captain.

'Oh, is it!' returned Sam, with supreme good humour, and just the least suspicion of a laugh. 'A box like that would be uncommonly useful to me.'

'I expect, young man, the guineas would!'

'Right you are, captain.'

But Captain Cockermuth regarded this mocking pleasantry as particularly ill-timed. He believed the young man was putting it on to divert suspicion from himself.

'Who did take the box?' questioned he. 'Tell me that.'

'I wish I could, sir.'

'How could the box vanish off the table unless it was taken, I ask you?'

'That's a puzzling question,' coolly rejoined Sam. 'It was too heavy for the rats, I expect.'

'Oh, dear, but we have not rats in the house,' cried Miss Betty. 'I wish we had, I'm sure – and could find the box in their holes.' She was feeling tolerably uncomfortable. Placid and easy in a general way, serious worry always upset her considerably.

Captain Cockermuth's suspicions were becoming certainties. The previous night, when his brother had been telling him various items of news of the old town, as they sat confidentially over the fire after Miss Betty had gone to bed, Mr Cockermuth chanced to mention the fact that young Dene had been making a few debts. Not speaking in any ill-natured spirit, quite the contrary, for he liked the young man amazingly. Only a few, he continued; thoughtless young men would do so; and he had given him a lecture. And then he laughingly added the information that Mr Jacobson had imparted to him twelve months ago, in their mutual friendship – of the debts Sam had made in London.

No sensible person can be surprised that Charles Cockermuth recalled this now. It rankled in his mind. Had Sam Dene taken the box of guineas to satisfy these debts contracted during the past year at Worcester? It looked like it. And the longer the captain dwelt on it, the more and more likely it grew to look.

All the afternoon the search was kept up by the captain. Not an individual article in the parlour but was turned inside out; he wanted to have the carpet up. His brother and Sam Dene had returned to their work in the office as usual. The captain was getting to feel like a raging bear; three times Miss Betty had to stop him in a dreadful fit of swearing; and when dinner-time came he could not eat. It was a beautiful slice of Severn salmon, which had its price, I can tell you, in Worcester then, and minced veal, and a jam tart, all of which dishes Charles Cockermuth especially favoured. But the loss of the sixty guineas did away with his appetite. Mr Cockermuth, who took the loss very cooly, laughed at him.

The laughing did not mend the captain's temper: neither did the hearing that Sam Dene had departed for home as usual at five o'clock. Had Sam been innocent, he would at least have come to the parlour and enquired whether the box was found, instead of sneaking off home to tea.

Fretting and fuming, raging and stamping, disturbing the parlour's peace and his own, strode Charles Cockermuth. His good-humoured brother John bore it for an hour or two, and then told him he might as well go outside and stamp on the pavement for a bit.

'I will,' said Charles. Catching up his hat, saying nothing to anybody, he strode off to see the Sergeant of Police – Dutton – and laid the case concisely before him: The box of guineas was on the table where his sister sat at work; her work being at one end, the box at the other. Sam Dene was also in the room, copying a letter at the writing-table. Miss Betty was called upstairs; she went, leaving the box on the table. It was the last thing she saw as she left the room; the servant, who had come to call her, also saw it standing there. Presently young Dene also left the room and the house; and from that moment the box was never seen.

'What do you make of that, Mr Dutton?' summed up Captain Cockermuth.

'Am I to understand that no other person entered the room after Mr Dene quitted it?' enquired the sergeant.

'Not a soul. I can testify to that myself.'

330

'Then it looks as though Mr Dene must have taken the box.'

'Just so,' assented the complainant, triumphantly. 'And I shall give him into custody for stealing it.'

Mr Dutton considered. His judgement was cool; the captain's hot. He thought there might be ins and outs in this affair that had not yet come to the surface. Besides that, he knew young Dene, and did not much fancy him the sort of individual likely to do a thing of this kind.

'Captain Cockermuth,' said he, 'I think it might be best for me to come up to the house and see a bit into the matter personally, before proceeding to extreme measures. We experienced officers have a way of turning up scraps of evidence that other people would never look at. Perhaps, after all, the box is only mislaid.'

'But I tell you it's *lost*,' said the captain. 'Clean gone. Can't be found high or low.'

'Well, if that same black box is lost again, I can only say it is the oddest case I ever heard of. One would think the box had a demon inside it.'

'No, sergeant, you are wrong there. The demon's inside him that took it. Listen while I whisper something in your ear – that young Dene is over head and ears in debt: he has debts here, debts there, debts everywhere. For some little time now, as I chance to know, he has been at his very wits' end to think where or how he can pick up some money to satisfy the most pressing; fit to die of fear, lest they should travel to the knowledge of his uncle at Elm Farm.'

'*Is* it so?' exclaimed Mr Dutton, severely. And his face changed, and his opinion also. 'Are you sure of this, sir?'

'Well, my informant was my brother; so you may
judge whether it is likely to be correct or not,' said
the captain. 'But, if you think it best to make some
enquiries at the house, come with me and do so.'

They walked to Foregate together. The sergeant
looked a little at the features of the parlour, where the
loss had taken place, and heard what Miss Betty had
to say, and questioned Susan. This did not help the
suspicion thrown on Sam Dene, saving in one point –
their joint testimony that he and the box were left
alone in the room together.

Mr Cockermuth had gone out, so the sergeant did
not see him: but, as he was not within doors when the
loss occurred, he could not have aided the investigation
in any way.

'Well, Dutton, what do you think now?' asked
Captain Cockermuth, strolling down the street with
the sergeant when he departed.

'I confess my visit has not helped me much,' said
Dutton, a slow-speaking man, given to be cautious.
'If nobody entered the room between the time when
Miss Cockermuth left it and you entered it, why then,
sir, there's only young Dene to fall back upon.'

'I tell you nobody did enter it,' cried the choleric
captain; 'or *could*, without my seeing them. I stood at
the front-door. Ward was busy at the house that
morning, dodging perpetually across the top of the
passage, between the kitchen and brew-house: he,
too, is sure no stranger could have come in without
being seen by him.'

'Did you see young Dene leave the room, sir?'

'I did. Hearing somebody come out of the parlour, I
looked round and saw it was young Dene with some
papers in his hand. He went into the office for a minute

332

or two and then passed me, remarking, with all the impudence in life, that he was going to the town hall. He must have had my box in his pocket then.'

'A pity you didn't go into the parlour at once, captain,' remarked the sergeant. 'If only to put the box in safety – provided it was there.'

'But I thought it was safe. I thought my sister was there. I did go in almost directly.'

'And you never stirred from the door – from first to last?'

'I don't say that. When I first stood there I strolled about a little, talking with one person and another. *But I did not stir from the door after I saw Sam Dene leave the parlour.* And I do not think five minutes elapsed before I went in. Not more than five, I am quite certain. What are you thinking about, Dutton? – you don't seem to take me.'

'I take you well enough, sir, and all you say. But what is puzzling me in the matter, strikes me as strange, in fact, is that Mr Dene should do the thing (allowing that he has done it) in so open and bare-faced a manner, laying himself open to immediate suspicion. Left alone in the room with the box by Miss Betty, he must know that if, when he left it, the box vanished with him, only one inference would be drawn. Most thieves exercise some caution.'

'Not when they are as hard up as Dene is. Impudence with them is the order of the day, and often carries luck with it. Nothing risk, nothing win, they cry, and they *do* risk – and win. Dene has got my box, sergeant.'

'Well, sir, it looks dark against him; almost *too* dark; and if you decide to give him into custody, of course we have only too – Good-evening, Badger!'

They had strolled as far as the Cross, and were standing on the pavement in front of St Nicholas's Church, about to part, when that respectable gentleman Jonas Badger passed by. A thought struck the captain. He knew the man was a moneylender in a private way.

'Here, Badger, stop a minute,' he hastily cried. 'I want to ask you a question about young Dene – my brother's clerk, you know. Does he owe you money? – Much?'

Mr Badger, wary by nature and by habit, glanced first at the questioner and then at the police-sergeant, and did not answer. Whereupon Captain Cockermuth, as an excuse for his curiosity, plunged into the history of what had occurred: the finding of the box of guineas yesterday and the losing it again today, and the doubt of Sam.

Mr Badger listened with interest; for the news of that marvellous find had not yet reached his ears. He had been shut up in his office all the morning, very busy over his account-books; and in the afternoon had walked over to Kempsey, where he had a client or two, getting back only in time for tea.

'That long-lost box of guineas come to light at last!' he exclaimed. 'What an extraordinary thing! And Mr Dene is suspected of – Why, good gracious!' he broke off in fresh astonishment, 'I have just seen him with a guinea in his pocket!'

'Seen a guinea in Sam Dene's pocket!' cried Captain Cockermuth, turning yellow as the gas-flame under which they were standing.

'Why yes, I have. It was – '

But there Mr Badger came to a full stop. It had suddenly struck him that he might be doing harm to

Sam Dene; and the rule of his life was not to harm anyone, or to make an enemy, if his own interest allowed him to avoid it.

'I won't say any more, Captain Cockermuth. It is no business of mine.'

But here Mr Sergeant Dutton came to the fore. 'You must, Badger. You must say all you know that bears upon the affair; the law demands it of you. What about the guineas?'

'Well, if you force me to do so – putting it in that way,' returned the man, driven into a corner.

Mr Badger had just been down to Edgar Street to pay another visit to Sam. Not to torment him; he did not do that more than he could help; but simply to say he would accept smaller instalments for the liquidation of his debt – which of course meant giving to Sam a longer time to pay the whole in. This evening he was admitted to Sam's sitting-room. During their short conversation, Sam, searching impatiently for a pencil in his waistcoat-pocket, drew out with it a few coins in silver money, and one coin in gold. Mr Badger's hungry eyes saw that it was an old guinea. These particulars he now imparted.

'What did he *say* about the guinea?' cried Captain Cockermuth, his own eye glaring.

'Not a word,' said Badger; 'Neither did I. He slipped it back into his pocket.'

'I hope you think there's some proof to go upon *now*,' were Charlies Cockermuth's last words to the police-officer as he wished him good-night.

On the following morning, Sam Dene was apprehended, and taken before the magistrates. Beyond his being formally charged, very little was done; Miss Betty was in bed with a sick headache, brought on by the worry, and could not appear to give evidence so he was remanded on bail until Saturday.

I'm sure you might have thought all his rick-yards were on fire by the way old Jacobson came bursting in. It was Saturday morning, and we were at breakfast at Dyke Manor. He had run every step of the way from Elm Farm, two miles nearly, not having patience to wait for his gig, and came in all excitement, the *Worcester Herald* in his hand. The Squire started from his chair; Mrs Todhetley, then in the act of pouring out a cup of coffee, let if flow over on to the tablecloth.

'What on earth's amiss, Jackson?' cried the Squire.

'Ay, what's amiss?' stuttered Jacobson in answer; '*this* is amiss,' holding out the newspaper. 'I'll prosecute the editor as sure as I'm a living man. It is a conspiracy got up to sell it; a concocted lie. It can't be anything else, you know, Todhetley. And I want you to go off with me to Worcester. The gig's following me.'

When we had somewhat collected our senses, and could look at the newspaper, there was the account as large as life. Samson Reginald Dene had been had up before the magistrates on Thursday morning on a charge of stealing a small box of carved ebony, containing sixty guineas in gold, from the dwelling house of Lawyer Cockermuth; and he was to be brought up again that day, Saturday, for examination.

'A pretty thing this is to see, when a man opens his weekly newspaper at his breakfast-table?' gasped Jacobson, flicking the report with his angry finger. 'I'll have the law of them – accusing *my* nephew of such a thing as that! You'll go with me, Squire!'

'Go! of course I'll go!' returned Squire, in his hot

partisanship. 'We were going to Worcester, anyway;
I've things to do there. Poor Sam! Hanging would
be too good for the printers of that newspaper,
Jacobson.'

Mr Jacobson's gig was heard driving up to the gate
at railroad speed; and soon our own carriage was
ready. Old Jacobson sat with the Squire, I behind
with Giles; the other groom, Blossom, drove. Tod
followed in the gig; and away we went in the blustering
March wind. Many people, farmers and others, were
on the road, riding or driving to Worcester market.

Well, we found it was true. And not the mistake of
the newspaper: they had but reported what passed
before the magistrates at the town hall.

The first person we saw was Miss Cockermuth. She
was in a fine way, not knowing what to think or
believe, and sat in the parlour in that soft green gown
of twilled silk (that might have been a relic of the silk
made in the time of the Queen of Sheba), her cap and
front all awry. Rumour said old Jacobson had been a
sweetheart of hers in their young days; but I'm sure I
don't know. Anyway they were very friendly with one
another, and she sometimes called him 'Frederick'.
He sat down by her on the horsehair sofa, and we
took chairs.

She recounted the circumstances (ramblingly) from
beginning to end. Not that the end had come yet by a
long way. And – there it was, she would up, when the
narrative was over: the box had disappeared, just for
all the world as mysteriously as it disappeared in the
days gone by.

Mr Jacobson had listened patiently. He was a fine,
upright man, with a healthy colour and bright dark
eyes. He wore a blue frock-coat today, with metal

337

buttons, and top-boots. As yet he did not see how they had got grounds for accusing Sam, and he said so.

'To be sure,' cried the Squire. 'How's that, Miss Betty?'

'Why, it's this way,' said Miss Betty – 'that nobody was here in the parlour but Sam when the box vanished. It is my brother Charles who had done it all; he is so passionate, you know. John has properly quarrelled with him for it.'

'It is not possible, you know, Miss Betty, that Sam Dene could have done it,' struck in Tod, who was boiling over with rage at the whole thing. 'Some thief must have stolen in at the street door when Sam had left the room.'

'Well, no, they could hardly have done that, seeing that Charles never left the street door,' returned Miss Betty, mildly. 'It appears to be a certain fact that not a soul entered the room after the young man left it. And there lies the puzzle of it.'

The case being as Miss Betty put it – and I may as well say here that nothing turned up, then or later, to change the facts – it looked rather suspicious for Sam Dene. I think the Squire saw it.

'I suppose you are sure the box was on the table when you left the room, Miss Betty?' said he.

'Why, of course I am sure, Squire,' she answered. 'It was the last thing my eyes fell on; for, as I went through the door, I glanced back to see that I had left the table tidy. Susan can bear witness to that. Dutton, the police-sergeant, thinks some demon of mischief must be in that box – meaning the deuce, you know. Upon my word it looks like it.'

Susan came in with some glasses and ale as Miss

Betty spoke, and confirmed the testimony – which did not need confirmation. As she closed the parlour-door, she said, after her mistress had passed out, she noticed the box standing on the table.

'Is Sam here today – in the office?' asked Mr Jacobson.

'Oh, my goodness, no,' cried Miss Betty in a fluster. 'Why, Frederick, he has not been here since Thursday, when they had him up at the Guildhall. He couldn't well come while the charge is hanging over him.'

'Then I think we had better go out to find Sam, and hear what he has to say,' observed Mr Jacobson, drinking up his glass of ale.

'Yes, do,' said Miss Betty. 'Tell poor Sam I'm as sorry as I can be – pestered almost out of my mind over it. And as to their having found one of the guineas in his pocket, please just mention to him that I say it might have slipped in accidentally.'

'One of the guineas in Sam's pocket!' exclaimed Mr Jacobson, taken aback.

'Well, I hear so,' responded Miss Betty. 'The police searched him you see.'

As the Squire and Mr Jacobson went out, Mr Cockermuth was coming in. They all turned into the office together, while we made a rush to Sam Dene's lodgings in Edgar Street: as much of a rush, at least, as the Saturday's street would let us make. Sam was out, the young servant said when we got there, and while we were parleying with her Mrs Parslet opened her sitting-room door.

'I do not suppose Mr Dene will be long,' she said. 'He has to appear at the town hall this morning, and I think it likely he will come home first. Will you walk in and wait?'

She handed us into her parlour, where she had been busy marking sheets and pillow-cases and towels with 'prepared' ink; the table was covered with them. Tod began telling her that Mr Jacobson was at Worcester, and went on to say what a shame it was that Sam Dene should be accused of this thing.

'We consider it so,' said Mrs Parslet, who was a capable, pleasant-speaking woman, tall and slender. 'My husband says it has upset Mr Cockermuth more than anything that has occurred for years past. He tells his brother that he should have had it investigated privately, not have given Mr Dene into custody.'

'Then why did he let him do it, Mrs Parslet?'

She looked at Tod, as if surprised at the question. 'Mr Cockermuth knew nothing of it, you may be sure of that. Captain Cockermuth had the young man at the Guildhall and was preferring the charge before Mr Cockermuth heard a word of what was afoot. Certainly that is a most mysterious box! It seems fated to give trouble.'

At this moment the door opened, and a young lady came into the parlour. It was Maria. What a nice face she had! – what sweet, thoughtful eyes! – what gentle manners! Sam's friends in the town were accusing him of being in love with her – and small blame to him.

But Sam did not appear to be coming home, and time was getting on. Tod decided not to wait longer, and said good-morning.

Flying back along High Street, we caught sight of the tray of Dublin buns, just put fresh on the counter in Rousse's shop, and made as good a feast as time allowed. Some people called them Doubling buns (from their shape, I take it), and I don't know to this day which was right.

Away with fleet foot again, past the bustle round the town hall and market house, till we came to the next confectioner's and saw the apple-tarts. Perhaps somebody remembers yet how delicious those apple-tarts were. Bounding in, we began upon them.

While the feast was in progress, Sam Dene went by, walking very fast. We dashed out to catch him. Good Mrs Mountford chanced to be in the shop and knew us, or they might have thought we were decamping without payment.

Sam Dene, in answer to Tod's hasty questions, went into a passion, swearing at the world in general and Captain Cockermuth in particular, as freely as though the justices, then taking their places in the Guildhall, were not as good as within earshot.

'It is a fearful shame, Todhetley! – to bring such a charge against me, and to lug me up to the criminal bar like a felon. Worse than all, to let it go forth to the town and county in today's glaring newspapers that I, Sam Dene, am a common thief!'

'Of course it is a fearful shame, Sam – it's infamous, and all your friends know it is,' cried Tod, with eager sympathy. 'My father wishes he could hang the printers. I say, what do you think has become of the box?'

'Become of it! – why, that blundering Charles Cockermuth has got it. He was off his head with excitement at its being found. He must have come into the room and put it somewhere and forgotten it; or else he put it into his pocket and got robbed of it in the street. That's what I think. Quite off his head, I give you my word.'

'And what fable is it the wretches have got up about finding one of the guineas in your pocket, Sam?'

'Oh, bother that! It was my own guinea. I swear it – there! I can't stay now,' went on Sam, striding off down High Street. 'I am due at the town hall this minute; only out on bail. You'll come with me.'

'You go in and pay for the tarts, Johnny,' called back Tod, as he put his arm within Sam Dene's. I looked in, pitched a shilling on the counter, said I didn't know how many we had eaten; perhaps ten; and that I couldn't wait for change.'

Crushing my way amidst the market women and their baskets in the Guildhall yard, I came upon Austin Chance. His father held some post connected with the law as administered there, and Austin said he would get me in.

'Can it be true that the police found one of the guineas about him?' I asked.

Chance pulled a long face. 'It's true they found one when they searched him – '

'What right had they to search him?'

'Well, I don't know,' said Austin, laughing a little; 'they did it. To see perhaps whether all the guineas were about him. And I am afraid, Johnny Ludlow, that the finding of that guinea will make it rather hard for Sam. It is said that Maria Parslet can prove the guinea was Sam's own, and that my father has had a summons served on her to appear here today. He has taken Sam's case in hand; but he is closer than wax, and tells me nothing.'

'You don't think he can have stolen the box, Chance?'

'I don't. I shouldn't think him capable of anything so mean; let alone the danger of it. Not but that there are circumstances in the case that tell uncommonly strong against him. And where the deuce the box can have got to, otherwise, is more than mortal man can guess at. Come along.' Not for a long while had Worcester been stirred as it was over this affair of Samson Dene's. What with the curious discovery of the box of guineas after its mysterious disappearance of years, and then its second no less mysterious loss, with the suspicion that Sam Dene stole it, the Faithful City was so excited as hardly to know whether it stood on its head or its heels.

When the police searched the prisoner on Thursday morning, after taking him into custody, and found the guinea upon him (having been told that he had one about him), his guilt was thought to be as good as proved. Sam said the guinea was his own, an heirloom, and stood to this so indignantly resolute that the police let him have it back. But now, what did Sam go and do? When released upon bail by the magistrates – to come up again on the Saturday – he went straight off to a silversmith's, had a hole stamped in the guinea and hung it to his watch-chain across his waistcoat, that the public might feast their eyes upon it. It was in this spirit of defiance – or, as the town call it, bravado – that he met the charge. His lodgings had been searched for the rest of the guineas, but they were not found.

The hour for the Saturday's examination – twelve o'clock – was striking, as I struggled my way with Austin Chance through the crush round the Guildhall. But that Austin's father was a man of consequence with the doorkeepers, we should not have got in at all.

The accused, arraigned by his full name, Samson Reginald Dene, stood in the place allotted to prisoners, cold defiance on his handsome face. As near to him as might be permitted, stood Tod, just as defiant as he. Captain Charles Cockermuth, a third in defiance, stood opposite to prosecute; while lawyer Cockermuth, who came in with Sam's uncle, Mr Jacobson, openly wished his brother at Hanover. Squire Todhetley, being a county magistrate, sat on the bench with the city magnates, but not to interfere.

The proceedings began. Captain Cockermuth related how the little box, his property, containing sixty golden guineas, was left on the table in a sitting-room in his brother's house, the accused being the only person in the room at the time, and that the box disappeared. He, himself (standing at the front-door), saw the accused quit the room; he went into it almost immediately, but the box was gone. He swore that no person entered the room after the prisoner left it.

Miss Betty Cockermuth, flustered and red, appeared next. She testified that she was in the room nearly all the morning, the little box being upon the table; when she left the room, Mr Dene remained in it alone, copying a letter for her brother; the box was still on the table. Susan Edwards, housemaid at Lawyer Cockermuth's spoke to the same fact. It was she who had fetched her mistress out, and she saw the box standing upon the table.

The accused was asked by one of the magistrates what he had to say to this. He answered, speaking freely, that he had nothing to say in contradiction, except that he did not know what became of the box.

'Did you see the box on the table?' asked the lawyer on the opposite side, Mr Standup.

'I saw it there when I first went into the room. Miss Betty made a remark about the box, which drew my attention to it. I was sitting at the far end of the room,

344

at Mr Cockermuth's little desk-table. I did not notice the box afterwards.'

'Did you not see it there after Miss Cockermuth left the room?'

'No, I did not; not that I remember,' answered Sam. 'Truth to say, I never thought about it. My attention was confined to the letter I was copying, to the exclusion of everything else.'

'Did anyone come into the room after Miss Cockermuth left it?'

'No one came into it. Somebody opened the door and looked in.'

This was fresh news. The town hall pricked up its ears.

'I do not know who it was,' added Sam. 'My head was bent over my writing, when the door opened quickly and as quickly shut again. I supposed somebody had looked in to see if Mr or Miss Cockermuth was there, and had retreated on finding they were not.'

'Could that person, whomsoever it might have been, have advanced to the table and taken the box?' asked the chief of the magistrates.

'No, sir. For certain, no!' – and Sam's tone here, he best knew why, was aggravatingly defiant. 'The person might have put his head in – and no doubt did – but he did not set a foot inside the room.'

Captain Cockermuth was asked about this: whether he had observed anyone go to the parlour and look in. He protested till he was nearly blue with rage (for he regarded it as Sam's invention) that such a thing never took place, that no one whatever went near the parlour-door.

Next came up the question of the guinea, which was hanging from his watch-guard, shining and bold as if it had been brass. Sam had been questioned about this by the justices on Thursday, and his statement in answer to them was just as bold as the coin.

The guinea had been given him by his late father's uncle, old Thomas Dene, who had jokingly enjoined him never to change it, always to keep it by him, and then he would never be without money. Sam had kept it; kept it from that time to this. He kept it in one pocket of an old-fashioned leather case, which contained some letters from his father, and two or three other things he valued. No, he was not in the habit of getting the guinea out to look at, he had retorted to a little badgering; had not looked at it (or at the case either, which lay in the bottom of his trunk) for months and months – yes, it might be years, for all he recollected. But on the Tuesday evening, when talking with Miss Parslet about guineas, he fetched it to show to her; and slipped in into his pocket afterwards, where the police found it on the Thursday. This was the substance of his first answer, and he related it now.

'Do you know who is said to be the father of lies, young man?' asked Justice Whitewicker in a solemn tone, suspecting that the prisoner was telling an out-and-out fable.

'I have heard,' answered Sam. 'Have never seen him myself. Perhaps you have, sir.' At which a titter went round the court, and it put his worships's back up. Sam went on to say that he had often thought of taking his guinea out to wear, and had now done it. And he gave the guinea a flick in the face of us all.

Evidently little good could come of a hardened criminal like this; and Justice Whitewicker, who thought nothing on earth so grand as the sound of his own voice from the bench, gave Sam a piece of his mind. In the midst of this a stir arose at the appearance of Maria Parslet. Mr Chance led her in; her father, sad and shrinking as usual, walked behind them. Lawyer Cockermuth – and I liked him for it – made a place for his clerk next to himself. Maria looked modest, gentle and pretty. She wore black silk, being in slight mourning, and a dainty white bonnet.

Mr Dene was asked to take tea with them in the parlour on the Tuesday evening, as a matter of convenience, Maria's evidence ran, in answer to questions, and she briefly alluded to the reason why. While waiting together, he and she, for her father to come in, Mr Dene told her of the finding of the ebony box of guineas at Mr Cockermuth's. She laughingly remarked that a guinea was an out-of-date coin now, and she was not sure that she had ever seen one. In reply to that, Mr Dene said he had one by him, given him by an old uncle some years before; and he went upstairs and brought it down to show to her. There could be no mistake, Maria added to Mr Whitewicker, who wanted to insinuate a word of doubt, and her sweet brown eyes were honest and true as she said it; she had touched the guinea and held it in her hand for some moments.

'Held it and touched it, did you, Miss Parslet?' retorted Lawyer Standup. 'Pray what appearance had it?'

'It was a thin, worn coin, sir,' replied Maria; 'thinner, I think, than a sovereign, but somewhat larger; it seemed to be worn thin at the edge.'

'Whose image was on it? - what king's?'

'George III's. I noticed that.'

'Now, don't you think, young lady, that the accused

took this marvellous coin from his pocket, instead of from some receptacle above stairs?' pursued Mr Standup.

'I am quite sure he did not take it from his pocket when before me,' answered Maria. 'He ran upstairs quickly, saying he would fetch the guinea; he had nothing in his hand then.'

Upon this Lawyer Chance enquired of his learned brother why he need waste time in useless questions; begging to remind him that it was not until Wednesday morning the box disappeared, so the prisoner could not well have had any of its contents about him on Tuesday.

'Just let my questions alone, will you,' retorted Mr Standup, with a nod. 'I know what I am about. Now, Miss Parslet, please attend to me. Was the guinea you profess to have seen a perfect coin, or was there a hole in it?'

'It was a perfect coin, sir.'

'And what became of it?'

'I think Mr Dene put it in his waistcoat-pocket. I did not particularly notice. Quite close upon that, my father came home, and we sat down to tea. No, sir, nothing was said to my father about the guinea; if it was, I did not hear it, but he and Mr Dene talked of the box of guineas that had been found.'

'Who was it that called while you were at tea?'

'Young Mr Chance called. We had finished tea then, and Mr Dene took him upstairs to his own sitting-room.'

'I am not asking you about young Mr Chance; we shall come to him presently,' was the rough-toned, but not ill-natured retort. 'Somebody else called: who was it?'

Maria, blushing and paling ever since she stood up to the ordeal, grew white now. Mr Badger had called at the door, she answered, and Mr Dene went out to speak to him. Worried by Lawyer Standup as to whether he did not come to ask for money, she said she believed so, but she did not hear all they said.

Quiet Mr Parslet was the next witness. He had to acknowledge that he did hear it. Mr Badger appeared to be pressing for some money owing to him; could not tell the amount, knew nothing about that. When questioned whether the accused owed him money, Parslet said not a shilling; Mr Dene had never sought to borrow from him, and had paid his monthly accounts regularly.

Upon that, Mr Badger was produced; a thin man with a neck as stiff as a poker; who gave his reluctant testimony in a sweet tone of benevolence. Mr Dene had been borrowing money from him for some time; somewhere about twenty pounds, he thought, was owing now, including interest. He had repeatedly asked for its repayment, but only got put off with (as he believed) lame excuses. Had certainly gone to ask for it on the Tuesday evening; was neither loud nor angry, oh dear no; but did tell the accused he thought he could give him some if he would, and did say that he must have a portion of it within a week, or he should apply to Mr Jacobson, of Elm Farm. Did not really mean to apply to Mr Jacobson, had no wish to do anyone an injury, but felt vexed at the young man's off-handedness, which looked like indifference. Knew besides that Mr Dene had other debts.

Now I'll leave you to judge how this evidence struck

on the ears of old Jacobson. He leaped to the conclusion that Sam had been going all sorts of ways, as he supposed he went when in London, and might be owing, the mischief only knew how much money; and he shook his fist at Sam across the justice-room.

Mr Standup next called young Chance, quite to young Chance's surprise; perhaps also to his father's. He was questioned upon no end of things – whether the accused had shown any guinea to him when he was in Edgar Street on the Tuesday night. Austin answered that he believed Mr Dene owed a little money, not a great deal, so far as he knew; and that he had not seen the guinea or heard of it. And in saying all this, Austin's tone was just as resentfully insolent to Mr Standup as he dared to make it.

Well, it is of no use to go on categorically with the day's proceedings. When they came to an end, the magistrates conferred pretty hotly in a low tone among themselves, some apparently taking up one opinion as to Sam's guilt or innocence and some the other. At length they announced their decision, and it was as follows.

'Although the case undoubtedly presents grave grounds of suspicion against the accused, Samsom Reginald Dene' – 'Very grave indeed,' interjected Mr Whitewicker, solemnly – 'we do not consider them to be sufficient to commit him for trial upon; therefore, we give him the benefit of the doubt and discharge him. Should any further evidence transpire, he can be brought up again.'

'It was Maria Parslet's testimony about the guinea that cleared him,' whispered the crowd, as they filed out.

And I think it must have been. It was just impossible

to doubt her truth, or the earnestness with which she gave it.

Mr Jacobson 'interviewed' Sam, as the Americans say, and the interview was not a loving one. Being in the mood, he said anything that came uppermost. He forbade Sam to appear at Elm Farm again ever, as 'long as oak and ash grew'; and he added that as Sam was bent on going to the deuce head foremost, he might do it upon his own means, for he'd never get any more help from him.

The way the Squire lashed up Bob and Blister when driving home – for, liking Sam hitherto, he was just as much put out as old Jacobson – was alarming, and the duet they kept together in abuse of his misdeeds was edifying to hear. Tod laughed; I did not. The gig was given over this return journey to the two grooms.

'I do not believe Sam took the box, sir,' I said to Jacobson, interrupting a fiery oration.

He turned round to stare at me. 'What do you say, Johnny Ludlow? *You do not believe he took the box?*'

'Well, to me it seems quite plain that he did not take it. I've hardly ever felt more sure of anything.'

'Plain!' struck in the Squire. 'How is it plain, Johnny? What grounds do you go upon?'

'I judge by his looks and his tones, sir, when denying it. They are to be trusted.'

They did not know whether to laugh or scoff at me. It was Johnny's way, said the Squire, always fancying he could read the riddles in a man's face and voice. But they'd have thrown up their two best market-going hats with glee to be able to think it true.

Samson Reginald Dene was relieved of the charge, as it was declared 'not proven'; all the same, Samson

Reginald Dene was ruined. Worcester said so. During the following week, which was Passion Week, its citizens talked more of him than of their prayers.

Granted that Maria Parslet's testimony had been honestly genuine, a theory cropped up to counteract it. Lawyer Standup had been bold enough to start it at the Saturday's examination: a hundred tongues were repeating it now. Sam Dene, as may be remembered, was present at the finding of the box on Tuesday; he had come up the passage and touched the golden guineas in it with the tips of his fingers; those fingers might have deftly extracted one of the coins. No wonder he could show it to Maria when he went home to tea! Captain Cockermuth admitted that in counting the guineas subsequently he had thought he counted sixty; but, as he knew there were (or ought to be) that number in the box, probably the assumption misled him, causing him to reckon them as sixty when in fact there were only fifty-nine. Which was a bit of logic.

Still, popular opinion was divided. If part of the town judged Sam to be guilty, part believed him to be innocent. A good deal might be said on both sides. To a young man who does not know how to pay his debts from lack of means, and debts that he is afraid of, too, sixty golden guineas may be a great temptation; and people did not shut their eyes to that. It transpired also that Mr Jacobson, his own uncle, his best friend, had altogether cast Sam off and told him he might now go to the dogs his own way.

Sam resented it all bitterly, and defied the world. Far from giving in or showing any sense of shame, he walked about with an air, his head up, and that brazen guinea dangling in front of him. He actually had the face to appear in the cathedral on Good Friday (the congregation looking askance at him) and sit out the cold service of the day: no singing, no organ, and the little chorister-boys in black surplices instead of white ones.

But the crowning act of boldness was to come. Before Easter week had lapsed into the past, Sam Dene had taken two rooms in a conspicuous part of the town and set-up in practice. A big brass plate on the outer door displayed his name: 'Mr Dene, Attorney-at-Law'. Sam's friends extolled his courage; Sam's enemies were amazed at his impudence. Captain Cockermuth prophesied that the ceiling of that office would come tumbling down on its crafty occupant's head: it was *his* gold that was paying for it.

The Cockermuths, like the town, were divided in opinion. Mr Cockermuth could not believe Sam guilty, although the mystery as to where the box could be puzzled him as few things had ever puzzled him in his life. He would fain have taken Sam back again, had it been a right thing to do. What the captain thought need not be enlarged upon. While Miss Betty felt uncertain; veering now to this belief, now to that, and much distressed either way.

There is one friend in this world that hardly ever deserts us – and that is a mother. Mrs Dene, a pretty little woman yet, had come flying to Worcester, ready to fight everybody in it on her son's behalf. Sam of course made his own tale good to her; whether it was a true one or not he alone knew, but not an angel from heaven could have stirred her faith in it. She declared that, to her positive knowledge, the old uncle had given Sam the guinea.

It was understood to be Mrs Dene who advanced

353

VINTAGE DETECTIVE STORIES

the money to Sam to set up with; it was certainly Mrs Dene who bought a shutting-up bed (at old Ward's), and a gridiron, and a tea-pot, and a three-legged table, and a chair of two, all for the back room of the little office, that Sam might go into housekeeping on his own account, and live upon sixpence a day, so to say, until business came in. To look at Sam's hopeful face, he meant to do it, and to live down the scandal.

Looking at the thing impartially, one might perhaps see that Sam was not swayed by impudence in setting-up so much as by obligation. For what else lay open to him? – no firm would engage him as clerk with that doubt sticking to his coat-tails. He paid some of his debts, and undertook to pay the rest before the year was out. A whisper arose that it was Mrs Dene who managed this. Sam's adversaries knew better; the funds came out of the ebony box; that, as Charles Cockermuth demonstrated, was as sure as heaven.

But now there occurred one thing that I, Johnny Ludlow, could not understand, and never shall: why Worcester should have turned its back, like an angry drake, upon Maria Parslet. The school where she was resident teacher wrote her a cool, polite note, to say she need not trouble herself to return after the Easter recess. That example was followed. Pious individuals looked upon her as a possible storyteller, in danger of going to the bad in Sam's defence, nearly as much as Sam had gone.

It was just a craze. Even Charles Cockermuth said there was no sense in blaming Maria: of course Sam had deceived her (when pretending to show the guinea as his own), just as he deceived other people. Next the town called her 'bold' for standing up before all eyes at the Guildhall to give her evidence. But how could Maria help that? It was not her own choice; she'd rather have locked herself up in the cellar. Lawyer Chance had burst in upon her that Saturday morning (not ten minutes after we left the house), giving nobody warning, and carried her off imperatively, never saying, 'Will you?' or, 'Won't you?' It was not his way.

Placid Miss Betty was indignant when the injustice came to her ears. What did people mean by it? she wanted to know. She sent for Maria to spend the next Sunday in Foregate Street, and marched with her arm in arm to church (St Nicholas's), morning and evening.

As the days and the weeks passed, commotion gave place to a calm; Sam and his delinquencies were let alone. One cannot be on the grumble for ever. Sam's lines were pretty hard; practice held itself aloof from him; and if he did not live upon the sixpence a day, he looked at every halfpenny that he had to spend beyond it. His face grew thin, his blue eyes wistful, but he smiled hopefully.

'You keep up young Dene's acquaintance, I perceive,' remarked Lawyer Chance to his son one evening as they were finishing dinner, for he had met the two young men together that day.

'Yes: why shouldn't I?' returned Austin.

'Think that charge was a mistaken one, I suppose?'

'Well I do, father. He has affirmed it to me in terms so unmistakable that I can but believe him. Besides, I don't think Dene, as I have always said, is the sort of fellow to turn rogue. I don't, indeed.'

'Does he get any practice?'

'Very little, I'm afraid.'

Mr Chance was a man with a conscience. On the

whole, he felt inclined to think Sam had not helped himself to the guineas, but he was by no means sure of it; like Miss Betty Cockermuth, his opinion veered, now on this side, now on that, like a haunted weather-cock. If Sam was not guilty, why, then, fate had dealt hardly with the young fellow – and what would the end be? These thoughts were running through the lawyer's mind as he talked to his son and sat playing with his bunch of seals, which hung down by a short, thick gold chain, in the old-fashioned manner.

'I should like to say a word to him if he'd come to me,' he suddenly cried. 'You might go and bring him, Austin.'

'What – this evening?' exclaimed Austin.

'Aye; why not? One time's as good as another.'

Austin Chance started off promptly for the new office, and found his friend presiding over his own tea-tray in the little back-room: the loaf and butter on the table, and a red herring on the gridiron.

'Hadn't time to get any dinner today; too busy,' was Sam's apology, given briefly with a flush of the face. 'Mr Chance wants me? Well, I'll come. What is it for?'

'Don't know,' replied Austin. And away they went.

The lawyer was standing at the window, his hands in the pockets of his pepper-and-salt trousers, tinkling the shillings and sixpences there. Austin supposed he was not wanted, and shut them in.

'I have been thinking of your case a good bit lately, Sam Dene,' began Mr Chance, giving Sam a seat and sitting down himself; 'and I should like to feel, if I can, more at a certainty about it, one way or the other.'

'Yes, sir,' replied Sam. And you must please to note that manners in those days had not degenerated to what they are in these. Young men, whether gentle or simple, addressed their elders with respect; young women also. 'Yes, sir,' replied Sam. 'but what do you mean about wishing to feel more at a certainty?'

'When I defended you before the magistrates, I did my best to convince them that you were not guilty; you had assured me you were not; and they discharged you. I believe my arguments and my pleadings went some way with them.'

'I have no doubt of it, sir, and I thanked you at the time with all my heart,' said Sam warmly. 'Some of my enemies were bitter enough against me.'

'But you should not speak in that way – calling people your enemies!' reproved the lawyer. 'People were only at enmity with you on the score of the offence. Look here, Sam Dene – did you commit it, or did you not?'

Sam stared. Mr Chance dropped his voice to a solemn key, his head pushed forward, gravity sat on his face.

'No, sir. No.'

The short answer did not satisfy the lawyer. 'Did you filch the box of guineas out of Cockermuth's room; or were you, and are you, as you assert, wholly innocent?' he resumed. 'Tell me the truth as before heaven. Whatever it be, I will shield you still.'

Sam rose. 'On my sacred word, sir, and before heaven, I have told nothing but the truth. I did not take or touch the box of guineas. I do not know what became of it.'

Mr Chance regarded Sam in silence. He had known young men, when under a cloud, prevaricate in a most extraordinary and unblushing manner; to look at them and listen to them, one might have said they were fit to be canonised. But he thought truth lay with Sam now.

'Sit down, sit down, Dene,' he said. 'I am glad to believe you. Where the deuce could the box have got to? It could not take flight through the ceiling up to the clouds, or down to the earth through the floor. *Whose hands took it?*'

'The box went in one of two ways,' returned Sam. 'If the captain did not fetch it out unconsciously, and lose it in the street, why, somebody must have entered the parlour after I left it and carried off the box. Perhaps the individual who looked into the room when I was sitting there.'

'A pity you didn't notice who that was.'

'Yes, it is. Look here, Mr Chance; a thought has more than once struck me – if that person did not come back and take the box, why has he not come forward and openly and honestly avowed it was himself who looked in?'

The lawyer gave his head a dissenting shake. 'It is a ticklish thing to be mixed up in, he may think, one that he had best keep out of – though he may be innocent as the day. How are you getting on?' he asked, passing abruptly from the subject.

'Oh, middling,' replied Sam. 'As well, perhaps, as I could expect to get on at first, with all the prejudice abroad against me.'

'Earning bread and cheese?'

'Not quite – yet.'

'Well, see here, Dene – and this is what I chiefly sent for you to say, if you could assure me on your conscience you deserved it – I may be able to put some little business in your hands. Petty matters are brought to us that we hardly care to waste time upon.

I'll send them to you in future. I dare say you'll be able to rub on by dint of patience. Rome was not built in a day, you know.'

'Thank you, sir; I thank you very truly,' breathed Sam. 'Mr Cockermuth sent me a small matter the other day. If I can make a bare living of it at present, that's all I ask. Fame and fortune are not rained down upon black sheep.'

Which was so true a remark as to need no contradiction.

May was nearing its close then, and the summer evenings were long and lovely. As Sam went forth from the interview, he thought he would take a walk by the river, instead of turning in to his solitary rooms. Since entering upon them he had been as steady as Old Time: the accusation and its attendant shame seemed to have converted him from a heedless, youthful man into a wise old sage of age and care. Passing down Broad Street towards the bridge, he turned to the left and sauntered along beside the Severn. The water glittered in the light of the setting sun; barges, some of them bearing men and women and children, passed smoothly up and down on it; the opposite fields, towards St John's, were green as an emerald; all things seemed to wear an aspect of brightness.

All of a sudden things grew brighter – and Sam's pulses gave a leap. He had passed the grand old red-stoned wall that enclosed the Bishop's Palace and was close upon the gates leading up to the Green, when a young lady turned out of them and came towards him with a light, quick step. It was Maria Parslet, in a pretty summer muslin, a straw hat shading her blushing face. For it did blush furiously at sight of Sam.

'Mr Dene!'

'Maria!'

She began to say, hurriedly, that her mother had sent her with a message to the dressmaker on the Parade, and she had taken that way, as being the shortest – as if in apology for having met Sam.

He turned with her, and they paced slowly along side by side, the colour on Maria's cheeks coming and going with every word he spoke and every look he gave her – which seemed altogether senseless and unreasonable. Sam told her of his conversation with Austin Chance's father, and his promise to put a few things in his way.

'Once let me be making two hundred a year, Maria, and then – '

'Then what?' questioned Maria innocently.

'Then I should ask you to come to me, and we'd risk it together.'

'Risk what?' stammered Maria, turning her head right round to watch a barge that was being towed by.

'Risk our luck. Two hundred a year is not so bad to begin upon. I should take the floor above as well as the ground-floor I rent now, and we should get along. Anyway, I hope to try it.'

'Oh, Mr Dene!'

'Now don't "Mr Dene" me, young lady, if you please. Why, Maria, what else can we do? A mean, malicious set of dogs and cats have turned their backs upon us both; the least we should do is to see if we can't do without them. I know you'd rather come to me than stay in Edgar Street.'

Maria held her tongue, as to whether she would or not. 'Mamma is negotiating to get me a situation at Cheltenham,' she said.

'You will not go to Cheltenham, or anywhere else, if I get any luck,' he replied dictatorially. 'Life would look very blue to me now without you, Maria. And many a man and wife, rolling in riches at the end, have rubbed on with less than two hundred a year at the beginning. I wouldn't say, mind, but we might risk it on a hundred and fifty. My rent is low, you see.'

'Ye–es,' stammered Maria. 'But – I wish that mystery of the guineas could be cleared up!'

Sam stood still, turned, and faced her. 'Why do you say *that*? You are not suspecting that I took them?'

'Oh dear, no,' returned Maria, losing her breath. 'I *know* you did not take them: could not. I was only thinking of your practice: so much more would come in.'

'Cockermuth has sent me a small matter or two. I think I shall get on,' repeated Sam.

They were at their journey's end by that time, at the dressmaker's door. 'Good-evening,' said Maria, timidly holding out her hand.

Sam Dene took it and clasped it. 'Goodbye, my darling. I am going home to my bread-and-cheese supper, and I wish you were there to eat it with me!'

Maria sighed. She wondered whether that wonderful state of things would ever come to pass. Perhaps no; perhaps yes. Meanwhile no living soul knew aught of these treasonable aspirations; they were a secret between her and Sam. Mr and Mrs Parslet suspected nothing.

Time went on. Lawyer Chance was as good as his word, and put a few small matters of business into the hands of Sam Dene. Mr Cockermuth did the same. The town came down upon him for it; though it let Chance alone, who was not the sort of man to be dictated to. 'Well,' said Cockermuth in answer, 'I don't believe the lad is guilty; never believed it. Had he been of a dishonest turn, he could have helped himself before, for a good deal of cash passed at times through his hands. And, given that he was innocent, he has been hardly dealt by.'

Sam Dene was grateful for these stray windfalls, and returned his best thanks to the lawyers for them. But they did not amount to much in the aggregate; and a gloomy vision began to present itself to his apprehension of being forced to give up the struggle, and wandering out in the world to seek a better fortune. The summer assizes drew near. Sam had no grand cause to come on at them, or small one either; but it was impossible not to give a thought now and again to what his fate might have been, had he stood committed to take his trial at them. The popular voice said that was only what he merited.

The assizes were held, and passed. One hot day, when July was nearing its meridian, word was brought to Miss Cockermuth – who was charitable – that a poor sick woman, whom she had befriended, was worse than usual, so she put on her bonnet and cloak to pay her a visit. The bonnet was a huge leghorn, which shaded her face well from the sun, its trimming of straw colour; and the cloak was of thin black 'taffeta', edged with narrow lace. It was a long walk on a hot afternoon, for the sick woman lived but just on this side Henwick. Miss Betty had got as far as the bridge, and was about to cross it when Sam Dene, coming over it at a strapping pace, ran against her.

'Miss Betty!' he cried. 'I beg your pardon.'

Miss Betty brought her bonnet from under the shade of her large grass-green parasol. 'Dear me, is it you, Sam Dene?' she said. 'Were you walking for a wager?'

Sam laughed a little. 'I was hastening back to my office, Miss Betty. I have no clerk, you know, and a client *might* come in.'

Miss Betty gave her head a twist, something between a nod and a shake; she noticed the doubtful tone in the 'might'. 'Very hot, isn't it?' said she. 'I'm going up to see that poor Hester Knowles; she's uncommon bad, I hear.'

'You'll have a warm walk.'

'Aye. Are you pretty well, Sam? You look thin.'

'Do I? Oh, that's nothing but the heat of the weather. I am quite well, thank you. Good-afternoon, Miss Betty.'

She shook his hand heartily. One of Sam's worst enemies, who might have run in a curricle with Charles Cockermuth as to an out-and-out belief in his guilt, was passing at the moment, and saw it.

Miss Betty crossed the bridge and turned off into Turkey, for it was through those classical regions that her nearest and coolest way lay, and so onwards to the sick woman's room. There she found the blazing July sun streaming in at the wide window, which had no blind, no shelter whatever from it. Miss Betty had had enough of the sun out-of-doors, without having it in. Done up with the walk and the heat, she sat down on the first chair, and felt ready to swoon right off.

'Dear me, Hester, this is bad for you!' she gasped.

'Did you mean the sun, ma'am?' asked the sick woman, who was sitting full in it, wrapped in a blanket or two. 'It is a little hot just now, but I don't grumble at it; I'm so cold mostly. As soon as the sun goes off the window, I shall begin to shiver.'

'Well-a-day!' responded Miss Betty, wishing she could be cool enough to shiver. 'But if you feel it cold now, Hester, what will you do when the autumn winds come in?'

'Ah, ma'am, please do not talk of it? I just can't tell what I shall do. That window don't fit tight, and the way the wind pours in through it upon me as I sit here at evening, or lie in my little bed there, passes belief. I'm coughing always then.'

'You should have some good thick curtains put up,' said Miss Betty, gazing at the bare window, which had a pot of musk on its sill. 'Woollen ones.'

The sick woman smiled sadly. She was very poor now, though it had not always been so; she might as well have hoped to buy the sun itself as woollen curtains – or cotton curtains either. Miss Betty knew that.

'I'll think about it, Hester, and see if I've any old ones that I could let you have. I'm not sure; but I'll look,' repeated she – and began to empty her capacious dimity pockets of a few good things she had brought.

By and by, when she was a little cooler, and had talked with Hester, Miss Betty set off home again, her mind running upon the half-promised curtains. 'They are properly shabby,' thought she, as she went along, 'but they'll serve to keep the sun and the wind off her.'

She was thinking of those warm green curtains that she had picked the braid from that past disastrous morning – as the reader heard of, and all the town as well. Nothing had been done with them since.

Getting home, Miss Betty turned into the parlour.

Susan – who had not yet found leisure to fix any time for her wedding – found her mistress fanning her hot face, her bonnet untied and tilted back.

'I've been to see that poor Hester Knowles, Susan,' began Miss Betty.

'Law, ma'am!' interposed Susan. 'What a walk for you this scorching afternoon! All up that wide New Road!'

'You may well say that, girl, but I went through Turkey. She's very ill, poor thing; and that's a frightfully staring window of hers, the sun on it like a blazing fire, and not as much as a rag for a blind; and the window don't fit, she says, and in cold weather the biting wind comes in and shivers her up. I think I might give her those shabby old curtains, Susan – that were up in Mr Philip's room, you know, before we got the new chintz ones in.'

'So you might, ma'am,' said Susan, who was not a bad-hearted girl, excepting to the baker's man. 'They can't go up at any of our windows as they be; and if you had 'em dyed, I don't know as they'd answer much, being so shabby.'

'I put them – let me see – into the spare ottoman, didn't I? Yes, that was it. And there I suppose they must by lying still.'

'Sure enough, Miss Betty.'

'With all the trouble that got into our house at the time, I couldn't give my mind to seeing after the old things, and I've not thought about them since. Come upstairs with me now, Susan; we'll see what sort of a state they are in.'

They went up; and Miss Betty took off her bonnet and cloak and put her cap on. The spare ottoman, soft, and red, and ancient, used as a receptacle for odds and ends that were not wanted, stood in a spacious linen-closet on the first-floor landing. It was built out over the back-door, and had a skylight above. Susan threw back the lid of the ottoman, and Miss Betty stood by. The faded old brown curtains, green once, lay in a heap at one end, just as Miss Betty had hastily flung them on that past day in March, when on her way to look at the chintzes.

'They're in a fine rabble, seemingly,' observed Susan, pausing to regard the curtains.

'Dear me!' cried Miss Betty, conscience-stricken, for she was a careful housewife. 'I let them drop in any way, I remember. I did mean to have them well shaken out of doors and properly folded, but that bother drove it all out of my head. Take them out, girl.'

Susan put her strong arms underneath the heap and lifted it out with a fling. Something heavy flew out of the curtains and dropped on the boarded floor with a crash. Letting fall the curtains, Susan gave a wild shriek of terror and Miss Betty gave a wilder, for the floor was suddenly covered with shining gold coins. Mr Cockermuth, passing across the passage below at the moment, heard the cries, wondered whether the house was on fire, and came hastening up.

'Oh,' said he coolly, taking in the aspect of affairs. 'So the thief was you, Betty, after all!'

He picked up the ebony box, and bent his head to look at the guineas. Miss Betty sank down on a three-legged stool – brought in for Philip's children – and grew as white as death.

Yes, it was the missing box of guineas, come to light in the same extraordinary and unexpected manner that it had come before, without having been (as may be said) truly lost. When Miss Betty gathered her curtains off the dining-room table that March morning, a cumbersome and weighty heap, she had unwittingly gathered up the box with them. No wonder Sam Dene had not seen the box on the table after Miss Betty's departure! It was a grievous misfortune, though, that he failed to take notice it was not there.

She had no idea she was not speaking the truth in saying she *saw* the box on the table as she left the room. Having seen the box there all the morning she thought it was there still, and that she saw it, being quite unconscious that it was in her arms. Susan, too, had noticed the box on the table when she opened the door to call her mistress, and believed she was correct in saying she saw it there to the last; the real fact being that she had not observed it was gone. So there the box with its golden freight had lain undisturbed, hidden in the folds of the curtains. But for Hester Knowles's defective window, it might have stayed there still, who can say how long?

Susan, no less scared than her mistress, stood back against the closet wall for safety, out of reach of those diabolical coins; Miss Betty, groaning and half-fainting on the three-legged stool, sat pushing back her cap and her front. The lawyer picked up the guineas and counted them as he laid them flat in the box. Sixty of them: not one missing. So Sam's guinea *was* his own! He had not, as Worcester whispered, trumped up the story with Maria Parslet.

'John,' gasped poor Miss Betty, beside herself with remorse and terror, 'John, what will become of me now? Will anything be done?'

'How "done"?' asked he.

'Will they bring me to trial – or anything like that – in poor Sam's place?'

'Well, I don't know,' answered her brother grimly; 'perhaps not this time. But I'd have you take more care in future, Betty, than to hide away gold in old curtains.'

Locking the box securely within his iron safe, Mr Cockermuth put on his hat and went down to the town hall, where the magistrates, after dispensing their wisdom, were about to disperse for the day. He told them of the wonderful recovery of the box of guineas, of how it had been lost, and that Sam Dene was wholly innocent. Their worships were of course charmed to hear it, Mr Whitewicker observing that they had only judged Sam by appearances, and that appearances had been sufficient (in theory) to hang him.

From the town hall, Mr Cockermuth turned off to Sam's office. Sam was making a great show of business, surrounded by a table full of imposing parchments, but with never a client to the fore. His old master grasped his hand.

'Well, Sam, my boy,' he said, 'the tables have turned for you. That box of guineas is found.'

Sam never spoke an answering word. His lips parted with expectation: his breath seemed to be a little short.

'Betty had got it all the time. She managed somehow to pick it up off the table with those wretched old curtains she had there, all unconsciously, of course, and it has lain hidden with the curtains upstairs in a lumber-box ever since. Betty will never forgive herself. She'll have a fit of the jaundice over this.'

Sam drew a long breath. 'You will let the public know, sir?'

'Aye, Sam, without the loss of an hour. I've begun

with the magistrates – and a fine sensation the news made amidst 'em, I can tell you; and now I'm going round to the newspapers; and I shall go over to Elm Farm the first thing tomorrow. The town took up the cause against you, Sam, take care it does not eat you now in its repentance. Look here, you'll have to come round to Betty, or she'll moan her heart out; you won't bear malice, Sam?'

'No, that I won't,' said Sam warmly. 'Miss Betty did not bear it to me. She has been as kind as can be all along.'

The town did want to eat Sam. It is the custom of the true Briton to go to extremes. Being unable to shake Sam's hands quite off, the city would fain have chaired him round the streets with honours, as it used to chair its newly returned members.

Captain Cockermuth, sent for post haste, came to Worcester all contrition, beseeching Sam to forgive him fifty times a day, and wanting to press the box of guineas upon him as a peace-offering. Sam would not take it: he laughingly told the captain that the box did not seem to carry luck with it.

And then Sam's troubles were over. And no objection was made by his people (as it otherwise might have been) to his marrying Maria Parslet by way of recompense. 'God never fails to bring good out of evil, my dear,' said old Mrs Jacobson to Maria, the first time they had her on a visit at Elm Farm. As to Sam, he had short time for Elm Farm, or anything else in the shape of recreation. Practice was flowing in quickly: litigants arguing, one with another, that a young man, lying for months under an imputation of theft, and then coming out of it with flying colours, must needs be a clever lawyer.

'But, Johnny,' Sam said to me, when talking of the past, 'there's one thing I would alter if I made the laws. No person, so long as he is only suspected of crime, should have his name proclaimed publicly. I am not speaking of murder, you understand, or charges of that grave nature; but of such a case as mine. My name appeared in full, in all the local newspapers, Samson Reginald Dene, coupled with theft, and of course it got a mark upon it. It is an awful blight upon a man when he is innocent, one that he may never quite live down. Suspicions must arise, I know that, of the innocent as well as the guilty, and they must undergo preliminary examinations in public and submit to legal enquiries; but time enough to proclaim who the man is when evidence strengthens against him, and he is committed for trial; until then let his name be suppressed. At least that is my opinion.'

E. W. HORNUNG

Out of Paradise

If I must tell more tales of Raffles, I can but go back to our earliest days together, and fill in the blanks left by discretion in existing annals. In so doing I may indeed fill some small part of an infinitely greater blank, across which you may conceive me to have stretched my canvas for the first frank portrait of my friend. The whole truth cannot harm him now. I shall paint in every wart. Raffles was a villain, when all is written; it is no service to his memory to glaze the fact; yet I have done so myself before today. I have omitted whole heinous episodes. I have dwelt unduly on the redeeming side. And this I may do again, blinded even as I write by the gallant glamour that made my villain more to me than any hero. But at least there shall be no more reservations, and as an earnest I shall make no further secret of the greatest wrong that even Raffles ever did me.

I pick my words with care and pain, loyal as I still would be to my friend, and yet remembering as I must those Ides of March when he led me blindfold into temptation and crime. That was an ugly office, if you will. It was a moral bagatelle to the treacherous trick he was to play me a few weeks later. The second offence, on the other hand, was to prove the less serious of the two against society, and might in itself have been published to the world years ago. There have been private reasons for my reticence. The affair was not only too intimately mine, and too discreditable to Raffles. One other was involved in it, one dearer to me than Raffles himself, one whose name shall not even now be sullied by association with ours.

Suffice it that I had been engaged to her before that mad March deed. True, her people called it 'an understanding', and frowned even upon that, as well they might. But their authority was not direct; we bowed to it as an act of politic grace; between us, all was well but my unworthiness. That may be gauged when I confess that this was how the matter stood on the night I gave a worthless cheque for my losses at baccarat, and afterwards turned to Raffles in my need. Even after that I saw her sometimes. But I let her guess that there was more upon my soul than she must ever share, and at last I had written to end it all. I remember that week so well! It was the close of such a May as we had never had since, and I was too miserable even to follow the heavy scoring in the papers. Raffles was the only man who could get a wicket up at Lord's, and I never once went to see him play. Against Yorkshire, however, he helped himself to a hundred runs as well; and that brought Raffles round to me, on his way home to the Albany.

'We must dine and celebrate the rare event,' said he. 'A century takes it out of one at my time of life; and you, Bunny, you look quite as much in need of your end of a worthy bottle. Suppose we make it the Café Royal, and eight sharp? I'll be there first to fix up the table and the wine.'

And at the Café Royal I incontinently told him of the trouble I was in. It was the first he had ever heard of my affair, and I told him all, though not before our bottle had been succeeded by a pint of the same exemplary brand. Raffles heard me out with grave attention. His sympathy was the more grateful for the tactful brevity with which it was indicated rather than expressed. He only wished that I had told him of this complication in the beginning; as I had not, he agreed with me that the only course was a candid and complete renunciation. It was not as though my divinity had a penny of her own, or I could earn an honest one. I had explained to Raffles that she was an orphan, who spent most of her time with an aristocratic aunt in the country, and the remainder under the repressive roof of a pompous politician in Palace Gardens. The aunt had, I believed, still a sneaking softness for me, but her illustrious brother had set his face against me from the first.

'Hector Carruthers!' murmured Raffles, repeating the detested name with his clear, cold eye on mine. 'I suppose you haven't seen much of him?'

'Not a thing for ages,' I replied. 'I was at the house two or three days last year, but they've neither asked me since nor been at home to me when I've called. The old beast seems a judge of men.' And I laughed bitterly in my glass.

'Nice house?' said Raffles, glancing at himself in his silver cigarette-case.

'Top shelf,' said I. 'You know the houses in Palace Gardens, don't you?'

'Not so well as I should like to know them, Bunny.'

'Well, it's about the most palatial of the lot. The old ruffian is as rich as Croesus. It's a country-place in town.'

'What about the window-fastenings?' asked Raffles casually.

I recoiled from the open cigarette-case that he

373

proffered as he spoke. Our eyes met; and in his there
was that starry twinkle of mirth and mischief, that
sunny beam of audacious devilment, which had been
my undoing two months before, which was to undo
me as often as he chose until the chapter's end. Yet
for once I withstood its glamour; for once I turned
aside that luminous glance with front of steel. There
was no need for Raffles to voice his plans. I read
them all between the strong lines of his smiling,
eager face. And I pushed back my chair in the equal
eagerness of my own resolve.

'Not if I know it!' said I. 'A house I've dined in – a
house I've seen *her* in – a house where *she* stays by the
month together! Don't put it into words, Raffles, or
I'll get up and go.'

'You mustn't do that before the coffee and liqueur,'
said Raffles laughing. 'Have a small Sullivan first: it's
the royal road to a cigar. And now let me observe that
your scruples would do you honour if old Carruthers
still lived in the house in question.'

'Do you mean to say he doesn't?'

Raffles struck a match, and handed it first to me. 'I
mean to say, my dear Bunny, that Palace Gardens
knows the very name no more. You began by telling
me you had heard nothing of these people all this
year. That's quite enough to account for our little
misunderstanding. I was thinking of the house, and
you were thinking of the people in the house.'

'But who are they, Raffles? Who has taken the
house, if old Carruthers has moved, and how do you
know that it is still worth a visit?'

'In answer to your first question – Lord Lochmaben,' replied Raffles, blowing bracelets of smoke
toward the ceiling. 'You look as though you had never

374

heard of him; but as the cricket and racing are the only part of your paper that you condescend to read, you can't be expected to keep track of all the peers created in your time. Your other question is not worth answering. How do you suppose that I know these things? It's my business to get to know them, and that's all there is to it. As a matter of fact, Lady Lochmaben has just as good diamonds as Mrs Carruthers ever had; and the chances are that she keeps them where Mrs Carruthers kept hers, if you could enlighten me on that point.'

As it happened, I could, since I knew from his niece that it was one on which Mr Carruthers had been a faddist in his time. He had made quite a study of the cracksman's craft, in a resolve to circumvent it with his own. I remembered myself how the ground-floor windows were elaborately bolted and shuttered, and how the doors of all the rooms opening upon the square inner hall were fitted with extra Yale locks, at an unlikely height, not to be discovered by one within the room. It had been the butler's business to turn and to collect all these keys before retiring for the night. But the key of the safe in the study was supposed to be in the jealous keeping of the master of the house himself. That safe was in its turn so ingeniously hidden that I never should have found it for myself. I well remember how one who showed it to me (in the innocence of her heart) laughed as she assured me that even her little trinkets were solemnly locked up in it every night. It had been let into the wall behind one end of the bookcase, expressly to preserve the barbaric splendour of Mrs Carruthers; without a doubt these Lochmabens would use it for the same purpose; and in the altered circumstances I had no hesitation in giving Raffles all the information he desired. I even drew him a rough plan of the ground-floor on the back of my menu-card.

'It was rather clever of you to notice the kind of locks on the inner doors,' he remarked as he put it in his pocket. 'I suppose you don't remember if it was a Yale on the front door as well?'

'It was not,' I was able to answer quite promptly. 'I happen to know because I once had the key when – when we went to a theatre together.'

'Thank you, old chap,' said Raffles sympathetically. 'That's all I shall want from you, Bunny, my boy. There's no night like tonight!'

It was one of his sayings when bent upon his worst. I looked at him aghast. Our cigars were just in blast, yet already he was signalling for his bill. It was impossible to remonstrate with him until we were both outside in the street.

'I'm coming with you,' said I, running my arm through his.

'Nonsense, Bunny!'

'Why is it nonsense? I know every inch of the ground, and since the house has changed hands I have no compunction. Besides, "I have been there" in the other sense as well: once a thief, you know! In for a penny, in for a pound!'

It was ever my mood when the blood was up. But my old friend failed to appreciate the characteristic as he usually did. We crossed Regent Street in silence. I had to catch his sleeve to keep a hand in his inhospitable arm.

'I really think you had better stay away,' said Raffles as we reached the other curb. 'I've no use for you this time.'

'Yet I thought I had been so useful up to now?'

'That may be, Bunny, but I tell you frankly I don't want you tonight.'

'Yet I know the ground and you don't! I tell you what,' said I: 'I'll come just to show you the ropes, and I won't take a pennyweight of the swag.'

Such was the teasing fashion in which he invariably prevailed upon me; it was delightful to note how it caused him to yield in his turn. But Raffles had the grace to give in with a laugh, whereas I too often lost my temper with my point.

'You little rabbit!' he chuckled. 'You shall have your share, whether you come or not; but, seriously, don't you think you might remember the girl?'

'What's the use?' I groaned. 'You agree there is nothing for it but to give her up. I am glad to say I saw that for myself before I asked you, and wrote to tell her so on Sunday. Now it's Wednesday, and she hasn't answered by line or sign. It's waiting for one word from her that's driving me mad.'

'Perhaps you wrote to Palace Gardens?'

'No, I sent it to the country. There's been time for an answer, wherever she may be.'

We had reached the Albany, and halted with one accord at the Piccadilly portico, red cigar to red cigar.

'You wouldn't like to go and see if the answer's in your rooms?' he asked.

'No. What's the good? Where's the point in giving her up if I'm going to straighten out when it's too late? It *is* too late, I *have* given her up, and I *am* coming with you!'

The hand that bowled the most puzzling ball in England (once it found its length) descended on my shoulder with surprising promptitude.

'Very well, Bunny! That's finished; but your blood be on your own pate if evil comes of it. Meanwhile we can't do better than turn in here till you have finished your cigar as it deserves, and topped up with such a cup of tea as you must learn to like if you hope to get on in your new profession. And when the hours are small enough, Bunny, my boy, I don't mind admitting I shall be very glad to have you with me.'

I have a vivid memory of the interim in his rooms. I think it must have been the first and last of its kind that I was called upon to sustain with so much knowledge of what lay before me. I passed the time with one restless eye upon the clock, and the other on the tantalus which Raffles ruthlessly declined to unlock. He admitted that it was like waiting with one's pads on; and in my slender experience of the game of which he was a world's master, that was an ordeal not to be endured without a general quaking of the inner man. I was, on the other hand, all right when I got to the metaphorical wicket; and half the surprises that Raffles sprang on me were doubtless due to his early recognition of the fact.

On this occasion I fell swiftly and hopelessly out of love with the prospect I had so gratuitously embraced. It was not only my repugnance to enter that house in that way, which grew upon my better judgement as the artificial enthusiasm of the evening evaporated from my veins. Strong as that repugnance became, I had an even stronger feeling that we were embarking on an important enterprise far too much upon the spur of the moment. The latter qualm I had the temerity to confess to Raffles; nor have I often loved him more than when he freely admitted it to be the most natural feeling in the world. He assured me,

however, that he had had my Lady Lochmaben and
her jewels in his mind for several months; he had sat
behind them at first nights, and long ago determined
what to take or to reject; in fine, he had only been
waiting for those topographical details which it had
been my chance privilege to supply. I now learned
that he had numerous houses in a similar state upon
his list; something or other was wanting in each case
in order to complete his plans. In that of the Bond
Street jeweller it was a trusty accomplice; in the
present instance, a more intimate knowledge of the
house. And lastly, this was a Wednesday night, when
the tired legislator gets early to his bed.

How I wish I could make the whole world see and
hear him, and smell the smoke of his beloved Sullivan,
as he took me into these, the secrets of his infamous
trade! Neither look nor language would betray the
infamy. As a mere talker, I shall never listen to the
like of Raffles on this side of the sod; and his talk was
seldom garnished by an oath, never in my remembrance by an unclean word. Then he looked like a
man who had dressed to dine out, not like one who
had long since dined; for his curly hair, though longer
that another's, was never untidy in its length; and
these were the days when it was still as black as ink.
Nor were there many lines as yet upon the smooth
and mobile face; and its frame was still that dear den
of disorder and good taste, with the carved bookcase,
the dresser and chests of still older oak, and the
Wattses and Rossettis hung anyhow on the walls.

It must have been one o'clock before we drove in a
hansom as far as Kensington Church, instead of
getting down at the gates of our private road to ruin.
Constitutionally shy of the direct approach, Raffles

was further deterred by a ball in full swing at the Empress Rooms, whence potential witnesses were pouring between dances into the cool deserted street. Instead he led me a little way up Church Street, and so through the narrow passage into Palace Gardens. He knew the house as well as I did. We made our first survey from the other side of the road. And the house was not quite in darkness: there was a dim light over the door and a brighter one in the stables, which stood still farther back from the road.

'That's a bit of a bore,' said Raffles. 'The ladies have been out somewhere – trust them to spoil the show! They would get to bed before the stable folk, but insomnia is the curse of their sex and our profession. Somebody's not home yet; that will be the son of the house; but he's a beauty, who may not come home at all.'

'Another Alick Carruthers,' I murmured, recalling the one I liked least of all the household, as I remembered it.

'They might be brothers,' rejoined Raffles, who knew all the loose fish about town. 'Well, I'm not sure that I shall want you after all, Bunny.'

'Why not?'

'If the front door's only on the latch, and you're right about the lock, I shall walk in as though I were the son of the house myself.'

And he jingled the skeleton bunch that he carried on a chain as honest men carry their latchkeys.

'You forget the inner doors and the safe.'

'True. You might be useful to me there. But I still don't like leading you in where it isn't absolutely necessary, Bunny.'

'Then let me lead you, I answered, and forthwith

marched across the broad, secluded road, with the great houses standing back on either side in their ample gardens, as though the one opposite belonged to me. I thought Raffles had stayed behind, for I never heard him at my heels, yet there he was when I turned round at the gate.

'I must teach you the step,' he whispered, shaking his head. 'You shouldn't use your heel at all. Here's a grass border for you: walk it as you would the plank! Gravel makes a noise, and flower-beds tell a tale. Wait – I must carry you across this.'

It was the sweep of the drive, and in the dim light from above the door, the soft gravel, ploughed into ridges by the night's wheels, threatened an alarm at every step. Yet Raffles, with me in his arms, crossed the zone of peril softly as the pard.

'Shoes in your pocket – that's the beauty of pumps!' he whispered on the step; his light bunch tinkled faintly; a couple of keys he stooped and tried, with the touch of a humane dentist; the third let us into the porch. And as we stood together on the mat, as he was gradually closing the door, a clock within chimed a half-hour in fashion so thrillingly familiar to me that I caught Raffles by the arm. My half-hours of happiness had flown to just such chimes! I looked wildly about me in the dim light. Hat-stand and oak settee belonged equally to my past. And Raffles was smiling in my face as he held the door wide for my escape.

'You told me a lie!' I gasped in whispers.

'I did nothing of the sort,' he replied. 'The furniture's the furniture of Hector Carruthers; but the house is the house of Lord Lochmaben. Look here!'

He had stooped, and was smoothing out the

discarded envelope of a telegram. 'Lord Lochmaben',
I read in pencil by the dim light; and the case was
plain to me on the spot. My friends had let their
house, furnished, as anybody but Raffles would have
explained to me in the beginning.

'All right,' I said. 'Shut the door.'

And he not only shut it without a sound, but drew
a bolt that might have been sheathed in rubber.

In another minute we were at work upon the study
door, I with the tiny lantern and the bottle of rock-oil,
he with the brace and the largest bit. The Yale lock he
had given up at a glance. It was placed high up in the
door, feet above the handle, and the chain of holes
with which Raffles had soon surrounded it was bored
on a level with his eyes. Yet the clock in the hall
chimed again and two ringing strokes resounded
through the silent house before we gained admittance
to the room.

Raffles's next care was to muffle the bell on the
shuttered window (with a silk handkerchief from
the hat-stand) and to prepare an emergency exit by
opening first the shutters and then the window itself.
Luckily it was a still night, and very little wind came
in to embarrass us. He then began operations on the
safe, revealed by me behind its folding screen of
books, while I stood sentry on the threshold. I may
have stood there for a dozen minutes, listening to the
loud hall clock and to the gentle dentistry of Raffles
in the mouth of the safe behind me, when a third
sound thrilled my every nerve. It was the equally
cautious opening of a door in the gallery overhead.

I moistened my lips to whisper a word of warning
to Raffles. But his ears had been as quick as mine,
and something longer. His lantern darkened as I

turned my head; next moment I felt his breath upon the back of my neck. It was now too late even for a whisper, and quite out of the question to close the mutilated door. There we could only stand, I on the threshold, Raffles at my elbow, while one carrying a candle crept down the stairs.

The study door was at right angles to the lowest flight, and just to the right of one alighting in the hall. It was thus impossible for us to see who it was until the person was close abreast of us; but by the rustle of the gown we knew that it was one of the ladies, and dressed just as she had come from theatre or ball. Insensibly I drew back as the candle swam into our field of vision; it had not traversed many inches when a hand was clapped firmly but silently across my mouth.

I could forgive Raffles for that, at any rate! In another breath I should have cried aloud: for the girl with the candle, the girl in her ball-dress, at dead of night, the girl with the letter for the post, was the last girl on God's wide earth whom I should have chosen thus to encounter – a midnight intruder in the very house where I had been reluctantly received on her account!

I forgot Raffles. I forgot the new and unforgivable grudge I had against him now. I forgot his very hand across my mouth, even before he paid me the compliment of removing it. There was the only girl in all the world: I had eyes and brains for no one and for nothing else. She had neither seen nor heard us, had looked neither to the right hand nor the left. But a small oak table stood on the opposite side of the hall; it was to this table that she went. On it was one of those boxes in which one puts one's letters for the post; and she stooped to read by her candle the times at which this box was cleared.

The loud clock ticked and ticked. She was standing at her full height now, her candle on the table, her letter in both hands, and in her downcast face a sweet and pitiful perplexity that drew the tears to my eyes. Through a film I saw her open the envelope so lately sealed and read her letter once more, as though she would have altered it a little at the last. It was too late for that; but of a sudden she plucked a rose from her bosom, and was pressing it in with her letter when I groaned aloud.

How could I help it? The letter was for me: of that I was as sure as though I had been looking over her shoulder. She was as true as tempered steel; there were not two of us to whom she wrote and sent roses at dead of night. It was her one chance of writing to me. None would know that she had written. And she cared enough to soften the reproaches I had richly earned, with a red rose warm from her own warm heart. And there, and there was I, a common thief who had broken in to steal! Yet I was unaware that I had uttered a sound until she looked up, startled, and the hands behind me pinned me where I stood.

I think she must have seen us, even in the dim light of the solitary candle. Yet not a sound escaped her as she peered courageously in our direction; neither did one of us move; but the hall clock went on and on, every tick like the beat of a drum to bring the house about our ears, until a minute must have passed as in some breathless dream. And then came the awakening – with such a knocking and a ringing at the front door as brought all three of us to our senses on the spot.

'The son of the house!' whispered Raffles in my ear, as he dragged me back to the window he had left open for our escape. But as he leaped out first a sharp cry stopped me at the sill. 'Get back! Get back! We're trapped!' he cried; and in the single second that I stood there, I saw him fell one officer to the ground, and dart across the lawn with another at his heels. A third came running up to the window. What could I do but double back into the house? And there in the hall I met my lost love face to face.

Till that moment she had not recognised me. I ran to catch her as she all but fell. And my touch repelled her into life, so that she shook me off, and stood gasping: 'You, of all men! You, of all men!' until I could bear it no more, but broke again for the study-window. 'Not that way – not that way!' she cried in an agony at that. Her hands were upon me now. 'In there, in there,' she whispered, pointing and pulling me to a mere cupboard under the stairs, where hats and coats were hung; and it was she who shut the door on me with a sob.

Doors were already opening overhead, voices calling, voices answering, the alarm running like wildfire from room to room. Soft feet pattered in the gallery and down the stairs about my very ears. I do not know what made me put on my own shoes as I heard them, but I think that I was ready and even longing to walk out and give myself up. I need not say what and who it was that alone restrained me. I heard her name. I heard them crying to her as though she had fainted. I recognised the detested voice of my bête noire, Alick Carruthers, thick as might be expected of the dissipated dog, yet daring to stutter out her name. And then I heard, without catching,

385

her low reply; it was in answer to the somewhat stern questioning of quite another voice; and from what followed I knew that she had never fainted at all.

'Upstairs, miss, did he? Are you sure?'

I did not hear her answer. I conceive her as simply pointing up the stairs. In any case, about my very ears once more there now followed such a patter and tramp of bare and booted feet as renewed in me a base fear for my own skin. But voices and feet passed over my head, went up and up, higher and higher; and I was wondering whether or not to make a dash for it, when one light pair came running down again, and in very despair I marched out to meet my preserver, looking as little as I could like the abject thing I felt.

'Be quick!' she cried in a harsh whisper, and pointed peremptorily to the porch.

But I stood stubbornly before her, my heart hardened by her hardness, and perversely indifferent to all else. And as I stood I saw the letter she had written, in the hand with which she pointed, crushed into a ball.

'Quickly!' She stamped her foot. 'Quickly – *if you ever cared*!'

This in a whisper, without bitterness, without contempt, but with a sudden wild entreaty that breathed upon the dying embers of my poor manhood. I drew myself together for the last time in her sight. I turned, and left her as she wished – for her sake, not for mine. And as I went I heard her tearing her letter into little pieces, and the little pieces falling on the floor.

Then I remembered Raffles, and could have killed him for what he had done. Doubtless by this time he was safe and snug in the Albany; what did my fate matter to him? Never mind; this should be the end between him and me as well; it was the end of everything, this dark night's work! I would go and tell him so. I would jump into a cab and drive to his accursed rooms. But first I must escape from the trap in which he had been so ready to leave me. And on the very steps I drew back in despair. They were searching the shrubberies between the drive and the road; a policeman's lantern kept flashing in and out among the laurels, while a young man in evening-clothes directed him from the gravel sweep. It was this young man whom I must dodge, but at my first step in the gravel he wheeled round, and it was Raffles himself.

'Hello!' he cried. 'So you've come up to join the dance as well! Had a look inside, have you? You'll be better employed in helping to draw the cover in front here. It's all right, officer – only another gentleman from the Empress Rooms.'

And we made a brave show of assisting in the futile search, until the arrival of more police and a broad hint from an irritable sergeant gave us an excellent excuse for going off arm in arm. But it was Raffles who had thrust his arm through mine. I shook him off as we left the scene of shame behind.

'My dear Bunny!' he exclaimed. 'Do you know what brought me back?'

I answered savagely that I neither knew nor cared.

'I had the very devil of a squeak for it,' he went on. 'I did the hurdles over two or three garden-walls, but so did the flyer who was on my tracks, and he drove me back into the straight and down to High Street like any lamplighter. If he had only had the breath to sing out it would have been all up with me then; as it was I pulled off my coat the moment I was round the corner, and took a ticket for it at the Empress Rooms.'

'I suppose you had one for the dance that was going on,' I growled. Nor would it have been a coincidence for Raffles to have had a ticket for that or any other entertainment of the London season.

'I never asked what the dance was,' he returned. 'I merely took the opportunity of revising my toilet, and getting rid of that rather distinctive overcoat, which I shall call for now. They're not too particular at such stages of such proceedings, but I've no doubt I should have seen someone I knew if I had gone right in. I might even have had a turn, if only I had been less uneasy about you, Bunny.'

'It was like you to come back to help me out,' said I. 'But to lie to me, and to inveigle me with your lies into that house of all houses – that was not like you, Raffles – and I never shall forgive it or you!'

Raffles took my arm again. We were near the High Street gates of Palace Gardens, and I was too miserable to resist an advance which I meant never to give him an opportunity to repeat.

'Come, come, Bunny, there wasn't much inveigling about it,' said he. 'I did my level best to leave you behind, but you wouldn't listen to me.'

'If you had told me the truth I should have listened fast enough,' I retorted. 'But what's the use of talking? You can boast of your own adventures after you bolted. You don't care what happened to me.'

'I cared so much that I came back to see.'

'You might have spared yourself the trouble! The wrong had been done. Raffles – Raffles – don't you know who she was?'

It was my hand that gripped his arm once more.

'I guessed,' he answered, gravely enough even for me.

'It was she who saved me, not you,' I said. 'And that is the bitterest part of all!'

Yet I told him that part with a strange sad pride in her whom I had lost – through him – for ever. As I ended we turned into High Street; in the prevailing stillness, the faint strains of the band reached us from the Empress Rooms; and I hailed a crawling hansom as Raffles turned that way.

'Bunny,' said he, 'it's no use saying I'm sorry. Sorrow adds insult in a case like this – if ever there was or will be such another! Only believe me, Bunny, when I swear to you that I had not the smallest shadow of a suspicion that *she* was in the house.'

And in my heart of hearts I did believe him; but I could not bring myself to say the words.

'You told me yourself that you had written to her in the country,' he pursued.

'And that letter!' I rejoined, in a fresh wave of bitterness: 'that letter she had written at dead of night, and stolen down to post, it was the one I have been waiting for all these days! I should have got it tomorrow. Now I shall never get it, never hear from her again, nor have another chance in this world or in the next. I don't say it was all your fault. You no more knew that she was there than I did. But you told me a deliberate lie about her people, and that I never shall forgive.'

I spoke as vehemently as I could under my breath. The hansom was waiting at the curb.

'I can say no more than I have said,' returned Raffles with a shrug. 'Lie or no lie, I didn't tell it to bring you with me, but to get you to give me certain information without feeling a beast about it. But, as a matter of fact, it was no lie about old Hector Carruthers and Lord Lochmaben, and anybody but you would have guessed the truth.'

'What is the truth?'

'I as good as told you, Bunny, again and again.'

'Then tell me now.'

'If you read your paper there would be no need; but if you want to know, old Carruthers headed the list of the Birthday Honours, and Lord Lochmaben is the title of his choice.'

And this miserable quibble was not a lie! My lip curled, I turned my back without a word, and drove home to my Mount Street flat in a new fury of savage scorn. Not a lie, indeed! It was the one that is half a truth, the meanest lie of all, and the very last to which I could have dreamt that Raffles would stoop. So far there had been a degree of honour between us, if only of the kind understood to obtain between thief and thief. Now all that was at an end. Raffles had cheated me. Raffles had completed the ruin of my life. I was done with Raffles, as she who shall not be named was done with me.

And yet, even while I blamed him most bitterly, and utterly abominated his deceitful deed, I could not but admit in my heart that the result was out of all proportion to the intent: he had never dreamt of doing me this injury, or indeed any injury at all. Intrinsically the deceit had been quite venial, the reason for it obviously the reason that Raffles had given me. It was quite true that he had spoken of this Lochmaben peerage as a new creation, and of the heir to it in a fashion only applicable to Alick Carruthers. He had given me hints, which I had been too dense to take, and he had certainly made more than one attempt to deter me from accompanying him on this fatal emprise; had he been more explicit, I might have made it my business to deter him. I could not say in my heart that Raffles had failed to satisfy such honour as I might reasonably expect to subsist between us. Yet it seems to me to require a superhuman sanity always and unerringly to separate cause from effect, achievement from intent. And I, for one, was never quite able to do so in this case.

I could not be accused of neglecting my newspaper during the next few wretched days. I read every word that I could find about the attempted jewel robbery in Palace Gardens, and the reports afforded me my sole comfort. In the first place, it was only an attempted robbery; nothing had been taken, after all. And then – and then – the one member of the household who had come nearest to a personal encounter with one of the intruders was unable to furnish any description of the man – had even expressed a doubt as to the likelihood of identification in the event of an arrest!

I will not say with what mingled feelings I read and dwelt on that announcement. It kept a certain faint glow alive within me until the morning that brought me back the only presents I had ever made her. They were but books; jewellery had been tabooed by the authorities. And the books came back without a word, though the parcel was directed in her hand.

I had made up my mind not to go near Raffles again, but in my heart I already regretted my resolve. I had forfeited love, I had sacrificed honour, and now I must deliberately alienate myself from the one being whose society might yet be some recompense for all that I had lost. The situation was aggravated by the state of my exchequer. I expected an ultimatum from my banker by every post. Yet this influence was nothing to the other. It was Raffles I loved. It was not the dark life we led together, still less its base rewards; it was the man himself, his gaiety, his humour, his dazzling audacity, his incomparable courage and resource. And a very horror of turning to him again in mere need or greed set the seal on my first angry resolution. But the anger was soon gone out of me, and when at length Raffles bridged the gap by coming to me, I rose to greet him almost with a shout.

He came as though nothing had happened; and, indeed, not very many days had passed, though they might have been months to me. Yet I fancied the gaze that watched me through our smoke a trifle less sunny than it had been before. And it was a relief to me when he came with few preliminaries to the inevitable point.

'Did you ever hear from her, Bunny?' he asked.

'In a way,' I answered. 'We won't talk about it, if you don't mind, Raffles.'

'That sort of way!' he exclaimed. He seemed both surprised and disappointed.

'Yes,' I said, 'that sort of way. It's finished. What did you expect?'

'I don't know,' said Raffles. 'I only thought that the girl who went so far to get a fellow out of a tight place might go a little further to keep him from getting into another.'

'I don't see why she should,' said I, honestly enough, yet with the irritation of a less just feeling deep down in my inmost consciousness.

'Yet you did hear from her?' he persisted.

'She sent me back my poor presents, without a word,' I said, 'if you call that hearing.'

I could not bring myself to own to Raffles that I had given her only books. He asked if I was sure that she had sent them back herself; and that was his last question. My answer was enough for him. And to this day I cannot say whether it was more in relief than in regret that he laid a hand upon my shoulder.

'So you are out of Paradise after all!' said Raffles. 'I was not sure, or I should have come round before. Well, Bunny, if they don't want you there, there's a little Inferno in the Albany where you will be as welcome as ever!'

And still, with all the magic mischief of his smile, there was that touch of sadness which I was yet to read aright.

Murder!

1

Many great ones of the earth have justified murder as
a social act, defensible and even laudable in certain
instances. There is something to be said for murder,
though perhaps not much. All of us, or nearly all of
us, have at one time or another had the desire and the
impulse to commit murder. At any rate, murder is
not an uncommon affair. On an average, two people
are murdered every week in England, and probably
about two hundred every week in the United States.
And forty per cent of the murderers are not brought
to justice. These figures take no account of the
undoubtedly numerous cases where murder has been
done but never suspected. Murders and murderesses
walk safely abroad among us, and it may happen to
us to shake hands with them. A disturbing thought!
But such is life, and such is homicide.

2

Two men, named respectively Lomax Harder and
John Franting, were walking side by side one autumn
afternoon on the Marine Parade of the seaside resort
and port of Quangate (English Channel). Both were
well dressed and had the air of moderate wealth, and
both were about thirty-five years of age. At this point
the resemblances between them ceased. Lomax
Harder had refined features, an enormous forehead,
fair hair and a delicate, almost apologetic manner.

John Franting was low-browed, heavy chinned, scowling, defiant, indeed what is called a tough customer. Lomax Harder corresponded in appearance with the popular notion of a poet – save that he was carefully barbered. He was in fact a poet, and not unknown in the tiny, trifling, mad world where poetry is a matter of first-rate interest. John Franting corresponded in appearance with the popular notion of a gambler, an amateur boxer and, in spare time, a deluder of women. Popular notions sometimes fit the truth.

Lomax Harder, somewhat nervously buttoning his overcoat, said in a quiet but firm and insistent tone: 'Haven't you got anything to say?'

John Franting stopped suddenly in front of a shop whose façade bore the sign: 'Gontle – Gunsmith'.

'Not in words,' answered Franting. 'I'm going in here.' And he brusquely entered the small, shabby shop.

Lomax Harder hesitated half a second, and then followed his companion.

The shopman was a middle-aged gentleman wearing a black velvet coat.

'Good afternoon,' he greeted Franting, with an expression and in a tone of urbane condescension which seemed to indicate that Franting was a wise as well as a fortunate man in that he knew of the excellence of Gontle's and had the wit to come into Gontle's.

For the name of Gontle was favourably and respectfully known wherever triggers are pressed. Not only along the whole length of the Channel coast but throughout England was Gontle's renowned. Sportsmen would travel to Quangate from the far north, and even from London, to buy guns. To say: 'I bought it at Gontle's,' or, 'Old Gontle recommended it,' was sufficient to silence any dispute concerning the merits of a firearm. Experts bowed the head before the unique reputation of Gontle. As for old Gontle, he was extremely and pardonably conceited. His conviction that no other gunsmith in the wide world could compare with him was absolute. He sold guns and rifles with the gesture of a monarch conferring an honour. He never argued; he stated; and the customer who contradicted him was as likely as not to be courteously and icily informed by Gontle of the geographical situation of the shop-door. Such shops exist in the English provinces, and nobody knows how they have achieved their renown. They could exist nowhere else.

' 'd afternoon,' said Franting gruffly, and paused.

'What can I do for you?' asked Mr Gontle, as if saying: 'Now don't be afraid. This shop is tremendous, and I am tremendous; but I shall not eat you.'

'I want a revolver,' Franting snapped.

'Ah! A revolver!' commented Mr Gontle, as if saying: 'A gun or a rifle, yes! But a revolver – an arm without individuality, manufactured wholesale! . . . However, I suppose I must deign to accommodate you.'

'I presume you know something about revolvers?' asked Mr Gontle, as he began to produce the weapons.

'A little.'

'Do you know the Webley Mark III?'

'Can't say that I do.'

'Ah! It is the best for all common purposes.' And Mr Gontle's glance said: 'Have the goodness not to tell me it isn't.'

Franting examined the Webley Mark III.

'You see,' said Mr Gontle, 'the point about it is that until the breach is properly closed it cannot be fired. So that it can't blow open and maim or kill the would-be murderer.' Mr Gontle smiled archly at one of his oldest jokes.

'What about suicides?' Franting grimly demanded.

'Ah!'

'You might show me just how to load it,' said Franting.

Mr Gontle, having found ammunition, complied with this reasonable request.

'The barrel's a bit scratched,' said Franting.

Mr Gontle inspected the scratch with pain. He would have denied the scratch, but could not.

'Here's another one,' said he, 'since you're so particular.' He simply had to put customers in their place.

'You might load it,' said Franting.

Mr Gontle loaded the second revolver.

'I'd like to try it,' said Franting.

'Certainly,' said Mr Gontle, and led Franting out of the shop by the back exit and down to a cellar where revolvers could be experimented with.

Lomax Harder was now alone in the shop. He hesitated a long time and then picked up the revolver rejected by Franting, fingered it, put it down, and picked it up again. The back-door of the shop opened suddenly, and startled, Harder dropped the revolver into his overcoat pocket: a thoughtless, quite unpremeditated act. He dared not remove the revolver. The revolver was as fast in his pocket as though the pocket had been sewn up.

'And cartridges?' asked Mr Gontle of Franting.

'Oh,' said Franting, 'I've only had one shot. Five'll be more than enough for the present. What does it weigh?'

'Let me see. Four-inch barrel? Yes. One pound four ounces.'

Franting paid for the revolver, receiving thirteen shillings in change from a five-pound note, and strode out of the shop, weapon in hand. He was gone before Lomax Harder decided upon a course of action.

'And for you, sir?' said Mr Gontle, addressing the poet.

Harder suddenly comprehended that Mr Gontle had mistaken him for a separate customer, who had happened to enter the shop a moment after the first one. Harder and Franting had said not a word to one another during the purchase, and Harder well knew that in the most exclusive shops it is the custom utterly to ignore a second customer until the first one has been dealt with.

'I want to see some foils.' Harder spoke stammeringly the only words that came into his head.

'Foils!' exclaimed Mr Gontle, shocked, as if to say: 'Is it conceivable that you should imagine that I, Gontle, gunsmith, sell such things as foils?'

After a little talk Harder apologised and departed – a thief.

'I'll call later and pay the fellow,' said Harder to his restive conscience. 'No. I can't do that. I'll send him some anonymous postal orders.'

He crossed the Parade and saw Franting, a small left-handed figure all alone far below on the deserted sands, pointing the revolver. He thought that his ear caught the sound of a discharge, but the distance was too great for him to be sure. He continued to watch,

and at length Franting walked westward diagonally
across the beach.

'He's going back to the Bellevue,' thought Harder,
the Bellevue being the hotel from which he had met
Franting coming out half an hour earlier. He strolled
slowly towards the white hotel. But Franting, who
had evidently come up the face of the cliff in the
penny lift, was before him. Harder, standing outside,
saw Franting seated in the lounge. Then Franting
rose and vanished down a long passage at the rear of
the lounge. Harder entered the hotel rather guiltily.
There was no hall-porter at the door, and not a soul
in the lounge or in sight of the lounge. Harder went
down the long passage.

3

At the end of the passage Lomax Harder found himself in a billiard-room – an extension built partly of
brick and partly of wood on a sort of courtyard behind
the main structure of the hotel. The roof, of iron and
grimy glass, rose to a point in the middle. On two
sides the high walls of the hotel obscured the light.
Dusk was already closing in. A small fire burned
feebly in the grate. A large radiator under the window
was steel-cold, for though summer was finished, winter
had not officially begun in the small economically-run
hotel: so that the room was chilly; nevertheless, in
deference to the English passion for fresh air and
discomfort, the window was wide open.

Franting, in his overcoat and with an unlit cigarette
between his lips, stood lowering with his back to the
bit of fire. At sight of Harder he lifted his chin in a
dangerous challenge.

'So you're still following me about,' he said resentfully to Harder.

'Yes,' said the latter, with his curious gentle primness of manner. 'I came down here specially to talk to you. I should have said all I had to say earlier, only you happened to be going out of the hotel just as I was coming in. You didn't seem to want to talk in the street; but there's some talking has to be done. I've a few things I must tell you.' Harder appeared to be perfectly calm, and he felt perfectly calm. He advanced from the door towards the billiard-table.

Franting raised his hand, displaying his square-ended, brutal fingers in the twilight.

'Now listen to me,' he said with cold, measured ferocity. 'You can't tell me anything I don't know. If there's some talking to be done I'll do it myself, and when I've finished you can get out. I know that my wife has taken a ticket for Copenhagen by the steamer from Harwich, and that she's been seeing to her passport, and packing. And of course I know that you have interests in Copenhagen and spend about half your precious time there. I'm not worrying to connect the two things. All that's got nothing to do with me. Emily has always seen a great deal of you, and I know that the last week or two she's been seeing you more than ever. Not that I mind that. I know that she objects to my treatment of her and my conduct generally. That's all right, but it's a matter that only concerns her and me. I mean that it's no concern of yours, for instance, or anybody else's. If she objects enough she can try and divorce me. I doubt if she'd succeed, but you can never be sure – with these new laws. Anyhow she's my wife till she does divorce me, and so she has the usual duties and responsibilities towards me – even though I was the worst husband in the world. That's how I look at it, in my old-fashioned way. I've just had a letter from her – she knew I was here, and I expect that explains how you knew I was here.'

'It does,' said Lomax Harder quietly.

Franting pulled a letter out of his inner pocket and unfolded it.

'Yes,' he said, glancing at it, and read some sentences aloud:

'I have absolutely decided to leave you, and I won't hide from you that I know you know who is doing what he can to help me. I can't live with you any longer. You may be very fond of me, as you say, but I find your way of showing your fondness too humiliating and painful. I've said this to you before, and now I'm saying it for the last time.

And so on and so on.'

Franting tore the letter in two, dropped one half on the floor, twisted the other half into a spill, turned to the fire, and lit his cigarette.

'That's what I think of her letter,' he proceeded, the cigarette between his teeth. 'You're helping her, are you? Very well. I don't say you're in love with her, or she with you. I'll make no wild statements. But if you aren't in love with her I wonder why you're taking all this trouble over her. Do you go about the world helping ladies who say they're unhappy just for the pure sake of helping? Never mind. Emily isn't going to leave me. Get that into your head. I shan't let her leave me. She has money, and I haven't. I've been living on her, and it would be infernally awkward for me if she left me for good. That's a reason for keeping her, isn't it? But you may believe me or not – it isn't my reason. She's right enough when she says I'm very fond of her. That's a reason for keeping her too. But it isn't my reason. My reason is that a wife's a wife, and she can't break her word just because everything isn't lovely in the garden. I've heard it said I'm unmoral. I'm not all unmoral. And I feel particularly strongly about what's called the marriage tie.' He drew the revolver from his overcoat pocket, and held it up to view. 'You see this thing. You saw me buy it. Now you needn't be afraid. I'm not threatening you; and it's no part of my game to shoot you. I've nothing to do with your goings-on. What I have to do with is the goings-on of my wife. If she deserts me – for you or for anybody or for nobody – I shall follow her, whether it's to Copenhagen or Bangkok or the North Pole, and I shall kill her – with just this very revolver that you saw me buy. And now you can get out.'

Franting replaced the revolver, and began to consume the cigarette with fierce and larger puffs.

Lomax Harder looked at the grim, set, brutal, scowling, bitter face, and knew that Franting meant what he had said. Nothing would stop him from carrying out his threat. The fellow was not an argufier; he could not reason; but he had unmistakable grit and would never recoil from the fear of consequences. If Emily left him, Emily was a dead woman; nothing in the end could protect her from the execution of her husband's menace. On the other hand, nothing would persuade her to remain with her husband. She had decided to go, and she would go. And indeed the mere thought of this lady to whom he, Harder, was utterly devoted, staying with her husband and continuing to suffer the tortures and humiliations which she had been suffering for years – this thought revolted him. He could not think it.

He stepped forward along the side of the billiard-table, and simultaneously Franting stepped forward to meet him. Lomax Harder snatched the revolver which was in his pocket, aimed and pulled the trigger.

Franting collapsed, with the upper half of his body somehow balanced on the edge of the billiard-table. He was dead. The sound of the report echoed in Harder's ear like the sound of a violin string loudly twanged by a finger. He saw a little reddish hole in Franting's bronzed right temple.

'Well,' he thought, 'somebody had to die. And it's better him than Emily.' He felt that he had performed a righteous act. Also he felt a little sorry for Franting.

Then he was afraid. He was afraid for himself, because he wanted not to die, especially on the scaffold; but also for Emily Franting, who would be friendless and helpless without him; he could not bear to think of her alone in the world – the central point of a terrific scandal. He must get away instantly . . .

Not down the corridor back into the hotel-lounge! No! That would be fatal! The window. He glanced at the corpse. It was more odd, curious, than affrighting. He had made the corpse. Strange! He could not unmake it. He had accomplished the irrevocable. Impressive! He saw Franting's cigarette glowing on the linoleum in the deepening dusk, and picked it up and threw it into the fender.

Lace curtains hung across the whole width of the window. He drew one aside, and looked forth. The light was much stronger in the courtyard than within the room. He put his gloves on. He gave a last look at the corpse, straddled the window-sill, and was on the brick pavement of the courtyard. He saw that the curtain had fallen back into the perpendicular.

He gazed around. Nobody! Not a light in any window! He saw a green wooden gate, pushed it; it yielded; then a sort of entry-passage . . . In a moment, after two half-turns, he was on the Marine Parade again. He was a fugitive. Should he fly to the right, to the left? Then he had an inspiration. An idea of genius for baffling pursuers. He would go into the hotel by the main-entrance. He went slowly and deliberately into the portico, where a middle-aged hall-porter was standing in the gloom.

'Good-evening, sir.'

'Good-evening. Have you got any rooms?'

'I think so, sir. The housekeeper is out, but she'll be back in a moment – if you'd like a seat. The manager's away in London.'

The hall-porter suddenly illuminated the lounge, and Lomax Harder, blinking, entered and sat down.

'I might have a cocktail while I'm waiting,' the murderer suggested with a bright and friendly smile. 'A Bronx.'

'Certainly, sir. The page is off duty. He sees to orders in the lounge, but I'll attend to you myself.'

'What a hotel!' thought the murderer, solitary in the chilly lounge, and gave a glance down the long passage. 'Is the whole place run by the hall-porter? But of course it's the dead season.'

Was it conceivable that nobody had heard the sound of the shot?

Harder had a strong impulse to run away. But no! To do so would be highly dangerous. He restrained himself.

'How much?' he asked of the hall-porter, who had

arrived with surprising quickness, tray in hand and
glass on tray.

'A shilling, sir.'

The murderer gave him eighteenpence, and drank
off the cocktail.

'Thank you very much, sir.' The hall-porter took
the glass.

'See here!' said the murderer. 'I'll look in again.
I've got one or two little errands to do.'

And he went, slowly, into the obscurity of the
Marine Parade.

4

Lomax Harder leant over the left arm of the sea-wall
of the man-made port of Quangate. Not another soul
was there. Night had fallen. The lighthouse at the
extremity of the right arm was occulting. The lights –
some red, some green, many white – of ships at sea
passed in both directions in endless processions.
Waves plashed gently against the vast masonry of the
wall. The wind, blowing steadily from the north-west,
was not cold. Harder, looking about – though he
knew he was absolutely alone, took his revolver from
his overcoat pocket and stealthily dropped it into the
sea. Then he turned round and gazed across the small
harbour at the mysterious amphitheatre of the lighted
town, and heard public clocks and religious clocks
striking the hour.

He was a murderer, but why should he not successfully escape detection? Other murderers had done so.
He had all his wits. He was not excited. He was not
morbid. His perspective of things was not askew. The
hall-porter had not seen his first entrance into the

hotel, nor his exit after the crime. Nobody had seen them. He had left nothing behind in the billiard-room. No fingermarks on the window-sill. (The putting-on of his gloves was in itself a clear demonstration that he had fully kept his presence of mind.) No footmarks on the hard, dry pavement of the courtyard.

Of course there was the possibility that some person unseen had seen him getting out of the window. Slight: but still a possibility! And there was also the possibility that someone who knew Franting by sight had noted him walking by Franting's side in the streets. If such a person informed the police and gave a description of him, enquiries might be made . . . No! Nothing in it. His appearance offered nothing remarkable to the eye of a casual observer – except his forehead, of which he was rather proud, but which was hidden by his hat.

It was generally believed that criminals always did something silly. But so far he had done nothing silly, and he was convinced that, in regard to the crime, he never would do anything silly. He had none of the desire, supposed to be common among murderers, to revisit the scene of the crime or to look upon the corpse once more. Although he regretted the necessity for his act, he felt no slightest twinge of conscience. Somebody had to die, and surely it was better that a brute should die than the heavenly, enchanting, martyrised creature whom his act had rescued for ever from the brute! He was aware within himself of an ecstasy of devotion to Emily Franting – now a widow and free. She was a unique woman. Strange that a woman of such gifts should have come under the sway of so obvious a scoundrel as Franting. But she was very young at the time, and such freaks of sex had happened before and would happen again; they were a widespread phenomenon in the history of the relations of men and women. He would have killed a hundred men if a hundred men had threatened her felicity. His heart was pure; he wanted nothing from Emily in exchange for what he had done in her defence. He was passionate in her defence. When he reflected upon the coarseness and cruelty of the gesture by which Franting had used Emily's letter to light his cigarette, Harder's cheeks grew hot with burning resentment.

A clock struck the quarter. Harder walked quickly to the harbour front, where there was a taxi-rank, and drove to the station . . . A sudden apprehension! The crime might have been discovered! Police might already be watching for suspicious-looking travellers! Absurd! Still, the apprehension remained despite its absurdity. The taxi-driver looked at him queerly. No! Imagination! He hesitated on the threshold of the station, then walked boldly in, and showed his return ticket to the ticket-inspector. No sign of a policeman. He got into the Pullman car, where five other passengers were sitting. The train started.

5

He nearly missed the boat-train at Liverpool Street because according to its custom the Quangate flyer arrived twenty minutes late at Victoria. And at Victoria the foolish part of him, as distinguished from the common-sense part, suffered another spasm of fear. Would detectives, instructed by telegraph, be waiting for the train? No! An absurd idea! The boat-train from Liverpool Street was crowded with travellers, and the platform crowded with senders-off. He gathered from scraps of talk overheard that an international conference was about to take place in Copenhagen. And he had known nothing of it – not seen a word of it in the papers! Excusable perhaps; graver matters had held his attention.

Useless to look for Emily in the vast bustle of the compartments! She had her through ticket (which she had taken herself, in order to avoid possible complications), and she happened to be the only woman in the world who was never late and never in a hurry. She was certain to be on the train. But was she on the train? Something sinister might have come to pass. For instance, a telephone message to the flat that her husband had been found dead with a bullet in his brain.

The swift two-hour journey to Harwich was terrible for Lomax Harder. He remembered that he had left the unburnt part of the letter lying under the billiard-table. Forgetful! Silly! One of the silly things that criminals did! And on Parkeston Quay the confusion was enormous. He did not walk, he was swept, on to the great shaking steamer whose dark funnels rose amid wisps of steam into the starry sky. One advantage: detectives would have no chance in that multitudinous scene, unless indeed they held up the ship.

The ship roared a warning, and slid away from the quay, groped down the tortuous channel to the harbour mouth, and was in the North Sea; and England dwindled to naught but a string of lights. He searched every deck from stem to stern, and could not find Emily. She had not caught the train, or, if she had caught the train, she had not boarded the steamer because he had failed to appear. His misery was intense. Everything was going wrong. And on the arrival at Esbjerg would not detectives be lying in wait for the Copenhagen train? . . .

Then he descried her, and she him. She too had been searching. Only chance had kept them apart. Her joy at finding him was ecstatic; tears came into his eyes at sight of it. He was everything to her, absolutely everything. He clasped her right hand in both his hands and gazed at her in the dim, diffused light blended of stars, moon and electricity. No woman was ever like her: mature, innocent, wise, trustful, honest. And the touching beauty of her appealing, sad, happy face, and the pride of her carriage! A unique jewel – snatched from the brutal grasp of that fellow – who had ripped her solemn letter in two and used it as a spill for his cigarette! She related her movements; and he his. Then she said: 'Well?'

'I didn't go,' he answered. 'Thought it best not to. I'm convinced it wouldn't have been any use.'

He had not intended to tell her this lie. Yet when it came to the point, what else could he say? He had told one lie instead of twenty. He was deceiving her, but for her sake. Even if the worst occurred, she was for ever safe from that brutal grasp. And he had saved her. As for the conceivable complications of the future, he refused to confront them; he could live in the marvellous present. He felt suddenly the amazing beauty of the night at sea, but beneath all his other sensations was the obscure sensation of a weight at his heart.

'I expect you were right,' she angelically acquiesced.

6

The Superintendent of Police (Quangate was the county town of the western half of the county) and a detective-sergeant were in the billiard-room of the Bellevue. Both wore mufti. The powerful green-shaded lamps usual in billiard-rooms shone down ruthlessly on the green table, and on the reclining body of John Franting, which had not moved and had not been moved.

A charwoman was just leaving these officers when a stout gentleman, who had successfully beguiled a policeman guarding the other end of the long corridor, squeezed past her, greeted the two officers and shut the door.

The superintendent, a thin man, with lips to match, and a moustache, stared hard at the arrival.

'I am staying with my friend Dr Furnival,' said the arrival cheerfully. 'You telephoned for him, and as he had to go out to one of those cases in which nature will not wait, I offered to come in his place. I've met you before, superintendent, at Scotland Yard.'

'Dr Austin Bond!' exclaimed the superintendent.

'He,' said the other.

They shook hands, Dr Bond genially, the super-intendent half-consequential, half-deferential, as one who had his dignity to think about; also as one who resented an intrusion, but dared not show resentment.

The detective-sergeant reeled at the dazzling name of the great amateur detective, a genius who had solved the famous mysteries of 'The Yellow Hat', 'The Three Towns', 'The Three Feathers', 'The Gold Spoon', etc., etc., etc., whose devilish perspicacity had again and again made professional detectives both look and feel foolish, and whose notorious friendship with the loftiest heads of Scotland Yard compelled all police forces to treat him very politely indeed.

'Yes,' said Dr Austin Bond, after detailed examination. 'Been shot about ninety minutes, poor fellow! Who found him?'

'That woman who's just gone out. Some servant here. Came in to look after the fire.'

'How long since?'

'Oh! About an hour ago.'

'Found the bullet? I see it hit the brass on that cue-rack there.'

The detective-sergeant glanced at the superintendent, who, however, resolutely remained unastonished.

'Here's the bullet,' said the superintendent.

'Ah!' commented Dr Austin Bond, glinting through his spectacles at the bullet as it lay in the superintendent's hand. 'Decimal 38, I see. Flattened. It would be.'

'Sergeant,' said the superintendent, 'you can get, help and have the body moved now Dr Bond has made his examination. Eh, doctor?'

'Certainly,' answered Dr Bond, at the fireplace. 'He was smoking a cigarette, I see.'

'Either he or his murderer.'

'You've got a clue?'

'Oh yes,' the superintendent answered, not without pride. 'Look here. Your torch, sergeant.'

The detective-sergeant produced a pocket electric-lamp, and the superintendent turned to the window-sill.

'I've got a stronger one than that,' said Dr Austin Bond, producing another torch.

The superintendent displayed fingerprints on the window-frame, footmarks on the sill, and a few strands of inferior blue cloth. Dr Austin Bond next produced a magnifying glass, and inspected the evidence at very short range.

'The murderer must have been a tall man – you can judge that from the angle of fire; he wore a blue suit, which he tore slightly on this splintered wood of the window-frame; one of his boots had a hole in the middle of the sole, and he'd only three fingers on his left hand. He must have come in by the window and gone out by the window, because the hall-porter is sure that nobody except the dead man entered the lounge by any door within an hour of the time when the murder must have been committed.' The superintendent proudly gave many more details, and ended by saying that he had already given instructions to circulate a description.

'Curious,' said Dr Austin Bond, 'that a man like John Franting should let anyone enter the room by the window! Especially a shabby-looking man!'

'You knew the deceased personally then?'

'No! But I know he was John Franting.'

'How, doctor?'

'Luck.'

'Sergeant,' said the superintendent, piqued. 'Tell the constable to fetch the hall-porter.'

Dr Austin Bond walked to and fro, peering everywhere, and picked up a piece of paper that had lodged against the step of the platform which ran round two sides of the room for the raising of the spectators' benches. He glanced at the paper casually, and dropped it again.

'My man,' the superintendent addressed the hall-porter. 'How can you be sure that nobody came in here this afternoon?'

'Because I was in my cubicle all the time, sir.'

The hall-porter was lying. But he had to think of his own welfare. On the previous day he had been reprimanded for quitting his post against the rule. Taking advantage of the absence of the manager, he had sinned once again, and he lived in fear of dismissal if found out.

'With a full view of the lounge?'

'Yes, sir.'

'Might have been in there beforehand,' Dr Austin Bond suggested.

'No,' said the superintendent. 'The charwoman came in twice. Once just before Franting came in. She saw the fire wanted making up and she went for some coal and then returned later with the scuttle. But the look of Franting frightened her, and she turned back with her coal.'

'Yes,' said the hall-porter. 'I saw that.'

Another lie.

At a sign from the superintendent he withdrew.

'I should like to have a word with that charwoman,' said Dr Austin Bond.

The superintendent hesitated. Why should the great amateur meddle with what did not concern him? Nobody had asked his help. But the superintendent thought of the amateur's relations with Scotland Yard, and sent for the charwoman.

'Did you clean the window here today?' Dr Austin Bond interrogated her.

'Yes, please, sir.'

'Show me your left hand.' The slattern obeyed. 'How did you lose your little finger?'

'In a mangle accident, sir.'

'Just come to the window, will you, and put your hands on it. But take off your left boot first.'

The slatten began to weep.

'It's quite all right, my good creature,' Dr Austin Bond reassured her. 'Your skirt is torn at the hem, isn't it?'

When the slattern was released from her ordeal and had gone, carrying one boot in her grimy hand, Dr Austin Bond said genially to the superintendent: 'Just a fluke. I happened to notice she'd only three fingers on her left hand when she passed me in the corridor. Sorry I've destroyed your evidence. But I felt sure almost from the first that the murderer hadn't either entered or decamped by the window.'

'How?'

'Because I think he's still here in the room.'

The two police officers gazed about them as if exploring the room for the murderer.

'I think he's there.'

Dr Austin Bond pointed to the corpse.

'And where did he hide the revolver after he'd killed himself?' demanded the thin-lipped superintendent icily, when he had somewhat recovered his aplomb.

'I'd thought of that, too,' said Dr Austin Bond, beaming. 'It is always a very wise course to leave a dead body absolutely untouched until a professional man has seen it. But *looking* at the body can do no harm. You see the left-hand pocket of the overcoat. Notice how it bulges. Something unusual in it. Something that has the shape of a – Just feel inside it, will you?'

The superintendent, obeying, drew a revolver from the overcoat pocket of the dead man.

'Ah! Yes!' said Dr Austin Bond. 'A Webley Mark III. Quite new. You might take out the ammunition.' The superintendent dismantled the weapon. 'Yes, yes! Three chambers empty. Wonder how he used the other two! Now, where's that bullet? You see? He fired. His arm dropped, and the revolver happened to fall into the pocket.'

'Fired with his left hand, did he?' asked the superintendent, foolishly ironic.

'Certainly. A dozen years ago Franting was perhaps the finest amateur lightweight boxer in England. And one reason for it was that he bewildered his opponents by being left-handed. His lefts were much more fatal than his rights. I saw him box several times.'

Whereupon Dr Austin Bond strolled to the step of the platform near the door and picked up the fragment of very thin paper that was lying there.

'This,' said he, 'must have been blown from the hearth to here by the draught from the window when the door was opened. It's part of a letter. You can see the burnt remains of the other part in the corner of the fender. He probably lighted the cigarette with it. Out of bravado! His last bravado! Read this.'

The superintendent read:

'... repeat that I realise how fond you are of me, but you have killed my affection for you, and I shall leave our home tomorrow. This is absolutely final. E.'

Dr Austin Bond, having for the nth time satisfactorily demonstrated in his own unique, rapid way that police officers were a set of numskulls, bade the superintendent a most courteous good-evening, nodded amicably to the detective-sergeant, and left in triumph.

7

'I must get some mourning and go back to the flat,' said Emily Franting.

She was sitting one morning in the lobby of the Palads Hotel, Copenhagen. Lomax Harder had just called on her with an English newspaper containing an account of the inquest at which the jury had returned a verdict of suicide upon the body of her late husband. Her eyes filled with tears.

'Time will put her right,' thought Lomax Harder, tenderly watching her. 'I was bound to do what I did. And I can keep a secret for ever.'

SIR BASIL THOMSON

The Hanover Court Murder

A whole week had passed since Mr Pepper – and the small boy – had spoilt Mr Cohen's scheme; and no one had come near the office. My chief spent the time in perfecting his scientific apparatus which had not been called into use since my short association with him. It was therefore with immense satisfaction that an opportunity for exercising Mr Pepper's higher art was thrown into my way.

An acquaintance at my club, finding me in the smoking-room when other people were working, took the chair opposite to mine and said, 'By the way, Jones, I hear that you dabble in detective work; that you have discovered a wonderful Yankee who wipes the eye of Scotland Yard. Why don't you make your name by solving this Hanover Court case?'

'I've never heard of it.'

'No, it hasn't got into the papers yet, but it will.'

He had himself heard of it only that morning. His landlord had a sister who let lodgings in Hanover Court. She had opened the luggage of a tenant who had gone abroad owing rent and had been horrified to find in one of the trunks what appeared to be the remains of a dismembered human body. She had run at once to her brother, who consulted my friend as to what she ought to do. He took the usual course of advising that she should report the matter to the police, but, as far as he knew, she had not yet done so because she had made the discovery only that morning at breakfast time. He gave me her address.

I seized my hat and took a taxi to Hanover Court. I found the poor landlady wringing her hands. 'You heard of the case through my brother, sir? Well, I am glad that you've come in time. I was just going off to the police, but it will ruin my business to have the police messing about the house, asking me a lot of questions and calling in the coroner. They would make me appear as a witness at the inquest and the papers would publish the address. Then what chance would there be of the best class of people taking rooms where there's been a murder? It is not respectable. Now if you'll take away the trunk and take all responsibility I shall breathe freely. Of course, if there *has* been a murder I must stand by it, but you will ferret it all out and I hope that I shall hear no more about it.'

I agreed to everything on the condition that she gave me all the information she possessed. She showed me the trunk which stood on the landing of the second floor. I opened it with trembling fingers. It contained a number of packages wrapped in dirty newspaper and enveloped in part of what appeared to be an old army blanket. I satisfied myself that they contained bones, probably human bones, and with her assistance carried the trunk downstairs for removal to our office. In the meantime she told me the story of her lodger.

'He was what they call an eccentric, sir – always going off without notice and writing letters asking me to reserve his room and take care of his luggage. He always sent me money for the rent while he was away. He would write from all sorts of places – Naples, Egypt, Athens, and one letter I had came from Peru.

I never knew him pack anything for his journeys. All he said was that he was called away on business and would I be sure and feed his cat?'

'You haven't told me his name, Mrs Auger.'

'To tell your the truth, I had almost forgotten it. We always called him "the doctor" because when he came to me five years ago he said something about being in the medical profession. But his real name was Allen – Henry Allen.'

'That sounds English enough.'

'Oh, there was nothing foreign about him except his hair – he never seemed to get it cut – and his eccentricity – for foreigners *are* eccentric, don't you think so, Mr Meddleston-Jones? His age? Well, that would be hard to say – something between thirty-five and fifty, I should say.'

'Had he no friends, no visitors?'

'That's the peculiar thing. He had none. No, I am wrong there. About three years ago a lady did call and ask for Dr Allen. I asked her what name I should give. She said, "Don't trouble; just tell me what floor he's on, and I'll find him myself." And up she walked, but of course he must have heard her voice. She soon came down again and said he wasn't there. Then I went up myself, and of course there he was, hiding under the bed. He said nothing to me, but I can't help thinking that that lady was his wife. She never came again, not to my knowledge.'

'Did he get no letters?'

'Yes, once a month, always on the second unless it was a Sunday, there would be a fat registered letter addressed "Henry Allen, Esq." – no 'Dr' on the envelope. I think it was from a bank, but I don't remember which. He never had a meal in the house, not even his breakfast, but he used to bring back a little meat for his cat. Where did he go all day? Well, sir, that's more than I can tell you. On weekdays I would hear him coming downstairs regular at nine – I could have set my clock by him. If he passed me he would say good-morning, but nothing else. On Sundays he would lie in bed all the morning, and go out punctually at twelve. Oh, he was eccentric, but not the sort to commit a cold-blooded murder; for it is cold-blooded, Mr Meddleston-Jones, whatever you may say, to cut up a person into little bits like that, now isn't it? He had no books in his room and he didn't leave a scrap of writing behind him. What he did all day is a mystery to me.'

'When did you see him last?'

'It would be back in April. Yes, it is just three months. He just walked out of the house as usual and when I went up to do his room I found that he had packed everything away in his trunks. "Off again, I suppose," I said to myself, and I was right – only this time I had no letter and he hadn't paid me for the room. I didn't think very much of that – he had been behind with the rent before. I thought that the money would come. But then as the weeks went by and I had no letter I began to get anxious and I thought I had better see what he had left behind him. There wasn't a scrap of writing in any of the trunks – only old clothes and – and what you saw.'

'But the letters from the bank?'

'That's the peculiar thing. Whenever he went off those letters stopped coming. There hasn't been a letter since he left. Do you think he can have committed suicide after the murder?'

'We have got to find out first if there has been a

murder, Mrs Auger. I suppose there has been no one missing in the neighbourhood?'

She thought for some moments and then shook her head. 'But I'm sure that lady who came to see him was his wife,' she said.

'Why?'

'Well, she had a masterful, disagreeable way with her and he got under the bed to hide from her. A man would never do that with anybody except his wife.' I forebore to evoke any confidences of Mrs Auger's own experience of the married state.

'And if she was his wife, what then?'

'Why, it might be her that's in the trunk.'

The taxi-driver knew nothing of what his burden contained. For an extra shilling he helped me upstairs with it into the office where my chief's face became a mark of interrogation until the man was gone. Then I told him the story and opened the trunk. I never saw him so much moved before. He laid the bones out on the table as if they were jewels, I noticed that desiccated flesh was adhering to some of them; it was quite inoffensive. At the bottom of the trunk was the skull carefully wrapped in newspaper by itself. We carried the remains into the laboratory and cleared a table for them. While he was arranging them in order I committed to paper what Mrs Auger had told me.

Now, if my chief had a fault it was that he tried to do too much himself rather than call in the expert. My instinct would have been to call in a surgeon or an anatomist and let him express his opinion on the bones, but when I ventured to suggest this, my chief flew up in the air. 'What does your surgeon know of plastic reconstruction?' he said, and not knowing what plastic reconstruction was I said that I didn't know. 'Well,' he said, 'I am going to show you.'

It was a great opportunity for me. When I was admitted to the laboratory the bones were disposed on the table like a complete skeleton. My chief's first words were disconcerting. 'Some of the bones are missing,' he said, 'but the curious thing is that the body was deformed. That ought to make our work easier, but it is a very remarkable case. This woman had a left leg three inches shorter than the right and a right arm two inches shorter than the left. She must have had a very odd appearance.

'But we'll soon see what she looked like,' said my chief, confidently, as he manipulated wax in a pan of warm water. The skull was secured in a wooden vice clamped to the table. With extraordinary dexterity he pinched off little cones from the lump of wax in the pan, warmed them over a spirit lamp, and stuck them all over the skull. Very gradually he began to build up a face; and after an hour's work it became under his skilled manipulation a human face certainly, but a face that one could only see in a nightmare. With her bodily deformities in addition she might have made a good living at a show.

'There,' he said, 'is the murdered woman as she was in life.' I had it on the tip of my tongue to say, 'Then she deserved to die,' but I restrained myself in time, and I suggested that Mrs Auger should be called to the office to see if she recognised her as Mrs Allen. But my chief thought that the time had not come for that. 'Let us find the murderer and confront him with his victim,' he said. 'In nine cases out of ten he is so startled that he makes a full confession.'

'And if he does, what then? Surely we should have to hand him over to the police.'

'Yes,' he mused, 'but in a case of felony it is the duty of any citizen to arrest the felon. You will make the arrest; I will call in the reporters, and then we will ring up your wonderful Scotland Yard.' There was the most subtle irony in his tone. He covered the remains with a sheet, and we sat down to consider the best way of finding Henry Allen. I was for advertising in the agony columns of *The Times*, the *Daily Telegraph* and the *Daily Mail*: 'Henry Allen. Come back and all will be forgiven.'

'He would plead at his trial that he had been promised a free pardon.'

'Then why not something like this? "If Henry Allen, late of 17 Hanover Court, will communicate with Pepper and Jones, Adelphi, London, he will hear of something to his advantage." ' My chief snorted with contempt; I feared that it might be because for the first time I had dared to couple our two names.

'Do you really suppose that a man who goes in daily fear that his crime will be discovered would reply to an advertisement?'

'Well, you see them in the newspapers every day when lawyers want to get hold of a man. Someone must reply to them or they wouldn't put them in.'

'No, Mr Meddleston-Jones; if we use the newspapers we will proceed in quite a different way. I have there' (he pointed to his card-index cabinet) 'the names and addresses of the principal newspapers of every country in the world – daily and weekly. We could prepare a little news paragraph, a snappy little thing about how an Englishman named Henry Allen had been named as residuary legatee to an eccentric lady who died leaving a million and a half, and that when the sole executor, Mr Pepper' (there was no mention of Meddleston-Jones in the proposed paragraph), 'wrote to the happy legatee he found that he had gone abroad leaving no address and the letter was returned by the Post Office. Under the provisions of the will, if Henry Allen failed to claim his legacy within six months, the whole of the money would go to found a home for starving cats in London. We would have this translated into every language and sent out through one of the press agencies. Everyone likes to read about unclaimed money.'

'Wouldn't you be inundated with false claimants?'

'All the better. We would confront them all with the corpse first, then with Mrs Auger, and they would be glad to get away alive.'

It seemed to me to be a very dilatory method of procedure, but my chief must have adopted it because a week or so later reporters connected with the press agency began to hang about the office and stop me in the street. This annoyed my chief very much. It appeared that he had made a confidential arrangement with the head of the agency that the paragraph should not be released to any newspaper in the United Kingdom, because he would have to confess that there was no eccentric millionaire lady in the case at all. But the paragraph must have appeared in foreign newspapers because later we received begging letters from abroad. An Englishwoman wrote from Leghorn to say that if Henry Allen failed to appear, there were more starving cats in Leghorn than there could possibly be in London, that they kept her awake at night by their miaowing, and that she would be glad to establish a home for them if she might have part of the money. A man signing himself Henry Allen wrote from Cooktown in Queensland, asking for the expenses necessary for him to come to England to establish his claim. Another wrote from Salt Lake City to say that, though he was known locally as Richard Doherty, he was satisfied that as his mother was an Allen he was the person named in the will, and he would be thankful if a payment could be made on account; and a lady, writing from Buenos Aires in the name of Mary Allen, claimed the legacy on the ground that when she was a girl her schoolfellows always called her Henry. But of the real Henry Allen not a word.

My chief was becoming impatient. He was engaged on several cases at the time and the remains of the murdered woman, taking up nearly half the laboratory, were in his way. He had added chestnut hair to his reconstruction of the head, and colour to the cheeks; in her current state she must certainly have been very trying to live with, even when covered with a sheet. One morning he said to me, 'Mr Meddleston-Jones, we are not getting on with this Allen case. Why don't you bring the landlady down to look at the victim? Then we might get on.'

Mrs Auger did not take at all kindly to my suggestion. She reminded me that our agreement was that she should not be troubled with the case any more, and I had some difficulty in getting her to the office. When I drew back the sheet she uttered a piercing scream and fell into a chair. 'Oh! My heart!' she sobbed. 'My poor heart!' and she tried to clutch that organ of her anatomy.

'You recognise her, Mrs Auger? Is she like the wife?'

'She is like nothing on earth,' she gasped, 'and after

seeing her I shall be ill for a week.' It was a great disappointment.

I persuaded my chief at last to take a photograph of the head and give it to an illustrated daily paper for circulation as a missing person about whom information was desired. He took the photograph, but ten minutes before I started with it for the newspaper office in Fleet Street, an event occurred which entirely changed the course of our enquiry. Mrs Auger reappeared.

She produced a picture postcard, bearing a Genoa postmark, from Henry Allen himself, saying that he would be in London within the week. 'And now,' she said, 'what am I to say to him when he asks for his trunk? I can't say that the police have taken it, can I? You had better pack up all those bones in the newspapers just as he left them and bring back the trunk.' To this proposition, of course, my chief would not agree. He pointed out that, according to the law, Mrs Auger herself was bound to arrest him as soon as he set foot in her house.

'Arrest him?' she exclaimed aghast. 'How can a woman arrest a man?'

'The law knows no difference between men and women, Mrs Auger,' I said. 'Women serve on juries; there are women police. All you have to do is to lay your hand on his shoulder and say, "Henry Allen, I arrest you for the wilful murder of a woman unknown, and I must caution you that anything you say will be taken down in writing and may be used against you at your trial." Then write down what he says, lock him up in his room, and telephone to Mr Pepper, Central 1202.'

'I could never do such a thing. Mr Meddleton-

Jones, were he a murderer three times over. You'll have to do this yourself.'

I looked at Mr Pepper and Mr Pepper looked at me. It seemed to me that this was the moment for calling in the regular police who are paid for doing these things, but I did not dare to say so. I had an uncomfortable feeling that I had read somewhere about a man being charged as an accessory after the fact, and I had a horrible presentiment that Pepper and I would find ourselves standing in the dock at the Old Bailey. We dismissed Mrs Auger with some difficulty on the plea that we had to consider our position. There were still four days before us. Mr Pepper was equally perturbed. The only solution which he could suggest was that I should wait at Mrs Auger's door day after day and as soon as Allen appeared accost him and induce him to come to the office to be confronted with his victim. We would then be guided by events. If he displayed signs of guilt, we might go so far as to telephone the police. It was the first time I had ever known him to contemplate lowering his dignity as a scientific detective, and I honoured him for it though I cannot say that I liked the role he had assigned to me. An extraordinary coincidence saved me. I owed my rescue to the same club acquaintance who had first introduced me to the man whom I shall continue to regard as the greatest detective of the age.

My friend was lunching at a table for two. As I passed him he sprang up and introduced me to his guest, a middle-aged man with a beard turning grey, and asked me to join them. In the course of conversation it emerged that his guest was the head of a well-known medical school in London, and that he was at the moment of my appearance relating an unpleasant incident at the school. My friend asked him to begin the story again. 'Mr Meddleston-Jones,' he was good enough to say, 'is the very man to advise you. He is associated with the best detective brains in London, besides being himself a man of very wide experience in crime.' It was rather oddly expressed, but my friend meant well.

'But I don't want to call in the police – at any rate until we know more.'

'Bless you, Mr Meddleston-Jones has no connection with Scotland Yard. He is an amateur – if I may say so, a brilliant amateur.'

Thus reassured, the doctor told his story. A young man, an assistant to the custodian of the anatomical school, had disappeared two days before. His character was exemplary; he handled no money; as far as the custodian knew, he had no private worries. He had put away the 'subjects' on the Monday evening and had remarked to the custodian that he thought it looked like rain. At eight next morning he should have returned to work for he was always punctual. It was a busy day and when the students arrived at ten everything was late; some of them complained to him, the doctor, that if their 'subjects' were not arranged for them, they could not expect to do well in the approaching examination. He sent for the custodian, and it was thus for the first time that he learned that John was missing. They sent to his home to enquire the cause; he had not been home. The whole day passed without news of him. The obvious course was to report his disappearance to the police, but, as we could easily understand, it would be very disturbing to the young minds of the students then in the throes of preparing for examination and destructive to the morale of the establishment to have detectives practically in charge of the place, questioning everybody and poking their noses into every part of the building. He wished to avoid it if possible. But there was one possibility that had occurred to him – he scarcely liked to breathe it – which would make the intervention of the police inevitable – if the poor lad had been the victim of foul play in the building itself – then –

'But why should you suspect that?'

'Well, I don't quite know. Perhaps it was that when I was going my rounds a few evenings ago I heard loud words coming from the laboratory. All the students had left for the day. I went to the door and I heard the custodian speaking very sharply to the boy, and he was answering much in the same tone. It was one of those quarrels about the details of duty in which a principal had better not interfere, and I went away. But I confess that it left a disagreeable impression on my mind. The custodian has always seemed to me an excellent servant – been with us for years – but he is short-tempered and I confess that his language on that occasion was rather a shock to me. Perhaps his duties tend to make a man callous.'

'But there is a wide gap between bad language and murder.'

'I know, I know. Only it occurred to me – I may be unduly imaginative – that for a man in his position, alone in the building with this boy till a late hour, there are so many facilities for disposing of a body – the furnace and so forth; it is nothing more than a vague suspicion.'

We were silent for some time, leaving our food untasted. Then my friend said, 'Why don't you ask Jones to go back with you? He could look over the place and tackle the porter in a way you could not. Let him represent himself as employed to find the missing boy.'

'Will you?' said the doctor, turning to me. 'It would take a great load off my mind, but I scarcely liked to suggest it.'

We wasted no further time over luncheon. The doctor had his car waiting and drove me to the school. 'If you don't mind,' I said, 'I should like you to introduce me to the custodian and leave him to show me round. I can put the necessary questions to him as we go. It will seem less formal and official.' This being precisely what the doctor wanted, he took me straight to the laboratory, where a middle-aged man was moving about in his shirt sleeves. 'Stokes,' he said, 'this is Mr Meddleston-Jones, who is enquiring into the disappearance of young Sopwith. He would like you to show him round the premises. I'll leave him with you.' He shook hands with me and disappeared.

Stokes seemed quite glad to see me. 'We had better not disturb the students in the operating-room, sir. They'll all be gone at five and in the meantime we can go over the basement. Queer business, this of young Sopwith. A better lad never stepped, but I had noticed lately that things had been going wrong with him. He had lost interest in his work.'

'Had he anything on his mind?'

'That's just what I think. From things he let drop I think he was gone on some young woman who wouldn't have him. One day he said, "What's the least that a young couple could live on in London, Mr Stokes?" And when I named two pounds a week, he just fell to pieces, as if I'd crushed him. He's never been the same lad since they refused him for the army. This is where they bring them in, sir.'

'Bring what in?'

'The subjects,' he said, in some surprise. We were in a vaulted tunnel in the basement. 'And this is the boiler house.' A furnace was glowing behind a red hot door.

'Whose duty is it to stoke the boiler?'

'That's just it, sir. It was young Sopwith's duty, but latterly he neglected it and it fell upon me. The same with the packing.'

'The packing?'

'Yes, packing the subjects into the coffins. Here is the packing room.' We were in a vaulted cellar. On one side was a pile of rough deal coffins stained black, on the other trays of bones and skulls with dried flesh adhering to them. 'They come down here from the operating-room like that, sir, and it was young Sopwith's duty to sort them out into some sort of body for each coffin; that is to say, he was supposed to be careful that, as far as he could, there should be only one head, two arms and two legs in each coffin before it was nailed up and taken to the cemetery, but he was very careless latterly and I've had to see to it myself.'

'You mean he mixed up the bodies?'

'Oh, no one could help doing that, sir. You can't keep them distinct, but we keep a register of the names and each coffin has the name of one of the subjects tacked on to it for funeral purposes. But of course it may not be their remains. Probably there is something belonging to ten or a dozen in each coffin.'

While we were holding this cheerful conversation, I was leaning on an enormous wooden box in the outer cellar. I ventured on a question.

'When they bring in the – the subjects, what is done with them?'

'If you will stand over there, sir, I'll show you. You are leaning on them.' I must have startled him by the speed of my movements. 'Oh, they won't bite, sir,' he said, smiling, as he lifted the heavy lid. I peeped over his shoulder. There on racks lay ten human bodies, old and young, stiff, nude and white, the debris of humanity, the homeless and friendless, who lead their lives in the London workhouses and probably are sorry to leave them in spite of the misery they have known. In their death they do more for humanity than they have ever done in life by furnishing material for each new generation of surgeons to work upon. 'We keep them fresh by injecting formalin,' he said, pointing to a wound in the neck of one of the corpses. He shut down the lid and looked at his watch. 'The students will be gone now, sir,' he said. 'I'll take you to the dissecting-room.' He led the way upstairs to a large room with high windows that ran the length of the building. A dozen tables, each covered with a sheet, held the subjects that were in the hands of students. One attracted my attention on account of its great bulk in comparison with the rest. The sheet scarcely sufficed to cover it. 'Oh that. That's a young elephant that died in the Zoo. One of the students who is sure of his final had a fancy for it.'

At the end of the room were a number of iron doors labelled 'Head', 'Arm', 'Leg', 'Pelvis', and so on. I asked Stokes about them, for they were a possible hiding-place for the body of the missing youth. He threw open one of the iron doors disclosing iron racks on which human remains were disposed in various stages of dissection.

'It's these that make our job of "assembling" so difficult downstairs. There's perhaps the arms of twenty people in there and there'll be twenty heads in the next cupboard but one. But it has to be like this so that a student can take up his work just where he left off.'

Something had caught my attention and I was scarcely listening. These human arms with desiccated flesh adhering to the bones. Where had I seem them? Then it came to me with a flash – the remains of the murdered woman in our office. I turned to Stokes.

'Do you ever lose any of these bodies?'

'Oh, now and again a student will take away a hand or foot in his bag to work on at home, but if he did such a thing without reporting it to me there'd be trouble, sir. You see, they can't get past my system of booking in and out. I make 'em all sign for what they have. You, for instance, sir, suppose you were a new student. You come to me and say, "Stokes, have you got a knee for me today?" "Yes," I say, "but you'll have to sign for a whole leg." And then you slip it into your bag and walk away with it. Then, the next morning you say, "Stokes, I think I'll work at the wrist and hand today. Have you got a nice forearm?" I look at my book and I say, "Mr Meddleston-Jones, not another bit do you get until I see that leg you had yesterday." ' He became silent and thoughtful. 'Mind you, I don't say that I've never had them get by me. There was that Allen, for instance – I'll have something to say to *him* when he comes back, if he ever does.'

'Tell me about Allen,' I said, trying hard to keep my voice even and steady.

'Oh, you should ask the principal about him. He'd have plenty to tell you. He got away with a whole body from me last year – more than a body – and I didn't find it out till I was going over my books afterwards. Cunning? I never knew a man to beat him. I'll tell you how he did it. On a Monday he'd ask for a head, and just before five I'd see him go to that locker with the head in his hand. Of course, I thought he'd put it back. On Tuesday I'd get a note from him to say he'd been called away. Would I keep the same head for him? He'd be away perhaps a week, and then he'd ask for an arm and so it went on. It wasn't for weeks that I found out what he'd been doing, and then it was too late: he'd gone abroad. He was always doing that – playing fast and loose with the institution. I can't understand why the principal lets him come back time after time. Well, if he comes back after this he'll have some questions to answer. I've got them all booked out and I'd know them anywhere. Look here, sir, a page all to himself.'

He turned over the leaves of his ledger and there, under the name of Henry Allen, were the entries: 'June 20th. Head No. 128, male. July 2nd. Forearm No. 43, female,' and so on.

'Would you know your – your specimens again if you saw them?'

'Know them? Yes, and could swear to every one of them. When Allen had a subject I put my private mark on it, so there should be no mistake. It's a theft, that's what it is, to say nothing of the trouble it meant for me if I couldn't make up the number for the funerals.'

I asked him whether the principal was still in the building. If so I must see him before he left. He looked at his watch.

'You'll just catch him if you are quick, sir. He leaves sharp at six. It's the second door on the left as you go down the passage.'

I was just in time; the doctor was brushing his hat. 'Well,' he said, 'any daylight?'

'I think I have cleared up one thing: young Sopwith has not been murdered on the premises.'

'And you think?'

'I think that you should report him to Scotland Yard as missing, giving his home address. It may be a case of suicide.' (I was justified next morning when Sopwith's body was found in the Thames, with a letter in the pocket addressed to the object of his affections.) 'But I came to ask you about another matter altogether. You had a student named Henry Allen!'

He threw down his hat and lifted his hands to heaven. 'Henry Allen! Has that fellow turned up again? I never met such a man in my life before. The most charitable view that one can take of Allen is to say that he is mad. Why, that man has been on our books for six years. He passed all his intermediate tests brilliantly, and I used to think that he would carry all before him in his final. Then, on the eve of the examination I would get a note from him saying that he was called abroad on business and we might see nothing of him for six months. I don't know whether it was stage fright or simply a love of roving; perhaps a little of both. He was a good deal older than the ordinary run of pupils, and was an interesting person if one got him to talk. But he made no friends here. He paid his fees regularly and worked hard. You should get Stokes to tell you about him. He accuses him of stealing some of his subjects.'

'And I think he is right about that. But I can get them back for you if you think it worth while. I know where they are.'

'Is there anything in London that you don't know? Of course, we'd like them back.'

'Can Stokes come and identify them?'

'Of course he can. Arrange it with him – any time you like. And now I must be off – one of these horrible early public dinners. I cannot thank you enough for coming.'

I found Stokes in the laboratory just sitting down to his tea. 'Let me get you a cup, sir. A drop of tea helps one through the evening.' He pushed back a jar containing a human eye to make room for my cup, and I found my appetite had left me. I declined the tea, but we talked while he ate and drank. It was a creepy sort of place, this laboratory: bottles from ceiling to floor all alike and all containing the intimate machinery of the human machine – the watch-springs of the human body – bleached and half-floating in yellowish liquid. They did not disturb Stokes's appetite in the least.

'You said just now that you could identify the – er – specimens that Allen took away.'

'Try me, sir.'

'That's exactly what I want to do if you'll come with me now.'

'You know where they are!' he exclaimed in astonishment. 'I'll go whenever you like.'

It was past seven when we reached the office, but a light showing beneath the door proved that my chief was still there. I asked Stokes to wait on the landing till I called him.

'I've been thinking over that Henry Allen case, Mr Meddleston-Jones,' said my chief before I could speak. 'I've been waiting for you all the afternoon. I am now satisfied that in Allen we have got Jack the Ripper. That woman in there is one of his victims.' I was very much taken aback, being about to produce Stokes. 'Yes,' my chief continued, 'everything points to it – the man's personal habits – his secretiveness – his sudden disappearances. When you arrest him bear in mind that he has a knife about him.'

'Don't say any more, Mr Pepper, till you've heard what I've got to tell you. I have a man here who says he can identify the bones. They are surgical specimens which Allen stole from him.' I have never seen a face so transfigured with noble indignation. After all, I was belittling one of the most important cases in his experience.

'Bring him in,' he said faintly, and he lighted up the laboratory, into which I led Stokes. My chief threw back the sheet while I watched Stokes. His was not usually an expressive face. First his eyes grew very round, then his whole frame was shaken with some strong emotion. He seemed quite unable to speak. When at last he found his voice it came harsh and loud. He picked up a thigh bone and said, 'You are right, sir; they're ours right enough. Here's my private mark,' and he showed me '118' scratched in minute figures on the bone. He looked hard at the face, and again his sturdy frame was shaken by a convulsive movement that began quite low down in his body

437

and seemed to deprive him of speech. If his face had not been so impassive, I should have said that he was rocking with suppressed laughter. When at last he had recovered command of his voice he said, 'You've made a fine woman of No. 48, but what about his beard? He had a long grey beard when he was with us.' I did not dare to look at my chief.

'I think,' I said very gently, 'that Mr Stokes had better take the bones away with him. They belong to his medical school, where Henry Allen was a student. They were, in fact, stolen, and the authorities may wish to prosecute.' My chief made no sign, and Stokes began to pack up the specimens in the trunk.

'When Mr Henry Allen comes home,' he said, 'and asks for his trunk, you might refer him to the principal, if you don't mind.' He took one long look at the head before he wrapped it up. 'I wouldn't damage this waxwork for the world: we'll put it in our museum.' As I was helping him down the stairs with the trunk, he said, 'Your friend must have been puzzled by the different sizes of the bones. One arm and one leg belonged to women.'

'He was a little puzzled. He thought that the murdered woman was deformed.'

'I suppose he didn't happen to notice that she had three hands. I see that he had put one of them where a foot was missing.'

When I reached Mrs Auger's door a man was ringing the bell. He was a thin, hunted-looking creature of about thirty, with three days' growth of beard. The door opened as I came up and Mrs Auger said, 'Oh, Mr Allen, where *have* you been?'

'I've been to Lisbon,' he said in a weak voice.

I laid my hand firmly on his shoulder and said,

'Henry Allen, you are wanted at the Medical School to explain why you are unlawfully in possession of certain anatomical specimens which are the property of the School and I must caution you that anything you say will be taken down in writing and may be used against you at your trial.'

He turned very white and Mrs Auger collapsed on her own doorstep.

But the principal declined to prosecute.

JACQUES FUTRELLE

The Phantom Motor Car

Two dazzling white eyes bulged suddenly through the night, as a motor car swept round a curve in the wide road, and laid a smooth, glaring pathway ahead. Even at this distance the rhythmical crackling-chug informed Special Constable Baker that it was a gasoline car, and the headlong swoop of the unblinking lights towards him made him instantly aware of the fact that the speed ordinance of Yarborough County was being a little more than broken – it was being obliterated.

Now the County of Yarborough was one wide expanse of summer estates and superbly kept roads, level as a floor, and offered distracting temptations to the dangerous pastime of racing. But against this was the fact that the County was particular about its speed laws, so particular, in fact, that it had stationed half a hundred men on its highways to abate the nuisance. Incidentally it had found that keeping record of infractions of the law was an excellent source of income.

'Forty miles an hour if an inch,' remarked Baker to himself.

He rose from a camp stool where he was wont to make himself comfortable on watch from six o'clock until midnight, picked up his lantern, turned up the light and stepped down to the edge of the road. He always remained on watch at the same place – at one end of a long stretch which motorists had unanimously dubbed the 'Trap'. The Trap was singularly tempting – a perfectly macadamised road bed lying

between two tall stone walls with only enough of a
sinuous twist in it to make each end invisible from the
centre. Another man, Special Constable Bowman,
was stationed at the other end of the Trap, and there
was telephonic communication between the points,
enabling the two to check each other and ensure that
if one failed to stop a car or get its number the other
would. That at least was the theory.

So now, with the utmost confidence, Baker waited
beside the road. The approaching lights were only a
couple of hundred yards away. At the proper instant
he would raise his lantern, the car would stop, its
occupants would protest, and then the county would
add a mite to its general fund for making the roads
even better and more tempting to motorists. Or sometimes the cars did not stop. In that event it was part of
the special constable's duty to get the number as it
flew past; subsequent reference to the monthly motor-
car register gave the name of the owner. An extra fine
was always imposed in such cases.

Without the slightest diminution of speed the car
came hurtling on towards him and swung wide so as
to take the straight path of the Trap at full speed. At
the psychological instant Baker stepped out into the
road and waved his lantern.

'Stop!' he commanded.

The crackling-chug came on, heedless of the cry.
The car was almost on him before he leaped out of
the road – a feat at which he was particularly expert –
then it flashed by and plunged into the Trap. Baker
was, at the instant, so busily engaged in getting out
of the way that he could not read the number, but he
was not disconcerted because he knew there was no
escape from the Trap. On the one side a solid stone

wall eight feet high marked the eastern boundary of
the John Phelps Stocker country estate, and on the
other side a stone wall nine feet high marked the
western boundary of the Thomas Q. Rogers country
estate. There was no turn out, no place, no possible
way for an auto to get out of the Trap except at one
of the two ends guarded by the special constables.
So Baker, perfectly confident of results, seized the
phone.

'Car coming through sixty miles an hour,' he
bawled. 'It won't stop. I missed the number. Look
out!'

'All right,' answered Special Constable Bowman.

For ten, fifteen, twenty minutes Baker waited expecting a call from Bowman at the other end. It did
not come and finally he picked up the phone again.
No answer. He rang several times, battered the box
and did some tricks with the receiver. Still no answer.
Finally he began to feel worried. He remembered
that at the same post one special constable had been
badly hurt by a reckless chauffeur who refused to stop
or turn his car when the officer stepped out into the
road. In his mind's eye he saw Bowman now lying
helpless, perhaps badly injured. If the car held the
pace at which it passed him it would be certain death
to anybody unlucky enough to get in its path.

With these thoughts running through his head, and
with genuine solicitude for Bowman, Baker at last
walked on along the Trap towards the other end. The
feeble rays of his lantern showed the unbroken line of
the cold stone walls on either side. There was no
shrubbery of any sort, only a narrow strip of grass
close to the wall. The more Baker considered the
matter the more anxious he became, and he increased

his pace a little. As he turned a gentle curve he saw a lantern in the distance coming slowly towards him. It was evidently being carried by someone who was looking carefully along each side of the road.

'Hello!' called Baker, when the lantern came within distance. 'That you, Bowman?'

'Yes,' came the welcome response.

The lanterns moved on and met. Baker's solicitude for the other constable was quickly changed to curiosity.

'What're you looking for?' he asked.

'That motor,' replied Bowman. 'It didn't come through my end, and I thought perhaps there had been an accident, so I walked along looking for it. Haven't seen anything.'

'Didn't come through your end?' repeated Baker in amazement. 'Why it must have. It didn't come back my way and I haven't passed it, so it must have gone through.'

'Well, it didn't,' declared Bowman conclusively. 'I was on the lookout for it, too, standing beside the road. There hasn't been a car through my end in an hour.'

Special Constable Baker raised his lantern until the rays fell full on the face of Special Constable Bowman, and for an instant they stared each at the other. Suspicion glowed from the keen, avaricious eyes of Baker.

'How much did they give you to let 'em by?' he asked.

'Give me?' exclaimed Bowman, in righteous indignation. 'Give me? Nothing. I haven't seen a car.'

A slight sneer curled the lips of Special Constable Baker.

'Of course that's all right to report at headquarters,' he said, 'but I happen to know that the motor came in here, that it didn't go back my way, that it couldn't get out except at the ends, therefore it went your way.' He was silent for a moment. 'And whatever you got, Jim, seems to me I ought to get half.'

Then the worm – i.e., Bowman – turned. A polite curl appeared about his lips and was permitted to show through the grizzled moustache.

'I guess,' he said deliberately, 'you think because you do that, everybody else does. I haven't seen any motors.'

'Don't I always give you half, Jim?' Baker demanded, almost pleadingly.

'Well I haven't seen any car, and that's all there is to it. If it didn't go back your way there wasn't any car.' There was a pause; Bowman was framing up something particularly unpleasant. 'You're seeing things, that's what's the matter.'

So was sown discord between two officers of the County of Yarborough. After a while they separated with mutual sneers and open derision, and went back to their respective posts. Each was thoughtful in his own way. At five minutes to midnight, just before they went off duty, Baker called Bowman on the phone again.

'I've been thinking this thing over, Jim, and I guess it would be just as well if we didn't report it or say anything about it when we go in,' said Baker slowly. 'It seems foolish, and if we did say anything about it it would give the boys the laugh on us.'

'Just as you say,' responded Bowman.

Relations between Special Constable Baker and Special Constable Bowman were strained on the morrow. But they walked along side by side to their respective posts. Baker stopped at his end of the Trap; Bowman did not even look around.

'You'd better keep your eyes open tonight, Jim,' Baker called as a last word.

'I had 'em open last night,' was the disgusted retort.

Seven, eight o'clock passed. Two or three cars had gone through the Trap at moderate speed and one had been warned by Baker. At a few minutes past nine he was staring down the road which led into the Trap when he saw something that brought him quickly to his feet. It was a pair of dazzling white eyes, far away. He recognised them – the mysterious car of the night before.

'I'll get her this time,' he muttered grimly, between closed teeth.

Then, when the on-rushing car was a full two hundred yards away, Baker planted himself in the middle of the road and began to swing the lantern. The car seemed, if anything, to be travelling even faster than on the previous night. At a hundred yards Baker began to shout. Still the car did not lessen speed, merely rushed on. Again at the psychological instant Baker jumped. The car whisked by as the chauffeur gave it a dexterous twist to prevent running down the special constable.

Safely out of its way Baker turned and stared after it, trying to read the number. He could see there was a number because a white board swung from the tail axle, but he could not make out the figures. Dust and a swaying car conspired to defeat him. And he did see, too, that there were four persons in the car dimly silhouetted against the light reflected from the road. It was useless, of course, to conjecture as to sex, for even as he looked the fast-receding car swerved around the turn and was lost to sight.

Again he rushed to the telephone; Bowman responded promptly.

'That car's gone in again,' Baker called. 'Ninety miles an hour. Look out!'

'I'm looking,' responded Bowman.

'Let me know what happens,' Baker shouted.

With the receiver at his ear he stood for ten or fifteen minutes, then Bowman came back on the other end.

'Well?' Baker responded. 'Get 'em?'

'No car passed through and there's none in sight,' said Bowman.

'But it went in,' insisted Baker.

'Well, it didn't come out here,' declared Bowman. 'Walk along the road till I meet you and look out for it.'

Then was repeated the search of the night before. When the two men met in the middle of the Trap their faces were blank – blank as the high stone walls which stared at them from either side.

'Nothing!' said Bowman.

'Nothing!' echoed Baker.

Special Constable Bowman perched his head on one side and scratched his grizzly chin.

'You're not trying to put up a job on me?' he enquired coldly. 'You did see a car?'

'I certainly did,' declared Baker, and a belligerent tone underlay his manner. 'I certainly saw it, Jim, and if it didn't come out your end, why – why – '

He paused and glanced quickly behind him. The action inspired a sudden similar one on Bowman's part.

'Maybe – maybe – ' said Bowman after a minute, 'maybe it's a – a spook car?'

'Well it must be,' mused Baker. 'You know as well as I do that no car can get out of this Trap except at the ends. That car came in here, it isn't here now, and it didn't go out your end. Now where is it?'

Bowman stared at him a minute, picked up his lantern, shook his head solemnly and wandered along the road back to his post. On his way he glanced around quickly, apprehensively, three times – Baker did the same thing four times.

On the third night the phantom car appeared and disappeared precisely as it had done previously. Again Baker and Bowman met halfway between posts and talked it over.

'I'll tell you what, Baker,' said Bowman in conclusion, 'maybe you're just imagining that you see a car. Maybe if I was at your end I couldn't see it.'

Special Constable Baker was distinctly hurt at the insinuation.

'All right, Jim,' he said at last, 'if you think that way about it we'll swop posts tomorrow night. We won't have to say anything about it when we report.'

'Now that's the talk,' exclaimed Bowman with an air approaching enthusiasm. 'I'll bet *I* don't see it.'

On the following night Special Constable Bowman made himself comfortable on Special Constable Baker's camp stool. And *he* saw the phantom car. It came upon him with a rush and the crackling-chug of the engine, and then sped on, leaving him nerveless. He called Baker over the wire and Baker watched half an hour for the phantom. It did not appear.

Ultimately all things reach the newspapers. So with the story of the phantom motor car. Hutchinson

Hatch, reporter, smiled incredulously when his city editor laid aside an inevitable cigar and tersely stated the known facts. The known facts in this instance were meagre almost to the disappearing point. They consisted merely of a corroborated statement that a motor car, solid and tangible enough to all appearances, had rushed into the Trap each night and totally disappeared.

But there was enough of the bizarre about it to pique the curiosity, to make one wonder, so Hatch journeyed down to Yarborough County, an hour's ride from the city, met and talked to Baker and Bowman and then, in broad daylight, strolled along the Trap twice. It was a leisurely, thorough investigation with the end in view of finding out how an automobile, once inside, might get out again without going out either end.

On the first trip through Hatch paid particular attention to the Thomas Q. Rogers side of the road. The wall, nine feet high, was an unbroken line of stone with not the slightest indication of a secret way through it anywhere. Secret way! Hatch smiled at the phrase. But when he reached the other end – Bowman's end – of the Trap he was perfectly convinced of one thing – that no motor car had left the hard, macadamised road to go over, under or through the Thomas Q. Rogers wall. Returning, still leisurely, he paid strict attention to the John Phelps Stocker side, and when he reached the other end – Baker's end – he was convinced of another thing – that no motor car had left the road to go over, under or through the John Phelps Stocker wall.

Hatch saw no shrubbery along the road, nothing but a strip of scrupulously cared-for grass, therefore the phantom car could not be hidden any time, night or day. Hatch failed, too, to find any holes in the road, so the car did not go down through the earth. At this point he involuntarily glanced up at the blue sky. Perhaps, he thought whimsically, the automobile was a strange sort of bird, or – or – and he stopped suddenly.

'By George!' he exclaimed. 'I wonder if – '

And the remainder of the afternoon he spent systematically making enquiries. He went from house to house, the Stocker house, the Rogers house, both of which were at the time unoccupied, then to cottage, cabin and hut in turn. But he did not seem overladen with information when he joined Special Constable Baker at his end of the Trap that evening about seven o'clock.

Together they rehearsed the strange points of the mystery as the shadows grew about them, until finally the darkness was so dense that Baker's lantern was the only bright spot in sight. As the chill of evening closed in, a certain awed tone crept into their voices. Occasionally a motor car bowled along, and each time as it hove in sight Hatch glanced at Baker questioningly. And each time Baker shook his head. And each time, too, he called Bowman, in this manner accounting for every car that went into the Trap.

'It'll come all right,' said Baker after a long silence, 'and I'll know it the minute it rounds the curve coming towards us. I'd know its two lights in a thousand.'

They sat still and smoked. After awhile two dazzling white lights burst into view far down the road and Baker, in excitement, dropped his pipe.

'That's her!' he declared. 'Look at her coming!'

449

And Hatch did look at her coming. The speed of the mysterious car was such as to make one look. Like the eyes of a giant the two lights came on towards them, and Baker perfunctorily went through the motions of attempting to stop it. The car fairly whizzed past them and the rush of air which tugged at their coats was convincing enough proof of its solidity. Hatch strained his eyes to read the number as the motor flashed by. But it was hopeless. The tail of the car was lost in an eddying whirl of dust.

'She certainly does travel,' commented Baker, softly.

'She does,' Hatch assented.

Then, for the benefit of the newspaper man, Baker called Bowman on the wire.

'Car's coming again,' he shouted. 'Look out and let me know!'

Bowman, at his end, waited twenty minutes, then made the usual report – the car had not passed. Hutchinson Hatch was a calm, cold, dispassionate young man, but now a queer, creepy sensation stole along his spinal column. He lighted a cigarette and pulled himself together with a jerk.

'There's one way to find out where it goes,' he declared at last, emphatically, 'and that's to place a man in the middle just beyond the bend of the Trap and let him wait and see. If the car goes up, down or even evaporates he'll see and can tell us.'

Baker looked at him curiously.

'I'd hate to be the man in the middle,' he declared. There was something of uneasiness in his manner.

'I rather think I would, too,' responded Hatch.

On the following evening, consequent on the appearance of the story of the phantom motor in Hatch's paper, there were twelve other reporters on hand. Most of them were openly, flagrantly sceptical; they even insinuated that no one had seen a car. Hatch smiled wisely.

'Wait!' he advised with deep conviction.

So when the darkness fell that evening the newspaper men of a great city had entered into a conspiracy to capture the phantom car. Thirteen of them, making a total of fifteen men with Baker and Bowman, were on hand, and they agreed to a suggestion for all to take positions along the road of the Trap from Baker's post to Bowman's, watch for the car, see what happened to it, and compare notes afterwards. So they scattered themselves along, a few hundred feet apart, and waited. That night the phantom did not appear at all and twelve reporters jeered at Hutchinson Hatch, and told him to light his pipe with the story. But next night when Hatch and Baker and Bowman alone were watching the phantom motor reappeared.

Whereupon, like a child with a troublesome problem, Hatch took the entire matter and laid it before Professor Van Dusen, the master brain which had, at various times, untangled facts from a score or more intricate affairs for his benefit. The Thinking Machine, with squint eyes turned steadily upward, and long, slender fingers pressed tip to tip, listened to the end.

'Now I know, of course, that motor cars don't fly,' Hatch burst out savagely, in conclusion, 'and if this one doesn't fly there is no earthly way for it to get out of the Trap, as they call it. I went over the thing carefully – I even went so far as to examine the ground and the tops of the walls to see if a runway had been let down for the auto to go over.'

The Thinking Machine squinted at him enquiringly. 'Are you sure you saw a motor car?'

'Certainly I saw it,' blurted the reporter. 'I not only saw it – I smelt it. Just to convince myself that it was real I tossed my cane in front of the thing and it smashed it to toothpicks.'

'Perhaps, then, if everything is as you say, the car actually *has* wings,' remarked the scientist.

The reporter stared into the calm, inscrutable face of the Thinking Machine, fearing first that he had not heard aright. Then he concluded that he had.

'You mean,' he enquired eagerly, 'that the phantom may be a motor-aeroplane affair, and that it actually does fly?'

'It's not at all impossible,' commented the scientist.

'I had an idea something like that myself,' Hatch explained, 'and questioned every soul within a mile or so, but I didn't get anything.'

'The perfect stretch of road there might be the very place for some daring experimenter to get up sufficient speed to soar a short distance in a light machine,' continued the scientist.

'Light machine?' Hatch repeated 'Didn't I tell you that this car had four people in it?'

'Four people!' exclaimed the scientist. 'Dear me! Dear me! That makes it very different. Of course four people would be too great a lift for an – '

For ten minutes he sat silent, and tiny, cobwebby lines appeared in his dome-like brow. Then he arose and passed into the adjoining room. After a moment Hatch heard the telephone bell jingle. Five minutes later the Thinking Machine appeared, and scowled upon him unpleasantly.

'I suppose what you really want to learn is if the car

is a – a material one, and to whom it belongs?' he queried.

'That's it,' agreed the reporter, 'and, of course, why it does what it does, and how it gets out of the Trap.'

'Do you happen to know a fast, long-distance bicycle rider?' demanded the scientist abruptly.

'A dozen of them,' replied the reporter promptly. 'I think I see the idea, but – '

'You haven't the faintest inkling of the idea,' declared the Thinking Machine positively. 'If you can arrange with a fast rider who can go a distance – it might be thirty, forty, fifty miles – we may end this little affair without difficulty.'

In these circumstances Professor Van Dusen, scientist and logician, met the famous Jimmie Thalhauer, the world's champion long-distance bicyclist. He held every record from five miles up to and including six hours, had twice won the six-day race and was, altogether, a master in his field. He came in chewing a toothpick. There were introductions.

'You ride the bicycle?' enquired the crusty little scientist.

'Well, *some*,' confessed the champion modestly with a wink at Hatch.

'Can you keep up with a motor car for a distance of, say, thirty or forty miles?'

'I can keep up with anything that ain't got wings,' was the response.

'Well, to tell you the truth,' volunteered Professor Van Dusen, 'there is a growing belief that this particular car has wings. However, if you can keep up with it – '

'Ah, quit your kiddin',' said the champion, easily.

'I can ride rings round anything on wheels. I'll start behind it and beat it where it's going.'

Professor Van Dusen examined the champion, Jimmie Thalhauer, as a curiosity. In the seclusion of his laboratory he had never had an opportunity of meeting just such another worldly young person.

'How fast *can* you ride, Mr Thalhauer?' he asked at last.

'I'm ashamed to tell you,' confided the champion in a hushed voice. 'I can ride so fast that I scare myself.' He paused a moment. 'But it seems to me,' he said, 'if there's thirty or forty miles to do I ought to do it on a motorcycle?'

'Now that's just the point,' explained Professor Van Dusen. 'A motorcycle makes a noise; if anything of that sort could have been used we should have hired a fast motorcycle. The proposition, briefly, is: I want you to ride, without lights, behind a motor car, which may also run without lights, and find out where it goes. No occupant of the car must suspect that it is followed.'

'Without lights?' repeated the champion. 'Gee! Rubber shoe, eh?'

The Thinking Machine looked his bewilderment.

'Yes, that's it,' Hatch answered for him.

'I guess it's good for a four-column head?' enquired the champion. 'Special pictures posed by the champion? Eh?'

'Yes,' Hatch replied.

' "Tracked on a Bicycle" sounds good to me. Eh?'

Hatch nodded.

So arrangements were concluded, and then and there Professor Van Dusen gave definite and conclusive instructions to the champion. While these apparently bore broadly on the problem in hand, they conveyed absolutely no inkling of his plan to the reporter. At the end the champion arose to go.

'You're a most extraordinary young man, Mr Thalhauer,' commented the scientist, not without admiration for the sturdy, powerful figure.

And as Hatch accompanied the champion out of the room and down the steps, Jimmie smiled with easy grace

'Nutty old guy, ain't he?'

Night! Utter blackness, relieved only by a white, ribbon-like road which winds away mistily under a starless sky. Shadowy hedges line either side, and occasionally a tree thrusts itself upward out of the sombreness. The murmur of human voices in the shadows, then the crackling-chug of an engine and a motor car moves slowly, without lights, into the road. There is the sudden clatter of an engine revving up, and the car rushes away.

From the hedge comes the faint rustle of leaves as of wind stirring, then a figure moves impalpably. A moment and it becomes a separate entity; a quick movement and the creak of a leather bicycle saddle. Silently the single figure, bent low over the handle bars, moves after the car with ever-increasing momentum.

Then a long, desperate race. For mile after mile, mile after mile the car goes on. The silent cyclist has crept up almost to the rear axle and hangs there doggedly as a racer to his pacer. On and on they rush together through the darkness, the chauffeur moving with a perfect knowledge of his road, the single rider behind clinging on grimly with set teeth. The powerful piston-like legs move up and down to the beat of the engine.

At last, with dust-dry throat and stinging, aching eyes, the cyclist feels the pace slacken and instantly he drops back out of sight. It is only by sound that he follows now. The car stops; the cyclist is lost in the shadows.

For two or three hours the car stands deserted and silent. At last the voices are heard again, the car stirs, moves away, and the cyclist drops in behind. Another race, which leads off in another direction. Finally, from a knoll, the lights of a city are seen. Ten minutes elapse, the motor car stops, the headlights flare up, and more leisurely it proceeds on its way.

On the following evening Professor Van Dusen and Hutchinson Hatch called upon Fielding Stanwood, president of the Fordyce National Bank. Mr Stanwood looked at them with interrogative eyes.

'We called to inform you, Mr Stanwood,' explained Professor Van Dusen 'that a box of securities, probably United States bonds, is missing from your bank.'

'What?' exclaimed Mr Stanwood, and his face paled. 'Robbery?'

'I only know the bonds were taken out of the vault tonight by Joseph Marsh, your assistant cashier,' said the scientist, 'and that he, together with three other men, left the bank with the box and are now at – a place I can name.'

Mr Stanwood was staring at him in amazement.

'You know where they are?' he demanded.

'I said I did,' replied the scientist, shortly.

'Then we must inform the police at once, and – '

'I don't know that there has been an actual crime,' interrupted the scientist. 'I do know that every night for a week these bonds have been taken out, through the connivance of your watchman, and in each instance have been returned, intact, before morning. They will be returned tonight. Therefore I would advise, if you act, not to do so until the four men return with the bonds.'

It was a singular party which met in the private office of President Stanwood at the bank just after midnight. Marsh and three companions, formally under arrest, were present, as were President Stanwood, Professor Van Dusen and Hutchinson Hatch, besides detectives. Marsh had the bonds under his arm when he was taken. He talked freely when questioned.

'I will admit,' he said without hesitation, 'that I have acted beyond my rights in removing the bonds from the vault here, but there is no ground for prosecution. I am a responsible officer of this bank and have violated no trust. Nothing is missing, nothing is stolen. Every bond that went out of the bank is here.'

'But why – why did you take the bonds?' demanded Mr Stanwood.

Marsh shrugged his shoulders.

'It's what has been called a "get-rich-quick" scheme,' said Professor Van Dusen. 'Mr Hatch and I made some investigations today. Mr Marsh and these other three are interested in a business venture which is ethically dishonest but which is within the law. They have sought backing for the scheme amounting to about a million dollars. Those four or five men of means with whom they have discussed the matter have called each night for a week at Marsh's country place. It was necessary to make them believe that there was already a million or so in the scheme, so these bonds were borrowed and represented to be owned by themselves. They were taken to and fro between the bank and his home in a kind of motor car. This is really what happened, based on knowledge which Mr Hatch has gathered, and what I myself developed by the use of a little logic.'

And his statement of the affair proved to be correct. Marsh and the others admitted it. It was while Professor Van Dusen was homeward bound that he explained the phantom-car affair to Hatch.

'The phantom car, as you call it,' he said, 'is the vehicle in which the bonds were moved about. The phantom idea came merely by chance. On the night the vehicle was first noticed it was rushing along – we'll say to reach Marsh's house in time for an appointment. A road map will show you that the most direct line from the bank to Marsh's was through the Trap. If an automobile should go half-way through there then cut across the Stocker estate to the other road the distance would be lessened by a good five miles. This saving at first was, of course, valuable, so the car in which they rushed into the Trap was merely taken across the Stocker estate to the road in front. Of course they always returned to the bank by another route.

'But how?' demanded Hatch. 'There's no road there.'

'I learned by phone from Mr Stocker that there is a narrow walk from a very narrow foot-gate in Stocker's wall on the Trap leading through the grounds to the other road. The phantom car wasn't really a motor at all – it was merely two motorcycles arranged with seats and a steering apparatus. The French army has been experimenting with them. The motorcycles are, of course, separate machines, and as such it was easy to trundle them through a narrow gate and across to the other road. The seats are light; they can be carried under the arm. I knew instantly what the "phantom" must be when I knew there was no road through the wall – only a gateway.'

'Oh!' exclaimed Hatch suddenly, then after a minute: 'But what did Jimmie Thalhauer do for you?'

'He waited in the road at the other end of the footpath – the opposite end from the Trap,' the scientist explained. 'When the auto was brought through and put together he followed it to Marsh's home and from there to the bank. The rest of it you and I worked out today. It's merely logic, Mr Hatch, logic.'

There was a pause.

'That Mr Thalhauer is really a marvellous young man, Mr Hatch, don't you think?'

ROBERT BARR

In the Grip of the Green Demon

Next morning I was in Paris, and next night I
attended the underground meeting of the anarchists,
held within a quarter of a mile of the Luxembourg. I
was known to many there assembled, but my
acquaintance, of course, was not so large as with the
London circle. They had half expected me the night
before, knowing that even going by the Hook of
Holland I might have reached Paris in time for
the conclave. I was introduced generally to the
assemblage as the emissary from England, who was
to assist the bomb-throwing brother to escape either
to that country, or to such other point of safety as I
might choose. No questions were asked me regarding
my doings of the day before, nor was I required to
divulge the plans for my fellow-member's escape. I
was responsible; that was enough. If I failed, through
no fault of my own, it was but part of the ill luck we
were all prepared to face. If I failed through treachery,
then I must expect a dagger in the back at the earliest
possible moment. We all knew the conditions of our
sinister contract, and we all recognised that the least
said the better.

The cellar was dimly lighted by one oil lamp
depending from the ceiling. From this hung a cord
attached to an extinguisher, and one jerk of the cord
would put out the light. Then, while the main entry
doors were being battered down by police, the
occupants of the room could escape through one of

three or four human rat holes provided for that purpose. If any Parisian anarchist does me the honour to read these jottings, I beg to inform him that while I remained in office under the Government of France there was never a time when I did not know the exit of each of these underground passages, and could, during any night there was a conference, have bagged the whole lot of those there assembled. It was never my purpose, however, to shake the anarchists' confidence in their system, for that merely meant the removal of the gathering to another spot, thus giving us the additional trouble of mapping out their new exits and entrances. When I did make a raid on anarchist headquarters in Paris, it was always to secure some particular man. I had my emissaries in plain clothes stationed at each exit. In every case, the rats were allowed to escape unmolested, sneaking forth with great caution into the night, but we always spotted the man we wanted and almost invariably arrested him elsewhere, having followed him from his kennel. On breaking in, my uniformed officers found a dark and empty cellar, and retired apparently baffled. But the coincidence that on the night of every raid some member there present was secretly arrested in another quarter of Paris, and perhaps given a free passage to Russia, never seemed to awaken suspicion in the minds of the conspirators.

I think the London anarchists' method is much better, and I have ever considered the English nihilist the most dangerous of this fraternity, for he is coolheaded and not carried away by his own enthusiasm, and consequently rarely carried away by his own police. The authorities of London meet no opposition in making a raid. They find a well-lighted room containing a more or less shabby coterie playing cards at cheap pine tables. There is no money visible, and, indeed, very little coin would be brought to light if the whole party were searched; so the police are unable to convict the players under the Gambling Act. Besides, it is difficult in any case to obtain a conviction under the Gambling Act, because the accused has the sympathy of the whole country with him. It has always been to me one of the anomalies of the English nature that a magistrate can keep a straight face while he fines some poor wretch for gambling, knowing that next race day (if the court is not sitting) the magistrate himself, in correct sporting costume, with binoculars hanging at his hip, will be on the lawn by the course backing his favourite horse.

After my reception at the anarchists' club in Paris, I remained seated unobtrusively on a bench, waiting until routine business was finished, after which I expected an introduction to the man selected to throw the bomb. I am a very sensitive person, and sitting there quietly I became aware that I was being scrutinised with more than ordinary intensity by someone, which gave me a feeling of uneasiness. At last, in the semi-obscurity opposite me, I saw a pair of eyes, as luminous as those of a tiger, peering fixedly at me. I returned the stare with such composure as I could bring to my aid, and the man, as if fascinated by a look as steady as his own, leaned forward and came more and more into the circle of light. Then I received a shock which it required my utmost self-control to conceal. The face, haggard and drawn, was none other than that of Adolph Simard, who had been my second assistant in the Secret Service of France during my last year in office.

He was a most capable and rising young man at that time, and, of course, he knew me well. Had he, then, penetrated my disguise? Such an event seemed impossible; he could not have recognised my voice, for I had said nothing aloud since entering the room, my few words to the president being spoken in a whisper. Simard's presence there bewildered me; by this time he should be high up in the Secret Service. If he were now a spy, he would, of course, wish to familiarise himself with every particular of my appearance, as in my hands lay the escape of the criminal. Yet, if such were his mission, why did he attract the attention of all members by this open-eyed scrutiny? That he recognised me as Valmont I had not the least fear; my disguise was too perfect; and, even if I were there in my own proper person, I had not seen Simard, nor he me, for ten years, and great changes occur in a man's appearance during so long a period. Yet I remembered with disquietude that Mr White recognised me, and here tonight I had recognised Simard. I could not move my bench farther back because it stood already against the wall. Simard, on the contrary, was seated on one of the few chairs in the room, and this he periodically hitched forward, the better to continue his examination, which now attracted the notice of others besides myself. As he came forward, I could not help admiring the completeness of his disguise so far as apparel was concerned. He was a perfect picture of the Paris wastrel, and, what was more, he wore on his head a cap of the Apaches, the most dangerous band of cut-throats that have ever cursed a civilised city. I could understand that even among lawless anarchists this badge of membership of the Apache band might well strike terror. I felt that before the meeting adjourned I must speak with him, and I determined to begin our conversation by asking him why he stared so fixedly at me. Yet even then I should have made little progress. I did not dare to hint that he belonged to the Secret Service; nevertheless, if the authorities had this plot in charge, it was absolutely necessary we should work together, or, at least, that I should know they were in the secret, and steer my course accordingly. The fact that Simard appeared with undisguised face was not so important as might appear to an outsider. It is always safer for a spy to preserve his natural appearance if that is possible, because a false beard or false moustache or wig runs the risk of being deranged or torn away. As I have said, an anarchist assemblage is simply a room filled with the atmosphere of suspicion. I have known instances where an innocent stranger was suddenly set upon in the midst of solemn proceedings by two or three impetuous fellow-members, who nearly jerked his own whiskers from his face under the impression that they were false. If Simard, therefore, appeared in his own scraggy beard and unkempt hair, it meant that he communicated with headquarters by some circuitous route. I realised, therefore, that a very touchy bit of diplomacy awaited me if I was to learn from himself his actual status.

While I pondered over this perplexity, it was suddenly dissolved by the action of the president, and another substituted for it. 'Will Brother Simard come forward?' asked the president.

My former subordinate removed his eyes from me, slowly rose from his chair, and shuffled up to the president's table.

'Brother Ducharme,' said that official to me in a quiet tone, 'I introduce you to Brother Simard, whom you are commissioned to see into a place of safety when he has dispersed the procession.'

Simard turned his fishy goggle-eyes upon me, and a grin disclosed wolflike teeth. He held out his hand, which, rising to my feet, I took. He gave me a flabby grasp, and all the time his enquiring eyes travelled over me.

'You don't look up to much,' he said. 'What are you?'

'I am a teacher of the French language in London.'

'Umph!' growled Simard, evidently in no wise prepossessed by my appearance. 'I thought you weren't much of a fighter. The gendarmes will make short work of this fellow,' he growled to the chairman.

'Brother Ducharme is vouched for by the whole English circle,' replied the president firmly.

'Oh, the English! I think very little of them. Still, it doesn't matter,' and with a shrug of the shoulders he shuffled to his seat again, leaving me standing there in a very embarrassed state of mind, my brain in a whirl. That the man was present with his own face was bewildering enough, but that he should be here under his own name was simply astounding. I scarcely heard what the president said. It seemed to the effect that Simard would take me to his own room, where we might talk over our plans. And now Simard rose again from his chair, and said to the president that if nothing more were wanted of him we would go. Accordingly we left the place of meeting together. I watched my comrade narrowly. There was now a trembling eagerness in his action, and without a word he hurried me to the nearest

465

café, where we sat down at a little iron table on the pavement.

'Garçon,' he shouted harshly, 'bring me four absinthes. What will you drink, Ducharme?'

'A café-cognac, if you please.'

'Bah!' cried Simard; 'better have absinthe.'

Then he cursed the waiter for his slowness. When the absinthe came he grasped one half-full glass and swallowed the liquid raw, a thing I had never seen done before. Into the next measure of the wormwood he poured water impetuously from the carafe, another thing I had never seen done before, and dropped two lumps of sugar into it. Over the third glass he placed a flat perforated plated spoon, piled the sugar on this bridge, and now quite expertly allowed the water to drip through, the proper way of concocting this seductive mixture. Finishing his second glass, he placed the perforated spoon over the fourth, and began now more calmly sipping the third, while the water dripped slowly into the last glass.

Here before my eyes was enacted a more wonderful change than the gradual transformation of transparent absinthe into an opaque opalescent liquid. Simard, under the influence of the drink, was slowly becoming the Simard I had known ten years before. Remarkable! Absinthe, having in earlier years made a beast of the man, was now forming a man out of the beast. His staring eyes took on an expression of human comradeship. The whole mystery became perfectly clear to me without a question asked or an answer uttered. This man was no spy, but a genuine anarchist. However it happened, he had become a victim of absinthe, one of many with whom I was acquainted, although I never met any so far sunk as he. He was into his fourth glass, and had ordered two more when he began to speak.

'Here's to us!' he cried, with something like a civilised smile on his gaunt face. 'You're not offended at what I said in the meeting, I hope?'

'Oh, no,' I answered.

'That's right. You see, I once belonged to the Secret Service, and if my chief had been there today, we would soon find ourselves in a cool dungeon. We couldn't trip up Eugene Valmont.'

At these words, spoken with sincerity, I sat up in my chair, and I am sure such an expression of enjoyment came into my face that, if I had not instantly suppressed it, I might have betrayed myself.

'Who was Eugene Valmont?' I asked, in a tone of assumed indifference.

Mixing his fifth glass he nodded sagely.

'You wouldn't ask that question if you'd been in Paris a dozen years ago. He was the Government's chief detective, and he knew more of anarchists, yes, and of Apaches, too, than either you or I do. He had more brains in his little finger than that whole lot babbling there tonight. But the Government, being a fool, as all governments are, dismissed him, and because I was his assistant, they dismissed me as well. They got rid of all his staff. Valmont disappeared. If I could have found him, I wouldn't be sitting here with you tonight; but he was right to disappear. The Government did all they could against us who had been his friends, and I for one came through starvation, and was near throwing myself in the Seine, which sometimes I wish I had done. Here, garçon, another absinthe! But by and by I came to like the gutter, and here I am. I'd rather have the gutter and

467

absinthe than the Luxembourg without it. I've had my revenge on the Government many times since, for I knew their ways, and often have I circumvented the police. That's why they respect me among the anarchists. Do you know how I joined? I knew all their passwords, and walked right into one of their meetings, alone and in rags.

' "Here am I," I said; "Adolph Simard, late second assistant to Eugene Valmont, chief detective to the French Government." '

'There were twenty weapons covering me at once, but I laughed.

' "I'm starving," I cried, "and I want something to eat, and more especially something to drink! In return for that I'll show you every rat hole you've got. Lift the president's chair, and there's a trapdoor that leads to the Rue Blanc. I'm one of you, and I'll tell you the tricks of the police."

'Such was my initiation, and from that moment the police began to pick their spies out of the Seine, and now they leave us alone. Even Valmont himself could do nothing against the anarchists since I have joined them.'

Oh, the incredible self-conceit of human nature. Here was this ruffian proclaiming the limitations of Valmont, who half an hour before had shaken his hand within the innermost circle of his order! Yet my heart warmed towards the wretch who had remembered me and my exploits.

It now became my anxious and difficult task to lure Simard away from this café and its absinthe. Glass after glass of the poison had brought him up almost to his former intellectual level, but now it was shoving him rapidly down the hill again. I must know where his room was situated, yet if I waited much longer the man would be in a state of drunken imbecility which would not only render it impossible for him to guide me to his room, but likely cause both of us to be arrested by the police. I tried persuasion, and he laughed at me; I tried threats, whereat he scowled and cursed me as a renegade from England. At last the liquor overpowered him, and his head sank on the metal table and the dark blue cap fell to the floor.

The Fate of the Picric Bomb

I was in despair, but now received a lesson which taught me that if a man leaves a city, even for a short time, he falls out of touch with its ways. I called the waiter, and said to him: 'Do you know my friend here?'

'I do not know his name,' replied the garçon, 'but I have seen him many times at this café. He is usually in this state when he has money.'

'Do you know where he lives? He promised to take me with him, and I am a stranger in Paris.'

'Have no discontent, monsieur. Rest tranquil; I will intervene.'

With this he stepped across the pavement in front of the café into the street and gave utterance to a low, peculiar whistle. The café was now nearly deserted, for the hour was very late, or, rather, very early. When the waiter returned I whispered to him in some anxiety: 'Not the police, surely?'

'But no!' he cried in scorn; 'certainly not the police.'

He went on unconcernedly taking in the empty chairs and tables. A few minutes later there swaggered up to the café two of the most disreputable, low-browed scoundrels I had ever seen, each wearing a dark blue cap, with a glazed peak over the eyes, caps exactly similar to the one which lay in front of Simard. The band of Apaches which now permeates all Paris has risen since my time, and Simard had been mistaken an hour before in asserting that Valmont was familiar with their haunts. The present Chief of Police in Paris and some of his predecessors confess there is a difficulty in dealing with these picked assassins, but I should very much like to take a hand in the game on the side of law and order. However, that is not to be; therefore the Apaches increase and prosper.

The two vagabonds roughly smote Simard's cap on his prone head, and as roughly raised him to his feet.

'He is a friend of mine,' I interposed, 'and promised to take me home with him.'

'Good! Follow us,' said one of them; and now I passed through the morning streets of Paris behind three cut-throats, yet knew that I was safer than if broad daylight was in the thoroughfare, with a meridian sun shining down upon us. I was doubly safe, being in no fear of harm from midnight prowlers, and equally free from danger of arrest by the police. Every officer we met avoided us, and casually stepped to the other side of the street. We turned down a narrow lane, then through a still narrower one, which terminated at a courtyard. Entering a tall building, we climbed up five flights of stairs to a landing, where one of the scouts kicked open a door into a room so miserable that there was not even a lock to protect its poverty. Here they allowed the insensible Simard to drop with a crash on to the floor, and then they left us alone without even an adieu. The Apaches take care of their own – after a fashion.

I struck a match and found part of a bougie stuck

in the mouth of an absinthe bottle, resting on a rough deal table. Lighting the bougie, I surveyed the horrible apartment. A heap of rags lay in a corner, and this was evidently Simard's bed. I hauled him to it, and there he lay unconscious, himself a bundle of rags. I found one chair, or, rather, stool, for it had no back. I drew the table against the lockless door, blew out the light, sat on the stool, resting my arms on the table, and my head on my arms, and slept peacefully till long after daybreak.

Simard awoke in the worst possible humour. He poured forth a great variety of abusive epithets at me. To make himself still more agreeable, he turned back the rags on which he had slept, and brought to the light a round black object, like a small cannon ball, which he informed me was the picric bomb that was to scatter destruction among my English friends, for whom he expressed the greatest possible loathing and contempt. Then, sitting up, he began playing with this infernal machine, knowing, as well as I, that if he allowed it to drop that would be the end of the two of us.

I shrugged my shoulders at this display, and affected a nonchalance I was far from feeling, but finally put an end to his dangerous amusement by telling him that if he came out with me I would pay for his breakfast and give him a drink of absinthe.

The next few days were the most anxious of my life. Never before had I lived on terms of intimacy with a picric bomb, that most deadly and uncertain of all explosive agencies. I speedily found that Simard was so absinthe-soaked I could do nothing with him. He could not be bribed or cajoled or persuaded or threatened. Once, indeed, when he talked with drunken affection of Eugene Valmont, I conceived a wild notion of declaring myself to him; but a moment's reflection showed the absolute uselessness of this course. It was not one Simard with whom I had to deal, but half a dozen or more. There was Simard sober, half sober, quarter sober, drunk, half drunk, quarter drunk or wholly drunk. Any bargain I might make with the one Simard would not be kept by any of the other six. The only safe Simard was Simard insensible through over-indulgence. I had resolved to get Simard insensibly drunk on the morning of the procession, but my plans were upset at a meeting of the anarchists, which luckily took place on an evening shortly after my arrival, and this gave me time to mature the plan which was actually carried out. Each member of the anarchists' club knew of Simard's slavery to absinthe, and fears were expressed that he might prove incapable on the day of the procession, too late for a substitute to take his place. It was therefore proposed that one or two others should be stationed along the route of the procession with bombs ready if Simard failed. This I strenuously opposed, and guaranteed that Simard would be ready to launch his missile. I met with little difficulty in persuading the company to agree, because, after all, every man among them feared he might be one of those selected, when selection was practically a sentence of death. I guaranteed that the bomb would be thrown, and this apparently was taken to mean that if Simard did not do the deed, I would.

This danger over, I next took the measurements and estimated the weight of the picric bomb. I then sought out a most amiable and expert pyrotechnist, a capable workman of genius, who with his own hand makes those dramatic firework arrangements which you sometimes see in Paris. As Eugene Valmont, I had rendered a great service to this man, and he was not likely to have forgotten it. During one of the anarchist scares a stupid policeman had arrested him, and when I intervened the man was just on the verge of being committed for life. France trembled in one of her panics, or, rather, Paris did, and demanded victims. This blameless little workman had indeed contributed with both material and advice, but any fool might have seen that he had done this innocently. His assistance had been invoked and secured under the pretence that his clients were promoting an amateur firework display, which was true enough, but the display cost the lives of three men, and intentionally so. I cheered up the citizen in the moment of his utmost despair, and brought such proof of his innocence to the knowledge of those above me that he was most reluctantly acquitted. To this man I now went with my measurement of the bomb and the estimate of its weight.

'Sir,' said I, 'do you remember Eugene Valmont?'

'Am I ever likely to forget him?' he replied, with a fervour that pleased me.

'He has sent me to you, and implores you to aid me, and that aid will wipe out the debt you owe him.'

'Willingly, willingly,' cried the artisan, 'so long as it has nothing to do with the anarchists or the making of bombs!'

'It has to do exactly with those two things. I wish you to make an innocent bomb which will prevent an anarchist outrage.'

At this the little man drew back, and his face became pale.

473

'It is impossible,' he protested; 'I have had enough of innocent bombs. No, no, and in any case how can I be sure you come from Eugene Valmont? No, monsieur, I am not to be trapped the second time.'

At this I related rapidly all that Valmont had done for him, and even repeated Valmont's most intimate conversation with him. The man was nonplussed, but remained firm.

'I dare not do it,' he said.

We were alone in his back shop. I walked to the door and thrust in the bolt; then, after a moment's pause, turned round, stretched forth my right hand dramatically, and cried: 'Behold Eugene Valmont!'

My friend staggered against the wall in his amazement, and I continued in solemn tones: 'Eugene Valmont, who by this removal of his disguise places his life in your hands as your life was in his. Now, monsieur, what will you do?'

He replied: 'Monsieur Valmont, I shall do whatever you ask. If I refused a moment ago, it was because I thought there was now in France no Eugene Valmont to rectify my mistake if I made one.'

I resumed my disguise, and told him I wished an innocent substitute for this picric bomb, and he at once suggested an earthenware globe, which would weigh the same as the bomb, and which could be coloured to resemble it exactly.

'And now, Monsieur Valmont, do you wish smoke to issue from this imitation bomb?'

'Yes,' I said, 'in such quantity as you can compress within it.'

'It is easily done!' he cried, with the enthusiasm of a true French artist. 'And may I place within some little design of my own which will astonish your friends the English and delight my friends the French?'

'Monsieur,' said I, 'I am in your hands. I trust the project entirely to your skill.' And thus it came about that four days later I substituted the bogus globe for the real one, and, unseen, dropped the picric bomb from one of the bridges into the Seine.

On the morning of the procession I was compelled to allow Simard several drinks of absinthe to bring him up to a point where he could be depended on, otherwise his anxiety and determination to fling the bomb, his frenzy against all government, made it certain that he would betray both of us before the fateful moment came. My only fear was that I could not stop him drinking when once he began, but somehow our days of close companionship, loathsome as they had been to me, seemed to have had the effect of building up again the influence I held over him in former days, and his yielding more or less to my wishes appeared to be quite unconscious on his part.

The procession was composed entirely of carriages, each containing four persons – two Englishmen sat on the back seats, with two Frenchmen in front of them. A thick crowd lined each side of the thorough-fare, cheering vociferously. Right into the middle of the procession Simard launched his bomb. There was no terrific explosion. The missile simply went to pieces as if it were an earthenware jar, and there arose a dense column of very white smoke. In the immediate vicinity the cheering stopped at once, and the sinister word 'bomb' passed from lip to lip in awed whispers. As the throwing had been unnoticed in the midst of the commotion, I held Simard firmly by the wrist, determined he should not draw attention to himself by his panic-stricken desire for immediate flight.

'Stand still, you fool!' I hissed into his ear, and he obeyed, trembling.

The pair of horses in front of which the bomb fell rose for a moment on their hind legs, and showed signs of bolting, but the coachman held them firmly, and uplifted his hand so that the procession behind him came to a momentary pause. No one in the carriages moved a muscle, then suddenly the tension was broken by a great and simultaneous cheer. Wondering at this, I turned my eyes from the frightened horses to the column of pale smoke in front of us, and saw that in some manner it had resolved itself into a gigantic canna lily, pure white, while from the base of this sprang the lilies of France, delicately tinted. Of course, this could not have happened if there had been the least wind, but the air was so still that the vibration of the cheering caused the huge lily to tremble gently as it stood there marvellously poised; the lily of peace, surrounded by the lilies of France! That was the design, and if you ask me how it was done, I can only refer you to my pyrotechnist, and say that whatever a Frenchman attempts to do he will accomplish artistically.

And now these imperturbable English, who had been seated, immobile, when they thought a bomb was thrown, stood up in their carriages to get a better view of this aerial phenomenon, cheering and waving their hats. The lily gradually thinned and dissolved in little patches of cloud that floated away above our heads.

'I cannot stay here longer,' groaned Simard, quaking, his nerves, like himself, in rags. 'I see the ghosts of those I have killed floating around me.'

'Come on, then, but do not hurry.'

There was no difficulty in getting him to London, but it was absinthe, absinthe, all the way, and when we reached Charing Cross I was compelled to help him, partly insensible, into a cab. I took him direct to the Imperial Flats, and up into my own set of chambers, where I opened my strong-room and flung him inside to sleep off his intoxication, and subsist on bread and water when he became sober.

I attended that night a meeting of the anarchists, and detailed accurately the story of our escape from France. I knew we had been watched, and so skipped no detail. I reported that I had taken Simard directly to my compatriot's flat; to Eugene Valmont, the man who had given me employment, and who had promised to do what he could for Simard, beginning by trying to break him of the absinthe habit, as he was now a physical wreck through over-indulgence in that stimulant.

It was curious to note the discussion which took place a few nights afterwards regarding the failure of the picric bomb. Scientists among us said that the bomb had been made too long; that a chemical reaction had taken place which destroyed its power. A few superstitious ones saw a miracle in what had happened, and they forthwith left our organisation. Then again, things were made easier by the fact that the man who constructed the bomb, evidently terror-stricken at what he had done, disappeared the day before the procession, and has never since been heard of. The majority of the anarchists believed he had made a bogus bomb, and had fled to escape their vengeance rather than to evade the justice of the law.

Simard will need no purgatory in the next world. I

kept him on bread and water for a month in my strong-room, and at first he demanded absinthe with threats, then grovelled, begging and praying for it. After that a period of depression and despair ensued, but finally his naturally strong constitution conquered and began to build itself up again. I took him from his prison one midnight, and gave him a bed in my Soho room, taking care in bringing him away that he would never recognise the place where he had been incarcerated. In my dealings with him I had always been that old man, Paul Ducharme. Next morning I said to him: 'You spoke of Eugene Valmont. I have learned that he lives in London, and I advise you to call upon him. Perhaps he can get you something to do.'

Simard was overjoyed, and two hours later, as Eugene Valmont, I received him in my flat, and made him my assistant on the spot. From that time forward, Paul Ducharme, language teacher, disappeared from the earth, and Simard abandoned his two As – anarchy and absinthe.

478

STACY AUMONIER

Miss Bracegirdle Does Her Duty

'This is the room, madame.'

'Ah, thank you . . . thank you.'

'Does it appear satisfactory to madame?'

'Oh, yes, thank you . . . quite.'

'Does madame require anything further?'

'Er – if not too late, may I have a hot bath?'

'*Parfaitement*, madame. The bathroom is at the end of the passage on the left. I will go and prepare it for madame.'

'There is one thing more . . . I have had a very long journey. I am very tired. Will you please see that I am not disturbed in the morning until I ring.'

'Certainly, madame.'

Millicent Bracegirdle was speaking the truth – she *was* tired. In the sleepy cathedral town of Easingstroke, from which she came, it was customary for everyone to speak the truth. It was customary, moreover, for everyone to lead simple, self-denying lives – to give up their time to good works and elevating thoughts. One had only to glance at little Miss Bracegirdle to see that in her were epitomised all the virtues and ideals of Easingstoke. Indeed, it was the pursuit of duty which had brought her to the Hôtel de l'Ouest at Bordeaux on this summer's night. She had travelled from Easingstoke to London, then without a break to Dover, crossed that horrid stretch of sea to Calais, entrained for Paris, where she of necessity had to spend four hours – a terrifying experience – and then

479

had come on to Bordeaux, arriving at midnight. The reason for this journey was that someone had to come to Bordeaux to meet her young sister-in-law, who was arriving the next day from South America. The sister-in-law was married to a missionary brother in Paraguay, but the climate not agreeing with her, she was returning to England. Her dear brother, the dean, would have come himself, but the claims on his time were so extensive, the parishioners would miss him so . . . it was clearly Millicent's duty to go.

She had never been out of England before, and she had a horror of travel, and an ingrained distrust of foreigners. She spoke a little French – sufficient for the purposes of travel and for obtaining any modest necessities, but not sufficient for carrying on any kind of conversation. She did not deplore this latter fact, for she was of the opinion that French people were not the kind of people that one would naturally want to have conversation with; broadly speaking, they were not quite 'nice', in spite of their ingratiating manners.

The dear dean had given her endless advice, warning her earnestly not to enter into conversation with strangers, to obtain all information from the police, railway officials – in fact, anyone in an official uniform. He deeply regretted to say that he was afraid that France was not a country for a woman to travel about in *alone*. There were loose, bad people about, always on the lookout . . . He really thought perhaps he ought not to let her go. It was only by the utmost persuasion, in which she rather exaggerated her knowledge of the French language and character, her courage and indifference to discomfort, that she managed to carry the day.

She unpacked her valise, placed her things about the room, tried to thrust back the little stabs of home-sickness as she visualised her darling room at the deanery. How strange and hard and unfriendly seemed these foreign hotel bedrooms – heavy and depressing, no chintz and lavender and photographs of . . . all the dear family, the dean, the nephews and nieces, the interior of the cathedral during harvest festival, no samplers and needlework or coloured reproductions of the paintings by Marcus Stone. Oh dear, how foolish she was! What did she expect?

She disrobed and donned a dressing-gown; then, armed with a sponge-bag and towel, she crept timidly down the passage to the bathroom, after closing her bedroom door and turning out the light. The gay bathroom cheered her. She wallowed luxuriously in the hot water, regarding her slim legs with quiet satisfaction. And for the first time since leaving home there came to her a pleasant moment – a sense of enjoyment in her adventure. After all, it *was* rather an adventure, and her life had been peculiarly devoid of it. What queer lives some people must live, travelling about, having experiences! How old was she? Not really old – not by any means. Forty-two? Forty-three? She had shut herself up so. She hardly ever regarded the potentialities of age. As the world went, she was a well-preserved woman for her age. A life of self-abnegation, simple living, healthy walking and fresh air, had kept her younger than these hurrying, pampered city people.

Love? yes, once when she was a young girl . . . he was a schoolmaster, a most estimable, kind gentleman. They were never engaged – not actually, but it was a kind of understood thing. For three years it went on, this pleasant understanding and friendship. He was so gentle, so distinguished and considerate. She would have been happy to have continued in this strain for ever. But there was something lacking. Stephen had curious restless lapses. From the physical aspect of marriage she shrank – yes, even with Stephen, who was gentleness and kindness itself. And then one day . . . one day he went away – vanished, and never returned. They told her he had married one of the country girls – a girl who used to work in Mrs Forbes's dairy – not a very nice girl, she feared, one of these fast, pretty, foolish women. Heigho! well, she had lived that down, destructive as the blow appeared at the time. One lives everything down in time. There is always work, living for others, faith, duty . . . At the same time she could sympathise with people who found satisfaction in unusual experiences.

There would be lots to tell the dear dean when she wrote to him on the morrow; nearly losing her spectacles in the restaurant car; the amusing remarks of an American child on the train to Paris; the curious food everywhere, nothing simple and plain; the two English ladies at the hotel in Paris who told her about the death of their uncle – the poor man being taken ill on Friday and dying on Sunday afternoon, just before teatime; the kindness of the hotel proprietor who had sat up for her; the prettiness of the chambermaid. Oh, yes, everyone was really very kind. The French people, after all, were very nice. She had seen nothing – nothing but was quite nice and decorous. There would be lots to tell the dean tomorrow.

Her body glowed with the friction of the towel. She again donned her night attire and her thick, woollen dressing-gown. She tidied up the bathroom carefully in exactly the same way she was accustomed to do at home, then once more gripping her sponge-bag and towel, and turning out the light, she crept down the passage to her room. Entering the room she switched on the light and shut the door quickly. Then one of those ridiculous things happened – just the kind of thing you would expect to happen in a foreign hotel. The handle of the door came off in her hand.

She ejaculated a quiet 'Bother!' and sought to replace it with one hand, the other being occupied with the towel and sponge-bag. In doing this she behaved foolishly, for thrusting the knob carelessly against the steel pin – without properly securing it – she only succeeded in pushing the pin farther into the door and the knob was not adjusted. She uttered another little 'Bother!' and put her sponge-bag and towel down on the floor. She then tried to recover the pin with her left hand, but it had gone in too far.

'How very foolish!' she thought. 'I shall have to ring for the chambermaid – and perhaps the poor girl has gone to bed.'

She turned and faced the room, and suddenly the awful horror was upon her. *There was a man asleep in her bed!*

The sight of that swarthy face on the pillow, with its black tousled hair and heavy moustache, produced in her the most terrible moment of her life. Her heart nearly stopped. For some seconds she could neither think nor scream, and her first thought was: 'I mustn't scream!'

She stood there like one paralysed, staring at the man's head and the great curved hunch of his body under the clothes. When she began to think she thought very quickly, and all her thoughts worked

483

together. The first vivid realisation was that it wasn't the man's fault; it was *her* fault. *She was in the wrong room*. It was the man's room. The rooms were identical, but there were all his things about, his clothes thrown carelessly over chairs, his collar and tie on the wardrobe, his great heavy boots and the strange yellow trunk. She must get out somehow, anyhow.

She clutched once more at the door, feverishly driving her fingernails into the hole where the elusive pin had vanished. She tried to force her fingers into the crack and open the door that way, but it was of no avail. She was to all intents and purposes locked in – locked in a bedroom in a strange hotel alone with a man . . . a foreigner . . . *a Frenchman*! She must think. She must think . . . She switched off the light. If the light was off he might not wake up. It might give her time to think how to act. It was surprising that he had not awakened. If he *did* wake up, what would he do? How could she explain herself? He wouldn't believe her. No one would believe her. In an English hotel it would be difficult enough, but here where she wasn't known, where they were all foreigners and consequently antagonistic . . . merciful heavens!

She *must* get out. Should she wake the man? No, she couldn't do that. He might murder her. He might . . . Oh, it was too awful to contemplate! Should she scream? Ring for the chambermaid? But no, it would be the same thing. People would come rushing. They would find her there in the strange man's bedroom after midnight – she, Millicent Bracegirdle, sister of the Dean of Easingstoke! Easingstoke!

Visions of Easingstoke flashed through her alarmed mind. Visions of the news arriving, women whispering around tea-tables: 'Have you heard, my dear? . . . Really no one would have imagined! Her poor brother! He will of course have to resign, you know, my dear. Have a little more cream, my love.'

Would they put her in prison? She might be in the room for the purpose of stealing or . . . She might be in the room for the purpose of breaking every one of the ten commandments. There was no explaining it away. She was a ruined woman, suddenly and irretrievably, unless she could open the door. The chimney? Should she climb up the chimney? But where would that lead to? And then she visualised the man pulling her down by her legs when she was already smothered in soot. Any moment he might wake up . . .

She thought she heard the chambermaid going along the passage. If she had wanted to scream, she ought to have screamed before. The maid would know she had left the bathroom some minutes ago. Was she going to her room? Suddenly she remembered that she had told the chambermaid that she was not to be disturbed until she rang the next morning. That was something. Nobody would be going to her room to find out that she was not there.

An abrupt and desperate plan formed in her mind. It was already getting on for one o'clock. The man was probably a quite harmless commercial traveller or businessman. He would probably get up about seven or eight o'clock, dress quickly, and go out. She would hide under his bed until he went. Only a matter of a few hours. Men don't look under their beds, although she made a religious practice of doing so herself. When he went he would be sure to open the door all right. The handle would be lying on the floor as though it had dropped off in the night. He would probably ring for the chambermaid or open it with a penknife. Men were so clever at those things. When he had gone she would creep out and steal back to her room, and then there would be no necessity to give any explanation to anyone. But heavens! What an experience! Once under the white frill of that bed she would be safe till the morning. In daylight nothing seemed so terrifying.

With feline precaution she went down on her hands and knees and crept towards the bed. What a lucky thing there was that broad white frill! She lifted it at the foot of the bed and crept under. There was just sufficient depth to take her slim body. The floor was fortunately carpeted all over, but it seemed very close and dusty. Suppose she coughed or sneezed! Anything might happen. Of course . . . it would be much more difficult to explain her presence under the bed than to explain her presence just inside the door. She held her breath in suspense. No sound came from above, but under this frill it was difficult to hear anything. It was almost more nerve-racking than hearing everything . . . listening for signs and portents. This temporary escape in any case would give her time to regard the predicament detachedly. Up to the present she had not been able to visualise the full significance of her action. She had in truth lost her head. She had been like a wild animal, consumed with the sole idea of escape . . . a mouse or a cat would do this kind of thing – take cover and lie low. If only it hadn't all happened *abroad*! She tried to frame sentences of explanation in French, but French escaped her. And then they talked so rapidly, these people. They didn't listen. The situation was intolerable. Would she be able to endure a night of it?

At present she was not altogether uncomfortable, only stuffy and . . . very, very frightened. But she had to face six or seven or eight hours of it – perhaps even then discovery in the end! The minutes flashed by as she turned the matter over and over in her head. There was no solution. She began to wish she had screamed or awakened the man. She saw now that that would have been the wisest and most politic thing to do; but she had allowed ten minutes or a quarter of an hour to elapse from the moment when the chambermaid would know that she had left the bathroom. They would want an explanation of what she had been doing in the man's bedroom all that time. Why hadn't she screamed before?

She lifted the frill an inch or two and listened. She thought she heard the man breathing but she couldn't be sure. In any case it gave her more air. She became a little bolder, and thrust her face partly through the frill so that she could breathe freely. She tried to steady her nerves by concentrating on the fact that – well, there it was. She had done it. She must make the best of it. Perhaps it would be all right after all.

'Of course I shan't sleep,' she kept on thinking, 'I shan't be able to. In any case it will be safer not to sleep. I must be on the watch.'

She set her teeth and waited grimly. Now that she had made up her mind to see the thing through in this manner she felt a little calmer. She almost smiled as she reflected that there would certainly be something to tell the dear dean when she wrote to him tomorrow. How would he take it? Of course he would believe it – he had never doubted a single word that she had uttered in her life – but the story would sound so . . . preposterous. In Easingstoke it would be almost impossible to envisage such an experience. She, Millicent Bracegirdle, spending a night under a strange man's bed in a foreign hotel! What would those women think? Fanny Shields and that garrulous old Mrs Rusbridger? Perhaps . . . yes, perhaps it would be advisable to tell the dear dean to let the story go no further. One could hardly expect Mrs Rushbridger to . . . not make implications . . . exaggerate.

Oh, dear! What were they all doing now? They would all be asleep, everyone in Easingstoke. Her dear brother always retired at ten-fifteen. He would be sleeping calmly and placidly, the sleep of the just . . . breathing the clear sweet air of Sussex, not this – oh, it *was* stuffy! She felt a great desire to cough. She mustn't do that. Yes, at nine-thirty all the servants were summoned to the library – a short service – never more than fifteen minutes, her brother didn't believe in a great deal of ritual – then at ten o'clock cocoa for everyone. At ten-fifteen bed for everyone. The dear sweet bedroom with the narrow white bed, by the side of which she had knelt every night as long as she could remember – even in her dear mother's day – and said her prayers.

Prayers! Yes, that was a curious thing. This was the first night in her life's experience that she had not said her prayers on retiring. The situation was certainly very peculiar . . . exceptional, one might call it. God would understand and forgive such a lapse. And yet after all, why . . . what was to prevent her saying her prayers? Of course she couldn't kneel in the proper devotional attitude, that would be a physical impossibility; nevertheless, perhaps her prayers might be just as efficacious . . . if they came from the heart. So little Miss Bracegirdle curved her body and placed her hands in a devout attitude in front of her face and quite inaudibly murmured her prayers under the strange man's bed.

'Our Father, which art in heaven, hallowed be Thy name. Thy kingdom come. Thy will be done in earth as it is in heaven. Give us this day our daily bread. And forgive us our trespasses . . . '

Trespasses! Yes, surely she was trespassing on this occasion, but God would understand. She had not wanted to trespass. She was an unwitting sinner. Without uttering a sound she went through her usual prayers in her heart. At the end she added fervently: 'Please God protect me from the dangers and perils of this night.'

Then she lay silent and inert, strangely soothed by the effort of praying. 'After all,' she thought, 'it isn't the attitude that matters – it is that which occurs deep down in us.'

For the first time she began to meditate – almost to question – church forms and dogma. If an attitude was not indispensable, why a building, a ritual, a church at all? Of course her dear brother couldn't be wrong, the church was so old, so very old, its roots deep buried in the story of human life; it was only that . . . well, outward forms *could* be misleading. Her own present position, for instance. In the eyes of the world she had, by one silly careless little action, convicted herself of being the breaker of every single one of the ten commandments.

She tried to think of one of which she could not be accused. But no – even to dishonouring her father and mother, bearing false witness, stealing, coveting her neighbour's . . . husband! That was the worst thing of all. Poor man! He might be a very pleasant honourable married gentleman with children and she – she was in a position to compromise him! Why hadn't she screamed? Too late! Too late!

It began to get very uncomfortable, stuffy, but at the same time draughty, and the floor was getting harder every minute. She changed her position stealthily and controlled her desire to cough. Her heart was beating rapidly. Over and over again recurred the vivid impression of every little incident and argument that had occurred to her from the moment she left the bathroom. This must, of course, be the room next to her own. So confusing, with perhaps twenty bedrooms all exactly alike on one side of a passage – how was one to remember whether one's number was 115 or 116?

Her mind began to wander idly off into her school-days. She was always very bad at figures. She disliked Euclid and all those subjects about angles and equations – so unimportant, not leading anywhere. History she liked, and botany, and reading about strange foreign lands, although she had always been too timid to visit them. And the lives of great people, *most* fascinating – Oliver Cromwell, Lord Beaconsfield, Lincoln, Grace Darling – *there* was a heroine for you – General Booth, a great, good man, even if a little vulgar. She remembered dear old Miss Trimming talking about him one afternoon at the vicar of St Bride's garden party. She was *so* amusing. She . . . *Good heavens!*

Almost unwittingly, Millicent Bracegirdle had emitted a violent sneeze!

It was finished! For the second time that night she was conscious of her heart nearly stopping. For the second time that night she was so paralysed with fear

490

that her mentality went to pieces. Now she would hear the man get out of bed. He would walk across to the door, switch on the light, and then lift up the frill. She could almost see that fierce moustached face glaring at her and growling something in French. Then he would thrust out an arm and drag her out. And then? O God in heaven! What then?

'I shall scream before he does it. Perhaps I had better scream now. If he drags me out he will clap his hand over my mouth. Perhaps chloroform . . . '

But somehow she could not scream. She was too frightened even for that. She lifted the frill and listened. Was he moving stealthily across the carpet? She thought – no, she couldn't be sure. Anything might be happening. He might strike her from above – with one of those heavy boots perhaps. Nothing seemed to be happening, but the suspense was intolerable. She realised now that she hadn't the power to endure a night of it. Anything would be better than this – disgrace, imprisonment, even death. She would crawl out, wake the man, and try and explain as best she could.

She would switch on the light, cough, and say: '*Monsieur!*'

Then he would start up and stare at her.

Then she would say – what should she say?

'*Pardon, monsieur, mais je –* ' What on earth was the French for 'I have made a mistake'.

'*J'ai tort. C'est la chambre –* er – incorrect. *Voulez-vous –* er – '

What was the French for 'doorknob', 'let me go'?

It didn't matter. She would turn on the light, cough and trust to luck. If he got out of bed, and came towards her, she would scream the hotel down.

The resolution formed, she crawled deliberately out at the foot of the bed. She scrambled hastily towards the door – a perilous journey. In a few seconds the room was flooded with light. She turned towards the bed, coughed, and cried out boldly: '*Monsieur!*'

Then, for the third time that night, little Miss Bracegirdle's heart all but stopped. In this case the climax of the horror took longer to develop, but when it was reached, it clouded the other two experiences into insignificance.

The man on the bed was dead!

She had never beheld death before, but one does not mistake death.

She stared at him bewildered, and repeated almost in a whisper: '*Monsieur! . . . Monsieur!*'

Then she tiptoed towards the bed. The hair and moustache looked extraordinarily black in that grey, wax-like setting. The mouth was slightly open, and the face, which in life might have been vicious and sensual, looked incredibly peaceful and far away. It was as though she were regarding the features of a man across some vast passage of time, a being who had always been completely remote from mundane preoccupations.

When the full truth came home to her, little Miss Bracegirdle buried her face in her hands and murmured: 'Poor fellow . . . poor fellow!'

For the moment her own position seemed an affair of small consequence. She was in the presence of something greater and more all-pervading. Almost instinctively she knelt by the bed and prayed.

For a few moments she seemed to be possessed by an extraordinary calmness and detachment. The burden of her hotel predicament was a gossamer trouble – a silly, trivial, almost comic episode, something that could be explained away.

But this man – he had lived his life, whatever it was like, and now he was in the presence of his Maker. What kind of man had he been?

Her meditations were broken by an abrupt sound. It was that of a pair of heavy boots being thrown down by the door outside. She started, thinking at first it was someone knocking or trying to get in. She heard the 'boots', however, stumping away down the corridor, and the realisation stabbed her with the truth of her own position. She mustn't stop there. The necessity to get out was even more urgent.

To be found in a strange man's bedroom in the night is bad enough, but to be found in a dead man's bedroom was even worse. They could accuse her of murder, perhaps. Yes, that would be it – how could she possibly explain to these foreigners? Good God! they would hang her. No, guillotine her, that's what they do in France. They would chop her head off with a great steel knife. Merciful heavens! She envisaged herself standing blindfold, by a priest and an executioner in a red cap, like that man in the Dickens story – what was his name? . . . Sydney Carton, that was it, and before he went on the scaffold he said: 'It is a far, far better thing that I do than I have ever done.'

But no, she couldn't say that. It would be a far, far worse thing that she did. What about the dear dean? Her sister-in-law arriving alone from Paraguay tomorrow? All her dear people and friends in Easingstoke? Her darling Tony, the large grey tabby cat? It was her duty not to have her head chopped off if it could possibly be avoided. She could do no good in the room. She could not recall the dead to life. Her only mission was to escape. Any minute people might arrive. The chambermaid, the boots, the manager, the gendarmes . . . Visions of gendarmes arriving armed with swords and notebooks vitalised her almost exhausted energies. She was a desperate woman. Fortunately now she had not to worry about the light. She sprang once more at the door and tried to force it open with her fingers. The result hurt her and gave her pause. If she was to escape she must *think*, and think intensely. She mustn't do anything rash and silly, she must just think and plan calmly.

She examined the lock carefully. There was no keyhole, but there was a slip-bolt, so that the hotel guest could lock the door on the inside, but it couldn't be locked on the outside. Oh, why didn't this poor dear dead man lock his door last night? Then this trouble could not have happened. She could see the end of the steel pin. It was about half an inch down the hole. If anyone was passing they must surely notice the handle sticking out on the other side! She drew a hairpin out of her hair and tried to coax the pin back, but she only succeeded in pushing it a little farther in. She felt the colour leaving her face and a strange feeling of faintness come over her.

She was fighting for her life, she mustn't give way. She darted round the room like an animal in a trap, her mind alert for the slightest crevice of escape. The window had no balcony and there was a drop of five storeys to the street below. Dawn was breaking. Soon the activities of the hotel and the city would begin. The thing must be accomplished before then.

She went back once more and stared at the lock. She stared at the dead man's property: his razors and brushes and writing materials. He appeared to have a lot of writing materials – pens and pencils and rubber and sealing-wax . . . Sealing-wax!

Necessity is truly the mother of invention. It is in any case quite certain that Millicent Bracegirdle, who had never invented a thing in her life, would never have evolved the ingenious little device she did, had she not believed that her position was utterly desperate. For in the end this is what she did. She got together a box of matches, a bar of sealing-wax and a hairpin. She made a little pool of hot sealing-wax, into which she dipped the end of the hairpin. Collecting a small blob on the end of it she thrust it into the hole, and let it adhere to the end of the steel pin. At the seventh attempt she got the thing to move. It took her just an hour and ten minutes to get that steel pin back into the room, and when at length it came far enough through for her to grip it with her fingernails, she burst into tears through the sheer physical tension of the strain. Very, very carefully she pulled it farther, and holding it firmly with her left hand she fixed the knob with her right, then slowly turned it. The door opened!

The temptation to dash out into the corridor and scream with relief was almost irresistible, but she forbore. She listened; she peeped out. No one was about. With beating heart, she went out, closing the door inaudibly. She crept like a little mouse to the room next door, stole in and flung herself on her bed. Immediately she did so it flashed through her mind that *she had left her sponge-bag and towel in the dead man's room!*

In looking back upon her experience she always considered that that second expedition was the worst of all. She might have left the sponge-bag and towel there, only that the towel – she never used hotel towels – had neatly inscribed in the corner 'M.B'.

With furtive caution she managed to retrace her steps. She re-entered the dead man's room, reclaimed her property and returned to her own. When this mission was accomplished she was indeed wellnigh spent. She lay on her bed and groaned feebly. At last she fell into a fevered sleep.

It was eleven o'clock when she awoke and no one had been to disturb her. The sun was shining, and the experiences of the night appeared a dubious night-mare. Surely she had dreamt it all?

With dread still burning in her heart she rang the bell. After a short interval of time the chambermaid appeared. The girl's eyes were bright with some uncontrollable excitement. No, she had not been dreaming. This girl had heard something.

'Will you bring me some tea, please?'

'Certainly, madame.'

The maid drew back the curtains and fussed about the room. She was under a pledge of secrecy, but she could contain herself no longer. Suddenly she approached the bed and whispered excitedly: 'Oh, madame, I have promised not to tell . . . but a terrible thing has happened! A man, a dead man, has been found in Room 117 – a guest. Please not to say I tell you. But they have all been there, the gendarmes, the doctors, the inspectors. Oh, it is terrible . . . terrible!'

The little lady in the bed said nothing. There was indeed nothing to say. But Marie Louise Lancret was too full of emotional excitement to spare her.

'But the terrible thing is – Do you know who he is,

madame? They say it is Boldhu, the man wanted for the murder of Jeanne Carreton in the barn at Vincennes. They say he strangled her, and then cut her up in pieces and hid her in two barrels which he threw into the river . . . Oh, but he was a bad man, madame, a terrible bad man . . . and he died in the room next door . . . Suicide, they think; or was it an attack of the heart? . . . Remorse, some shock perhaps . . . Did you say a *café complet*, madame?'

'No, thank you, my dear . . . just a cup of tea . . . strong tea . . . '

'*Parfaitement*, madame.'

The girl retired, and a little later a waiter entered the room with a tray of tea. She could never get over her surprise at this. It seemed so – well, indecorous for a man – although only a waiter – to enter a lady's bedroom. There was no doubt a great deal in what the dear dean said. They were certainly very peculiar, these French people – they had most peculiar notions. It was not the way they behaved at Easingstoke. She got farther under the sheets, but the waiter appeared quite indifferent to the situation. He put the tray down and retired.

When he had gone she sat up and sipped her tea, which gradually warmed her. She was glad the sun was shining. She would have to get up soon. They said that her sister-in-law's boat was due to berth at one o'clock. That would give her time to dress comfortably, write to her brother, and then go down to the docks. Poor man! So he had been a murderer, a man who cut up the bodies of his victims . . . and she had spent the night in his bedroom! They were certainly a most – how could she describe it? – people. Nevertheless she felt a little glad that at the end she had been there to kneel and pray by his bedside. Probably nobody else had ever done that. It was very difficult to judge people . . . Something at some time might have gone wrong. He might not have murdered the woman after all. People were often wrongly convicted. She herself . . . If the police had found her in that room at three o'clock that morning . . . It is that which takes place in the heart which counts. One learns and learns. Had she not learnt that one can pray just as effectively lying under a bed as kneeling beside it? . . . Poor man!

She washed and dressed herself and walked calmly down to the writing-room. There was no evidence of excitement among the other hotel guests. Probably none of them knew about the tragedy except herself. She went to a writing-table, and after profound meditation wrote as follows:

MY DEAR BROTHER – I arrived late last night after a very pleasant journey. Everyone was very kind and attentive, the manager was sitting up for me. I nearly lost my spectacle case in the restaurant car! But a kind old gentleman found it and returned it to me. There was a most amusing American child on the train. I will tell you about her on my return. The people are very pleasant, but the food is peculiar, nothing *plain and wholesome*. I am going down to meet Annie at one o'clock. How have you been keeping, my dear? I hope you have not had any further return of the bronchial attacks.

Please tell Lizzie that I remembered in the train on the way here that that large stone jar of marmalade that Mrs Hunt made is behind those empty tins on the top shelf of the cupboard next to the coach-house. I wonder whether Mrs Butler was able to come to evensong after all? This is a nice hotel, but I think Annie and I will stay at the Grand tonight, as the bedrooms here are rather noisy. Well, my dear, nothing more till I return. Do take care of yourself.

Your loving sister,

MILLICENT

Yes, she couldn't tell Peter about it, neither in the letter nor when she went back to him. It was her duty not to tell him. It would only distress him; she felt convinced of it. In this curious foreign atmosphere the thing appeared possible, but in Easingstoke the mere recounting of the fantastic situation would be positively . . . indelicate. There was no escaping that broad general fact – she had spent a night in a strange man's bedroom. Whether he was a gentleman or a criminal, even whether he was dead or alive, did not seem to mitigate the jar upon her sensibilities, or, rather, it would not mitigate the jar upon the peculiarly sensitive relationship between her brother and herself. To say that she had been to the bathroom, the knob of the door-handle came off in her hand, she was too frightened to awaken the sleeper or scream, she got under the bed – well, it was all perfectly true. Peter would believe her, but – one simply could not conceive such a situation in Easingstoke deanery. It would create a curious little barrier between them, as though she had been dipped in some mysterious solution which alienated her. It was her duty not to tell.

She put on her hat and went out to post the letter. She distrusted a hotel letter-box. One never knew who handled these letters. It was not a proper official way of treating them. She walked to the head post office in Bordeaux.

The sun was shining. It was very pleasant walking about amongst these queer, excitable people, so foreign and different-looking – and the cafés already crowded with chattering men and women, and the flower stalls, and the strange odour of – what was it? Salt? Brine? Charcoal? . . . A military band was playing in the square . . . very gay and moving. It was all life, and movement, and bustle . . . thrilling rather.

'I spent a night in a strange man's bedroom.'

Little Miss Bracegirdle hunched her shoulders, murmured to herself, and walked faster. She reached the post office and found the large metal plate with the slot for letters and 'R.F.' stamped above it. Something official at last! Her face was a little flushed – was it the warmth of the day or the contact with movement and life? – as she put her letter into the slot. After posting it she put her hand into the slot and flicked it round to see that there were no foreign contraptions to impede its safe delivery. No, the letter had dropped safely in. She sighed contentedly and walked off in the direction of the docks to meet her sister- in-law from Paraguay.

HERBERT JENKINS

The Surrey Cattle-Maiming Mystery

'Disguise,' Malcolm Sage had once remarked, 'is the chief characteristic of the detective of fiction. In actual practice it is rarely possible. I am a case in point. No one but a builder, or an engineer, could disguise the shape of a head like mine;' as he spoke he had stroked the top of his head, which rose above his strongly marked brows like a down-covered cone.

He maintained that a disguise can always be identified, although not necessarily penetrated. This in itself would be sufficient to defeat the end of the disguised man by rendering him an object of suspicion. Few men can disguise their walk or bearing, no matter how clever they might be with false beards, grease-paint and wigs.

In this Malcolm Sage was a bitter disappointment to William Johnson, the office junior. His conception of the sleuth hound had been tinctured by the vivid fiction with which he beguiled his spare time. In the heart of William Johnson there were three great emotions: his hero-worship of Malcolm Sage, his romantic devotion to Gladys Norman and his whole-some fear of the rumbustious humour of Tims. In his more imaginative moments he would create a world in which he was the recognised colleague of Malcolm Sage, the avowed admirer of Miss Norman and the austere employer of Tims – chauffeurs never took liberties with the hair of their employers, no matter how knut-like it might be worn.

It was with the object of making sure of the first turret of his castle in Spain, that William Johnson devoted himself to the earnest study of what he conceived to be his future profession. He read voraciously all the detective stories and police reports he came across. Every moment he could snatch from his official duties he devoted to some scrap of paper, booklet or magazine. He strove to cultivate his reasoning powers. Never did a prospective client enter the Malcolm Sage Bureau without automatically setting into operation William Johnson's mental induction-coil. With eyes that were covertly keen, he would examine the visitor as he sat waiting for the two sharp buzzes on the private telephone which indicated that Malcolm Sage was at liberty.

It mattered little to William Johnson that error seemed to dog his footsteps: that he had 'deduced' a famous pussyfoot admiral as a comedian addicted to drink; a lord, with a ten-century lineage, as a man selling something or other; a cabinet minister as a company promoter in the worst sense of the term; nothing could damp his zeal.

Malcolm Sage's 'cases' he studied as intimately as he could from his position as junior; but they disappointed him. They seemed lacking in that element of drama he found so enthralling in the literature he read and the films he saw.

Malcolm Sage would enter the office as Malcolm Sage, and leave it as Malcolm Sage, as obvious and as easily recognisable as St Paul's Cathedral. He seemed indifferent to the dramatic possibilities of disguise.

William Johnson longed for some decrepit and dirty old man or woman to enter the bureau, selling boot-laces or bananas, and, on being peremptorily ordered out, suddenly to straighten up, and in his chief's well-known voice remark, 'So you don't recognise me, Johnson – good.' There was romance.

He yearned for a 'property-room', where executive members of the staff would disguise themselves beyond recognition. In his more imaginative moments he saw come out from that mysterious room a full-blooded Kafir, whereas he knew that only Thompson had entered. He would have liked to see Miss Norman shed her pretty brunetteness and reappear as an old apple-woman, who besought him to buy of her wares. He even saw himself being transformed into a hooligan, or a smart RAF officer, complete with toothbrush moustache and 'swish'.

In his own mind he was convinced that, given the opportunity, he could achieve greatness as a master of disguise, rivalling the highly coloured exploits of Charles Peace. He had even put his theories to the test.

One evening as Miss Norman, who had been working late, was on her way to Charing Cross Underground Station, she was accosted by a youth with upturned collar, wearing a shabby cap and a queer Charlie Chaplin moustache that was not on straight. In a husky voice he enquired the way to the Strand.

'Good gracious, Johnnie!' she cried involuntarily. 'What on earth's the matter?'

A moment later, as she regarded the vanishing form of William Johnson, she wanted to kill herself for her lack of tact.

'Poor little innocent!' she had murmured as she continued down Villiers Street, and there was in her eyes a reflection of the tears she had seen spring to those of William Johnson, whose first attempt at disguise had proved so tragic a failure.

Neither ever referred to the incident subsequently – although for days William Johnson experienced all the unenviable sensations of Damocles.

From that moment his devotion to Gladys Norman had become almost worship.

But William Johnson was not deterred, either by his own initial failure or his chief's opinion. He resolutely stuck to his own ideas, and continued to expend his pocket-money upon tinted glasses, false moustaches and greasepaint; for hidden away in the inner recesses of his mind was the conviction that it was not quite playing the game, as the game should be played, to solve a mystery or bring a criminal to justice without having recourse to disguise.

It was to him as if Nelson had won the Battle of Trafalgar in a soft hat and a Burberry, or Wellington had met Blücher in flannels and silk socks.

Somewhere in the future he saw himself the head of a 'William Johnson Bureau', and in the illustrated papers a portrait of 'Mr William Johnson as he is', and beneath it a series of characters that would rival a Dickens novel with another legend reading: 'Mr William Johnson as he appears'.

With these daydreams, the junior at the Malcolm Sage Bureau would occupy the time when not actually engaged either in the performance of his by no means arduous duties, or in reading the highly coloured detective stories from which he drew his inspiration.

From behind the glass-panelled door would come the ticktack of Miss Norman's typewriter, whilst outside droned the great symphony of London, growing into a crescendo as the door was opened, dying away again as it swung to once more, guided by an automatic self-closer.

From these reveries William Johnson would be aroused either by peremptory blasts upon the buzzer of the private telephone, or by the entry of a client.

One morning, as he was hesitating between assuming the disguise of a naval commander or a street-hawker, a florid little man with purple jowl and a white, bristling moustache hurtled through the swing-door, followed by a tall, spare man, whose clothing indicated his clerical calling.

'Mr Sage in?' demanded the little man fiercely.

'Mr Sage is engaged, sir,' said the junior, his eyes upon the clergyman, in whose appearance there was something that caused William Johnson to like him on the spot.

'Take my card in to him,' said the little, bristly man. 'Tell him that General Sir John Hackblock wishes to see him immediately.' The tone was suggestive of the parade-ground rather than a London office.

At that moment Gladys Norman appeared through the glass-panelled door. The clergyman immediately removed his hat, the general merely turned as if changing front to receive a new foe.

'Mr Sage will be engaged for about a quarter of an hour. I am his secretary,' she explained. She, also, looked at the general's companion, wondering what sort of teeth were behind that gentle, yet firm mouth. 'Perhaps you will take a seat,' she added.

This time the clergyman smiled, and Gladys Norman knew that she too liked him. Sir John looked about him aggressively, blew out his cheeks several times, then flopped into a chair. His companion also seated himself, and appeared to become lost in a fit of abstraction.

William Johnson returned to his table and became engrossed, ostensibly in the exploits of an indestructible trailer of men, but really in a surreptitious examination of the two callers.

He had just succeeded in deducing from their manner that they were father and son, and from the boots of the younger that he was low church and a bad walker, when two sharp blasts on the telephone-buzzer brought him to his feet and halfway across the office in what was practically one movement. With Malcolm Sage there were two things to be avoided, delay in answering a summons and unnecessary words.

'This way, sir,' he said, and led them through the glass-panelled door to Malcolm Sage's private room.

With a short, jerky movement of his head Malcolm Sage motioned his visitors to be seated. In that one movement his steel-coloured eyes had registered a mental photograph of the two men. That glance embraced all the details: the dark hair of the younger, greying at the temples, the dreamy grey eyes, the gentle curves of a mouth that was, nevertheless, capable of great sternness, and the spare, almost lean frame; then the self-important, over-bearing manner of the older man. 'High Anglican, ascetic, out-of-doors', was Malcolm Sage's mental classification of the one, thus unconsciously reversing William Johnson's verdict. The other he dismissed as a pompous ass.

'You Mr Sage?' Sir John regarded the bald conical head and gold-rimmed spectacles as if they had been unpolished buttons on parade.

Malcolm Sage inclined his head slightly, and

proceeded to gaze down at his fingers spread out on the table before him. After the first appraising glance he rarely looked at a client.

'I am Sir John Hackblock; this is my friend, the Reverend Geoffrey Callice.'

Again a slight inclination of the head indicated that Malcolm Sage had heard.

Mr Llewellyn John would have recognised in Sir John Hackblock the last man in the world who should have been brought into contact with Malcolm Sage. The prime minister's own policy had been to keep Malcolm Sage from contact with other ministers, and thus reduce the number of embarrassing resignations.

'I want to consult you about a most damnable atrocity,' exploded the general. 'It's inconceivable that in this – '

'Will you kindly be as brief as possible?' said Malcolm Sage, fondling the lobe of his left ear. 'I can spare only a few minutes.'

Sir John gasped, glared across at him angrily then, seeming to take himself in hand, continued: 'You've heard of the Surrey cattle-maiming outrages?'

Malcolm Sage nodded.

'Well, this morning a brood-mare of mine was found hacked about in an unspeakable manner. Oh, the damn scoundrels!' he burst out as he jumped from his chair and began pacing up and down the room.

'I think it will be better if Mr Callice tells me the details,' said Malcolm Sage, evenly. 'You seem a little overwrought.'

'Overwrought!' cried Sir John. 'Overwrought! Dammit, so would you be if you had lost over a dozen beasts.' In the army he was known as 'Dammit Hackblock'.

Mr Callice looked across to the general, who, nodding acquiescence, proceeded to blow his nose violently, as if to bid Malcolm Sage defiance.

'This morning a favourite mare belonging to Sir John was found mutilated in a terrible manner – ' Mr Callice paused; there was something in his voice that caused Malcolm Sage to look up. The gentle look had gone from his face, his eyes flashed, and his mouth was set in a stern, severe line.

'Good preacher,' Malcolm Sage decided as he dropped his eyes once more, and upon his blotting pad proceeded to develop the Pons Asinorum into a church.

In a voice that vibrated with feeling and suggested great self-restraint, Mr Callice proceeded to tell the story of the latest outrage. How when found that morning the mare was still alive, of the terrible nature of her injuries, and how the perpetrator had disappeared leaving no trace.

'Her look, sir! Dammit!' the general broke in. 'Her eyes have haunted me ever since. They – ' His voice broke, and he proceeded once more to blow his nose violently.

Mr Callice went on to explain that after having seen the mare put out of her misery, Sir John had motored over to his lodgings and insisted that they should go together to Scotland Yard and demand that something be done.

'Callice is chairman of the Watchers' Committee,' broke in Sir John.

'I should explain,' proceeded Mr Callice, 'that some time ago we formed ourselves into a committee to patrol the neighbourhood at night in the hope of tracing the criminal. On the way up Sir John remembered hearing of you in connection with Department Z, and as he was not satisfied with his call at Scotland Yard, he decided to come on here and place the matter in your hands.'

'This is the twenty-ninth maiming?' Malcolm Sage remarked, as he proceeded to add a graveyard to the church.

'Yes, the first occurred some two years ago.' Then, as if suddenly realising what Malcolm Sage's question implied, he added: 'You have interested yourself in the affair?'

'Yes,' was the reply. 'Tell me what has been done.'

'The police seem utterly at fault,' continued Mr Callice. 'Locally we have organised watch-parties. My boys and I have been out night after night; but without result. I am a scoutmaster,' he explained. 'The poor beasts' sufferings are terrible,' he continued after a slight pause. 'It is a return to barbarism;' again there was the throb of indignation in his voice.

'You have discovered nothing?'

'Nothing,' was the response, uttered in a tone of deep despondency. 'We have even tried bloodhounds; but without result.'

'And now I want you to take up the matter, and don't spare expense,' burst out Sir John, unable to contain himself longer.

'I will consider the proposal and let you know,' said Malcolm Sage, evenly. 'At present, my time is fully occupied; but later – ' He never lost an opportunity of countering aggression by emphasising the democratic tendency of the times. Mr Llewellyn John had called it 'incipient Bolshevism'.

'Later!' cried Sir John in consternation. 'Why,

dammit, sir! there won't be an animal left in the county. This thing has been going on for two years now, and those damn fools at Scotland Yard – '

'If it were not for Scotland Yard,' said Malcolm Sage quietly, as he proceeded to shingle the roof of the church, the graveyard having proved a failure, 'we should probably have to sleep at night with pistols under our pillows.'

'Eh!' Sir John looked across at him with a startled expression.

'Scotland Yard is the headquarters of the most efficient and highly organised police force in the world,' was the quiet reply.

'But, dammit! if they're so clever why don't they put a stop to this torturing of poor dumb beasts?' cried the general indignantly. 'I've shown them the man. It's Hinds; I know it. I've just been to see that fellow Wensdale. Why, dammit! he ought to be cashiered, and I told him so.'

'Who is Hinds?' Malcolm Sage addressed the question to Mr Callice.

'He used to be Sir John's head gamekeeper – '

'And I discharged him,' exploded the general. 'I'll shoot a poacher or his dog; but, dammit! I won't set traps for them,' and he puffed out his cheeks aggressively.

'Hinds used to set traps to save himself the trouble of patrolling the preserves,' explained Mr Callice, 'and one day Sir John discovered him actually watching the agonies of a dog caught across the hindquarters in a mantrap.' Again there was a wave of feeling in the voice, and a stern set about the mouth.

'It's Hinds right enough,' cried the general with conviction. 'The man's a brute. Now will you – ?'

'I will let you know as soon as possible whether or no I can take up the enquiry,' said Malcolm Sage, rising. 'I fear that is the best I can promise.'

'But –' began Sir John; then he stopped and stared at Malcolm Sage as he moved towards the door. 'Dammit! I don't care what it costs,' he spluttered explosively. 'It'll be worth five hundred pounds to the man who catches the scoundrel. Poor Betty,' he added in a softer tone.

'I will write to you shortly,' said Malcolm Sage. There was dismissal in his tone.

With darkened jowl and bristling moustache Sir John strutted towards the door. Mr Callice paused to shake hands with Malcolm Sage, and then followed the general, who, with a final glare at William Johnson, as he held open the swing-door, passed out into the street, convinced that now the country was no longer subject to conscription it would go rapidly to the devil.

For the next half-hour Malcolm Sage pored over a volume of press-cuttings containing accounts of previous cattle-maimings.

Following his usual custom in such matters, he had caused the newspaper accounts of the various mutilations to be collected and pasted in a press-cutting book. Sooner or later he had determined to devote time to the affair.

Without looking up from the book he pressed three times in rapid succession a button of the private telephone. Instantly Gladys Norman appeared, note-book in hand. She had been heard to remark that if she were dead 'three on the buzzer' would bring her to life again.

'*Whitaker's* and Inspector Wensdale,' said Malcolm Sage, his eyes still on the book before him.

When deep in a problem, Malcolm Sage's economy with words made it difficult for anyone but his own staff to understand his requirements.

Without a word the girl vanished and, a moment later, William Johnson placed *Whitaker's Almanack* on the table, then he in turn disappeared as silently as Gladys Norman.

Malcolm Sage turned to the calendar, and for some time studied the pages devoted to the current month – June – and July. As he closed the book there were three buzzes from the house-telephone, the signal that he was through to the number required. Drawing the pedestal-instrument towards him, he put the receiver to his ear.

'That Inspector Wensdale? – Yes! Mr Sage speaking. It's about the new cattle-maiming business. – I've just heard of it. – I've not decided yet. I want a large-scale map of the district, with the exact spot of each outrage indicated, and the date. – Tomorrow will do. – Yes, come round. Give me half an hour with the map first.'

Malcolm Sage replaced the receiver as the buzzer sounded, announcing another client.

'So there is nothing?' Malcolm Sage looked up enquiringly from the map before him.

'Nothing that even a stage detective could turn into a clue,' said Inspector Wensdale, a big, clean-shaven man with hard, alert eyes.

Malcolm Sage continued his study of the map.

'Confound those magazine detectives!' the inspector burst out explosively. 'They've always got a dustpan full of clues ready made for 'em.'

'To say nothing of fingerprints,' said Malcolm Sage dryly. He never could resist a sly dig at Scotland Yard's faith in fingerprints as clues instead of means of identification.

'It's a bit awkward for me, too, Mr Sage,' continued the inspector, confidentially. 'Last time, the *Daily Telegram* went for us because – '

'You hadn't found a dustpan full of clues?' suggested Malcolm Sage, who was engaged in forming geometrical designs with spent matches.

'They're getting a bit restive, too, at the Yard,' he continued. He was too disturbed in mind for flippancy. 'It was this cattle-maiming business that sent poor old Scott's number up,' he added, referring to Detective Inspector Scott's failure to solve the mystery. 'Now the general's making a terrible row. Threatens me with the commissioner.'

For some seconds Malcolm Sage devoted himself to his designs.

'Any theory?' he enquired at length, without looking up.

'I've given up theorising,' was the dour reply.

In response to a further question as to what had been done, the inspector proceeded to detail how the whole neighbourhood had been scoured after each maiming, and how, night after night, watchers had been posted throughout the district, but without result.

'I have had men out night and day,' continued the inspector gloomily. 'He's a clever devil, whoever he is. It's my opinion the man's a lunatic,' he added.

Malcolm Sage looked up slowly.

'What makes you think that?' he asked.

'His cunning, for one thing,' was the reply. 'Then,

it's so senseless. No,' he added with conviction, 'he's no more an ordinary man than Jack the Ripper was.'

He went on to give details of his enquiries among those living in the district. There was absolutely nothing to attach even the remotest suspicion to any particular person. Rewards had been offered for information; but all without producing the slightest evidence or clue.

'This man Hinds?' enquired Malcolm Sage, looking about for more matches.

'Oh! the general's got him on the brain. Absolutely nothing in it. I've turned him inside out. Why, even the deputy commissioner had a go at him, and if he can get nothing out of a man, there's nothing to get out.'

'Well,' said Malcolm Sage rising, 'keep the fact to yourself that I am interested. I suppose, if necessary, you could arrange for twenty or thirty men to run down there?' he queried.

'The whole blessed Yard if you like, Mr Sage,' was the feeling reply.

'We'll leave it at that for the present then. By the way, if you happen to think you see me in the neighbourhood you needn't remember that we are acquainted.'

The inspector nodded comprehendingly and, with a heart lightened somewhat of its burden, he departed. He had an almost childlike faith in Malcolm Sage.

For half an hour Malcolm Sage sat engrossed in the map of the scene of the maimings. On it were a number of red-ink crosses with figures beneath. In the left-hand bottom corner was a list of the various outrages, with the date and the time, as near as could be approximated, against each.

The numbers in the bottom corner corresponded with those beneath the crosses.

From time to time he referred to the two copies of *Whitaker's Almanack* open before him, and made notes upon the writing-pad at his side. Finally he ruled a square upon the map in red ink, and then drew two lines diagonally from corner to corner. Then, without looking up from the map, he pressed one of the buttons of the private telephone. 'Tims,' he said through the mouthpiece.

Five minutes later Malcolm Sage's chauffeur was standing opposite his chief's table, ready to go anywhere and do anything.

'Tomorrow will be Sunday, Tims.'

'Yessir.'

'A day of rest.'

'Yessir!'

'We are going out to Hempdon, near Selford,' Malcolm Sage continued, pointing to the map. Tims stepped forward and bent over to identify the spot. 'The car will break down. It will take you or any other mechanic two hours to put it right.'

'Yessir,' said Tims, straightening himself.

'You understand,' said Malcolm Sage, looking at him sharply, 'you *or any other mechanic*?'

'Yessir,' repeated Tims, his face sphinx-like in its lack of expression.

He was a clean-shaven, fleshless little man who, had he not been a chauffeur, would probably have spent his life with a straw between his teeth, hissing lullabies to horses.

'I shall be ready at nine,' said Malcolm Sage, and with another 'Yessir', Tims turned to go.

'And, Tims.'

'Yessir.' He about-faced smartly on his right heel.
'You might apologise for me to Mrs Tims for depriving
her of you on Sunday. Take her out to dinner on
Monday and charge it to me.'

'Thank you, sir, very much, sir,' said Tims, his face
expressionless.

'That is all, Tims, thank you.'

Tims turned once more and left the room. As he
walked towards the outer door he winked at Gladys
Norman and, with a sudden dive, made a frightful
riot of William Johnson's knut-like hair. Then, without
change of expression, he passed out to tune up the car
for its run on the morrow.

Malcolm Sage's staff knew that when 'the chief'
was what Tims called 'chatty' he was beginning to see
light, so Tims whistled loudly at his work: for he, like
all his colleagues, was pleased when 'the chief' saw
reason to be pleased.

The following morning, as they trooped out of
church, the inhabitants of Hempdon were greatly
interested in the breakdown of a large car, which
seemed to defy the best efforts of the chauffeur to
coax into movement. The owner drank cider at the
Spotted Woodpigeon and talked pleasantly with the
villagers, who, on learning that he had never even
heard of the Surrey cattle-maimings, were at great
pains to pour information and theories into his
receptive ear.

The episode quite dwarfed the remarkable sermon
preached by Mr Callice, in which he exhorted his
congregation to band themselves together to track
down whoever was maiming and torturing God's
creatures and defying the Master's merciful teaching.

It was Tom Hinds, assisted by a boy scout, who

conducted Malcolm Sage to the scene of the latest outrage. It was Hinds who described the position of the mare when she was discovered, and it was he who pocketed two half-crowns as the car moved off Londonwards.

That evening Malcolm Sage sat long and late at his table, engrossed in the map that Inspector Wensdale had sent him.

Finally he subjected to a thorough and exhaustive examination the thumb-nail of his right hand. It was as if he saw in its polished surface the tablets of destiny.

The next morning he wrote a letter that subsequently caused Sir John Hackblock to explode into a torrent of abuse against detectives in general, and one investigator in particular. It stated in a few words that, owing to circumstances over which he had no control, Malcolm Sage would not be able to undertake the enquiry with which Sir John Hackblock had honoured him until the end of the month following. He hoped, however, to communicate further with his client soon after the twenty-third of that month.

Nearly a month had elapsed, and the cattle-maiming mystery seemed as far off solution as ever. The neighbourhood in which the crimes had been committed had once more settled down to its usual occupations, and Scotland Yard had followed suit.

Sir John Hackblock had written to the chief commissioner and a question had been asked in the House.

Inspector Wensdale's colleagues had learned that it was dangerous to mention in his presence the words 'cattle' or 'maiming'. The inspector knew that the affair was referred to as 'Wensdale's Waterloo', and his failure to throw light on the mystery was beginning to tell upon his nerves.

For three weeks he had received no word from Malcolm Sage. One morning on his arrival at Scotland Yard he was given a telephone message asking him to call round at the bureau during the day.

'Nothing new?' queried Malcolm Sage ten minutes later, as the inspector was shown into his room by Thompson.

The inspector shook a gloomy head and dropped his heavy frame into a chair.

Malcolm Sage indicated with a nod that Thompson was to remain.

'Can you borrow a couple of covered government lorries?' queried Malcolm Sage.

'A couple of hundred if necessary,' said the inspector dully.

'Two will be enough,' was the dry rejoinder. 'Now listen carefully, Wensdale. I want you to have fifty men housed some ten miles away from Hempdon on the afternoon of the twenty-second. Select men who have done scouting, ex-boy scouts, for preference. Don't choose any with bald heads or with very light hair. See that they are wearing dark clothes and dark shirts and, above all, no white collars. Take with you a good supply of burnt cork such as is used by negro minstrels.'

Malcolm Sage paused, and for the fraction of a second there was a curious fluttering at the corners of his mouth.

Inspector Wensdale was sitting bolt upright in his chair, gazing at Malcolm Sage as if he had been requested to supply two lorry-loads of archangels.

'It will be moonlight, and caps might fall off,' explained Malcolm Sage. 'You cannot very well ask a man to black his head. Above all,' he continued evenly, 'be sure you give no indication to anyone why you want the men, and tell them not to talk. You follow me?' he queried.

'Yes,' said the inspector, 'I – I follow.'

'Don't go down Hempdon way again, and tell no one in the neighbourhood; *no one*, you understand, is to know anything about it. Don't tell the general, for instance.'

'Him!' There was a world of hatred and contempt in the inspector's voice. Then he glanced a little oddly at Malcolm Sage.

Malcolm Sage went on to elaborate his instructions. The men were to be divided into two parties, one to form a line north of the scene of the last outrage, and the other to be spread over a particular zone some three miles the other side of Hempdon. They were to blacken their faces and hands, and observe great care to show no light colouring in connection with their clothing. Thus they would be indistinguishable from their surroundings.

'You will go with one lot,' said Malcolm Sage to the inspector, 'and my man Finlay with the other. Thompson and I will be somewhere in the neighbourhood. You will be given a password for purposes of identification. You understand?'

'I think so,' said the inspector in a tone which suggested that he was very far from understanding.

'I'll have everything typed out for you, and scale-plans of where you are to post your men. Above all, don't take anyone into your confidence.'

Inspector Wensdale nodded and looked across at Thompson, as if to assure himself that after all it really was not some huge joke.

'If nothing happens on the twenty-second, we shall carry on the second, third and fourth nights. In all probability we shall catch our man on the twenty-third.'

'Then you know who it is?' spluttered the inspector in astonishment.

'I hope to know on the twenty-third,' said Malcolm Sage dryly, as he rose and walked towards the door. Directness was his strong point. Taking the hint, Inspector Wensdale rose also and, with the air of a man not yet quite awake, passed out of the room.

'You had better see him tomorrow, Thompson,' said Malcolm Sage, 'and explain exactly how the men are to be disposed. Make it clear that none must show themselves. If they actually see anyone in the act, they must track him, not try to take him.'

Thompson nodded his head comprehendingly.

'Make it clear that they are there to watch; but I doubt if they'll see anything,' he added.

At eleven o'clock on the night of July the twenty-third, two motor lorries glided slowly along, some three miles distant from one another. From their interiors silent forms dropped noiselessly on to the moon-white road. A moment later, slipping into the shadow of the hedge, they disappeared. All the previous night men had watched and waited; but nothing had happened. Now they were to try again.

Overhead the moon was climbing the sky, struggling against masses of cloud that from time to time swung themselves across her disc.

In the village of Hempdon all was quiet. The last light had been extinguished, the last dog had sent forth a final challenging bark, hoping that some neighbouring rival would answer and justify a volley of canine protest.

On the western side of the highway, and well behind the houses, two figures were standing in the shadow cast by a large oak. Their faces and hands were blackened, rendering them indistinguishable from their surroundings.

One wore a shade over a pair of gold-rimmed spectacles, a precaution against the moonlight being reflected on the lenses.

Half an hour, an hour, an hour and a half passed. They waited. Presently one gripped the arm of the other and pointed. At the back of the house immediately opposite there was a slight movement in the shade cast by a hedge. Then the line readjusted itself and the shadow vanished. A moment later it reappeared in a patch of moonlight, looking like a large dog.

Stooping low Malcolm Sage and Thompson followed the dog-like form, themselves taking advantage of every patch of shadow and cover that offered.

The mysterious form moved along deliberately and without haste, now disappearing in the shadow cast by some tree or bush, now reappearing once more on the other side.

It was obviously taking advantage of everything that tended to conceal its movements.

Once it disappeared altogether, and for five minutes the two trackers lay on their faces and waited.

'Making sure he's not being followed,' whispered Thompson, and Malcolm Sage nodded.

Presently the figure appeared once more and, as if reassured, continued its slow and deliberate way.

Once a dog barked, a short, sharp bark of un-
certainty. Again there was no sign of the figure for
some minutes. Then it moved out from the surrounding shadows and continued its stealthy progress.

Having reached the outskirts of the village, it continued its crouching course along the western side of
the hedge flanking the roadside.

Malcolm Sage and Thompson followed under the
shadow of a hedge running parallel.

For a mile the slow and laborious tracking continued. Suddenly Malcolm Sage stopped. In the field
on their right two horses were grazing in the moonlight. It was the scene of the tragedy of the previous
month!

For some minutes they waited expectantly.
Suddenly Malcolm Sage gripped Thompson's arm
and pointed. From under the hedge a dark patch was
moving slowly towards the nearer of the two animals.
It was apparently the form of a man, face downwards,
wriggling along inch by inch without bending a limb.

'Get across. Cut off his retreat,' whispered Sage.
'Look out for the knife.'

Thompson nodded and slid away under cover of the
hedge separating the field in which the horses were
from that along which the watchers had just passed.

Slowly the form approached its quarry. Once the
horse lifted its head as though scenting danger; but
the figure was approaching up-wind.

Suddenly it raised itself, appearing once more like a
large dog. Then with a swift, panther-like movement
it momentarily disappeared in the shadow cast by the
horse.

There was a muffed scream and a gurgle, as the
animal collapsed, then silence.

A minute later the form seemed to detach itself from the carcase and wriggled along towards the hedge, a dark patch upon the grass.

Malcolm Sage was already halfway through the second field, keeping well under the shelter of the hedge. He reached a spot where the intersecting hedge joined that running parallel with the high road. There was a hole sufficiently large for a man to crawl through from one field to the other. By this Malcolm Sage waited, a life-preserver in his hand.

At the sound of the snapping of a twig, he gripped his weapon; a moment later a round, dark shape appeared through the hole in the hedge. Without hesitating Malcolm Sage struck.

There was a sound, half grunt, half sob, and Malcolm Sage was on his feet gazing down at the strangest creature he had ever encountered.

Clothed in green, its face and hands smeared with some pigment of the same colour, lay the figure of a tall man. Round the waist was a belt from which was suspended in its case a Gurkha's kukri.

Malcolm Sage bent down to unbuckle the belt. He turned the man on his back. As he did so he saw that in his hand was a small, collapsible tin cup covered with blood; blood also stained his lips and chin, and dripped from his hands, while the front of his clothing was stained in dark patches.

'I wonder who he is,' muttered Thompson, as he gazed down at the strange figure.

'Locally he is known as the Reverend Geoffrey Callice,' remarked Malcolm Sage quietly.

And Thompson whistled.

'And that damned scoundrel has been fooling us for two years.' Sir John Hackblock glared at Inspector Wensdale as if it were he who was responsible for the deception.

They were seated smoking in Sir John's library after a particularly early breakfast.

'I always said it was the work of a madman,' said the inspector in self-defence.

'Callice is no more mad than I am,' snapped Sir John. 'I wish I were going to try him,' he added grimly. 'The scoundrel! To think – ' His indignation choked him.

'He is not mad in the accepted sense,' said Malcolm Sage, as he sucked meditatively at his pipe. 'I should say that it is a case of race-memory.'

'Race-memory! Dammit! What's that?' Sir John Hackblock snapped out the words in his best parade-ground manner. He was more purple than ever about the jowl, and it was obvious that he was prepared to disagree with everyone and everything. As Lady Hackblock and her domestics would have recognised without difficulty, Sir John was angry.

'How the devil did you spot the brute?' he demanded, as Malcolm Sage did not reply immediately.

'Race-memory,' he remarked, ignoring the second question, 'is to man what instinct is to animals; it defies analysis or explanation.'

Sir John stared; and it was Inspector Wensdale who spoke. 'But how did you manage to fix the date, Mr Sage?' he enquired.

'By the previous outrages,' was the reply.

'The previous outrages!' cried Sir John. 'Dammit! how did they help you?'

'They all took place about the time the moon was

full. There were twenty-eight in all.' Malcolm Sage
felt in his pocket and drew out a paper. 'These are the
figures.'

In his eagerness Sir John snatched the paper from
his hand, and with Inspector Wensdale looking over
his shoulder, read:

Day before full moon	4
Full moon	15
Day after	7
Second day after	2
Total	28

'Well, I'm damned!' exclaimed Sir John, looking
up from the paper at Malcolm Sage, as if he had
solved the riddle of the universe.

The inspector's only comment was a quick in-
drawing of breath. Sir John continued to stare at
Malcolm Sage, the paper still held in his hand.

'That made matters comparatively easy,' continued
Malcolm Sage. 'The outrages were clearly not acts of
revenge upon any particular person; for they involved
nine different owners. They were obviously the work
of someone subject to a mania, or obsession, which
gripped him when the moon was at the full.'

'But how did you fix the actual spot?' burst out
Inspector Wensdale excitedly.

'Each of the previous acts had been either in a
diametrically opposite direction from that immediately
preceding it, or practically on the same spot. For
instance, the first three were north, east and south of
Hempdon, in the order named. Then the cunning of
the perpetrator prompted him to commit a fourth,
not to the west but to the south, within a few yards
of the previous act. The criminal argued, probably

VINTAGE DETECTIVE STORIES

subconsciously, that he would be expected to complete the square.'

'But what made you fix on Hempdon as the head-quarters of the blackguard?' enquired Sir John.

'That was easy,' remarked Malcolm Sage, polishing the thumb-nail of his left hand upon the palm of his right.

'Easy!' The exclamation burst involuntarily from the inspector.

'You supplied me with a large-scale map showing the exact spot where each of the previous maimings had taken place. I drew a square to embrace the whole. Lines drawn diagonally from corner to corner gave me the centre of gravity.'

'But – ' began the inspector.

Ignoring the interruption Malcolm Sage continued.

'A man committing a series of crimes from a given spot was bound to spread his operations over a fairly wide area in order to minimise the chance of discovery. The longer the period and the larger the number of crimes, the greater the chance of his being located somewhere near the centre of his activities.'

'Well, I'm damned!' remarked Sir John for the second time. Then suddenly turning to Inspector Wensdale, 'Dammit!' he exploded, 'why didn't you think of that?'

'There was, of course, the chance of his striking in another direction,' continued Malcolm Sage, digging into the bowl of his pipe with a penknife, 'so I placed the men in such a way that if he did so he was bound to be seen.'

Inspector Wensdale continued to gaze at him, eager to hear more.

'But what was that you said about race-memory?'

Sir John had quietened down considerably since Malcolm Sage had begun his explanation.

'I should describe it as a harking back to an earlier phase. It is to the mind what atavism is to the body. In breeding, for instance' – Malcolm Sage looked across to Sir John – 'you find that an offspring will manifest characteristics, or a taint, that is not to be found in either sire or dam.'

Sir John nodded.

'Well, race-memory is the same thing in regard to the mental plane, a sort of subconscious wave of reminiscence. In Callice's case it was in all probability the memory of some sacrificial rite of his ancestors centuries ago.'

'A case of heredity.'

'Broadly speaking, yes. At the full moon this particular tribe, whose act Callice has reproduced, was in the habit of slaughtering some beast, or beasts, and drinking the blood, probably with the idea of absorbing their strength or their courage. Possibly the surroundings at Hempdon were similar to those where the act of sacrifice was committed in the past.

'It must be remembered that Callice was an ascetic, and consequently highly subjective. Therefore when the wave of reminiscence is taken in conjunction with the surroundings, the full moon and his high state of subjectivity, it is easy to see that material considerations might easily be obliterated. That is why I watched the back entrance to his lodgings.'

'And all the time we were telling him our plans,' murmured the inspector half to himself.

'Yes, and he would go out hunting himself,' said Sir John. 'Damn funny, I call it. Anyway, he'll get seven years at least.'

'When he awakens he will remember nothing about it. You cannot punish a man for a subconscious crime.'

Sir John snorted indignantly; but Inspector Wensdale nodded his head slowly and regretfully.

'Anyway, I owe you five hundred pounds,' said Sir John to Malcolm Sage; 'and, dammit! it's worth it,' he added.

Malcolm Sage shrugged his shoulders as he rose to go. 'I was sorry to have to hit him,' he said regretfully, 'but I was afraid of that knife. A man can do a lot of damage with a thing like that. That's why I told you not to let your men attempt to take him, Wensdale.'

'How did you know what sort of knife it was?' asked the inspector.

'Oh! I motored down here, and the car broke down. Incidentally I made a lot of acquaintances, including Callice's patrol-leader, a bright lad. He told me a lot of things about Callice and his ways. A remarkable product the boy scout,' he added. 'Kipling calls him "the friend of all the world".'

Sir John looked across at Inspector Wensdale, who was strongly tempted to wink.

'Don't think too harshly of Callice,' said Malcolm Sage as he shook hands with Sir John. 'It might easily have been you or I, had we been a little purer in mind and thought.'

And with that he passed out of the room with Inspector Wensdale, followed by Sir John Hackblock, who was endeavouring to interpret the exact meaning of the remark.

'They said he was a clever devil,' he muttered as he returned to the library after seeing his guests off, 'and, dammit! they were right.'

The Secrets of the Black Brotherhood

It was a bitter night in December, now years ago, that a young and handsome man called upon me in great distress, to seek my advice and assistance. It was the third day after Christmas, and having dined, and dined well, I had ensconced myself in my favourite easy-chair, before a cheerful fire, and was engaged in the perusal of Charles Dickens's *The Cricket on the Hearth*, when my visitor was unceremoniously ushered into the room. He held his dripping hat in his hand, and the heavy topcoat he wore was white with snow, which was falling heavily outside. He was well proportioned, of blond complexion, and his face at once attracted me by its frank, open expression. He had clear, honest eyes, and a graceful moustache shaded a well-formed mouth.

'Pardon me for intruding upon you,' he said, in a somewhat excited tone, as he placed his wet hat on the table and began to pull off his thick woollen gloves; 'but the fact is, I am in a frame of mind bordering upon distraction. Let me introduce myself, however. My name is Harold Welldom Kingsley; Welldom being an old family name. I am the son of the late Admiral Kingsley, who, as you may possibly be aware, distinguished himself greatly in the service of his queen and country.'

'Yes,' I answered. 'I knew your father by reputation, and I remember that when he died some years ago his remains were accorded a public funeral. I am pleased

to make the acquaintance of the son of so distinguished a man. Pray remove your coat and be seated,
and let me know in what way I can serve you.'

'I am in the Admiralty Office,' my visitor continued,
as he divested himself of his damp coat and, placing
it on the back of a chair, sat down. Thereupon I
pushed the shaded lamp that stood on the table
nearer to him, tilting the shade slightly so that the
light might fall upon his face, for it is my habit always
to study the face of the person with whom I am in
conversation. 'I live with my mother and two sisters
in Kensington. For three years I have been engaged
to a young lady, who is, I may venture to say, the
sweetest woman who ever drew the breath of life.'

'Ah!' I murmured, with a smile, as I closely watched
my visitor, and saw his face light up with enthusiasm
as he thus referred to his fiancée, 'it is the old story:
love is blind and sees no faults until too late.'

'In my case it is not so,' he exclaimed, with a force of
emphasis that carried conviction of his perfect sincerity
and a belief in his own infallible judgement. 'But we
will not discuss that point,' he continued. 'The business
that has brought me here is far too serious for time to
be wasted in argument. The young lady who is pledged
to me as my wife is, at present, under arrest on the
serious charge of having stolen some very valuable
jewellery from a well-known firm of jewellers.'

'That is a grave charge, indeed,' I remarked, with
growing interest in my visitor; 'but presumably there
must have been good prima facie evidence to justify
her arrest.'

'Yes,' Mr Kingsley exclaimed, with an agonised
expression, 'that is the most terrible part of the whole
affair. I am afraid that legally the evidence will go

against her; and yet morally I will stake my very soul on her innocence.'

'You speak somewhat paradoxically, Mr Kingsley,' I said, with a certain amount of professional sternness, for it seemed to me he was straining to twist facts to suit his own views.

'To you it will seem so,' he answered; 'but if you have the patience to listen to me, I will tell you the whole story, and I think you will say I am right.'

I intimated that I was quite prepared to listen to anything he had to say, and leaning back in my chair with the tips of my fingers together and my eyes half closed – an attitude I always unconsciously assume when engaged in trying to dissect some human puzzle – I waited for him to continue.

'The lady's name is Beryl Artois,' he went on. 'She was born in France. Her mother was an English lady highly connected; and her father was a Frenchman of independent means. They lived surrounded with every luxury in a small château on the banks of the Seine, not far from St Germain. Unhappily, Monsieur Artois was fatally fond of a life of ease and pleasure, and dying suddenly after a night of revel in Paris, at a *bal masqué* during the *mi-carême*, it was found that he had dissipated his fortune, and left his widow and child totally unprovided for. Even his château was mortgaged up to the hilt, and on his furniture was a bill of sale. Not wishing to be dependent on his relations, Madame Artois and her daughter came to London. Beryl at that time was only six years of age. She was a delicate girl, and needed all her mother's care and attention. For a few years madame earned her living as a teacher of French, music and drawing, and every spare moment she had she devoted to the education and training of her daughter. Unhappily, before Beryl was twelve years of age her doting mother died, and a bachelor uncle, her mother's only brother, took Beryl under his care, and as he was well off he engaged a highly qualified governess for her. I first became acquainted with her when she was eighteen years of age. That is now a little over six years ago; and though I have proved the soundness of the old adage which says that the course of true love never did run smooth, I have every reason to congratulate myself, for, as I have before hinted, Beryl is goodness itself.'

'In what way has your wooing been ruffled?' I asked.

'Well, Mr Tamworth, her uncle, refused for some time to countenance our engagement and threw every obstacle in the way; and as Beryl was much under his influence, she struggled between what she considered her duty to her uncle and foster father, and love for me. The love has triumphed, and Mr Tamworth has consented to our union on condition that we wait three years, and I obtain the promotion I hope to obtain in the government service in that time.'

'This is a very pretty, even a romantic, story,' I remarked; 'it is as old as the hills, and yet, like all love stories, ever new. But now for the sequel. How comes it that this well-nurtured and well-cared-for young lady has fallen under the suspicion of being a thief?'

'Ah! that is where the mystery comes in,' exclaimed Mr Kingsley in great distress. 'I ask you now, is it likely that Beryl, who has everything she requires – for her uncle is wealthy – and who would shudder at anything that by any possible means could be construed as wrongdoing, would descend to purloin jewellery from a jeweller's shop?'

I could not help smiling at what seemed to be the

sweet simplicity of this love-stricken young man, nor could I refrain from saying: 'In answer to your question, Mr Kingsley, permit me to say that the annals of crime contain many such cases. Unhappily, neither education nor moral training is sufficient safeguard against transgression, where the tendency to wrongdoing exists. In the case in point, it is very possible that the lady's vanity and love of display have tempted her to her fall.'

'For heaven's sake, Mr Donovan, don't drive me mad,' cried my visitor, with an outburst of passionate distress that begot my fullest sympathy. 'If all the angels in heaven were to come down and proclaim Beryl's guilt, I would still believe her innocent.'

'May I venture to remark,' I answered, 'that in all probability this sentiment does more credit to your heart than your head?'

'I tell you, sir,' exclaimed Kingsley, almost fiercely, 'that Beryl Artois is as innocent as you are!'

'Well, now, Mr Kingsley,' I observed, 'as we have had the sentimental and poetical side of the affair, let us go into the more vulgar and prosaic part of the business. Therefore please give me a plain, straight-forward answer to the questions I shall put to you. First, where does Mr Tamworth reside?'

'He resides at Linden House, Thames Ditton.'

'You say he is well off?'

'Yes. He keeps numerous servants, rides to hounds, drives his carriage, and is very highly respected.'

'Has he always been kind to his niece?'

'In every possible way, I believe.'

'And has supplied her with all she has wanted?'

'Yes. I do not think any reasonable request of hers has ever been refused.'

'And now, as regards the charge she has to meet. Give me full particulars of that.'

'It appears that the day before yesterday she came up to town in the brougham, and drove to Whitney, Blake and Montague, the well-known jewellers of Regent Street. There she stated that she wished to purchase a diamond bracelet for a New Year's gift, and some costly things were shown to her. But after more than an hour spent in the shop she could not make up her mind, for though she saw what she wanted, the price was higher than she cared to go to; and, before committing herself to the purchase of the article, she was anxious to consult her uncle, since she is necessarily dependent upon him for her pocket-money. Consequently, she told the assistant in the shop that she would call again the next day and decide. She thereupon took her departure, and entered the brougham, but had not proceeded very far before the assistant tore down the street, accompanied by a policeman, overtook the brougham, which had been brought to a standstill owing to the congested traffic, and accused Miss Artois of having purloined a diamond pendant worth nearly a thousand pounds. Of course, she most indignantly denied it. But the shopman insisted on giving her in charge.'

'And was the pendant found either in the brougham or on her person?'

'Oh, dear, no. Miss Artois begged that the policeman and the shopman would get into the brougham, and that they should drive straight to Scotland Yard. This was done; and though the young lady and the brougham were alike searched, the pendant was not forthcoming. Nevertheless, the shopman persisted in

534

his accusation, and so there was no alternative but to place Miss Artois under arrest.'

'This is a very remarkable story,' I answered, 'and may prove a very serious business indeed for the firm of jewellers if they cannot justify their charge.'

'They will never be able to do that,' said Kingsley, warmly, 'and you may depend upon it, they will have to pay dearly for their error. They maintain, however, that they have certainly lost the jewel; that no one else could possibly have taken it except Miss Artois; and that she must have managed to secrete it in some way. The whole charge, however, is preposterous, and I wish you thoroughly to prove the young lady's innocence in order that an action may be commenced against Whitney, Blake and Montague.'

Having secured my promise that I would do my utmost in his interests, my visitor took his departure; whereupon, lighting a cigar, I fell to pondering on this – as I had to admit to myself – very remarkable case, assuming that all the facts were as stated by Mr Kingsley.

It was too late to take any steps that night, but immediately after breakfast the following morning I jumped into a hansom and drove to Whitney, Blake and Montague's place. As everyone knows, they are a firm of worldwide renown, and I could not imagine them committing such a grave error as to accuse a lady of theft, unless they had very strong reasons for believing they were right. I requested an interview with Mr Whitney, and his version of the affair was substantially the same as that told me by Mr Kingsley.

'Of course,' added Mr Whitney, 'we rely entirely upon the statement of our manager, Mr John Coleman, who attended to the lady. Mr Coleman, I may inform you, has been with the firm since he was seventeen years of age, and he is now over fifty. And as he is a partner in the firm, our faith in him is justified. However, you shall see Coleman and judge for yourself.'

Mr Whitney sounded his bell and requested that Mr Coleman would come to the room. In a few minutes Coleman entered. He at once struck me as being a very shrewd, keen-eyed man of business. Without any unnecessary verbiage he gave me his account of the affair, according to which he devoted special attention to the young lady as he thought she was going to be a good customer. There were other customers in the shop at the time, but he conducted her to one end of the counter where there was no one else. She caused him a good deal of trouble, and looked at a large number of things, but did not seem to know her own mind; and at last went away without purchasing anything.

For some few moments just before she left, his attention was drawn off by one of the assistants coming to him to ask a question, and during that time he had little doubt she availed herself of the opportunity to abstract the pendant from the jewel tray upon which he had displayed the things for her inspection.

On her deciding not to purchase then, he placed the tray temporarily in the glass case on the counter, locked the case, putting the key in his pocket, and then conducted Miss Artois to her brougham. He was certainly not absent more than five minutes. By the time he returned there were very few people in the shop, and he proceeded immediately to the case, took out the tray and began to sort the jewels preparatory to restoring them to their respective positions amongst the stock. It was then he missed the pendant which Miss Artois had examined with eager interest, asking him many questions about the quality of the stones, their intrinsic value, and their setting. The pendant had originally been made to the order of a lady of title from specially selected stones, but she died before the order was completed; her executors declined to take the pendant, and, therefore, in order to dispose of it quickly, the firm had offered it for sale at the low price of one thousand pounds.

As soon as he discovered the loss Mr Coleman ran out of the shop and down the street, and passing a policeman on the way, he demanded his services. As it was the busiest part of the day there was a great deal of traffic, and Miss Artois's brougham had been unable to proceed very far. So convinced was he in his own mind that she was guilty, that though he was fully alive to the risks he ran if he made a mistake, he did not hesitate to give her into custody, and he was quite prepared to stand or fall by his act.

Although I subjected Mr Coleman to a very close questioning, I could not shake his evidence in any way. I pointed out to him that there was one serious fact in connection with the case, and that was, he had failed to find the pendant either in the brougham or on Miss Artois's person; and that, however morally certain he might be that the young lady was guilty, no magistrate would convict her on such evidence.

'I am aware of that,' answered Mr Coleman, 'but I have employed Detective Spieglemann, of Scotland Yard, to make some enquiries about the lady, and he informs me that on various occasions when she has visited the shops of well-known tradesmen, goods have afterwards been missed. The victims have almost invariably been jewellers, and the property purloined has generally been of great value.'

'If that is correct there is prima facie evidence,' I answered; 'but still, suspicion is not proof, and unless you have something better to offer, I have no hesitation in saying you will fail to secure a conviction.'

Mr Coleman appeared, for the first time, to be a little disconcerted, and I fancied that I detected signs in his face that he felt he had been somewhat hasty. Nevertheless, he reasserted his belief that the young lady was guilty, though he was utterly unable to suggest what had become of the stolen pendant. Female searchers had subjected Miss Artois to the most rigorous examination, and every nook and cranny of the brougham had been searched.

'May I ask, Mr Coleman, if Spieglemann was present when the search was made?' I enquired pointedly.

'Oh, yes,' exclaimed Coleman. 'He happened to be in the Yard at the time, and conducted the search.'

'Indeed. And did he think of searching the coachman who drove the brougham?'

As I asked this question, a pallor of alarm spread itself over Coleman's face, and he and Mr Whitney looked at each other as each saw, for the first time, that a grave oversight had been committed.

Detective Spieglemann was a German, who had long been attached to the force of Scotland Yard. But though he bore the reputation of being almost preternaturally acute, I had never been able to regard him in any other light than as a very ordinary person, whose German stolidity prevented him from getting out of well-worn grooves.

THE SECRETS OF THE BLACK BROTHERHOOD

Of course, this expression of opinion will be denounced as mere professional jealousy, but I shall be able to justify my view by hard and indisputable facts.

I have always maintained that the unravelling of anything like a mystery is capable of being elevated to the position of a fine art. Spieglemann, on the other hand, asserted that the whole process was merely a mechanical one, and that only a mechanical mind could succeed. On these points we totally differed, and as I had frequently had the good fortune to be successful where my rival had failed, I was entitled to claim that my process was the correct one. Mr Coleman's answer was another item of evidence in my favour. He confessed with unmistakable concern that the coachman had not been searched, and that nobody had suggested that he should be. In fact, no suspicion had fallen upon him. I really could not resist something like a smile as I remarked: 'That was really a most extraordinary oversight, and may prove very serious for you. For, assuming that you are right, and that Spieglemann is right in his statement that the lady lies under suspicion of having been concerned in other cases of a similar kind, is it not highly probable that the coachman has been in collusion with her, and she passed the stolen property to him? If this is not so, how did she get rid of the pendant? Nothing is truer than that in criminal cases it is the seemingly improbable that is most probable.

'Certainly, on the face of it nothing could seem more improbable than that a young lady, well connected and well off, afflicted with kleptomania, should make a confidant of her coachman. Yet it is the most probable thing imaginable, but both you and Spieglemann have overlooked it.'

Mr Coleman was perfectly crestfallen, and freely admitted that a very grave oversight had been committed. Thanking him and Mr Whitney I withdrew, and it was perfectly clear to me that I left the two gentlemen in a very different frame of mind from that they had been in when I first saw them.

In passing all the facts, as I now knew them, under review, I could not deny that circumstances looked dark against Miss Artois; and putting aside the possibility that somebody else might have stolen the pendant, I admitted the strong probability that she was in reality the thief. That being so, the idea struck me – and it evidently had not struck anyone else, not even the renowned Spieglemann – that she was a confederate, more likely than not a victim, of the coachman. On this supposition I determined to act, and my next step was to seek an interview with Miss Artois, in order that I might form some opinion of her from personal knowledge. I obtained this interview through the solicitors who had been engaged on her behalf by her devoted lover, Harold Kingsley. Although prepared to find her good looking, I certainly was not prepared for the type of beauty she represented.

I don't think I ever looked upon a more perfect, a sweeter and I will go so far as to say a more angelic face than she possessed, while her form and mould were such that an artist would have gone into raptures about her. I was informed that she had undergone a preliminary examination before the police magistrate, who had remanded her without bail, although bail had been offered to an unlimited amount by her uncle; but the magistrate had stated that he would consider the question of bail the next time she came before him.

As I entered the little cell she occupied at the police station, and introduced myself, giving her to understand at the same time that I was there by request of Mr Kingsley, she rose from the table at which she had been sitting engaged in the perusal of a book, which I subsequently discovered to be a well-thumbed, dilapidated and somewhat dirty copy of Moore's *Lallah Rookh,* and bowing with exquisite grace she said in a low, musical and touchingly pathetic voice: 'It is good of you to come, and more than kind of Mr Kingsley to send you; but I am sorry that you have come, and I wish that you would leave me without another word.'

Her soft, gazelle-like eyes, although apparently bent upon me, had a far-away look in them; and she spoke as a person in a trance might speak. Altogether there was something about her that at once aroused my curiosity and interest.

'That is a somewhat strange wish, Miss Artois,' I answered. 'I am here in your interest; and surely you cannot be indifferent to the grave charge that is hanging over you.'

'I am not indifferent,' she murmured, with a deep sigh.

'Then let me urge you to confide in your solicitors,' I said, 'and withhold nothing from them that may enable them to prepare your defence.'

'I shall confide in no one,' she replied in the same indifferent, same sweetly pathetic tone.

'But think of the consequences,' I urged.

'I have thought of everything.'

'Remember also, Miss Artois, your silence and refusal to give information will be tantamount to a tacit confession of guilt.'

For a moment her dreamy eyes seemed to lose their

dreaminess and to be expressive of an infinite pain, as she answered with quite a fiery energy – 'I am *not* guilty!' She laid peculiar emphasis on the word 'not'.

'Then,' said I, quickly, 'do all you possibly can to prove your guiltlessness;' and, in order that there should be no ambiguity in my meaning, I added, 'If you are the victim of anyone, for heaven's sake let it be known. For the sake of your lover conceal not the truth.'

'For the sake of my lover and the love I bear him, I would die,' she murmured, with the dreaminess which seemed peculiar to her.

'Then withhold nothing from your solicitors,' I repeated.

'Go!' she said, peremptorily, as she sank into her seat again, and resumed her reading.

'Have you no message to send to Mr Kingsley?' I asked.

'Go!' she repeated, without looking at me.

'Let me take some comforting word from you to Mr Kingsley,' I entreated.

She made no reply, but apparently was deeply absorbed in the book. Feeling that it would be useless to remain any longer, I withdrew, and as I did so she did not even look up from the book, nor did she make any response when I bade her adieu.

I had promised to call upon Mr Kingsley and acquaint him with the result of my interview with Miss Artois; and I carried out this promise with a sense of distress that I could hardly describe, because I was quite unable to give him the assurance he so much wanted that his fiancée was guiltless. Guiltless she was, in one sense, I was sure; but I was conscious of the fact that I was confronted with as complicated a human problem as I had ever been called upon to find a solution to.

I put the best face I could on matters while talking to young Kingsley; and on leaving him I felt convinced that my first surmise with reference to the coachman being a party to the robbery was a correct one. I had not been slow to determine that Miss Artois's temperament was one of those deeply sympathetic and poetic ones which are peculiarly subject to the influence of stronger wills.

In short, I came to the conclusion that the coachman was the really guilty person, and Miss Artois was his victim. He – in my opinion – had exercised some strange mesmeric influence over her, and she had been entirely under his sway. I was confirmed in this view when I learnt that the great Spieglemann had gathered up a mass of circumstantial evidence which tended to prove that Miss Artois had been in the habit for a long time of visiting some of the leading tradesmen in all quarters of London, and that these tradesmen had been robbed of property which in the aggregate represented many thousands of pounds.

It was altogether a peculiar case, as it presented two startling phases of human nature; for if Miss Artois had sinned, she had sinned not because her inclinations tended that way, but because her non-resisting, sympathetic nature had been made an instrument for the profit and gain of a debased and wicked man who did not scruple to use this beautiful girl as a means to an end.

My next step was to hurry off to Linden House at Thames Ditton, in order that I might get full particulars from Mr Tamworth of his coachman, before having the man arrested. Linden House was a large house, standing in its own grounds, and everything about the place was suggestive of wealth and comfort. I was ushered into an elegantly furnished drawing-room, and a few minutes later the door opened and a little, podgy, bald-headed man, wearing gold eye-glasses and dressed in a large-patterned dressing-gown and Turkish slippers, entered, and eyed me with a pair of strangely keen and hawk-like eyes. It was Mr Tamworth, and in many respects he was a striking and remarkable man, for his face was strongly marked, his eyes of unusual, almost unnatural brilliancy, the mouth firm, the square jaw indicative of an iron will. He was perfectly clean shaved, so that every feature, every line and angle were thrown into stronger prominence.

I had not sent my name up to him, but simply an urgent message that a gentleman wished to see him on very pressing and important business.

'Whom have I the pleasure to address?' he enquired as he bowed stiffly.

'My name is Dick Donovan,' I answered. 'I am –'

He interrupted me by exclaiming: 'Oh, yes, I have heard of you. You are a detective.' I bowed. 'Presumably,' he continued, 'you have come here in connection with the case of my dear niece?' He seemed to be overcome by emotion, and turning towards the window he applied a large bandana handkerchief to his eyes.

'I am not indifferent to the fact,' I answered, 'that the subject is necessarily a delicate and painful one. But from an interview I had with your niece I am forced to the conclusion that she is only guilty in degree.'

'How do you mean?' he asked, turning quickly

towards me, with an expression of mental suffering on his face.

'I mean that she is a victim of the machinations of a villain.'

'A victim,' he echoed, hoarsely. 'A victim of whom?'

'Of your coachman.'

He almost reeled at this announcement, and passed his hand over his bald head in a confused, distressed way; and then, with something like a wail, he exclaimed: 'My God, this is an awful revelation.'

He rushed towards the bell and was about to ring it when I stopped him by saying: 'What are you going to do?'

'Send for Tupper, the coachman.'

'Wait a bit,' I said. 'I should like to have some particulars of Tupper. What is his Christian name?'

'John.'

'Has he been with you long?'

'Just twelve months, I think.'

'Have you ever had occasion to suspect his honesty?'

'Never for a single instant.'

'Is he married?'

'I cannot tell you. I know absolutely nothing about his family affairs.'

'Well now, I have a suggestion to make, Mr Tamworth. I should like you to send for Tupper, and question him closely about what happened on the day that the pendant was stolen. And particularly I would like you to put this question to him, after you have skilfully led up to it: "Is it possible, Tupper, that my unhappy and misguided niece handed you the pendant, and you know what has become of it?"'

'I will do so,' answered Mr Tamworth, as he went towards the bell.

'Stop a minute, sir,' I said. 'There is one other important point. It is desirable that Tupper should not see me. Can you conceal me behind that screen in the corner, and in such a position that I can see without being seen? And you must not forget to place Tupper in such a way that I can get a full view of his face.'

'I don't think there will be any difficulty in that,' Mr Tamworth answered, and he requested me to follow him behind the screen. I did so, and taking out his penknife he bored a hole in one leaf of the screen, so that anyone looking through the hole commanded a full view of the room.

'There,' he said, 'I think that will answer your purpose. And now we will have the old villain here.'

He rang the bell, and a very respectable-looking manservant appeared.

'Robert,' said Mr Tamworth, peremptorily, 'send the coachman here.'

'Tupper's away, sir.'

'Away!'

'Yes. He went out last night and didn't come back.'

'Where has he gone to?' roared Mr Tamworth, in his excitement.

'I haven't the remotest idea, sir,' answered Robert.

'The double-dyed villain,' hissed Mr Tamworth between his clenched teeth. 'The double-dyed villain,' he repeated. 'But by heaven he shall be brought back, even if it takes all my fortune to effect his capture. That will do, Robert. You may go.'

As the man took his departure and closed the door I stepped from behind the screen. Mr Tamworth seemed terribly distressed.

'This is an awful bit of business,' he exclaimed;

'you see the arch villain has anticipated this discovery and bolted. What is to be done now?'

'We must arrest him in his flight,' was my answer. 'And to facilitate that you must furnish me with a full description of him.'

'Unless the rascal has removed it,' said Mr Tamworth, 'his likeness hangs over the mantelpiece in his room above the stable. I will go and get it. You will excuse me.'

He hurried from the room, and was absent nearly a quarter of an hour. Then he returned bearing a framed photograph in his hand. It was the likeness of a short, thickset man in coachman's garb. He had grey whiskers and moustache, and grey hair; and rather a scowling expression of face. I asked Mr Tamworth if it was a good likeness of John Tupper, and he assured me it was a most excellent likeness.

Promising Mr Tamworth to do all I could to effect Tupper's arrest, I left Linden House, taking the photograph with me. As soon as I got back to London I hailed a hansom and drove to Whitney, Blake and Montague's.

'My surmise about the coachman is correct,' I said, as I showed them the likeness, and told them that the man had fled. They acknowledged that the likeness was a very striking one, and as I intended to have it reproduced and sent broadcast all over the country, I was hopeful that I should be able speedily to bring about Tupper's arrest.

I lost no time in putting the photo in hand for reproduction; in the meantime Miss Artois was again brought up before the magistrate, and in view of the facts the solicitors were able to lay before him with reference to Tupper's flight, he no longer hesitated to admit the young lady to bail, her uncle being accepted for two thousand pounds. Two days after her release, young Kingsley called upon me again. He was terribly agitated, and throwing himself into a chair he rocked himself to and fro, and groaned with the anguish that tortured him. When he had somewhat calmed down, he exclaimed in a voice that was broken up with the passion of his grief: 'Mr Donovan, help me with your advice, or I think I shall go mad. And above all, do not betray the confidence I am going to repose in you.' I assured him that he might trust me, and he proceeded.

'Miss Artois came to me yesterday, and acknowledged that she was an unconscious victim in this terrible business, and said that I must give her up. In spite of my entreaties, my prayers, my tears, she most resolutely declined to tell me whose victim she was, and with a great shudder she said her lips were sealed with a seal she dare not break. I urged her to fly with me. I told her we would be married at once, and seek some corner of the earth where she would be safe, and her answer was that nowhere in the world would she be safe except in the grave.'

'You did wrong in urging her to fly,' I answered.

'I care not. Wrong, or no wrong, I will take her,' he cried, passionately. 'I tell you, Mr Donovan, that there is some hideous mystery about this affair, and I will move heaven and earth to save Miss Artois from the machination that is destroying her body and soul.'

'Your devotion, your chivalry do you infinite credit,' I replied. 'Miss Artois shall be saved if it is possible to save her, but, believe me, she cannot be saved by flight. She must remain here subject to the law. To defy the law will be a fatal mistake.'

Although he did not seem to be quite convinced of the soundness of my advice, he promised to be entirely guided by me, and in a little while he took his departure, and then I sat down to reflect and ponder, and endeavour to unravel the threads of this tangled skein. One thing I resolved on was to go down to Thames Ditton early on the morrow and have an interview with Miss Artois in the presence of her uncle. In a little while my servant entered the room and handed me a postal packet, which, on opening, I found was from the lithographers who were reproducing the photograph. It contained the original and a note to say that the reproductions would be ready for distribution the first thing in the morning.

Placing the photo of Tupper on the table, I lit my pipe, and once more throwing myself in my favourite easy-chair, I tried by the aid of smoke to solve the mystery surrounding Miss Artois. Presently I found myself almost unconsciously gazing on the photo that lay on the table, in the full rays of the shaded lamp. Suddenly that face presented itself to me as one I had seen before; and I beat my brains, so to speak, to try and think where and when. 'Whose face is it? Where have I seen it?' This was the question that, mentally, I repeated over and over again.

After much cogitation, I threw away the stump of my cigar, went to my desk, and taking out a powerful magnifying glass, I returned to the table and examined the likeness of John Tupper by means of the glass, until suddenly, like an inspiration, it flashed upon me where and when I had seen the face. It is not often I get excited, but I think I did on that occasion, for I felt certain that I had got hold of a clue to the mystery. I did not sleep much that night, and was up betimes in the morning, and hastened to call upon Mr Kingsley, to assure him that I believed I was in a fair way to solving the mystery, and I hoped all would be well with Miss Artois.

A week later, on a night in January as dark and stormy as any that winter, I was in an upper room in an old, untenanted house in the Borough. The owner of the house was Mr Tamworth, of Thames Ditton. Stretched at full length on the dusty floor, with my eye glued to a hole that enabled me to command a view of the room beneath, I was witness to one of the most remarkable and dramatic scenes I had ever looked upon. Thirteen men were in the room, seated at a long deal table. Six sat on one side, six on the other. The thirteenth sat at the head, and was evidently the president. Every man's face was concealed by a hood that entirely covered up the head, two holes being pierced for the eyes. Before the president was a china bowl, and laid across the bowl was a naked dagger.

A small lamp was suspended from the ceiling and threw a feeble light over the scene. In a few minutes one of the men arose and placed a bull's-eye lantern on a shelf in a corner of the room, in such a position that its rays fell full upon the doorway. That done the president rapped on the table with a wooden mallet. Then the door opened and three men appeared. Two were hooded like the rest. The third was not hooded, and was placed at the end of the table opposite the president, so that the light of the bull's-eye fell full upon his face. It was a cruel, cunning, almost fierce face. The man was without coat or waistcoat, and his shirt was opened and turned down, exposing his breast, while round his neck was a rope with the free end hanging behind. In a few minutes the president rose, and addressing the bareheaded man, said: 'Your name is Henry Beechworth?'

'It is.'

'Are you willing, Henry Beechworth, to join the Black Brotherhood?'

'I am.'

'And you are willing to take the oath that will bind you to us?'

'I am.'

'Then listen, and I will read the oath to you.' Here the president unrolled a little scroll of paper he had held in his hand, and read out as follows: ' "I, Henry Beechworth, hereby, of my own free will, join the Black Brotherhood, and I vow solemnly by heaven and earth to be true to it, and never utter a single word or give a sign that would be likely to betray any individual of the Brotherhood, or the Brotherhood collectively. And that at any time, should I be arrested, I will give no information against the Brothers, even though my life is at stake. Everything I obtain I will add to the common treasury, and I will at all times be subject to the ruling of the president, whoever he may be. These things I swear to do; and should at any time I break my oath, I hope that I shall go blind. I am aware that the rope I now have round my neck is a symbol that in the event of my betraying the Brotherhood their vengeance will pursue me to the ends of the earth, and that my life will be forfeited." '

'You have heard what I have read?' asked the president.

'I have,' answered Beechworth.

'And you will subscribe your name to it?'

'I will.'

Here the president made a sign, and one of the

two hooded men at the head of the table approached, and receiving the bowl and the dagger, he returned to the novitiate, who, instructed by the president, bent forward. Then the man took up the dagger and with its sharp point made a wound in the fleshy part of the novitiate's breast. Beechworth then bent right over the bowl, so that the blood dropped into it. And when a little had thus been caught, a new quill pen was dipped into it, and handed to Beechworth, who thereupon wrote his name with his own blood on the scroll. This senseless ceremony ended, the wound in the man's breast was sponged, a piece of plaster placed upon it, and he was told that he was now one of the Black Brotherhood, that his interests were bound up with theirs and that he must stand or fall with them.

'It only remains now for me to give you the sign,' the president added, 'by which you may always know a Brother. It is changed every month. For the current month it is the index finger of the left hand placed in the palm of the right hand, thus.' Here he gave a practical illustration of how it was to be done. 'Then we have a password, also changed every month. The one in use at present is "Croesus". We meet here again in three weeks' time, when you will be expected to contribute to the common fund value or money to the extent of a hundred pounds.'

The business being ended, all the members of this precious Brotherhood removed their hoods, and the hand of the new member was shaken by the others. Among them I recognised the fellow called Robert, who had acted the part of the servant at Linden House when I went there. In a little while the lights were extinguished and the Brotherhood commenced to leave the house, but as they reached the street, to their utter amazement and consternation, they were arrested, for the house was surrounded by a cordon of policemen.

It will, of course, be asked how it was I managed to unearth the secrets of the strange society, whose members were banded together with the sole object of enriching themselves by plundering their fellow-men. The question is easily answered. On the night when it dawned upon me that I had seen the face represented by the photograph of John Tupper somewhere before, I was enabled to detect by aid of the magnifying glass that the whiskers were not natural. There were two or three places where the hair did not adhere to the face. I came to the conclusion at once that Tupper was none other than Tamworth, disguised by false whiskers and moustache, and a wig. The dark piercing eyes, too, I was perfectly convinced were Tamworth's eyes. It was naturally a very startling discovery, and I immediately took steps to prove it right or wrong. For several days I shadowed Mr Tamworth, and at last followed him to the old house in the Borough.

Later on I obtained entrance to the house by means of a false key. In a drawer in a table I found a written circular summoning a meeting for a certain night and I resolved not only to witness that meeting, but as there could not be a shadow of a doubt that the Black Brotherhood, as they chose to call themselves, met for an unlawful purpose, I took means to have every man jack of them arrested.

At first when the news leaked out people were inclined to think that the Brotherhood was a hoax, but the revelations that were gradually made of their doings caused intense excitement throughout the country. Not only were they bound together by oath, which each man signed with his blood, but they had a formal set of rules and regulations for their guidance. Tamworth was the president, and he, with two others, took charge of all the things that were stolen.

Periodically this property was conveyed to the Continent by some of the members, and there disposed of, the proceeds of the sales being equally divided. In the event of a man being arrested the Brotherhood secretly provided funds for his defence; and if it was a bailable case the bail was always forthcoming, but the accused invariably disappeared unless he felt pretty sure he would only get a light sentence.

The Brotherhood owed its origin and success entirely to the arch villain Tamworth, who had, by some strange mesmeric influence he possessed, been enabled to obtain entire control over the will of his unfortunate niece Beryl Artois. In order to keep up this influence, he drove his own brougham disguised as a coachman, and whatever she obtained she handed to him immediately and he concealed it. Of course, nothing bulky was ever taken on such occasions. The plunder was either precious stones or jewellery.

In spite of their oath, three of the gang turned queen's evidence, and the conviction of the rest was secured. Tamworth, as the ringleader, was sentenced to life, and the others were dealt with only a little less severely. Tamworth was one of the most accomplished and consummate villains I ever had to deal with; his power of acting a part, and of concealing his true feelings, was simply marvellous, and would have made him a fortune if he had gone upon the stage.

In the face of the exposure I was thus enabled to make, and which left not the slightest doubt that poor Miss Artois had been an unconscious victim of the strange power possessed by her uncle, she was, after being committed for trial and duly tried, acquitted, and her faithful lover, Kingsley, lost no time in making her his wife. And as great sympathy was shown for him and her, a position was found for him abroad, whither he removed with his beautiful bride until time should have wiped the scandal out of the public memory.

R. AUSTIN FREEMAN

The Seal of Nebuchadnezzar

'I suppose, Thorndyke,' said I, 'footprints yield quite a lot of information if you think about them enough?'

The question was called forth by the circumstance of my friend halting and stooping to examine the little pit made in the loamy soil of the path by the walking stick of some unknown wayfarer. Ever since we had entered this path – to which we had been directed by the station-master of Pinwell Junction as a short cut to our destination – I had noticed my friend scanning its surface, marked with numerous footprints, as if he were mentally reconstructing the personalities of the various travellers who had trodden it before us. This I knew to be a habit of his, almost unconsciously pursued; and the present conditions certainly favoured it, for here, as the path traversed a small wood, the slightly moist, plastic surface took impressions with the sharpness of moulding wax.

'Yes,' he answered, 'but you must do more than think. You need to train your eyes to observe conspicuous characteristics.'

'Such as these, for instance,' said I, with a grin, pointing to a blatant print of a Cox's 'Invicta' rubber sole with its prancing-horse trademark.

Thorndyke smiled. 'A man,' said he, 'who wears a sole like that is a mere advertising agent. He who runs may read those characteristics, but as there are thousands of persons wearing "Invicta" soles, the

556

observation merely identifies the wearer as a member of a large genus. It has to be carried a good deal further to identify him as an individual; indeed, a standardised sole is apt to be rather misleading than helpful. Its gross distinctiveness tends to divert the novice's attention from the more specific characteristics which he would seek in a plain footprint like that of this man's companion.'

'Why companion?' I asked. 'The two men were walking the same way, but what evidence is there that they were companions?'

'A good deal, if you follow the series of tracks, as I have been doing. In the first place, there is the stride. Both men were rather tall, as shown by the size of their feet, but both have a distinctly short stride. Now the leather-soled man's short stride is accounted for by the way in which he put down his stick. He held it stiffly, leaning upon it to some extent and helping himself with it. There is one impression of the stick to every two paces; every impression of his left foot has a stick impression opposite to it. The suggestion is that he was old, weak or infirm. But the rubber-soled man walked with his stick in the ordinary way – one stick impression to every four paces. His abnormally short stride is not to be accounted for excepting by the assumption that he stepped short to keep pace with the other man.

'Then the two sets of footprints are usually separate. Neither man has trodden nor set his stick on the other man's tracks, excepting in those places where the path is too narrow for them to walk abreast, and there, in the one case I noticed the rubber soles treading on the prints of the leather soles, whereas at this spot the prints of the leather soles are imposed on those of the rubber soles. That, of course, is conclusive evidence that the two men were here at the same time.'

'Yes,' I agreed, 'that settles the question without troubling about the stride. But after all, Thorndyke, this is a matter of reasoning, as I said; of thinking about the footprints and their meaning. No special acuteness of observation or training of vision comes into it. The mere facts are obvious enough; it is their interpretation that yields the knowledge.'

'That is true so far,' said he, 'but we haven't exhausted our material. Look carefully at the impressions of the two sticks and tell me if you see any thing remarkable in either of them?'

I stooped and examined the little pits that the two sticks had made in the path, and, to tell the truth, found them extremely unilluminating.

'They seem very much alike,' I said. 'The rubber-soled man's stick is rather larger than the other and the leather-soled man's stick has made deeper holes – probably because it was smaller and he was leaning on it more heavily.'

Thorndyke shook his head. 'You've missed the point, Anstey, and you've missed it because you have failed to observe the visible facts. It is quite a neat point, too, and might in certain circumstances be a very important one.'

'Indeed,' said I. 'What is the point?'

'That,' said he, 'I shall leave you to infer from the visible facts, which are these: first, the impressions of the smaller stick are on the right-hand side of the man who made them, and second, that each impression is shallower towards the front and the right-hand side.'

I examined the impressions carefully and verified Thorndyke's statement.

Well,' I said, 'what about it? What does it prove?'

Thorndyke smiled in his exasperating fashion. 'The proof,' said he, 'is arrived at by reasoning from the facts. My learned friend has the facts. If he will consider them, the conclusion will emerge.'

'But,' said I, 'I don't see your drift. The impression is shallower on one side, I suppose, because the ferrule of the stick was worn away on that side. But I repeat, what about it? Do you expect me to infer why the fool that it belonged to wore his stick away all at one side?'

'Now, don't get irritable, Anstey,' said he. 'Preserve a philosophic calm. I assure you that this is quite an interesting problem.'

'So it may be,' I replied. 'But I'm hanged if I can imagine why he wore his stick down in that way. However, it doesn't really matter. It isn't my stick – and by Jingo, here is old Brodribb – caught us in the act of wasting our time on academic chin-wags and delaying his business. The debate is adjourned.'

Our discussion had brought us to the opening of the wood, which now framed the figure of the solicitor. As he caught sight of us, he hurried forward, holding out his hand.

'Good men and true!' he exclaimed. 'I thought you would probably come this way, and it is very good of you to have come at all, especially as it is a mere formality.'

'What is?' asked Thorndyke. 'Your telegram spoke of an "alleged suicide". I take it that there is some ground for enquiry?'

'I don't know that there is,' replied Brodribb. 'But the deceased was insured for three thousand pounds, which will be lost to the estate if the suicide is confirmed. So I put it to my fellow that it was worth an expert's fee to make sure whether or not things are what they seem. A verdict of death by misadventure will save us three thousand pounds. *Verbum sap.*' As he concluded, the old lawyer winked with exaggerated cunning and stuck his elbow into my ribs.

Thorndyke ignored the facetious suggestion of bribery and corruption and enquired dryly: 'What are the circumstances of the case?'

'I'd better give you a sketch of them before we get to the house,' replied Brodribb. 'The dead man is Martin Rowlands, the brother of my neighbour in New Square, Tom Rowlands. Poor old Tom found the telegram waiting when he got to his office this morning and immediately rushed into my office with it and begged me to come down here with him. So I came. Couldn't refuse a brother solicitor. He's waiting at the house now.

'The circumstances are these. Last evening, when he had finished dinner, Rowlands went out for a walk. That is his usual habit in the summer months – it is light until nearly half-past nine nowadays. Well, that is the last time he was seen alive by the servants. No one saw him come in. But there was nothing unusual in that, for he had a private entrance to the annexe in which his library, museum, study and workroom were situated, and when he returned from his walk, he usually entered the house that way and went straight to his study or workroom and spent the evening there. So the servants very seldom saw him after dinner.

'Last night he evidently followed his usual custom. But, this morning, when the housemaid went to his bedroom with his morning tea, she was astonished to find the room empty and the bed undisturbed. She at once reported to the housekeeper, and the pair made their way to the annexe. There they found the study door locked, and as there was no answer after repeated knockings, they went out into the grounds to reconnoitre. The study window was closed and fastened, but the workroom window was unbolted, so that they were able to open it from outside. Then the housemaid climbed in and went to the side door, which she opened and admitted the housekeeper. The two went to the workroom, and as the door which communicated with the study was open, they were able to enter the latter, and there they found Martin Rowlands, sitting in an armchair by the table, stone-dead, cold and stiff. On the table were a whisky decanter, a siphon of soda water, a box of cigars, an ash-bowl with the stump of a cigar in it, and a bottle of photographic tabloids of cyanide of potassium.

'The housekeeper immediately sent off for a doctor and dispatched a telegram to Tom Rowlands at his office. The doctor arrived about nine and decided that the deceased had been dead about twelve hours. The cause of death was apparently cyanide poisoning, but, of course, that will be ascertained or disproved by the post-mortem. Those are all the known facts at present. The doctor helped the servants to place the body on a sofa, but as it is as stiff as a frozen sheep, they might as well have left it where it was.'

'Have the police been communicated with?' I asked.

'No,' replied Brodribb. 'There were no suspicious circumstances, so far as any of us could see, and I don't know that I should have felt justified in sending for you – though I always like to have Thorndyke's opinion in a case of sudden death – if it had not been for the insurance.'

Thorndyke nodded. 'It looks like a straightforward

case of suicide,' said he. 'As to the state of deceased's affairs, his brother will be able to give us any necessary information, I suppose?'

'Yes,' replied Brodribb. 'As a matter of fact, I think Martin has been a bit worried just lately; but Tom will tell you about that. This is the place.'

We turned in at a gateway that opened into the grounds of a substantial though unpretentious house, and as we approached the front door, it was opened by a fresh-coloured, white-haired man whom we both knew pretty well in our professional capacities. He greeted us cordially, and though he was evidently deeply shocked by the tragedy, struggled to maintain a calm, businesslike manner.

'It is good of you to come down,' said he; 'but I am afraid we have troubled you rather unnecessarily. Still, Brodribb thought it best – *ex abundantia cautelae,* you know – to have the circumstances reviewed by a competent authority. There is nothing abnormal in the affair excepting its having happened. My poor brother was the sanest of men, I should say, and we are not a suicidal family. I suppose you had better see the body first?'

As Thorndyke assented, he conducted us to the end of the hall and into the annexe, where we entered the study, the door of which was now open, though the key was still in the lock. The table bore the things that Brodribb had described, but the chair was empty, and its late occupant lay on a sofa, covered with a large tablecloth. Thorndyke advanced to the sofa and gently drew away the cloth, revealing the body of a man, fully dressed, lying stiffly and awkwardly on its back, with the feet raised and the stiffened limbs extended. There was something strangely and horribly artificial in the aspect of the corpse, for, though it was lying down, it had the posture of a seated figure, and thus bore the semblance of a hideously realistic effigy which had been picked up from a chair and laid down. I stood looking at it from a little distance with a layman's distaste for the presence of a dead body, but still regarding it with attention and some curiosity. Presently my glance fell on the soles of the shoes – which were, indeed, exhibited plainly enough – and I noted, as an odd coincidence, that they were 'Invicta' rubber soles, like those which we had just been discussing in the wood; that it was even possible that those very footprints had been made by the feet of this grisly lay figure.

'I expect, Thorndyke,' Brodribb said tactfully, 'you would rather make your inspection alone. If you should want us, you will find us in the dining-room,' and with this he retired, taking Mr Rowlands with him.

As soon as they were gone I drew Thorndyke's attention to the rubber soles.

'It is a queer thing,' said I, 'but we may have actually been discussing this poor fellow's own prints.'

'As a matter of fact, we were,' he replied, pointing to a drawing-pin that had been trodden on and had stuck into one of the rubber heels. 'I noticed this at the time, and apparently you did not, which illustrates what I was saying about the tendency of these very distinctive types of sole to distract attention from those individual peculiarities which are the ones that really matter.'

'Then,' said I, 'if they were his footprints, the man with the remarkable stick was with him. I wonder who he was. Some neighbour who was walking home from the station with him, I expect.'

'Probably,' said Thorndyke, 'and as the prints were quite recent – they might even have been made last night – that person may be wanted as a witness at the inquest as the last person who saw the deceased alive. That depends on the time the prints were made.'

He walked back to the sofa and inspected the corpse very methodically, giving close attention to the mouth and hands. Then he made a general inspection of the room, examined the objects on the table and the floor under it, strayed into the adjoining workshop, where he peered into the deep laboratory sink, took an empty tumbler from a shelf, held it up to the light and inspected the shelf – where a damp ring showed that the tumbler had been put there to drain – and from the workshop wandered into a little lobby and from thence out at the side door, down the flagged path to the side gate and back again.

'It is all very negative,' he remarked discontentedly, as we returned to the study, 'except that bottle of tabloids, which is pretty positive evidence of pre-meditation. That looks like a fresh box of cigars. Two missing. One stump in the ashtray and more ash than one cigar would account for. However, let us go into the dining-room and hear what Rowlands has to tell us,' and with this he walked out and crossed the hall and I followed him.

As we entered the dining-room the two men looked at us and Brodribb asked: 'Well, what is the verdict?'

'At present,' Thorndyke replied, 'it is an open verdict. Nothing has come to light that disagrees with the obvious appearances. But I should like to hear more of the antecedents of the tragedy. You were saying that the deceased had been somewhat worried lately. What does that amount to?'

It amounts to nothing,' said Rowlands 'at least, I should have thought so, in the case of a level-headed man like my brother. Still, as it is all there is, so far as I know, to account for what has happened, I had better give you the story. It seems trivial enough.

'Some short time ago, a Major Cohen, who had just come home from Mesopotamia, sold to a dealer named Lyon a small gold cylinder seal that he had picked up in the neighbourhood of Baghdad. The Lord knows how he came by it, but he had it and he showed it to Lyon, who bought it of him for a matter of twenty pounds. Cohen, of course, knew nothing about the thing, and Lyon didn't know much more, for although he is a dealer, he is no expert. But he is a very clever faker – or rather, I should say, restorer, for he does quite a legitimate trade. He was a jeweller and watch-jobber originally, a most ingenious workman, and his line is to buy up damaged antiques and restore them. Then he sells them to minor collectors, though quite honestly as restorations, so I oughtn't to call him a faker. But, as I said, he has no real knowledge of antiques, and all he saw in Cohen's seal was a gold cylinder seal, apparently ancient and genuine, and on the strength of that he bought it for about twice the value of the gold and thought no more of it.

'About a fortnight later, my brother Martin went to his shop in Petty France, Westminster, to get some repairs done, and Lyon, knowing that my brother was a collector of Babylonian antiquities, showed him the seal; and Martin, seeing at once that it was genuine and a thing of some interest and value, bought it straight-way for forty pounds without examining it at all minutely, as it was obviously worth that much in any case. But when he got home and took a rolled impression of it on moulding wax, he made a most astonishing discovery. The impression showed a mass of minute cuneiform characters, and on deciphering these he learned with amazement and delight that this was none other than the seal of Nebuchadnezzar.

'Hardly able to believe in his good fortune, he hurried off to the British Museum and showed his treasure to the keeper of the Babylonian Antiquities, who fully confirmed the identity of the seal and was naturally eager to acquire it for the Museum. Of course, Martin wouldn't sell it, but he allowed the keeper to take a record of its weight and measurements and to make an impression on clay to exhibit in the case of seal-rollings.

'Meanwhile, it seems that Cohen, before disposing of the seal, had amused himself by making a number of rolled impressions on clay. Some of these he took to Lyon, who bought them for a few shillings and put one of them in his shop window as a curio. There it was seen and recognised by an American Assyriologist, who went in and bought it and then began to question Lyon closely as to whence he had obtained it. The dealer made no secret of the matter, but gave Cohen's name and address, saying nothing, however, about the seal. In fact, he was unaware of the connection between the seal and the rollings as Cohen had sold him the latter as genuine clay tablets which he said he had found in Mesopotamia. But, of course, the expert saw that it was a recent rolling and that someone must have the seal.

'Accordingly, off he went to Cohen and questioned him closely, whereupon Cohen began to smell a rat. He admitted that he had had the seal, but refused to say what had become of it until the expert told him what it was and how much it was worth. This the expert did, very reluctantly and in strict confidence, and when Cohen learned that it was the seal of Nebuchadnezzar and that it was worth anything up to ten thousand pounds, he nearly fainted; and then he and the expert together bustled off to Lyon's shop.

'But now Lyon smelt a rat, too. He refused absolutely to disclose the whereabouts of the seal; and having, by now, guessed that the seal-rollings were those of the seal, he took one of them to the British Museum, and then, of course, the murder was out. And further to complicate the matter, the Assyriologist, Professor Bateman, seems to have talked freely to his American friends at his hotel, with the result that Lyon's shop was besieged by wealthy American collectors, all eager to acquire the seal perfectly regardless of cost. Finally, as they could get no change out of Lyon, they went to the British Museum, where they learned that my brother had the seal and got his address – or rather mine, for he had, fortunately for himself, given my office as his address. Then they proceeded to bombard him with letters, as also did Cohen and Lyon.

'It was an uncomfortable situation. Cohen was like a madman. He swore that Lyon had swindled him and he demanded to have the seal returned or the proper price paid. Lyon, for his part, went about like a roaring lion of Judah, making a similar demand; and the millionaire collectors offered wild sums for the seal. Poor Martin was very much worried about it. He was particularly unhappy about Cohen, who had actually found the seal and who was a disabled soldier – he had been wounded in both legs and was permanently lame. As to Lyon, he had no grievance,

567

for he was a dealer and it was his business to know the value of his own stock; but still it was hard luck even on him. And then there were the collectors, pestering him daily with entreaties and extravagant offers. It was very worrying for him. They would probably have come down here to see him, but he kept his private address a close secret.

'I don't know what he meant to do about it. What he did was to arrange with me for the loan of my private office and have a field day, interviewing the whole lot of them – Lyon, the professor and the assorted millionaires. That was three days ago, and the whole boiling of them turned up; and by the same token one of them was the kind of pestilent fool that walks off with the wrong hat or umbrella.'

'Did he walk off with your hat?' asked Brodribb.

'No, but he took my stick; a nice old stick that belonged to my father.'

'What sort of stick did he leave in its place?' Thorndyke asked.

'Well,' replied Rowlands, 'I must admit that there was some excuse, for the stick that he left was almost a facsimile of my own. I don't think I should have noticed it but for the feel. When I began to walk with it, I was aware of something unusual in the feel of it.'

'Perhaps it was not quite the same length as yours,' Thorndyke suggested.

'No, it wasn't that,' said Rowlands. 'The length was all right, but there was some more subtle difference. Possibly, as I am left-handed and carry my stick on the left side, it may in the course of years have acquired a left-handed bias, if such a thing is possible. I'll go and get the stick for you to see.'

He went out of the room and returned in a few

moments with an old-fashioned Malacca cane, the ivory handle of which was secured by a broad silver band. Thorndyke took it from him and looked it over with a degree of interest and attention that rather surprised me, for the loss of Rowlands's stick was a trivial incident and no concern of ours. Nevertheless, my colleague inspected it most methodically, handle, silver band and ferrule; especially the ferrule, which he examined as if it were quite a rare and curious object.

'You needn't worry about your stick, Tom,' said Brodribb with a mischievous smile. 'Thorndyke will get it back if you ask him nicely.'

'It oughtn't to be very difficult,' said Thorndyke, handing back the stick, 'if you have a list of the visitors who called that day.'

'Their names will be in the appointments book,' said Rowlands. 'I must look them up. Some of them I remember – Cohen, Lyon, Bateman and two or three of the collectors. But to return to our history. I don't know what passed at the interviews or what Martin intended to do, but I have no doubt he made some notes on the subject. I must search for them, for, of course, we shall have to dispose of the seal.'

'By the way,' said Thorndyke, 'where is the seal?'

'Why, it is here in the safe,' replied Rowlands; 'and it oughtn't to be. It should have been taken to the bank.'

'I suppose there is no doubt that it is in the safe?' said Thorndyke.

'No,' replied Rowlands; 'at least – ' He stood up suddenly. 'I haven't seen it,' he said. 'Perhaps we had better make sure.'

He led the way quickly to the study, where he halted and stood looking at the shrouded corpse. 'The key will be in his pocket,' he said, almost in a whisper. Then, slowly and reluctantly, he approached the sofa, and gently drawing away the cover from the body, began to search the dead man's pockets.

'Here it is,' he said at length, producing a bunch of keys and separating one, which he apparently knew. He crossed to the safe, and inserting the key, threw open the door.

'Ha!' he exclaimed with evident relief, 'it is all right. Your question gave me quite a start. Is it necessary to open the packet?'

He held out a little sealed parcel on which was written 'The Seal of Nebuchadnezzar', and looked enquiringly at Thorndyke.

'You spoke of making sure,' the latter replied with a faint smile.

'Yes, I suppose it would be best,' said Rowlands; and with that, he cut the thread with which it was fastened, broke the seal and opened the package, disclosing a small cardboard box in which lay a cylindrical object rolled up in a slip of paper.

Rowlands picked it out, and removing the paper, displayed a little cylinder of gold pitted all over with minute cuneiform characters. It was about an inch and a quarter long by half an inch thick and had a hole bored through its axis from end to end.

'This paper, I see,' said Rowlands, 'contains a copy of the keeper's description of the seal – its weight, dimensions and so on. We may as well take care of that.'

He handed the little cylinder to Thorndyke, who held it delicately in his fingers and looked at it with a gravely reflective air. Indeed, small as it was, there was something very impressive in its appearance and in the thought that it had been handled by and probably worn on the person of the great king in those remote, almost mythical times, so familiar and yet so immeasurably far away. So I reflected as I watched Thorndyke inspecting the venerable little object in his queer, exact, scientific way, examining the minute characters through his lens, scrutinising the ends and even peering through the central hole.

'I notice,' he said, glancing at the paper which Rowlands held, 'that the keeper has given only one transverse diameter, apparently assuming that it is a true cylinder. But it isn't. The diameter varies. It is not quite circular in section and the sides are not perfectly parallel.'

He produced his pocket calliper-gauge, and closing the jaws on the cylinder, took the reading of the vernier. Then he turned the cylinder, on which the gauge became visibly out of contact.

'There is a difference of nearly two millimetres,' he said when he had again closed the gauge and taken the reading.

'Ah, Thorndyke,' said Brodribb, 'that keeper hadn't got your mathematically exact eye; and, in fact, the precise measurements don't seem to matter much.'

'On the other hand,' retorted Thorndyke, 'inexact measurements are of no use at all.'

When we had all handled and inspected the seal, Rowlands repacked it and returned it to the safe, and we went back to the dining-room.

'Well, Thorndyke,' said Brodribb, 'how does the insurance question stand? What is our position?'

'I think,' Thorndyke replied, 'that we will leave the question open until the inquest has been held. You must insist on an expert analysis, and perhaps that may throw fresh light on the matter. And now we must be off to the station. I expect you have plenty to do.'

'We have,' said Brodribb, 'so I won't offer to walk with you. You know the way.'

Politely but firmly declining Rowlands's offer of material hospitality, Thorndyke took up his research-case, and having shaken hands with our hosts, we followed them to the door and took our departure.

'Not a very satisfactory case,' I remarked as we set forth along the road, 'but you can't make a bull's-eye every time.'

'No,' he agreed; 'you can only observe and note the facts. Which reminds me that we have some data to collect in the wood. I shall take casts of those foot-prints in case they should turn out to be of importance. It is always a useful precaution, seeing that footprints are fugitive.'

It seemed to me an excessive precaution, but I made no comment; and when we arrived at the footpath through the wood and he had selected the sharpest footprints, I watched him take out from his case the plaster-tin, water-bottle, spoon and little rubber bowl, and wondered what was in his mind. The 'Invicta' footprints were obviously those of the dead man. But what if they were? And of what use were the casts of the other man's feet? The man was unknown, and as far as I could see, there was nothing suspicious in his presence here. But when Thorndyke had poured the liquid plaster into the two pairs of footprints, he went on to a still more incomprehensible proceeding. Mixing some fresh plaster, he filled up with it two adjoining impressions of the strange man's stick. Then, taking a reel of thread from the case, he cut off about two yards, and stretching it taut, held it exactly across the middle of the two holes, until the plaster set and fixed it in position. After waiting for the plaster to set hard, and having, meanwhile, taken up and packed the casts of the footprints, he gently raised, first the one and then the other cast; each of which was a snowy-white facsimile of the tip of the stick which had made the impression, the two casts being joined by a length of thread which gave the exact distance apart of the two impressions.

'I suppose,' said I, as he made a pencil mark on one of the casts, 'the thread is to show the length of the stride?'

'No,' he answered. 'It is to show the exact direction in which the man was walking and to mark the front and back of the stick.'

I could make nothing of this. It was highly ingenious, but what on earth was the use of it? What could it possibly prove?

I put a few tentative questions, but could get no explanation beyond the obvious truth that it was of no use to postpone the collection of evidence until after the event. What event he was referring to, I did not gather; nor was I any further enlightened when, on arriving at Victoria, he hailed a taxicab and directed the driver to set him down at Scotland Yard.

'You had better not wait,' he said, as he got out. 'I have some business to talk over with Miller or the Assistant Commissioner and may be detained some time. But I shall be at home all the evening.'

Taking this as an invitation to drop in at his chambers, I did so after dinner and made another ineffectual attempt to pump him.

'I am sorry to be so evasive,' said he, 'but this case

573

is so extremely speculative that I cannot come to any definite conclusion until I have more data. I may have been theorising in the air. But I am going forth tomorrow morning at half-past eight in the hope of putting some of my inferences to the test. If my learned friend would care to lend his distinguished support to the expedition, his society would be appreciated. But it will be a case of passive observation and quite possibly nothing will happen.'

'Well, I will come and look on,' said I. 'Passive observation is my speciality;' and with this I took my departure, rather more mystified than ever.

Punctually, next morning at half-past eight, I arrived at the entry of Thorndyke's chambers. A taxicab was already waiting at the kerb, and, as I stepped on the threshold, my colleague appeared on the stairs. Together we entered the cab which at once moved off, and proceeding down Middle Temple Lane to the Embankment, headed westward. Our first stopping-place was New Scotland Yard, but there Thorndyke remained only a minute or two. Our further progress was in the direction of Westminster, and in a few minutes we drew up at the corner of Petty France, where we alighted and paid off the taxi. Sauntering slowly westward and passing a large, covered car that was drawn up by the pavement, we presently encountered no less a person than Mr Superintendent Miller, dressed in the height of fashion and smoking a cigar. The meeting was not, apparently, unexpected, for Miller began, without preamble: 'It's all right, so far, doctor, unless we are too late. It will be an awful suck-in if we are. Two plain-clothes men have been here ever since you called yesterday evening, and nothing has happened yet.'

'You mustn't treat it as a certainty, Miller,' said Thorndyke. 'We are only acting on reasonable probabilities. But it may be a false shot, after all.'

Miller smiled indulgently. 'I know, sir. I've heard you say that sort of thing before. At any rate, he's there at present; I saw him just now through the shop window – and, by gum! here he is!'

I followed the superintendent's glance and saw a tallish, elderly man advancing on the opposite side of the street. He walked stiffly with the aid of a stick and with a pronounced stoop as if suffering from some weakness of the back, and he carried in his free hand a small wooden case suspended by a rug-strap. But what instantly attracted my attention was his walking-stick, which appeared, so far as I could remember, to be an exact replica of the one that Tom Rowlands had shown us.

We continued to walk westward, allowing Mr Lyon – as I assumed him to be – to pass us. Then we turned back and followed at a little distance; and I noticed that two tall, military-looking men whom we had met kept close behind us. At the corner of Petty France Mr Lyon hailed a taxicab; and Miller quickened his pace and bore down on the big covered car.

'Jump in,' he said, opening the door as Lyon entered the cab. 'We mustn't lose sight of him,' and with this he fairly shoved Thorndyke and me into the car, and having spoken a word to the driver, stepped in himself and was followed by the two plain-clothes men. The car started forward, and having made a spurt which brought it within a few yards of the taxi, slowed down to the pace of the latter and followed it through the increasing traffic until we turned into Whitehall, where our driver allowed the taxi to draw ahead somewhat. At Charing Cross, however, we closed up and kept immediately behind our quarry in the dense traffic of the Strand; and when it turned to cross opposite the Acropolis Hotel, we still followed and swept past it in the hotel courtyard so that we reached the main entrance first. By the time that Mr Lyon had paid his fare we had already entered and were waiting in the hall of the hotel.

As he followed us in, he paused and looked about him until his glance fell on a stoutish, clean-shaved man sitting in a wicker chair, who, on catching his eye, rose and advanced towards him. At this moment Superintendent Miller touched him on the shoulder, causing him to spin round with an expression of very distinct alarm.

'Mr Maurice Lyon, I think,' said Miller. 'I am a detective officer.' He paused and looked hard at the dealer, who had turned deathly pale. Then he continued: 'You are carrying a walking-stick which I believe is not your property.'

Lyon gave a gasp of relief. 'You are quite right,' said he. 'But I don't know whose property it is. If you do, I shall be pleased to return it in exchange for my own, which I left by mistake.'

He held it out in an irresolute fashion, and Miller took it from him and handed it to Thorndyke.

'Is that the stick?' he asked.

Thorndyke looked the stick over quickly, and then, inverting it, made a minute examination of the ferrule, finishing up by taking the dimensions of two diameters and comparing the results with some written notes.

Mr Lyon fidgeted impatiently. 'There's no need for all this fuss,' said he. 'I have told you that the stick is not mine.'

'Quite so,' said Miller, 'but we must have a few words privately about that stick.'

Here he turned to a hotel official, who had just arrived under the guidance of one of the plain-clothes men, and who suggested rather anxiously that our business would be better transacted in a private room at the back of the building than in the public hall. He was just moving off to show us the way when the clean-shaved stranger edged up to Lyon and extended his hand towards the wooden case.

'Shall I take this?' he asked suavely.

'Not just now, sir,' said Miller, firmly fending him off. 'Mr Lyon will talk to you presently.'

'But that case is my property,' the other objected truculently; 'and who are you, anyway?'

'I am a police officer,' replied Miller. 'But if that is your property, you had better come with us and keep an eye on it.'

I have never seen a man look more uncomfortable than did the owner of that case – with the exception of Mr Lyon; whose complexion had once more taken on a tallowy whiteness. But as the manager led the way to the back of the hall the two men followed silently, shepherded by the superintendent and the rest of our party, until we reached a small, marble-floored lobby or ante-room, when our conductor shut us in and retired.

'Now,' said Miller, 'I want to know what is in that case.'

'I can tell you,' said the stranger. 'It is a piece of sculpture, and it belongs to me.'

Miller nodded. 'Let us have a look at it,' said he.

There being no table, Lyon sat down on a chair, and resting the case on his knees, unfastened the strap with trembling fingers on which a drop of sweat fell now and again from his forehead. When the case was free, he opened the lid and displayed the head of a small plaster bust, a miniature copy of Donatello's *St Cecilia*, the shoulders of which were wedged in with balls of paper. These Lyon picked out clumsily, and when he had removed the last of them, he lifted out the bust with infinite care and held it out for Miller's inspection. The officer took it from him tenderly – after an eager glance into the empty case – and holding it with both hands, looked at it rather blankly.

'Feels rather damp,' he remarked with a somewhat nonplussed air; and then he cast an obviously enquiring glance at Thorndyke, who took the bust from him, and holding it poised in the palm of his hand, appeared to be estimating its weight. Glancing past him at Lyon, I noticed with astonishment that the dealer was watching him with a ghastly stare of manifest terror, while the stranger was hardly less disturbed.

'For God's sake, man, be careful!' the latter exclaimed, starting forward. 'You'll drop it!'

The prediction was hardly uttered before it was verified. Drop it he did; and in a perfectly deliberate, purposeful manner, so that the bust fell on its back on the marble floor and was instantly shattered into a hundred fragments. It was an amazing affair. But what followed was still more amazing. For, as the snowy fragments scattered to right and left, from one of them a little yellow metal cylinder detached itself and rolled slowly along the floor. The stranger darted forward and stooped to seize it; but Miller stooped, too, and I judged that the superintendent's cranium was the harder, for he rose, rubbing his head with one hand and with the other holding out the cylinder to Thorndyke.

'Can you tell us what this is, doctor?' he asked.

'Yes,' was the reply. 'It is the seal of Nebuchadnezzar, and it is the property of the executors of the late Martin Rowlands, who was murdered the night before last.'

As he finished speaking, Lyon slithered from his chair and lay upon the floor insensible, while the stranger made a sudden burst for the door, where he was instantly folded in the embrace of a massive plain-clothes man, who held him immovable while his colleague clicked on the handcuffs.

'So,' I remarked, as we walked home, 'your casts of the stick and the footprints were not wanted after all.'

'On the contrary,' he replied, 'they are wanted very much. If the seal should fail to hang Mr Lyon, the casts will assuredly fit the rope round his neck.' (This, by the way, actually happened. The defence that Lyon received the seal from some unknown person was countered by the unexpected production in court of the casts of Lyon's feet and the stick, which proved that the prisoner had been at Pinwell and in the company of the deceased at or about the date of the murder and secured his conviction.)

'By the way,' said I, 'how did you fix this crime on Lyon? It began, I think, with those stick impressions in the wood. What was there peculiar about those impressions?'

'Their peculiarity was that they were the impressions of a stick which apparently did not belong to the person who was carrying it.'

'Good Lord, Thorndyke!' I exclaimed, 'is that

possible? How could an impression on the ground suggest ownership?'

'It is a curious point,' he replied, 'though essentially simple, which turns on the way in which the ferrule of a stick becomes worn. In a plain, symmetrical stick without a handle, the ferrule wears evenly all round; but in a stick with a crook or other definite handle, which is grasped in a particular way and always put down in the same position, the ferrule becomes worn on one side – the side opposite the handle, or the front of the stick. But the important point is that the bevel of wear is not *exactly* opposite the handle. It is slightly to one side, for this reason. A man puts his stick down with the handle fore and aft; but as he steps forward, his hand swings away from his body, rotating the stick slightly outward. Consequently, the wear on the ferrule is slightly inward. That is to say, that in a right-handed man's stick the wear is slightly to the left and in a left-handed man's stick the wear is slightly to the right. But if a right-handed man walks with a left-handed stick, the impression on the ground will show the bevel of wear on the right side – which is the wrong side; and the right-handed rotation will throw it still farther to the right. Now in this case, the impressions showed a shallow part, corresponding to the bevel of wear, on the right side. Therefore it was a left-handed stick. But it was being carried in the right hand. Therefore it – apparently – did not belong to the person who was carrying it.

'Of course, as the person was unknown, the point was merely curious and did not concern us. But see how quickly circumstantial evidence mounts up. When we saw the feet of deceased, we knew that the foot-prints in the wood were his. Consequently, the man with the stick was in his company; and that man at once came into the picture. Then Tom Rowlands told us that he had lost his stick and that he was left-handed; arid he showed us the stick that he had got in exchange, and behold! that is a right-handed stick, as I ascertained by examining the ferrule. Here, then, is a left-handed man who has lost a stick and got a right-handed one in exchange; and there, in the wood, was a right-handed man who was carrying a left-handed stick and who was in company with the deceased. It was a striking coincidence. But further, the suggestion was that this unknown man was one of those who had called at Tom's office, and therefore one who wanted to get possession of the seal. This instantly suggested the question, Did he succeed in getting possession of the seal? We went to the safe and at once it became obvious that he did.'

'The seal in the safe was a forgery, of course?'

'Yes; and a bad forgery, though skilfully done. It was an electrotype; it was unsymmetrical; it did not agree with the keeper's measurements; and the perforation, though soiled at the ends, was bright in the middle from the boring tool.'

'But how did you know that Lyon had made it?'

'I didn't. But he was by far the most probable person. He had a seal-rolling, from which an electro could be made, and he had the great skill that was necessary to turn a flat electro into a cylinder. He was an experienced faker of antiques, and he was a dealer who would have facilities for getting rid of the stolen seal. But it was only a probability, though, as time pressed, we had to act on it. Of course, when we saw him with the stick in his hand, it became virtually a certainty.'

'And how did you guess that the seal was in the bust?'

'I had expected to find it enclosed in some plaster object, that being the safest way to hide it and smuggle it out of this country and into the United States. When I saw the bust, it was obvious. It was a hastily-made copy of one of Brucciani's busts. The plaster was damp – Brucciani's bake theirs dry – and had evidently been made only a few hours. So I broke it. If I had been mistaken I could have replaced it for five shillings, but the whole circumstances made it practically a certainty.'

'Have you any idea as to how Lyon administered the poison?'

'We can only surmise,' he replied. 'Probably he took with him some solution of cyanide – if that was what was used – and poured it into Rowlands's whisky when his attention was otherwise occupied. It would be quite easy; and a single gulp of a quick-acting poison like that would finish the business in a minute or two. But we are not likely ever to know the details.'

The evidence at the inquest showed that Thorndyke was probably right, and his evidence at the trial clenched the case against Lyon. As to the other man – who proved to be an American dealer well known to the New York customs officials – the case against him broke down from lack of evidence that he was privy either to the murder or the theft. And so ended the case of Nebuchadnezzar's seal: a case that left Mr Brodribb more than ever convinced that Thorndyke was either gifted with a sixth sense which enabled him to smell out evidence or was in league with some familiar demon who did it for him.